Praise for Laura Griffin

DESPERATE GIRLS

"Intensely suspenseful . . . Griffin pulls out all the stops in a phenomenal twist ending that will leave the readers stunned."

—*Publishers Weekly* (starred and boxed review)

"*Desperate Girls* by Laura Griffin is a keeper; I know because I carried it everywhere with me until I'd finished it. It has chills, thrills, action, and romance."

—*New York Times* bestselling author Linda Howard

"It takes great mastery to combine the terror of a scary killer with a fun, sexy romance. Griffin handles the balance perfectly in *Desperate Girls*. A nail-biting page-turner."

—*New York Times* bestselling author J.T. Ellison

"Each development will leave you breathless . . . right up to the twist you won't see coming!"

—Kathleen Barber, author of *Are You Sleeping*

"*Desperate Girls* is another winner from Laura Griffin!"

—Chanel Cleeton, author of *Next Year in Havana*

TOUCH OF RED

"Griffin never disappoints with her exciting, well-researched, fast-paced romantic thrillers. . . . An engrossing story full of twists, turns, and sexy interludes."

—*Publishers Weekly*

"Scorching-hot chemistry and a happily-ever-after you'll enjoy rooting for."

—*Kirkus Reviews*

"A carefully constructed mystery with high-stakes tension throughout will have readers eagerly turning the pages. Once again, Griffin delivers another top-notch thriller."

—*RT Book Reviews*

"Masterful writing."

—*The Romance Reviews*

"A killer mystery makes hearts pound faster . . . a fast-paced thrill!"

—*BookPage*

AT CLOSE RANGE

"A compelling mystery that will grip the reader from the start with her crisp storytelling, natural dialogue, and high-stakes tension . . . fiercely electric."

—*RT Book Reviews*

"Explosive, seductive, and totally empowering . . . *At Close Range* has it all."

—*Romance Junkies*

SHADOW FALL

"An expert at creating mystery and suspense that hooks readers from the first page, Griffin's detailed description, well-crafted, intriguing plot, and clear-cut characters are the highlights of her latest."

—*RT Book Reviews*

"Great lead characters and a spooky atmosphere make this a spine-tingling, stand-out novel of romantic suspense."

—*BookPage*

FAR GONE

"Perfectly gritty. . . . Griffin sprinkles on just enough jargon to give the reader the feel of being in the middle of an investigation, easily merging high-stakes action and spicy romance with rhythmic pacing and smartly economic prose."

—*Publishers Weekly* (starred review)

"Be prepared for heart palpitations and a racing pulse as you read this fantastic novel. Fans of Lisa Gardner, Lisa Jackson, Nelson DeMille, and Michael Connelly will love [Griffin's] work."

—*The Reading Frenzy*

"A tense, exciting romantic thriller that's not to be missed."

—*New York Times* bestselling author Karen Robards

"Griffin has cooked up a delicious read that will thrill her devoted fans and earn her legions more."

—*New York Times* bestselling author Lisa Unger

More praise for the Tracers series

"Explodes with action. . . . Laura Griffin escalates the tension with each page, each scene."

—*The Romance Reviews*

"With a taut story line, believable characters, and a strong grasp of current forensic practice, Griffin sucks readers into this drama and doesn't let go."

—*RT Book Reviews* (Top Pick)

"The perfect mix of suspense and romance."

—*Booklist*

"The science is fascinating, the sex is sizzling, and the story is top-notch, making this clever, breakneck tale hard to put down."

—*Publishers Weekly*

Books by Laura Griffin

The Tracers Series
Stone Cold Heart

Touch of Red

At Close Range

Deep Dark

Shadow Fall

Beyond Limits

Exposed

Scorched

Twisted

Snapped

Unforgivable

Unstoppable*

Unspeakable

Untraceable

————

Desperate Girls

Far Gone

Whisper of Warning

Thread of Fear

One Wrong Step

One Last Breath

Deadly Promises (anthology)

————

The Alpha Crew Series
Total Control*

Cover of Night*

Alpha Crew: The Mission Begins*

*ebook only

HER
DEADLY
SECRETS

A NOVEL

LAURA GRIFFIN

G

GALLERY BOOKS

New York   London   Toronto   Sydney   New Delhi

Gallery Books
An Imprint of Simon & Schuster, Inc.
1230 Avenue of the Americas
New York, NY 10020

First Gallery Books hardcover edition July 2019

GALLERY BOOKS and colophon are registered trademarks of Simon & Schuster, Inc.

For information about special discounts for bulk purchases, please contact Simon & Schuster Special Sales at 1-866-506-1949 or business@simonandschuster.com.

The Simon & Schuster Speakers Bureau can bring authors to your live event. For more information or to book an event, contact the Simon & Schuster Speakers Bureau at 1-866-248-3049 or visit our website at www.simonspeakers.com.

Interior design by Davina Mock-Mansicalco

Manufactured in the United States of America

10 9 8 7 6 5 4 3 2 1

The Library of Congress has cataloged the trade paperback edition as follows:

Names: Griffin, Laura, author.
Title: Her deadly secrets / Laura Griffin.
Description: First Gallery Books hardcover edition. | New York : Gallery Books, 2019. |
   Series: Tracers series
Identifiers: LCCN 2019006761 (print) | LCCN 2019009380 (ebook) | ISBN 9781501162442
   (ebook) | ISBN 9781501162435 (trade pbk.) | ISBN 9781501190391 (hardcover) |
   ISBN 9781982123666 (mass market pbk.)
Subjects: LCSH: Criminal investigation—Fiction. | GSAFD: Suspense fiction. | Mystery fiction.
Classification: LCC PS3607.R54838 (ebook) | LCC PS3607.R54838 H47 2019 (print) |
   DDC 813/.6—dc23
LC record available at https://lccn.loc.gov/2019006761

ISBN 978-1-5011-9039-1
ISBN 978-1-5011-6243-5 (pbk)
ISBN 978-1-5011-6244-2 (ebook)

For Lauren

HER
DEADLY
SECRETS

CHAPTER

ONE

KIRA VANCE gripped the steering wheel and navigated the slick streets. The summer downpour had come out of nowhere, catching her off guard. She'd wanted to make a good impression, and now she was going to arrive not just late but soaking wet in a white T-shirt that was nearly transparent.

Water dripped onto her shoulder as she reached a stoplight, and she glared up at her leaky sunroof. There was no denying it—she needed a new car. Her little Celica had six-digit mileage and a bad transmission, but she refused to trade it in. She couldn't afford an upgrade, and the car had been with her through so many ups and downs she was sentimental about it.

The phone chimed on the seat beside her, but she ignored it because it was Ollie, her shrewd, rude, and sometimes infuriating boss. She didn't want to talk to him on the phone. She needed a face-to-face.

As Kira skidded away from the intersection, her car's engine warning light flashed on.

"Son of a bitch," she muttered.

She'd just had it in for an oil change, and the guy had said he'd checked everything.

But people lied. Often. If they didn't, she'd be out of a job.

Kira's work was a search for the truth—the good, the bad, and the ugly. She dug up the facts and let the lawyers deal with them in court. Or not. Sometimes her discoveries meant a witness wouldn't be called to testify. Or the defense team would develop a new strategy. Sometimes her discoveries poked big fat holes in the case of a zealous prosecutor.

The truth cut both ways, and that's what she liked about it. Finding that truth gave her a heady rush that made up for the downsides of PI work, such as dealing with cheating spouses and deadbeat dads and insurance scams. Those were the cases that made her pissed off and cynical.

Another thing that pissed her off? Unpaid invoices. Ollie was three weeks behind on a big one, and he was the master of the dodge, which was one reason she'd decided to track him down in person tonight to deliver her news.

Kira reached the street that turned into River Oaks, where stately houses sat far back on manicured lawns. The thunderstorm had brought an early evening, and the thick St. Augustine grass looked almost neon green in the eerie light.

Cars lined both sides of the street. Someone down the block was having a party, apparently, which seemed odd for a Tuesday. A red Jaguar glided up to the curb ahead, and a valet sprang out and sprinted past her.

Kira spotted Ollie's no-nonsense Ford parked at the base of a steep driveway. She wedged her car between a pair of Mercedes SUVs and cut the engine as she looked around.

This was it. Mount Logan. Named for Brock Logan, managing partner at the law firm that had hired Ollie to investigate its big cases. Kira had thought the name was a reference to Brock Logan's oversize ego, but she saw now that she'd been wrong, at least partially. The house perched atop a hill on a large corner lot, elevated above the other mansions in Houston's most exclusive neighborhood.

Kira had never set foot inside a River Oaks home, and her curiosity was mixed with professional ambition. Besides confronting Ollie, she was here to do some business development. It was high time for her to meet Ollie's big-fish client, who'd been keeping her in Ramen noodles and Netflix these past three years. She'd never met the man because Ollie liked her to stay behind the scenes. But those days were over.

Kira grabbed her files and glanced in the rearview mirror. This extreme humidity was not her friend. Her mascara was smudged, and her long dark hair was a frizzy mess. She smoothed her hair down and swiped on some red lipstick. Nothing she could do about her damp skinny jeans, but she grabbed her tailored black blazer from the back seat, hoping to hide the wet-T-shirt look she had going on. After trading her cheap flip-flops for strappy black sandals, she pushed open the door with a squeak.

The torrent had let up, but it was drizzling as another valet ran past her. Not far behind him was a plodding jogger in a soaked gray hoodie. Kira waited for him to pass and then crossed the street to Logan's house.

The homes here sat on huge lots, and each seemed to have its own theme. To Logan's left was a Mississippi Plantation with tall white columns. To his right was a Stuffy New England Brick with a steep roof, no doubt to accommodate Houston's frequent snowstorms. Logan's house fell squarely into the Tacky California category, a sprawling mass of yellow adobe with a red-tiled roof. Tall palm trees surrounded it, towering obnoxiously over the neighborhood's namesake oaks.

The air smelled of rain and fresh-cut grass as Kira trekked up the stone path. She passed through a pair of concrete lions into a court-yard, where she faced an imposing carved wooden door.

This was it. Brock Logan. She had to nail this meeting. She took a rubber band from her pocket, pulled her hair into a ponytail, and hoped for the best as she squared her shoulders and rang the bell.

Brock Logan had made a fortune defending wealthy people ac-cused of serious crimes. The cases were high stakes, high pay, and Lo-gan's current project was a prime example: a prominent heart surgeon accused of murdering his wife. According to the prosecution's theory, the mild-mannered doctor was actually an abusive control freak. When his wife threatened to leave him, he killed her.

The story had a catchy ring to it, kind of like a cable docudrama. But Logan planned to counter it with an airtight alibi: his client had been having drinks at his golf club with a fellow doctor at the time of his wife's murder.

The door jerked back, and Ollie stood there in his typical short-sleeved button-down and dark pants. He had a gray buzz cut and a paunch that hung over his belt.

"Christ, what are you doing here? You coming from the court-house? Get your ass in here." He took her elbow and pulled her inside. "You could've called me, you know. You didn't have to drive all the way here in the rain."

"I needed to talk to you."

"Oh, yeah?" Ollie smirked. "And I'm guessing you wanted to meet the Big Kahuna, too, right?"

"I'm here for my money, Ollie. I've got rent due, and you've been dodging me."

"I was just about to write your check."

She crossed her arms.

"Hey, you know I'm good for it." He made a sweeping gesture at the entrance foyer, attempting to distract her. "So what do you think of this place?"

"It's nice."

The foyer was large and airy, and Kira's living room would have fit inside it, no problem. An ornate staircase curved over a tall archway that led into the back of the house. To Kira's left was a formal dining room, and to her right was a spacious living area with oversize sofas.

"Beats working at the office," Ollie said, leading her through the archway. "We've got Hunan coming. Logan's outside on the phone."

"In this weather?"

"Covered patio."

Kira stepped into the kitchen and stopped short, dazzled by the endless white countertops, sleek new appliances, and massive cooking island. In the breakfast room, financial news droned from a wall-mounted TV, and she noted the long wooden table blanketed with files and legal pads. Logan and Ollie were already neck-deep in trial prep.

Kira glanced around the kitchen. "You could cook for an army in here." Not that she cooked, but hypothetically. "Is he even married?"

"Divorced." Ollie rolled his eyes. "He made out better than I did, though. Pays to be a lawyer. Want a beer?"

"I'm good. Listen, we've got a problem."

"One sec." Ollie took his phone from his pocket and frowned down at it as he scrolled through a message. He muttered something and looked up. "What is it?"

Kira set her files on the island. "Robert Peck. The defendant's doctor friend."

"The golf-buddy alibi. What about him?" Ollie grabbed a beer bottle off the counter and took a swig.

"I was at the courthouse, and I dug up an old divorce," she said.

"How old?"

"Fourteen years."

Ollie set his beer down. "I didn't know Peck had been married before."

"Yeah, guess he forgot to mention it. The marriage only lasted eight months."

"So what's the problem?"

"In the filing, Peck's ex-wife alleges infidelity, along with mental and physical cruelty. She got a temporary restraining order against him."

Ollie's face didn't change.

"It's not going to look good if the defendant's alibi witness is guilty of spousal abuse," she said, pointing out the obvious. "Undermines his credibility."

Ollie looked down at his phone again, and Kira gritted her teeth. She'd spent her afternoon combing through filings, and what she'd discovered could potentially sink Logan's case, or at least damage it.

"Ollie? You listening?"

He rubbed his chin as he continued reading. "We're dealing with something bigger right now."

"Bigger than your alibi witness being a wife-beating dirtbag?"

"If this pans out, Peck won't matter."

"If *what* pans out?"

He looked up, and something flashed in his eyes. It was a look she recognized, and her pulse quickened.

Ollie had something.

The doorbell rang, and he glanced toward the foyer. "That's our food. You staying?"

"I'm not leaving without my money."

"You act like I'm some deadbeat. Jesus."

He grabbed his beer and went to answer the door, leaving her alone in the huge kitchen. She hadn't planned to stay for dinner, but she wasn't going anywhere until she heard more about this new lead.

And met the Big Kahuna.

As if on cue, the back door opened, and Brock Logan stepped inside. The forty-something trial lawyer was tall and lean and had his sleeves rolled up to reveal tanned forearms. If he was surprised to find a strange woman in his kitchen, he didn't show it.

"You must be Kira."

"That's me."

The side of his mouth curved in a sexy half-smile, and she remembered all the rumors she'd heard about him. Logan was a player, and meeting him in person, it was easy to see why.

A crash came from the front door. Kira whirled around.

"Ollie?"

She rushed into the foyer and found him sprawled on his back, clutching his chest, a puddle of beer and glass beside him. Kira dropped to her knees. Had he had a heart attack? A stroke?

Blood seeped between his fingers, and Kira's breath caught.

"*Ollie!* Oh, my God!"

Something moved in her peripheral vision. She swiveled toward it just in time to see a dark figure sprinting through the dining room.

"Hey!" Logan, who had followed behind her, bolted back into the kitchen to intercept the intruder.

A wet gurgle jerked her attention back to Ollie. Blood trickled from his mouth now. His eyes were wide with shock as he pushed his phone into her hand. The device was slick with blood, and it clattered to the floor before she managed to pick it up and call 911.

A crash in the kitchen. Then a sharp yelp, followed by two low sucking sounds that Kira recognized instantly.

Gunshots, but the gun had a silencer.

A vase shattered nearby. Something stung her cheek. She scrambled into the living room, diving behind a sofa and smacking her head on an end table.

The intruder was *shooting* at her.

Another crash from the kitchen, and Kira's heart skittered. Was that Logan? The gunman?

She tried to think. The phone glowed in her hand, and she realized the call had connected. She muted the volume with her thumb and ducked low, trying not to make a sound. Where was the shooter? Inching to the end of the sofa, she peered around it. She could see Ollie in the foyer, and he wasn't moving.

Kira crawled back to him, hoping he'd stay quiet and then hating herself for hoping that. His face was slack and ashen. She stripped off her blazer and pressed it against the crimson stain on his chest.

Ollie, please.

She heard more commotion at the back of the house as she desperately tried to stanch the bleeding, but the wadded fabric was already soaked through.

Kira's stomach twisted, and she pictured the gunman walking up behind her and putting a bullet in her skull. Blood, warm and sticky, covered her hands now, and she felt a surge of panic. This couldn't be happening. She checked the phone again, hoping they were tracing the call. The line was still open, but she had it on mute. If the shooter was nearby, she didn't want to draw him in here.

Ollie, come on. Open your eyes.

He wasn't moving, wasn't blinking, wasn't making a sound. The rest of the house had gone quiet, too. She prayed the shooter wouldn't come back. Had he fled out the back door? Was he in another wing of the house? Where the hell was Logan? She pictured him dead in the kitchen, and her blood turned cold.

Everything was quiet. Too quiet. The only sound was the frantic pounding of her own heart.

Don't be dead. Don't be dead. Don't be dead.

The quiet ended with an earsplitting shriek.

CHAPTER

TWO

CHARLOTTE SPEARS pulled up to the curb and surveyed the action. This was not her lucky night. She counted five patrol units and two SUVs, but the CSI van was nowhere in sight.

She got out of the car, tucking a notebook into her pocket just as a media van turned the corner and rolled to a stop beside the police barricade.

"Oh for two," she murmured.

Charlotte studied the house. The sidewalk leading to the front door had been cordoned off with yellow crime-scene tape, so she picked her way up the steep lawn, cursing as her heels sank into the grass. She'd considered going with flats today because of the soggy weather but had ditched the idea. She'd learned to accept the dull pantsuits her job required, but she would never be a gumshoe.

Charlotte paused beside a pair of cement lions and noted the open French doors on the far end of the courtyard. Ken Phan stood in the doorway talking to another uniform.

Okay, so maybe her luck was changing. She liked working with

Phan. He had an eye for detail and didn't have a problem with female authority figures.

Phan looked up and waved her over to the alternative entry point. Something must have gone down near the front door.

"Welcome back, Detective. How was your break?"

"Too short," Charlotte said, trading her heels for paper booties. She stepped through the French doors into a formal dining room with a table big enough for twenty.

"What have we got?" she asked.

"Shooter rang the bell. Guy who answered took it in the chest, point-blank range," Phan reported.

She sniffed the air. "Smells like a fraternity party in here."

"Vic dropped his beer when he got shot. There's glass everywhere."

Charlotte stepped closer to the entry foyer, where a crime-scene photographer in a white Tyvek suit was crouched beside a dark red puddle. She snapped a photograph of the blood, then stood and stepped carefully around some shards of brown glass.

"Where'd she come from?" Charlotte asked. "I didn't see the van outside."

"They parked around the corner. Street was a mess when we got here. Looks like someone's having a party down the block."

Which would add even more chaos to an already hectic scene, no doubt. But maybe they'd catch a break and one of the partygoers had seen something.

Charlotte nodded toward the foyer. "Is our victim the homeowner?"

"No. Homeowner was in the kitchen. He had some kind of confrontation with the perp, who got a couple shots off and left him bleeding on the floor."

The photographer continued taking pictures from various angles. The puddle was smeared, and it looked like emergency personnel had already managed to muck up the blood evidence.

"Are the victims a couple?" Charlotte asked.

"The vic works for the homeowner." Phan smiled. "And last I heard, Brock Logan likes women."

She turned around. "Brock Logan the lawyer?"

"You didn't know?"

"No."

"Guy from the foyer is Logan's investigator, apparently."

Charlotte disliked lawyers in general and defense attorneys in particular. She'd never met Logan personally, but she'd gone toe-to-toe with plenty of defense attorneys in court over the years, and it was about as fun as a migraine.

Phan led her through the dining room and into a spacious kitchen. Most of the room had been taped off, including another bloody patch of flooring near the granite cooking island.

"Logan went down there." Phan nodded at the spot. Once again, there was a great deal of blood. Near a door to the utility room, Charlotte noticed a smear of red on the wall beside a keypad.

"After the shooter fled out the back, Logan managed to get up and set off the alarm," Phan said.

"What's the status on him?"

"Both vics were transported to Hermann Hospital. I don't have an update."

"Get one."

Phan stepped away and spoke into his radio as Charlotte studied the scene. The breakfast table was a mess of legal pads and index cards. File folders were strewn across the floor, along with loose papers and a FedEx envelope. Charlotte noted two black power cords plugged into the wall but no computers in sight.

"We're getting an update," Phan reported.

"Two laptops stolen?"

"Looks like. But nothing obviously missing in the rest of the house. There's a bunch of high-end electronics everywhere. He's got a gold Rolex sitting on the dresser in the master bedroom and a pistol in the top drawer of the nightstand, so not your typical burglary."

Charlotte didn't like the sound of that.

"There's a partial footprint on the FedEx envelope on the floor there," Charlotte said. "Make sure the techs see it."

"I did."

She shook her head. "So this guy just rings the bell, shoots Logan's PI, comes in here and shoots Logan, then helps himself to some computers?" She glanced through the archway into the entry foyer. "Why'd the PI open the door in the first place?"

"Witness said they were expecting a food delivery."

Charlotte's gaze snapped to Phan. "What witness?"

"There was a girl here, too."

"A child?"

"No, a woman. Sorry." Phan cleared his throat. "She was here the whole time. The perp shot at her and missed."

"Is she injured?"

"No."

"Where the hell is she?"

Kira sat motionless on the patio chair.

Motionless except for her hands, which wouldn't stop shaking. She clamped them between her knees but couldn't get them to still.

The scene before her seemed far away. Detached. She was surrounded by people and noises and clipped commands, and she felt like she was on a movie set, watching a cast of characters rush this way and that. She kept thinking someone would jump into the action and yell "Cut!" and it would all be over.

But the people around her weren't actors. They carried real badges and real guns with real bullets that could tear through flesh.

Kira's stomach roiled, and she leaned forward, hoping she wouldn't puke. She glanced at the huddle of cops on the other side of Logan's patio. The pool lights cast their skin in a bluish hue, and again she felt like she was in some alternative universe. She was sitting on Brock Logan's patio in a borrowed Harris County EMT sweatshirt with Ollie's blood all over her jeans.

Police had arrived shortly after the alarm sounded, and Kira didn't know whether it was her phone call or the security system that summoned them. Maybe both. Ollie had been loaded onto a gurney and whisked away. Logan, too. He'd been conscious, at least, and cops had pelted him with questions as paramedics wheeled him out.

Ollie hadn't been conscious at all. Hadn't been moving or even breathing, as far as Kira could tell.

She tucked her hands under her thighs, but still they trembled. She stared down at the little bits of glass embedded in her knees.

Kira took a deep breath to steady herself and got a whiff of chlorine. Logan must have just had his pool shocked. She looked out over the blue expanse, and again she felt like she was on a movie set.

As she watched the group of police officers, the patio door opened, and a tall woman with short blond hair stepped out. She wore pants and an HPD windbreaker, and she towered over her male counterparts, including the heavyset uniform who'd interviewed Kira earlier. Hanson? Hamlin? Kira couldn't remember his name. Her brain was only minimally functioning, and her answers to his questions had come out garbled and disjointed. Embarrassed, she'd asked him for some water, and he'd given her a look of disapproval before he'd flipped shut his notebook and walked off.

The woman turned, and her gaze rested on Kira. She broke free from the others and walked over.

"You're Kira Vance?"

"Yes."

"Detective Spears, HPD." She took a notebook from her pocket. "Can you tell me what time you arrived at the residence?"

"Where's Ollie?" Kira sat up straighter and squared her shoulders. "Oliver Kovak. He had a pulse when they took him out of here. I heard the paramedics talking."

The detective looked her over. "He's been transported to Hermann Hospital. That's all I know."

Kira's chest squeezed. A tremor went through her, and she broke out in a cold sweat.

"We should know more soon," the detective said. "Can you tell me what time you arrived at the residence?"

Kira took a deep breath. "Around six forty."

"And you were coming from . . . ?"

"Work."

The detective nodded. "Where do you work?"

"I work for myself. Not, like, for a company. I'm a licensed PI."

The woman's eyebrow tipped up as she scribbled in her notebook. "And you were coming from . . . ?"

"Downtown," Kira said. "I had some papers for Ollie that I knew he'd want for tonight's meeting."

The detective flipped a page in her notebook. "Officer Hanlin tells me you got a look at the shooter." Her eyes locked with Kira's. "Can you describe him?"

"It was a blur, really. I didn't see much."

"Was he white? Black? Tall? Short?"

"I don't know."

"Did you get a look at his clothing?"

"He wore a gray sweatshirt. He—" Kira halted. Her throat went dry.

"Ms. Vance?"

"I saw him before."

The detective's gaze sharpened. "When?"

"When I pulled up. He was jogging. He had a gray hoodie and shorts, and he was jogging down the street right in front of the house." The words spilled out of Kira's mouth, and she was sweating again. "I had a fleeting thought about how that takes discipline, jogging in the rain like that, but maybe . . . I don't know."

"You think he was casing the house?"

Kira nodded.

Spears eased closer, her gaze intent now. "What else do you remember?"

"He was white." Kira visualized the jogger. "Caucasian but . . . tan. He was tall. And he was wearing these tinted glasses. Amber-colored." Which was odd, now that she thought about it, given the weather. "I didn't notice his hair because of the hoodie."

Officer Hanlin was back, and he looked Kira over as he handed her a bottle of water. Spears motioned for him to step away with her, and they spoke together in low voices.

Kira twisted the top off the water and took a gulp. It felt cool on her throat, and she realized how thirsty she was. She guzzled half the bottle. Then she poured the remainder over her fingers, trying not to think about Ollie's blood as she wiped her hands on her jeans.

Another cop approached. He talked to Spears, and Kira overheard the words "Kovak" and "hospital." She held her breath as the detective stepped over.

"Ms. Vance? We just got word about your friend."

One look at her eyes, and Kira knew.

CHAPTER

THREE

THE WHINE of the Cessna's engine made conversation impossible as the plane banked and descended, and that suited him fine. Jeremy Owen didn't like small talk, and he had a special aversion now, as he closed in on hour forty-two of a trip that had bounced him around the globe. He'd started in Jakarta and been through three airports before getting waylaid in San Jose and catching a lift home on a client's jet.

Jeremy was on edge. He needed food, a shower, and about three days of uninterrupted sleep before he was fit for human contact. He glanced at his teammate across the aisle, who was in worse shape than he was, dealing not only with extreme fatigue but with a dislocated shoulder that was going to knock him out of active duty for the foreseeable future. It had been a grueling job. Things had started out crappy and gone shitty from there, and Jeremy was ready to put the entire op in his rearview mirror.

He scrubbed his hand over his itchy beard and looked out the window. The morning sun gleamed off the bayou, and he squinted at the glare. Last time he'd had a bird's-eye view of Houston's Buffalo Bayou, he'd been in a helo packed with veterans en route to a staging area. It was two days after a hurricane had dumped fifty-two inches of rain on the city, stranding thousands of people in flooded houses until a volunteer army had pulled them out in skiffs, airboats, and kayaks—anything that would float. Jeremy had been drained that week, too, but not nearly as exhausted as he was right now.

The Cessna swooped low over the trees, and Jeremy tried to shake off the daze as the ground loomed closer. It was a pissant airfield with a too-short runway, but the pilot coasted in for a perfect landing, and Jeremy wasn't surprised, because he was a former Marine.

At the end of the runway was a twin-engine Otter. Catching sight of the familiar pickup parked beside it, Jeremy went from dog-tired to alert in less than a heartbeat.

The plane taxied to a stop. Jeremy grabbed his duffel as his teammate exited ahead of him. Jeremy shook hands with the pilot, then trudged down the stairs, his attention locked on the man waiting beside the truck.

Erik Morgan was dressed as usual in black BDUs and boots, with a SIG P220 on his hip. But the look in his eyes made it clear something unusual was up.

Jeremy crossed the tarmac and stopped in front of him. "Tell me you're kidding."

"Nope."

Jeremy tipped his head back. He wanted to howl at the sky. Or punch something. Or turn around and walk away.

"Fuck," he said.

"Get in." Erik nodded. "I'll explain on the way."

Jeremy tossed his duffel in back and slid into the truck. Erik quickly got moving, veering around the Otter and speeding across the tarmac to the exit.

"The rest of Bravo Team is in Los Angeles, and Alpha just started a training rotation," Erik said.

"What about Lopez?" Jeremy asked.

"Special assignment in Aspen."

"What about Keith?"

"He's in already."

"Trent?"

"In already. So is Joel, and Cody's sidelined with the shoulder injury. That leaves me and you."

"*Five* agents?"

"Six, including Liam."

Jeremy stared at him. "Who's the client?" Not that he gave a damn, but it had to be someone big for their CO to be directly involved.

"Brock Logan."

Jeremy rubbed his eyes. "I've heard that name."

"He's an attorney in Houston. Involved in some big murder trial that's about to start."

"The doctor who killed his wife. I read about it." Jeremy shook his head.

"Someone tried to take out his legal team last night, killed one of them," Erik said. "Now his law firm's scrambling to hire protection. They've got an in with Liam, so everything's code red, rapid response."

Jeremy leaned his head back against the seat. Physically and mentally, he was whipped. He was in a black mood, too, and the dead last thing he wanted any part of was a hastily organized op for some VIP client. A well-connected attorney, no less. Shit, shoot him now.

He looked at Erik. His friend was tense. Determined. And he hadn't budged a millimeter on anything.

"Our entire op went to shit," Jeremy reminded him. "We haven't even done a full debriefing yet."

"Liam's aware. He wants you anyway."

"Then he's getting a compromised agent."

Erik looked at him. "Are you?"

Was he?

Deep down, Jeremy knew he was solid. He had four tours in Afghanistan under his belt and five years with one of the world's most elite security firms. He was trained to take a hit and get right back in the fight. Plus, he wasn't the one who'd made the mistake that screwed everything up. But still, he felt rattled. Pissed off. Morose. And all that was in addition to being tired beyond belief.

"I'm not a hundred percent," Jeremy said. It was the closest he could come to admitting he had some work to do to get his head straight.

"Get there." Erik looked at him. "We need you on this one."

Kira awoke with sun in her face and a screaming headache. She closed her eyes, trying to quiet the noise, but it only grew louder, and she sat up, wincing.

She hadn't felt this hungover since . . . when? Her brother's wedding? The World Series? But she wasn't hungover. She'd banged her head on Logan's table when she'd *dodged a bullet* last night.

A hard lump formed in her throat. She wished it was merely a case of too many tequila shots.

Kira swung her legs out of bed and glanced at the clock. Ten fifty.

She'd come home at two and fallen into bed without even pulling the covers down. The crumpled jeans on her floor brought back a flood of memories, and the noise in her head intensified.

Kira turned the shower to cold and jumped under the spray. Three minutes later, she was wide awake. Wrapping herself in a towel, she hazarded a glance in the mirror.

"Crap," she murmured, leaning close to the glass.

She looked—and felt—like she'd been in a bar fight. Her hazel eyes were bloodshot and puffy, and she had a cut on her cheekbone where a chunk of porcelain had grazed her. Her hair concealed the ugly goose egg on the side of her head, but it hurt like hell.

A low sound pulled her attention to the bedroom. Her jeans were buzzing. She grabbed them off the floor and dug a cell phone from the back pocket.

Ollie's phone. One of them, anyway—he had at least three. In the chaos of last night, she'd forgotten stuffing it into her pocket. Kira sank onto the bed and stared at the blood-smeared device. She didn't recognize the number, and she wouldn't have answered it if she did. God, what if it was his daughter? Had police notified his next of kin?

Kira pinched the bridge of her nose. She needed to turn the phone over to investigators. She'd do it when she went back to the station later. Despite five long hours of interviews, they wanted her back today.

She found a clean pair of jeans in her closet. In deference to the humidity, she layered a thin white blouse over a tank top and slipped her feet into sandals. Her phone chimed from the charger in the kitchen, and she rushed to answer it.

Dread tightened her stomach as she read the caller ID: LOGAN & LOCKE. Was it more bad news?

She closed her eyes. "Kira Vance."

"Kira, it's Brock Logan."

She breathed a sigh and leaned back against the counter. "Hi. How are you?"

"I've been better, actually. How are you?"

"Fine." The pounding in her head started up again, calling BS on that.

"Listen, we need to meet with you. How soon can you get down here?"

"You mean downtown?"

"Yes, here at the firm. We're having a meeting at noon. Can you make it?"

Kira glanced at the coffeepot and felt a bone-deep yearning. She ignored it as she processed Logan's request. He wanted her downtown. She'd assumed he'd spent the night at the hospital, where he'd been treated for a gunshot wound to his arm, but evidently he was out and about and organizing meetings.

"Kira?"

"Absolutely. I'll be there."

"Good. And bring your case files. Everything you have."

He clicked off, and Kira stared at her phone. Her "case files" consisted of a few slim folders she'd left at Logan's house last night. Plus a spiral notebook jammed with research she'd gleaned online. But whatever. She'd wing it, like she always did. Her more pressing issue was transportation. A detective had given her a ride to the police station, and Kira had caught an Uber home, which meant her car was still parked in River Oaks.

Cursing, she glanced at her watch. Maybe she could get Gina to drive her. Kira went to the window and parted the mini blinds to check out Gina's side of the duplex. The windows were dark, and their shared carport was empty. Kira scanned the street and didn't see Gina's car there, either. But she *did* see her landlord's shiny black pickup.

"Damn it," she muttered.

Bruce Garvis owned four properties on this street and made house calls when rent was late. He'd probably seen the empty carport and assumed Kira wasn't home.

Kira grabbed her keys and picked up her messenger bag. She stepped through the back door into the muggy August air and instantly began to sweat. It was going to be one of those days.

Kira poked her head around the corner of the house. No Bruce. She quickly unlocked the storage closet at the back of the carport and disentangled her bike from a strand of Christmas lights. It was a Specialized Sirrus Comp with an aluminum frame, and her Lazer helmet dangled from the handlebar. The seat was dusty, but the tires looked fine. She went straight for the back fence, wedged open the gate, and cut through the neighbors' side yard. They'd already left for work, and only their yappy terrier noticed her squeezing past the trash cans.

Kira hadn't been on her bike in months, maybe a year. Her head pounded, and her system pleaded for caffeine. But at least she was alive.

A lump lodged in her throat as she walked down the driveway. *You gotta work when the work's there.* It was one of Ollie's mantras, and she wasn't sure why it had popped into her head right now.

Kira reached the street and looked for any sign of a black pickup. She looped her messenger bag over her head so that it crossed her body. Then she pulled on her helmet, fastened the chin strap, and took off.

CHAPTER

FOUR

THE RIDE did her good. Not as much good as a greasy breakfast would have, but better than nothing, and she felt better by the time she reached downtown. She coasted down Allen Parkway. This was the easy part, but it was about to get rough.

Kira hit the incline near Tranquility Park and pulled herself out of the saddle. She pumped the pedals for two blocks, then hung a right onto Rusk, where she hit bumper-to-bumper traffic. Peering ahead, she spied orange cones and a utility truck, so she hopped the curb and cut over to McKinney, where traffic was slow but moving.

Sweat stung her eyes, and she squinted, wishing she'd remembered her sunglasses. She watched the gaps between bumpers, judging time and distance. Slicing between cars, she ignored dirty looks from drivers.

Kira loved her bike. It was fast and durable, and the tires felt grippy. She'd shelled out eleven hundred dollars for it back when she'd been riding three hundred miles a week as a court runner, racing legal documents around town. It was an investment in her first job, and it had more than paid off over the years.

The light ahead turned yellow, and the cars on either side of her surged to catch it. She pumped furiously, getting a burst of adrenaline as she made it through, just like old times. Glancing up, she saw a forest of steel and concrete, and the soaring glass skyscraper she wanted was just up ahead.

Kira shifted her weight, swerving around a van belching black fumes. She kept an eye on parked cars, careful not to get doored. She used the empty fire lane for the last half block and then hopped the curb and zipped through a concrete pocket park dotted with trees that grew through cutouts in the pavement. She glided between a pair of modern sculptures—big bronze arcs that had always reminded her of eagles. As she passed the giant fountain, she savored the cool mist on her skin and coasted to a stop by the wall of glass. Kira hopped off, lashed her bike to a rack with a heavy-duty chain, and rushed inside the building.

The air inside was an arctic blast, and she stood still for a moment as the sweat dried on her skin. Kira's thighs quivered. Her car had spoiled her, and she'd let herself forget how it felt to ride all day—the sore muscles, the burning eyes, the layer of grime that clung to her skin like plastic wrap. But there was some good, too. The bike made her feel revved and alert. It brought out her competitive edge, which she desperately needed on a day like today.

Kira took off her helmet and shook out her long hair as she assessed the lobby. The building had fifty-nine stories served by eight elevators. Crowds of people waited in front of each one.

The lunch rush. She was later than she'd thought.

Kira attached her helmet to the strap of her bag and made a beeline for the service elevator. She caught it just in time, jumping through the doors to find herself alone with two large men—a maintenance worker and a DHL guy, judging by their uniforms. She didn't recognize either of them, but her helmet and messenger bag said she was an insider, one of them, sure as hell not a stuffed shirt who worked inside one of the lofty offices with a city view.

"Floor?" DHL asked her.

"Thirty-seven."

They soared up, and Kira held her stomach, afraid of losing the breakfast she hadn't eaten. They stopped at thirty for the maintenance guy, and then it was a quick hop to her floor. The doors pinged open.

"Later." Kira smiled and stepped off. She followed the corridor around to the real elevators used by people in suits and ties.

Across from the elevator bank, shiny brass letters spelled out LOGAN & LOCKE. The firm had the entire floor, and a young receptionist with blond corkscrew curls sat at a glass desk in the waiting room.

Kira stepped over. "Hey, Sydney. I'm here for—"

Sydney gasped. "Oh, my *God.* What happened to you?"

Kira remembered the cut on her face. And that she probably looked a bit disheveled, having just hopped off her bike.

"Looks worse than it is," Kira said. She didn't want to get into the whole story, but realization seemed to come over Sydney's face, and Kira saw that it was going to be inevitable.

"Were you *there* last night? At Mr. Logan's?" Sydney asked.

"Yes."

"Oh, my God." She pressed her hand to her chest. "I heard about Ollie. I'm so sorry."

Kira's stomach knotted. "Thanks. Listen, I'm—"

"One sec." Sydney adjusted her headset. "Logan and Locke. How may I direct your call?" She paused. "One moment, please." Then to Kira, "What were you saying?"

"I'm here for an appointment with Logan."

"He's in a meeting, but have a seat, and I'll let him know you're here."

Kira bypassed the modern leather chairs and ducked into the restroom to smooth her hair and put on some lipstick. Once she was presentable again, she crossed the waiting room to the Keurig. She spun the coffee carousel and selected a pod. As the machine hissed and slurped, she noticed the man standing by the doorway watching her.

Tall. Bulky. He looked like a bouncer, only less friendly. He wore a dark suit and tie, and clearly he was some sort of hired muscle, because she noticed the bump of a gun at his hip but didn't see a badge. Kira dumped sugar into her coffee as the man pulled out his cell phone and answered a call.

"Mr. Logan will be with you soon," Sydney told her.

Kira walked back to the desk. "So who's the beefcake?"

Sydney slid a glance at him. "Don't know." She leaned closer and lowered her voice. "They showed up an hour ago, right after the police got here. Speaking of."

A pair of plainclothes detectives crossed the waiting room to the elevator bank. Kira recognized one of them from last night, but neither seemed to notice her. She was good at escaping attention.

Sydney's phone bleated.

"You can go on back now," she said. "Last office on the right. You can't miss it."

Kira took a long sip of coffee and dropped her cup in a trash can. "Thanks."

She walked to the back, passing several offices with closed doors before she reached a windowed conference room with people seated around a long black table. Logan's office was just across the hall, and

Sydney was right—you couldn't miss it. It was a corner office, and a desk sat in front of it, probably for an administrative assistant, who wasn't there. Logan's door was open, though. He caught her eye and waved her in.

The attorney was on the phone, and he didn't get up as she entered. He looked shockingly similar to how he'd looked last night, in a light blue dress shirt with his sleeves rolled up. His left arm was in a sling, which was the only overt evidence of his near-death experience.

Overt evidence. The grim look on his face told Kira he was dealing with some fallout.

She glanced around his office, pretending to admire the decor as she collected details about the man, starting with his wall of diplomas and awards.

Brock Logan was a legend in legal circles. He had an Irish-American father and a Puerto Rican mother, and he'd been raised Catholic, or so she'd heard. She'd also heard he'd inherited his mother's good looks and his father's taste for booze.

Logan's dad had run an auto-repair place in Beaumont that was rumored to be a chop shop. When he wasn't knocking his kids around, he managed to make decent money. Logan wasn't interested in his dad's business, so he left home at eighteen and worked two jobs to put himself through school.

Kira didn't like everything she knew about Logan, but she couldn't help but be impressed with what he'd done for himself. Despite his well-heeled clients, he'd come from a working-class background, which meant that at trial, he typically had more in common with the people in the jury box than with the client sitting beside him at the defense table. Logan was fluent in Spanish—which became known during jury selection when he pronounced names correctly—and he had an instinct for people. Jurors found him relatable, which didn't necessarily make them fall in love with his clients, but it helped.

Kira looked him over now, taking in the black sling and the small white bandage on his hand from an IV. Any other man might look sickly today, but he didn't. If he still had the sling during the trial—which was bound to be postponed—Kira had no doubt he'd find a way to use it to his advantage.

He ended his call and stood up, resting his good hand on his hip. "Kira, hi. We didn't really meet last night. You're Ollie's partner?"

"Associate."

Was. She *was* Ollie's associate. She felt a sharp pang in her chest.

"We started working together about three years ago," she told him. Ollie liked to keep her behind the scenes, so she wouldn't poach his clients. He gave her the work he didn't want, especially the online stuff, which he hated doing, even though it was becoming a bigger and bigger part of every job. Kira hadn't minded the arrangement when she'd been a brand-new PI just starting out, but she'd recently upped her rate and started pressuring Ollie to treat her as an equal.

"Sit down." Logan gestured to a chair. "I assume you noticed the detectives on your way in?"

"I did." Kira took a seat and nodded at the conference room across the hall, where another linebacker-size guy was now stationed beside the door. "I noticed them, too. Who are they?"

"Private security." He leaned back in his chair. "We hired them this morning."

Kira looked at the conference room again and counted nine people seated around a table. Everyone wore suits, but the bodyguards were easy to pick out because of their muscular builds and military haircuts.

"Lot of manpower," she said.

"It's a big job. Our team has four attorneys and a paralegal."

Kira didn't comment. No matter how many people they had staffed to the case, she knew when it came to trial, it would be just Logan and the client at the defense table. He was known as "Lone Logan" because he always liked to play up his client's underdog status.

She checked her watch. "You said there was something urgent?"

He smiled slightly. "In a hurry today?"

"I've got a meeting at the police station, and I still have to retrieve my car from your house."

"No, you don't."

"What do you mean?"

"It's not there. They towed it this morning. One of the neighbors must have called."

Kira cursed inwardly. Just what she needed today.

"Listen, Kira." Logan leaned forward, resting his good arm on the desk. "I spent several hours this morning with the detectives investigating Ollie's murder."

"Any arrests?"

"No."

"Suspects?"

"Not yet. I assume you talked to them, too?"

"Five hours last night at the station."

He nodded. "I was in surgery then. It was a through-and-through bullet wound. Messy but not too serious, so they discharged me early this morning."

"Glad you're okay," she said. "Were you able to give a good description?"

"Not really, since he was wearing a ski mask."

Kira must have looked startled, because he frowned. "What, you didn't notice?"

"It was a blur," she said. "I didn't see much of anything."

"The detectives told me the gunman, whoever he was, took the laptops and cell phones, along with some files off the table," Logan said. "They're working the theory that he was after information. Particularly information about the Quinn case. They think someone might be trying to throw a wrench into the doctor's defense by gunning down his legal team and stealing the case files."

Kira just stared at him.

"You follow?"

"Sure, but if that was the purpose, why aren't you dead?"

He looked taken aback. "I don't know. Luck, I guess? I acted dead on the floor, so maybe he bought it. Or maybe he just wanted the hardware. It's possible he was after something we have but don't necessarily *know* we have yet. In that case, we might have been collateral damage, and the real goal may have been the electronics."

Kira watched him, trying to get her head around the idea. Was that really what all this was about? Laptops and cell phones?

"Which brings me to my next question," he said. "Why were you at my house last night?"

"I had info for Ollie."

"What info? He told me he'd just come up with something big that was going to help Quinn, but he hadn't filled me in yet."

"I found some new background on your alibi witness, Robert Peck."

He looked disappointed. "That's it?"

"He's your star witness. I'd say he's key to Quinn's defense."

Logan watched her, and he looked like he was trying to decide something.

"I'll cut to the chase here, Kira. We'd like to hire you to replace Ollie."

She scoffed. "You can't just *replace* Ollie. He had twenty-five years on the job."

"We're in a jam. The trial starts in five days. This judge is a former prosecutor, and he favors the state. I plan to ask for a continuance, but—"

"You won't get it." Kira's heart thudded as she saw where he was going with this. "And Ollie wasn't Quinn's counsel, so his death isn't going to warrant a delay."

"That's correct. So you see my problem." He paused for dramatic effect—always the trial lawyer. "Ollie knew my case inside out. He knew every report, every witness. He knew my trial strategy. I don't have time to get anyone else up to speed."

"You want to hire me."

"That's right, I'd like to bring you in. You'd work for Logan and Locke."

"I work for myself." The thought of losing her autonomy brought a surge of panic. She hated face time and suits and being under someone's thumb, especially a man's. "And anyway, Ollie is not my only client."

Her heart was racing now. She was trying to play hardball here, but she worried that Logan could see right through her.

He gave her an appraising look. "What was your arrangement with Ollie?"

"I charged him by the hour. But I work for an insurance company and several other lawyers in town, too."

"That's a no-go. You'd work for us exclusively," he said, as she'd known he would. "What was Ollie paying you?"

She tossed out her overtime rate.

"I'll double it."

Kira stared at him, trying not to react.

"You know details of what Ollie was working on recently?" Logan asked.

"Not all, but I can get up to speed." God, was she really going to agree to this?

"I assume you have access to his office?"

"Of course."

Triumph sparked in his eyes. "Good. I want an update by end of today. Email works fine if you don't have a chance to get back here."

"I'll need an advance," she blurted.

"Done. Would a thousand cover it? Two?"

"A thousand is fine." *Holy hell.*

"I'll have Bev take you by accounting. Then we'll get you briefed on the security arrangement."

"Security arrangement?"

"The firm we brought in. Wolfe Security." He nodded toward the conference room. "They'll provide an agent and take a look at your home security setup, your transportation, the works."

Her *setup*? She started to laugh, but the look on his face stopped her.

"You're serious?"

"Absolutely."

"That sounds . . . thorough."

"Yes. And we expect your cooperation." His face looked grim again, as it had when she'd first stepped in here. "This trial starts in five days. We've had a serious breach, and we can't afford another one. The opposition already has the advantage."

"You act like you think the other side had something to do with Ollie."

He didn't respond.

"You don't actually believe that, do you?"

He leaned back in his chair. "Have you met Gavin Quinn?"

"No."

"He's one of the city's top heart surgeons. He's spent his career saving lives, not ending them."

She rolled her eyes. "Look, I'm not a juror here. I just dig up the facts and deliver them to you guys."

"My client is one hundred percent innocent, and I probably don't have to tell you how rare that is."

"I'm aware."

"Gavin Quinn didn't murder his wife, and I plan to prove that at trial." Logan's voice was impassioned, and she felt like she was getting a glimpse of his opening statement. "And you know what else? I think the prospect of him being acquitted has somebody running scared."

Somebody. In other words, whoever really killed Quinn's wife? Kira was reading between the lines, but she felt sure that was what he meant.

"You've worked on the case," he said. "What's your take?"

"My *take* is that this doctor must be a pretty smooth talker for you to believe your own bullshit."

Logan's lip quirked. "Ollie mentioned you were outspoken."

"My job isn't to spin things, Mr. Logan. It's to track down facts. And speaking of, I really need to—"

"I'll get Bev." He hit a button on his phone and stood up. "Welcome aboard. And since we'll be working together, you should call me Brock."

A woman strode into the room. She had short brown hair and a take-charge look in her eyes.

"This is Beverly," he said. "She'll take you by accounting. I'll call and give them the heads-up."

Kira exchanged pleasantries with Bev and then followed her through a maze of offices. Kira's head was spinning. Logan, the investigation, the job offer.

The security team.

She'd deal with that later. Or maybe she wouldn't. For now, she had to focus on the logistics of her bank account, which, according to the firm's bespectacled accountant, was going to be getting a wire transfer by close of business today.

After leaving the accounting office, Kira ducked into a restroom to get away from prying eyes as she came up with a plan.

Brock Logan had hired her. He was about to pay her a boatload of money. All she had to do was figure out what Ollie had been working on right before he was killed.

Kira's chest felt tight. Maybe this was wrong. Too soon.

But Ollie's client needed her. And *she* needed the money. Her bank account was running on fumes, and the money Ollie owed her as of yesterday she could probably kiss goodbye.

I want an update by end of today.

Kira took a deep breath and straightened her shoulders. She could do this. She had to. She had to get through the day, the week. She could fall apart later when she had time.

She opened the door a crack and checked the corridor. Empty. She unhooked the helmet from her messenger bag. Holding it at her side as a prop, she strode through the reception area and past the shiny gold elevators to the corridor where the service elevator opened. She tapped the button to summon it and held her breath as she waited.

The elevator was empty, thank goodness, and she jabbed the button for U2, or parking level two. Her stomach plummeted as the car whisked down.

The underground parking garage was dim and humid and smelled of diesel fumes. She went straight to the stairwell, hurried up two flights, and stepped through the door into the blazing sun.

She blinked up, disoriented. Traffic hummed, horns blared, and the scent of hot dogs wafted over from a nearby food truck. She located the bicycle rack and race-walked toward it, relieved when she spotted her bike waiting for her. She knelt beside it and quickly unlocked the chain.

A shadow fell across the pavement.

Kira glanced up. A man towered over her, blocking out the sun.

He folded his arms over his chest. "Where we going?"

CHAPTER

FIVE

EXCUSE ME?"

"You're Kira Vance?"

She stood up, which put her eye-level with his neck. "Who are you?"

"Jeremy Owen. Wolfe Security."

Kira stepped back to look at him. Shaggy brown hair, tanned skin. He had a square jaw covered with at least a week's worth of beard.

"I'm head of your security detail," he said. "We were supposed to meet upstairs at the briefing. Which you skipped."

His blue eyes looked irritated and bloodshot and together with the scruff made him seem like he was coming off a weekend bender. Except for the gun. He wore jeans and an untucked black T-shirt that did little to conceal the holster at his hip.

"My *detail*?" she asked.

"That's right. I'm—"

A jackhammer sounded nearby, drowning him out. Kira waited patiently until the noise stopped.

"Look, Mr. . . ." What had he said?

"Jeremy."

"Not to be rude, Jeremy, but I don't have time for this now. I have a police interview, and I'm late to pick up my car." At least some of that was true, but he looked unmoved. "Let's reschedule for tonight. Maybe around six? I should be clear by then, and we can go over whatever it is." She stuffed the chain into her bag and jerked her bike from the rack.

He plucked it out of her hand, holding it by the frame.

"No deal."

"Excuse me? You want to put that down, please?"

"No."

"*No?*"

"Come with me."

He turned and walked back to the building, carrying her bike like it weighed nothing. He held the door open and waited, clearly expecting her to follow him.

She snatched up her helmet and complied, ducking under his arm into the air-conditioned lobby, where he guided her out of the traffic flow and set down her bike.

"Rescheduling isn't an option," he said as she glared up at him. Damn, he was tall. "But I'll make this quick if you want, and we can get to your interview."

She crossed her arms.

"Let's start over." He held his hand out. "I'm Jeremy Owen, lead security specialist with Wolfe Security."

It seemed petty not to shake his hand, so she did.

"Kira Vance."

"Good to meet you." He rested his hands on his hips and gazed down at her. "I understand you're on the defense team that was targeted yesterday evening."

"Yes and no."

His eyebrows tipped up.

"It's a long story." She huffed out a breath. "Look, is this really necessary? I don't need a bodyguard, and I'm very, very late for something, so can we—"

"If you don't like the arrangement, take it up with your boss."

"Brock Logan is not my boss."

"His law firm, then. They hired us to protect Logan's team, and I was told you're on it. Or am I wrong about that?"

She thought of the wire transfer hitting her account right about now. By taking the money, she'd tacitly agreed to all this.

And she thought about the likelihood that Jeremy had driven himself here.

"No, you're right, I'm on it." She blew out a sigh. "Sorry, it's been one of those mornings."

"No problem."

"Hey, so Jeremy, any chance you have a car here?"

"Yes." He picked up her bike again. "Tell me where we're going."

———

Kira Vance wanted nothing to do with him, and under normal circumstances, that might have intrigued him. Right now, though, it was all he could do to keep his eyes open as he navigated the traffic-choked streets of downtown.

"Hang a left at the intersection," she instructed.

Jeremy ran a yellow turn light.

"Pull over up here by the bank. Anywhere is fine."

He cut around a delivery truck and whipped into a no-parking zone.

"I'll just be a sec."

"Wait." Jeremy hopped out and went around to her door, glancing at the bike now strapped into the bed of his pickup with a bungee cord. Kira was already out of the truck, and he scanned the surrounding area as she crossed the sidewalk to the ATM vestibule. It was empty, and she walked straight to a machine.

Jeremy stationed himself beside the door as she shoved in her card.

"Are you guys always this attentive?" she asked.

He looked at her as she tapped at the screen. She was short and slender, with dark hair that cascaded down her back.

"Attentive?"

"You know, hovering." She glanced at him. "It's broad daylight, and there're about three security cams in here."

"Standard procedure. Which you would know if you hadn't skipped the meeting."

She shot him an annoyed look as the machine spit out bills. She briskly counted them before tucking the money into the front pocket of her jeans.

"Like I said, I'm in a rush today." She stepped past him. He caught her arm, and she gave him a startled look.

"Wait."

He pushed open the door and checked the area before walking her back to the truck, where she climbed in and yanked the door shut.

Jeremy went around and slid behind the wheel. Looking at her phone, she rattled off an address as he pulled away from the curb.

"Okay, so catch me up, since I missed the meeting," she said. "Are you guys really going to be shadowing Logan's team through the entire trial?"

"That's the plan."

"Sounds like overkill."

Jeremy didn't comment. The plan wasn't up for debate, and she wasn't a decision-maker anyway, so it wouldn't have mattered. He kept his mouth shut and his eyes open as he cut through downtown. Tall office towers gave way to low-rise buildings, which then gave way to strip centers and warehouses. They reached a vast parking lot surrounded by a fence topped with razor wire.

"This is it," Kira said.

Jeremy turned into the entrance and rolled over a strip of tire-shredding teeth. He crossed a potholed parking lot to a dilapidated shed bristling with satellite dishes and security cameras.

"I hate this place," she said.

"You've been here before?"

"Unfortunately." She pushed open her door. "You coming?"

She hopped out and approached the shed, where a guy in an Astros cap was seated behind yellowing plexiglass. Jeremy eyed the property's security measures, which weren't much. Then he eyed the line of cars parked toward the front of the lot—presumably the recent drop-offs—and tried to guess which one was hers.

After handling the paperwork, she returned to where Jeremy stood waiting. She looked up at him, using her hand to shield her eyes from the sun, and again he noticed the bruise on her cheekbone beside a small cut. Looked like she'd caught some shrapnel last night.

"So what now?" she asked. "Are you really going to follow me around all day?"

"I really am."

Annoyance flashed in her hazel eyes.

"Is there any chance I can talk you out of this?"

"No."

She blew out a sigh and glanced over her shoulder as a battered white car rumbled to a stop beside them. The Astros cap kid slid from behind the wheel and shot a wary look at Jeremy before disappearing back into his shack.

Jeremy looked at Kira. He'd been off by a mile.

"This is you?"

"Yep." She stepped over to the car and tossed her bag inside.

"Hold up."

"Why?"

"You've got a knock in your engine, and your tires are low. Not to mention bald." He eased past her and ducked his head to check out the car's interior. The engine light was on, which might be something minor, but still. He switched off the ignition and pulled out the key. "New plan."

"What? Why? I'm already late."

"You'll be later if you break down on the side of the road. I'll drive."

"But what about my car?"

"I'll have someone get it." He handed her the key and nodded at the attendant. "Let him know."

Jeremy turned away before she could protest and made a call to Trent. When he got off the phone, Kira collected her bag and stalked back to his pickup, clearly pissed.

Jeremy got behind the wheel.

"What time is your interview?" he asked.

"Two. That's in *twelve* minutes. There's no way—"

"Substation or main?"

"Main."

"Buckle up. We'll make it."

Ollie's phone buzzed from the depths of Kira's bag, and she pulled it out. It was a text this time. Again, she didn't recognize the number, but she took out a notepad and jotted it down. She was starting a list.

"Don't know the passcode?"

She looked at Jeremy. "It's Ollie's phone."

He lifted an eyebrow.

"What?" she asked.

"Withholding evidence in a homicide investigation could land you in trouble."

"Not something you need to worry about."

He didn't comment, just kept his gaze trained on the road. He wore mirrored sunglasses, and it was hard to read his expression, but she definitely sensed some disapproval.

Kira looked away, irritated. It was none of his damn business. Anyway, she'd turn the phone over soon, but in the meantime, she needed to get whatever she could from it. Ollie had definitely been distracted by something on his phone last night. Kira took out her own cell phone and did a search for the number that had just texted. No hits.

Why had she promised Brock an update so soon? She didn't have a clue what Ollie was working on, and there was no way she'd figure it out by today. She'd be lucky if she had anything by tomorrow, especially when all her time was being sucked up by errands and police interviews.

Maybe she'd been wrong to take this assignment. It seemed too soon. Disrespectful, somehow.

And yet she wanted the job. She *needed* the job. And if the roles were reversed, she knew Ollie would have jumped on this assignment.

He would have gone to the ends of the earth to investigate what happened. Knowing Ollie's skills, he would have figured it out, too. He wouldn't be sitting here clueless right now, wondering what to do next.

She slipped Ollie's phone into her bag, wishing she had access to his voice messages. Or his email password so she could check his inbox. Ollie was always forgetting passwords and usernames, so he jotted them down on sticky notes that he stashed in the top drawer of his desk.

Kira looked at Jeremy. "We need to make a detour."

"I thought you were late."

"It's important." She glanced over her shoulder. They'd just passed the street she wanted. "Hang a right at the next light."

Jeremy switched lanes without comment. She directed him through downtown, past the courthouse and the convention center to where the skyscrapers petered out. Their surroundings got seedier and seedier, and then the street she was looking for came into view.

"Take a left at the next intersection."

He made the turn, and Kira scanned the buildings. She hadn't been in this neighborhood in months. A yellow sign came into view advertising bail bonds in both English and Spanish.

"Ollie's office is in the two-story brown building. See?"

"Yeah."

"You can park here on the right."

Ollie's building was the next one down, a 1970s walk-up, and his office was directly above a Korean restaurant. No signage anywhere because Ollie didn't believe in advertising. He got his business purely through referrals.

Jeremy sailed past the building, and Kira looked at him.

"Why didn't you stop?"

"It's under surveillance."

"What?" She glanced over her shoulder.

"Gray Taurus. One block south."

He was right. Kira saw a man's silhouette behind the wheel of the car. How had she missed that?

Jeremy braked at a stoplight, and Kira checked the side mirror.

"Looks like a cop," she said.

"Maybe."

A black car slowed in front of Ollie's building. It was an unmarked four-door with a spotlight mounted to the windshield—clearly a police unit. The sedan parked in front of the building, and a pair of detectives got out, along with a uniformed officer holding a long black tool that looked like a crowbar.

"What do you want to do?" Jeremy asked.

"Keep going."

The light turned green, and Kira watched in the mirror as the cops filed up the metal staircase to Ollie's office.

She felt a surge of outrage. "Are they going to break down the door?"

"Maybe they have a warrant."

Kira looked ahead, picturing them jimmying open Ollie's door and going through his things. Just the thought of it made her irate.

"I have a key," she said.

"Want me to go back?"

"No. I'll come back later." She glanced at him, not sure why she'd told him that. Not sure why she trusted him at all.

All she knew was that she didn't want to go in with the cops there. When she went through Ollie's belongings, she didn't want police looking over her shoulder. Or trying to prevent her from doing it. Yes, she had a key to his office, but her name wasn't on the lease, and she wasn't officially his business partner. Legally, it was a gray area. Kira encountered those a lot, and she'd learned it was easier to ask forgiveness than permission.

"How'd you get into this?"

She looked at Jeremy. "What, PI work?"

"Yeah."

"I was a court runner while I was in college at U of H. It's like a bike messenger, running docs around town between the law firms and courthouses. I met Ollie at one of the firms."

"So you knew him a while?"

"Six years. We've been working together the last three." Her chest tightened. It seemed like ages ago, but it really wasn't such a long time.

Ollie had spotted her when she'd been at loose ends and frustrated, in a dead-end job that paid the bills but barely allowed her to keep her head above water. Kira had once planned on going to law school, but the more lawyers she saw up close, the more she realized she didn't want to be one. Ollie had noticed she had an eye for detail and a knack for talking herself into places where she had no business being. He told her she'd be good at detective work.

Kira looked out the window as the buildings whisked by. She checked her watch. "I'm definitely going to be late now."

Jeremy didn't comment, and she snuck a glance at him again. His eyes were squinty behind the sunglasses, and his mouth was set in a firm line. He looked to be in dire need of some sleep.

They pulled into the police station at two twenty. He swung into a visitor's space, then reached into the back of his truck and rummaged through a duffel bag, pulling out a gray flannel shirt. To conceal his holster? Probably. It was ninety-five degrees out, so that had to be it. He slid his arms into the sleeves, and she watched his long fingers move deftly over the buttons.

Jeremy scanned their surroundings as he accompanied her across the lot to the building. When they entered the lobby, Kira stopped to let her eyes adjust to the dimness.

"Where to?" Jeremy asked, peeling off his shades.

"My interview's on three," she said. "And FYI, they're never going to let you up with that gun."

"I'll wait in the lobby."

She glanced around. The visitors here covered the spectrum, with people in everything from cutoff shorts to business suits, plus an array of cops from various jurisdictions.

She turned to Jeremy, who was watching her closely.

"Well, I should be plenty safe here." She smiled, but he didn't smile back. "You can probably take off if you've got stuff to do."

"I'm not taking off."

"Really, it could get tedious. I was here for five hours last night."

"I'll manage."

"Suit yourself."

She left him by the door and crossed to the front desk, where she checked in and was directed through security. She rode the elevator up, thinking about Jeremy.

He didn't fit her idea of a private bodyguard. For one thing, he had a boulder-size chip on his shoulder about something. She didn't get the sense that it had to do with her, but who knew? Maybe he'd wanted to be assigned to a hotshot like Logan, who worked in a luxury office and went out for martini lunches. Any danger that arose would likely be directed at him. His house had been targeted last night, and everything indicated that this threat, whatever it was, had something to do with his case.

Which Kira was now working on.

She pictured Ollie's colorless face as he lay bleeding on that floor. She felt a wave of queasiness and tried to shake it off as the elevator slid open.

Detective Spears stood waiting by a row of chairs, arms crossed. She wore a black pantsuit and heels, giving her several inches on the detective beside her.

"Ms. Vance, so glad you could make it," she said pointedly. "You remember Detective Alex Diaz."

"Hi." Kira nodded at the detective, who wore a dress shirt and a tie today instead of the jeans and golf shirt he'd had on last night.

Spears led the way down a familiar hallway and into an interview room. It was a different one from yesterday but furnished the same, with a laminate table and cheap plastic chairs.

"Can we get you some coffee? Water?" Spears checked her watch.

"No, thanks."

Everyone sat, and Diaz pulled out a file folder. Kira looked the detective over. Short dark hair, clean shave, no rings. He was probably five years younger than Spears, which made him late twenties.

"We'll get straight to it," Spears said. "Our investigation is still in the preliminary stages, but everything indicates this was not a typical armed robbery."

Kira suddenly wished she'd asked for that water.

"We're treating it as a targeted hit," Diaz said. He opened the folder in front of him and leveled a look at her.

"You don't seem surprised," Spears commented.

"Brock told me," Kira said. "That's why his firm hired security."

"Yeah, we heard about that." Spears looked at her partner.

"You think he's overreacting?" Kira asked.

"No, as a matter of fact, it's not a bad idea, given the circumstances." Spears tipped her head to the side. "You don't agree?"

"Seems overboard to put security on the whole team. But whatever. I'm not paying the bill."

Spears watched her, and Kira could tell she wasn't buying her nonchalant act.

Diaz flipped open a notebook. "We want to know if you've noticed any suspicious persons hanging around lately. Maybe near your home or office?"

"*My* office? No."

"You're sure?"

"Yes."

"What about phone calls or messages?" he continued. "Any suspicious vehicles following you?"

"No. Why?" She looked at Spears.

"Ollie's office was hit," she said.

"What do you mean, 'hit'?"

"Ransacked."

"Someone trashed it," Diaz said. "They were looking for something, and we don't know whether they found it."

An icy trickle of fear slid down Kira's spine. "When did this happen?"

"We just learned about it," he said. "We don't know when it happened, but we're checking with nearby businesses to see if anyone heard or saw anything."

"It leads us to wonder," Spears said, "if Ollie might have been the true target of last night's attack. Not Logan, as we originally thought."

Kira stared at her. She'd assumed this was all about Brock Logan. He was the one whose name was in the news all the time.

"We think maybe Ollie Kovak *had* something, or maybe he *knew* something . . ." Diaz trailed off, as if he expected Kira to fill in the blank.

"Something that got him killed," she stated.

Diaz nodded.

"Any thoughts?" Spears asked.

"I have no idea."

"Did he have any enemies that you know of? People who'd threatened him or might have a grudge?"

"Sure," Kira said. "Try every cheating husband he ever tracked down."

"I thought he did criminal defense work," Spears said.

"He does now, but he started out with domestic cases and insurance fraud, like most of us do. Still works a case like that from time to time if he gets a special request."

Diaz flipped a page in his notebook. "Ms. Vance, back to the shooter. Can you be sure he isn't someone you've seen before? Maybe while going about your normal routine?"

"I told you. I didn't recognize him."

"We'd like you to sit down with a sketch artist," Spears said, "and see if we can get a more detailed description."

"I keep telling you, I barely saw the guy. Caucasian, sunglasses, hoodie. That's all I saw. Any sketch is going to look like the Unabomber."

Spears nodded. "Nevertheless, we'd like to try. We have confidence in our artist."

"You've known Ollie, what? Five or six years?" Diaz asked her.

"Yes."

"And he personally mentored you after you got your PI's license, am I right?"

"What's your point?"

He shrugged. "Just that I'd think you'd want to help us catch the person or persons responsible for his homicide."

His copspeak was starting to grate on her nerves. And she didn't appreciate the guilt trip.

Kira closed her eyes and took a deep breath. They were doing their jobs, and it wasn't their fault her nerves were raw today.

"Of course, I want to help however I can," she said. "I just don't know what you want me to tell an artist. The guy was jogging in the rain, and I really only saw him for a second. But if you think it might be helpful—"

"We do." Spears pushed her chair back. "We'll set it up and get back to you with a time."

"Wait." Kira reached for her messenger bag. She pulled out Ollie's cell phone and slid it across the table. It still had blood smears on it, and the detectives were instantly riveted.

Spears leaned closer. "Is that—"

"Ollie's phone," Kira said.

"I thought it was stolen. Logan told us their phones were taken from the kitchen with the laptops."

"That was probably a burner," Kira told her. "Ollie kept a bunch of phones. He was always juggling numbers."

"Why?" Diaz asked.

"PI work. You don't always want someone to know who's on the other end."

"Why didn't you give us this last night?" Spears asked.

"I forgot I had it."

Her gaze narrowed with suspicion. "Do you have the passcode?"

"No."

The door opened, and a uniformed officer leaned her head in. "Diaz, the captain wants to see you."

He shot a look at his partner and left the room.

"Did you try to unlock it?" Spears asked.

"I told you, I don't know his code."

Not really an answer, and she could tell the detective noticed.

"Well, thank you," Spears said. "This is potentially very useful."

The detective stood, clearly eager to end the meeting so she could get the phone to some techie who might be able to crack it.

"We'll call you with an appointment time," she said. "It'll probably be this evening."

Kira shouldered her bag, thinking about the report she'd promised Brock. He wanted an update on Ollie's big break, and Kira still knew absolutely nothing about it. She didn't relish the prospect of dancing around questions with a veteran trial attorney.

"This evening's no good. I'm slammed," Kira said. "It'll have to be tomorrow."

"Early, then. The sooner the better." She gave Kira a sharp look. "In the meantime, be careful."

"I will."

"And I wouldn't turn down that security detail if I were you."

CHAPTER

SIX

DIAZ CAUGHT up to Charlotte as she left the squad room.

"Where are we headed?" he asked.

"To twist some arms," Charlotte said. "What did the captain want?"

"Ballistics came back on the Kovak murder. The weapon is a Beretta nine-mil, but no hits from those shell casings."

Charlotte stepped into the concrete stairwell. It smelled like BO, but she'd learned to ignore it. She'd been taking the stairs lately in an effort to squeeze in extra cardio because she never seemed to find time to get to the gym.

"Not surprising the gun's not in the system, right?" Diaz said behind her. "Guy used a suppressor and wore a ski mask, so sounds like maybe a pro."

"I'm not sure about that. Four shots and only two hits? Half our rookies could beat that."

They reached the ground level and cut through booking before stepping outside, where a wall of hot air hit them. Charlotte's silk T-shirt was damp by the time she reached her car.

"What do you think of Kira Vance?" Diaz asked, sliding into the passenger seat.

"I don't trust her." Charlotte waited impatiently for a couple of uniforms to pass and then shot backward out of the space. "She's dragging her feet on the suspect sketch. And I don't like that she kept the vic's phone overnight."

"Maybe she really didn't realize she had it," Diaz said.

"Or maybe she wanted a chance to wipe something she didn't want us to see."

"If that was it, why'd she give it to us at all?"

Charlotte looked at him. "You just like her because she's pretty."

He rolled his eyes, and Charlotte could tell she'd nailed it. Kira Vance was totally his type. The sexy long hair, the attitude. Plus, she was shorter than he was, and Diaz was self-conscious about his height.

"She said she didn't know the code," Diaz said.

"She could easily be lying."

He shook his head. "That wasn't my read. And why are you so cynical?"

"Fifty percent of the stuff people tell me is bullshit. That's why."

"So, what, you think she's a suspect?"

Charlotte shrugged, mainly to irritate him.

"Get serious."

"She didn't pull the trigger, but that doesn't mean she's not involved. I happened to notice she's the only one who got out of there last night without taking a bullet."

Diaz shook his head, and she could tell she was getting on his nerves. Which was good. He did better work when he was trying to prove her wrong about something.

"Speaking of liars, we're headed to the Hunan place," Charlotte informed him. "The delivery kid is due back at work at four."

Diaz pulled a notebook from his pocket and flipped it open. "Ryan Conyers, eighteen years old. He was a block from Logan's house at the time of the murder but claims he didn't see anything." Diaz looked at her. "You don't think he gave us a straight story?"

"Not even kinda."

———————

Jeremy didn't say a word as they left the police station, which was fine, because Kira didn't feel like talking. Ollie's phone had been the best lead she had, and she'd willingly handed it over to the police, who probably wouldn't even be able to open it. What a waste.

She cast a glance at Jeremy as he pulled out of the parking lot. She couldn't believe she was riding around in a truck with a perfect stranger who was armed and outweighed her by at least a hundred pounds.

He had an intensity about him, and his movements and posture signaled years of training. Simply put, he looked dangerous. Not to *her*, specifically, but to anyone who threatened him—although why anyone would was a mystery. You'd have to be crazy. Or have a death wish. In his line of work, he'd probably encountered people from both camps.

She wondered what sort of clients he protected. Rock stars? Actors? Famous athletes? If so, this assignment was going to bore him to tears. He'd probably already figured that out.

Jeremy shot a look at her but didn't talk. More of that cheery attitude.

"I need to go by my office," Kira told him. "It's on McKinney Street, south of—"

"I know."

He shifted lanes, but instead of turning at the next light, he kept going. Half a block later, he swung into a restaurant parking lot.

"What's this?" she asked.

"Food stop."

"I'm not hungry."

"We're stopping."

He got out, and Kira huffed out a breath as she pushed open her door. Space City Diner, according to the sign. The building was long and silver, designed to look like an Airstream camper.

Jeremy led her to the entrance and held the door open. Kira stepped into the narrow restaurant that had two rows of booths on either side of an aisle packed with tables. Ignoring the PLEASE WAIT TO BE SEATED sign, Jeremy touched her elbow and steered her to a booth behind the cash register, where he slid into the seat facing the door.

Kira stood beside the table for a moment before scooting in across from him. He rubbed his hand over his unshaven face and reached for a menu.

"What's with the power trip?"

He didn't look up. "I need food. So do you. You look strung out."

She barked out a laugh. "*I* look strung out? Have you seen a mirror lately?"

He glanced up, and his brows furrowed.

A waitress walked over. She had bleached-blond hair and a brisk manner that said she didn't appreciate time wasters. She wiped down their table and tucked a tip into her apron pocket.

"Get y'all some drinks?"

"Coffee, please," Kira said.

"Water."

The waitress walked off, and Jeremy slid his menu behind the condiment bottles.

"I had Trent drop off your car at your house," he told her.

"Who's Trent?"

"The other half of your detail. He was in the meeting you skipped."

Kira sighed. "And how does he know where I live?"

"It's in your file."

Great, they had a file already. It probably included her office address, along with a bunch of personal information about her.

"You need to get your car looked at," Jeremy continued. "Trent says it sounds like a transmission problem."

"I'll add it to my list."

The waitress returned with their drinks.

"What do you recommend here?" Kira asked her.

"Breakfast or lunch?"

"Either."

"Space City Hash. Best thing on the menu."

"Done," Kira said.

"Same," Jeremy said.

She jotted their orders and was flagged down by a cop at a neighboring table. Half the people in the place were cops, which made Kira hopeful about the coffee.

She tore open a sugar packet and looked at Jeremy.

She didn't like that a team of strangers had a file on her. It was her own fault for agreeing to all this, but still. She didn't want a constant escort, especially one who was a stickler for rules. She had to bend rules occasionally to get her job done.

"Listen, Jeremy. I appreciate Brock Logan's concern for his team's safety, and it's generous of the firm to hire you guys. But this arrangement isn't going to work for me. Not without some changes."

Jeremy watched her.

"I have to fly under the radar in this job," she said. "That's going to be hard to do with a supersized bodyguard tagging along behind me all the time."

His face remained blank.

"Hello? Do you have a response?"

"No."

"Why not?"

"This is not a relevant discussion."

She tipped her head to the side. "Are you always this rude?"

He looked at her, and she caught a flicker of remorse in his eyes.

"Sorry." He rubbed his chin and sighed. "I'm jet-lagged. Haven't slept in forty-eight hours."

That piqued her interest. And his roadkill look made a little more sense now.

"Where have you been?" she asked.

"Working."

"Where?"

He watched her, as if debating whether to reveal more, which was ironic considering he had a freaking *file* on her.

"Spent the last three weeks in Southeast Asia with a client," he said.

"Oh, yeah?" She sipped her coffee. It was hot and strong, just what she needed. "And what kind of clients do you guys have? I don't know the first thing about you."

"It varies. We get politicians, celebrities, business moguls." He leaned back against the booth and seemed to loosen up, although he continued to glance at the door.

"Sounds exciting."

"Not usually."

"So was this client a celebrity or—"

"Tech CEO."

"Anyone I'd know?"

"Doubtful." His gaze drifted over her shoulder, and she got the feeling he wanted to change the subject, which made her determined to pursue it.

"Try me. What's he do?"

Jeremy sighed. "You ever heard of Cloud Corp?"

The name rang a bell. She'd read something in the news recently.

"Oh, my God, *that* guy? Leo What's-his-name? Rollins?"

"Roland."

"Didn't someone *kidnap* him or something in Kuala Lumpur? I saw something about it online."

"Attempted kidnapping." Jeremy's tone was grim. "They didn't succeed."

She watched him expectantly, but he didn't say more, even though it had been all over the news. She'd have to hunt down more details online.

The waitress reappeared and set down two huge platters heaped with hash browns and veggies, plus two strips of bacon and a steamy fried egg on top.

"Anything else?" she asked.

"No, thanks," Kira said as Jeremy shook hot sauce over his food.

Kira dug in. The potatoes were crisp and golden, and she realized she was famished. For several minutes, they focused on eating, and she went over what she'd learned.

A few hours ago, this man had been halfway around the world

protecting a tech billionaire from armed extremists. Now he was sitting in a greasy-spoon diner with an underemployed PI who'd just drained her bank account to get her car out of impound. Kira had always thought *her* work was unpredictable, but a job like Jeremy's would give her whiplash.

She watched him eat, wondering about his background. Was he ex-military? Secret service? Despite his scruff, the way he carried himself made her think military. She'd find out. If there was one thing she excelled at, it was digging up intel on people, whether they wanted her to or not.

Jeremy looked at her over a bite, and she was struck by how blue his eyes were.

"Tell me about last night," he said.

Her throat suddenly felt tight. She forced herself to swallow. "What about it?"

"I want to know what happened."

He was watching her intently, and she sipped coffee to stall for time.

"Did you see the police report?" she asked.

"I was briefed on it."

"It happened really fast," she said, pretty sure she could get through an abbreviated version. "We were in the kitchen at Logan's. The doorbell rang. I heard a crash. Next thing I knew, Ollie was on the floor." She looked down at her plate. "There was so much blood everywhere. Then the paramedics were whisking him away."

"You left out a few parts. Like when the killer took a shot at you?"

She thought of the vase exploding beside her head. Her hands felt sweaty again, and she tucked them into her lap.

"Yeah, well. He missed."

He stared at her, clearly expecting more. But what else was there to say?

A chime sounded from inside her bag. She reached for her phone, welcoming the interruption until she saw her mother's number.

Shit.

She took a deep breath. "Hey, what's up?"

"Kira, thank God. Are you all right?"

"Fine. Why?" she asked, although the tone of her mom's voice told her everything she needed to know.

"I just got off the phone with Ruth. She saw on the news that Oliver Kovak was murdered last night. Isn't that the private detective you work with?"

"It is."

Silence.

"Hello?"

"Well, what *happened*?"

"The police are still investigating."

Her mom apparently didn't know that Kira had been at the scene, and she wasn't about to enlighten her. She looked at Jeremy, who was eavesdropping as he pretended to focus on his food.

"Those people are dangerous, Kira."

Those people.

"I can't really talk right now. I'm taking over some of Ollie's cases, so things are really busy."

"That doesn't sound like a good idea."

"It's fine. Insurance work, mostly. Let's catch up tomorrow, okay? I have to run."

"Well, be careful."

"I will. Love you."

Kira put her phone away and pinched the bridge of her nose. "I'm going to hell for lying to my mother."

Jeremy winced. "That case, we're probably all going to hell."

She looked at him, taking in his lean face and muscular build. He came across as such a badass, and she couldn't imagine him having a regular mom.

He pushed his plate away. "So what's the issue?"

"She hates my job."

"Why?"

"Too fringe." She drained her coffee. "PIs are right up there with repo men and bounty hunters, as far as she's concerned. She thinks I should get a real estate license."

The corner of his mouth curved. It was the first hint of a smile she'd seen from him, and she felt a warm pull in the pit of her stomach.

Kira turned to look for the waitress so she wouldn't stare at him. Jeremy was hot, no question. Yet another reason this bodyguard thing was a bad idea. Brock had handed her the case of a lifetime, and she couldn't afford any distractions. Or limitations.

A man stepped into the restaurant and peeled off his sunglasses. Tall, business suit, military-straight posture. He zeroed in on their table and walked over.

"Ms. Vance, I'm Liam Wolfe," he said, offering a handshake.

Kira darted a look at Jeremy before shaking the man's hand.

"May I?" Liam asked.

"Sure."

He pulled a chair from the table beside them and sat down.

"We didn't have a chance to meet earlier, and it's important you be briefed on the security arrangements."

Kira sighed, once again regretting having skipped that damn meeting.

"We've found things go smoother when the client has a clear understanding of what's going on."

"I bet," she said. "Although I'm not really your client, because I'm not paying you."

He nodded. "Technically, you're considered a protectee."

She looked from Liam to Jeremy and decided she was done trying to wiggle out of this. These guys were here. They were serious. She needed this job, and the best she could hope for would be to establish some boundaries.

"I'm all ears," she told Liam. "Tell me how this works."

CHAPTER

SEVEN

KIRA'S BODY language was defensive, and Jeremy could tell Liam picked up on it. She didn't want protection, and they'd had clients like that before.

"The law firm has requested round-the-clock surveillance for Brock Logan and everyone on his team," Liam was telling her, "as well as an agent on each of you whenever you venture out."

"*Venture?*" She arched a pretty eyebrow. "My whole job is a venture. This isn't the kind of thing you do from behind a desk."

"Understood."

"And what exactly do you mean by 'surveillance'?"

"We'll have an agent monitoring your home and your place of business. And accompanying you when you go off-site."

"That's fine, but they can't get in the way. Which means they can't be visible," she said. "Most of what I do requires me to keep a low profile, and you guys look like the Avengers."

Liam darted a glance at Jeremy. "That shouldn't be a problem. Our agents are used to keeping a low profile. Most of the time, you won't even know they're there."

Kira crossed her arms and looked skeptical.

Of course she'd know they were there. Yes, Jeremy and his men were trained to be discreet, but this woman wasn't your typical civilian. She was a PI. A good one, too, judging by how determined Logan had been to get her on his team. And if she was any good at what she did, she'd spot her detail's every move, even if they tried to stay in the shadows.

Liam walked her through the logistics, including the security system that would be installed at her house and monitored remotely. To Jeremy's surprise, she didn't push back on that at all.

Kira Vance was an odd mix. Quiet one minute. Opinionated the next. Her body language was all over the map—open, defensive, friendly, evasive. He got the feeling she was hiding something, but he didn't know what.

Whatever it was, he'd find out.

Liam shot him a look, and Jeremy knew he'd picked up on it, too. Despite her seeming cooperation, Kira wasn't on board with this plan, and that made her a wild card.

"And what about you guys?" she asked Liam.

"What about us?"

"You've got a whole crew of people covering us, round-the-clock surveillance, rolling shift changes. Are you guys local, or is this a traveling assignment?"

"We're based about a hundred miles north of here in Cypress Springs. You know it?"

"I've driven through," she said. "Not much to it."

"We're headquartered there, and we've got room to spread out. Simulations, firearms training, whatever we need to do. We're on the road about forty weeks a year, and the rest of the time we're training."

"That's a lot of travel."

"Our agents are used to it," Liam said. "In this case, we've got a block of rooms at an extended-stay motel near downtown."

"Extended-stay." She looked at Jeremy. "So does that mean you all *will* definitely be covering us through the Quinn trial?"

"Under the current plan, yes," Liam said.

She didn't look happy with this news, but she was done resisting. At least openly.

"That about covers it." Liam checked his watch. "Do you have any more questions?"

"No." She smiled. "Think I'm all set."

"Good. Then I'll leave you to it." Liam stood and gave Jeremy a warning look before walking away. It was subtle, but Jeremy caught it because he'd been working with Liam for years.

Kira watched him go. Then she turned to Jeremy as he pulled out his wallet.

"Thanks for the ambush," she said.

"Anytime. You ready?"

She wasn't ready for any of this, but it looked like she was going to fake it.

"Absolutely." She grabbed her bag. "Let's go."

Hunan Court was a narrow storefront between a lash studio and a high-end dog groomer called Mud Puppies.

"How do you want to play this?" Diaz asked. "You want me to go in there and ask for him?"

"Let's wait," Charlotte said, pausing by the grooming place. The window display featured an array of frosted dog treats that looked far more appetizing than the protein bar she'd had for lunch. "We need him away from his boss, so he'll feel free to talk to us."

She glanced up and down the sidewalk. At one end of the strip center was a dry cleaner, and at the other was a boutique coffee shop.

The restaurant door opened, and Ryan Conyers emerged. He held a pair of brown shopping bags in one hand and a cell phone in the other.

Diaz stepped forward. "Mr. Conyers."

The kid glanced up, startled. His gaze jumped to Charlotte.

"Us again." She beamed a smile at him. "Hope you don't mind if we talk for a minute."

He glanced over his shoulder. "I'm not supposed to—"

"We insist." She stepped between him and the little blue hatchback with the delivery sign on top. "This shouldn't take long. Let's grab a seat over there."

She and Diaz corralled him to the coffee shop, where they snagged a table under a red umbrella. Ryan looked uneasy as he set his bags on the table.

"I really have to get this delivery out."

"We understand." Charlotte sat down and pushed a chair toward him, and he gave her a wary look as he sank into it.

Ryan had long blond surfer locks, which went well with his sun-brown skin and faded Rip Curl T-shirt. Diaz was looking him over, probably noticing the pipe-size bulge in the pocket of his cargo shorts. He took a chair next to the witness, scooting it just a little too close for comfort.

"We checked out what you told us," Diaz said. "According to your manager, you left the restaurant at six ten to make a delivery to three ninety-two Stone Brook Trail in River Oaks. The time's printed on the order receipt."

Ryan drummed his fingers on the arms of the chair. "That's right."

"You had a delivery before that." Charlotte took out her notebook and flipped it open. "Three eighty-eighty Lark Street, one block over, correct? James and Lisa Macey."

The kid paled under his tan.

"You remember who answered the door?" Charlotte asked.

"Uh, the woman who placed the order? Mrs. Macey?"

"Do you remember what time?"

"I don't know."

"You told the officer last night that you went immediately from that delivery to the Logan residence on Stone Brook," Diaz said, "and that there were already police cars on the street."

"Uh, I—"

"An officer saw you pull up at six fifty-two. That sound about right?"

He glanced from Diaz to Charlotte, total deer-in-the-headlights.

"We're just curious about the timing," Charlotte said. "Say it takes five minutes to get from here to River Oaks. Call it ten in traffic. That puts you at the Macey residence about six twenty." She shrugged. "Seems to be a chunk missing in there."

He swallowed.

"How long does it usually take you to make a delivery?" Diaz asked.

"About, I don't know, ten minutes."

"Ten? Really?" Charlotte tipped her head. "Even when a woman invites you inside?"

He looked at Diaz for help, but the detective just stared at him.

"Look, Ryan." Charlotte leaned forward. "We don't care what you and Mrs. Macey were doing in her bedroom—"

"It wasn't her bedroom!" His voice cracked on the last word. "I swear. We were out by the pool."

"Wasn't it raining?" Charlotte looked at Diaz.

"Think so." Diaz shook his head. "That doesn't really add up, Ryan."

"No, I swear. She has this big patio. She offered me a joint, and what was I supposed to do? She's a good tipper."

They watched him, letting his words hang there.

"Why'd you lie to us?" Charlotte asked.

"I didn't. We hung out for, like, fifteen minutes, tops. I left before the sirens."

Bingo. Charlotte looked at her partner.

The Maceys' street backed right up to Logan's. The shortest driving route between the two houses went straight down Lark Street, which was where detectives believed the killer had made his escape after fleeing through Logan's back door and scaling the fence.

"Then what?" Charlotte asked.

"Then . . . I don't know. I chilled in my car for a minute and checked some baseball scores and then headed over to Stone Brook. There were some sirens, and when I got there, there were already a couple cop cars in front of the address."

Charlotte stared at him, trying to drill a hole into his soul, where she hoped he had some sort of a conscience.

"Come on, Ryan." Diaz softened his tone. "Think about the timing. You had to have seen something."

Ryan's shoulders drooped, and Charlotte felt a surge of adrenaline.

"There was a guy, okay?" He looked at Charlotte.

"Where?"

"Down the block. Lark Street. When I came out of the house, he was getting into his car."

Charlotte tamped down the urge to jump all over him. Maybe the guy was a valet. Or a neighbor. Or a guest at the party two blocks away.

"What did this man look like?" she asked.

"I don't know. He was walking away from me."

"What was he wearing?"

Ryan sighed and rested his arms on his knees, like he was struggling to remember. "Shorts. And a gray sweatshirt with a hood."

Diaz leaned forward. "Did he have a ski mask or gloves on?"

"What? No!" He looked panicked now. "Nothing like that. I would have said something."

"What else?" Charlotte asked. "Race? Hair color?"

"He was a white guy, okay? Brown hair. He had a gym bag with him. I figured he was going to work out."

"Are you sure you didn't see his face?" Charlotte searched his eyes, but it felt like he was telling the truth now. "Not even from the side?"

"No."

"Are you certain?"

"Yes."

"What about his car?"

He nodded. "Sure, *that* I could see. It was a black BMW."

Kira stood naked in her steamy bathroom, relieved to be away from people for the first time in hours. She wiped the foggy mirror with her hand and checked out her face. Without makeup, it looked worse than this morning. The bruise on her cheek had turned blackish purple, and her cut had reopened, so there was a brand-new scab where she'd caught the chunk of porcelain. She dampened a tissue and cleaned it up as best she could, but there was no getting around the fact that for the foreseeable future, she was going to look like she'd run into a big fat fist.

Another reason to duck out of seeing her parents this weekend. She'd have to think of a plausible excuse. She also needed to dodge her brother, who'd left a message on her phone this afternoon.

Kira, it's me, pick up. What the hell? I heard you were at the scene of a shooting last night.

Jack was a firefighter with Houston FD and had friends in law enforcement, so his sources were a touch more informed than Ruth Hovis, their parents' neighbor. Kira needed to make sure Jack didn't relay whatever he knew to their parents. The last thing she needed this week was a barrage of worried phone calls.

Kira wrapped herself in a towel and stepped out of the bathroom, letting the steam escape. She crossed the hall to her bedroom and checked her phone on the dresser, hoping for something from Ollie's mystery caller. She'd dialed the number earlier and left a message on a generic voicemail but hadn't heard back. She hadn't heard from anyone, in fact, since Brock had called wanting his update, and Kira had convinced him to give her more time.

Kira rubbed eucalyptus-scented moisturizer on her arms and legs. She took her wide-tooth comb into the living room and stood in front of the TV, combing her hair as she caught the tail end of *House Hunters*. A couple was looking at a home in Atlanta, with the wife proclaiming that the countertops were "unbearable" and the entire kitchen needed to be gutted. Kira imagined what the woman would say about Kira's 1980s appliances and warped linoleum floor.

Her phone chimed, and she grabbed it. It was her brother again.

"Hi, Jack."

"'Hi'? That's it? Why didn't you call me back?"

"Sorry." She sat down on the sofa and tossed her comb onto the table. "I've been slammed today."

"Jesus, Kira. What happened last night? Are you okay?"

"I'm fine." But her brother knew her too well to believe that. "Shaken, mostly. And Ollie—" Her voice broke on the word.

"I'm really sorry."

"Thank you." She cleared her throat. "They're still investigating, but they think it's related to this trial he'd been working on."

"The Quinn murder."

"Yeah."

"Aren't you working on that, too?"

"Yeah."

"Kira . . ." He had that protective-older-brother tone now, and she needed to change the subject.

"How's Aiden?" she asked.

"Sick. Emily took him to the doctor today. Another ear infection."

"Oh, poor thing."

"And you're changing the subject."

"I know. And I'm sorry, but I'm really wiped out tonight. Can we talk about this later?"

"I'll try you tomorrow. I'm off through Saturday."

"Sounds good. Give Aiden a hug for me."

"Be careful, Kira."

"Same goes for you."

She hung up and stared down at the phone. She and Jack were straight with each other, always had been. He didn't hound her about the hazards of her job, and she showed him the same courtesy. Their mother gave them both enough grief already, and they didn't need any more. But Kira knew Jack worried about her. More than a few times, she'd been confronted by an angry husband after she'd uncovered details of an affair. And a deadbeat dad had taken a baseball bat to her windshield one time. She'd never proved who did it, but she knew it was him. So, yeah, her job wasn't exactly risk-free, but whose was? Her brother put out fires for a living, and he accepted the risks with a stoic nonchalance that Kira admired.

She crossed her messy living room and parted the blinds to check the carport. Still no Gina, and it was almost eleven, so she was probably at her boyfriend's tonight. Kira also saw no sign of her security detail, even though Trent had told her he'd be in the area.

After the diner, Kira's workday had been a bust. She'd made the rounds by Ollie's office and his house, but both locations still had police units parked out front, and she'd decided to cut her losses. Jeremy had delivered her home, where they found a Wolfe Security crew parked in front of her house in a black Suburban, waiting to install the new security system. After making introductions and handing her off to Trent, Jeremy had taken off, no doubt to catch up on some much-needed sleep.

Trent turned out to be the guy from the lobby at Brock's firm. He gave her a crash course in her new system, which included sensors on every window and surveillance cams for the doors, all of which could be monitored remotely.

Kira loved it. She'd always been a geek about gadgets and spy tools, and getting her PI's license had only given her cause to indulge. The trunk of her car was filled with all sorts of cameras and listening devices, but the equipment Wolfe's crew brought over put her collection to shame.

Kira peered out the front window now, searching up and down the street again for any sign of a Wolfe agent. They were running a combination of fixed surveillance and drive-bys. Kira had to admit, they were keeping a low profile, which she knew firsthand wasn't easy to do.

She checked her watch. It was time. She'd convinced Brock to give her until tomorrow to meet, but if she didn't come up with something by then, he'd know she was bluffing and boot her off the job. She was out of excuses, and she needed intel.

Kira threw on her darkest jeans, a black long-sleeved shirt, and some old black boots unearthed from the depths of her closet. She collected a few supplies and zipped everything into a black backpack. Her hair was still damp, and she didn't want to take the time to dry it, so she scooped it into a ponytail and grabbed a baseball cap on her way out the door.

Stepping into her carport, Kira popped the locks on her car. Still no sign of Trent, but her phone vibrated as she backed out of the driveway.

She recognized the number Trent had given her.

Where to?

She texted back: *Dropping by a friend's. Won't take long.*

Would he be content to stay outside? Or would he insist on coming in? Kira very much hoped not. She was accustomed to doing her job solo, and having her movements tracked made her feel claustrophobic. Everything made her feel claustrophobic right now. Emotions churned inside her—sadness, anger, disbelief—but they hadn't bubbled to the surface yet. She hadn't cried since Ollie died, and she didn't know why. Her feelings, like everything else in her life right now, seemed to be on lockdown.

Kira opened the window to get some fresh air circulating. Hearing her car's knocks and pings, she felt a wave of uneasiness. Trent and Jeremy had confirmed her suspicion that she needed to get her car looked at. Maybe next week she'd get her head above water long enough to think about it.

Sure. That would definitely happen. Brock's trial started Monday, and she'd probably be running around fetching rocks for him all week.

Unless he fired her before that. Then she'd have all the time in the world to fix her car but no money.

Avoiding the freeways, Kira stayed at a comfortable forty miles per hour all the way to Ollie's neighborhood. It was very much like hers. Small lots, big trees, a mix of single- and multifamily homes. Due to Houston's crazy zoning, it wasn't unusual to see business and residential mixed together in the older areas, and Ollie's house was three doors down from a used-book store that offered tarot card readings.

Kira slowed and surveyed the area. No Trent, so maybe he was keeping himself invisible. Also, no pedestrians out tonight, only a cigarette-smoking man standing on the porch of the bookstore. Kira rolled to a stop in front of Ollie's and waved at the man as she got out.

Ollie's house was a one-story ranch that had a tidy lawn and could have used a paint job. Kira jangled her keys and strode confidently up the driveway as if she belonged there.

She scanned the garage and the covered breezeway leading to the back door. No sign of forced entry, no yellow police tape. She let herself through the unlocked gate and took a moment to look around.

It was a small yard, taken up mostly by a brick patio that Ollie had put down himself. Beside a neatly coiled hose was a gas grill protected by a canvas cover that was coated in pollen. Kira peered through the kitchen window, being careful not to touch the glass. Everything looked normal, and she saw nothing to suggest the place had been ransacked like Ollie's office. It looked as though the police who'd been here earlier had been searching for clues in the homicide case, not responding to a break-in.

Kira reached under the grill and felt around for the magnetic box. She found it and slipped out the hide-a-key.

A dog barked. Kira froze.

The sound was high-pitched, like maybe a poodle, but it was persistent. Kira held her breath and listened. The dog sounded at least one house away, maybe two.

Kira replaced the magnetic box beneath the grill, then crept over to the garage. She discovered the door unlocked, so she slipped the key into her pocket for later.

The stuffy garage smelled of dust and grass clippings. Kira stepped around a tool bench and noted the old push mower parked beside the door. Half the garage was empty—just a brown oil stain where Ollie typically parked the Ford sedan that was still being processed by police. The other half of the garage was taken up by the gray Dodge minivan that Ollie jokingly called his cool car because he used it for undercover work.

The van was a soccer-mom mobile, right down to the BABY ON BOARD hangtag on the rearview mirror. It was versatile, though, and could be quickly transformed into a utility van or a delivery truck, depending on Ollie's needs.

Kira walked around the back, casting a glance through the grimy row of windows at the top of the garage door. She stepped into the shadows along the driver's side and unzipped her backpack. After tugging on a latex glove, she took out her slim jim, wedged it between the window and the rubber seal, and fished around until she heard the telltale *click*. Then she opened the door and slid inside.

The van smelled of French fries and Old Spice, and the familiar combination put a pang in her chest. Ollie would never sit here again. And whatever he'd been doing last time he sat here might have gotten him killed.

She couldn't believe he was gone. *Gone.* The gray pallor of his face the last time she'd seen him was ingrained in her mind, and yet she still couldn't quite believe it.

Kira switched on her mini flashlight. It emitted a soft red glow, and she swept it over the floor littered with newspapers, food wrappers, and drinking straws. She popped open the glove box and was surprised to find it empty. She would have expected him to keep a map there or an owner's manual, or his insurance paperwork, at least.

Kira felt around under the seats and came up with a snack-size Snickers and a receipt for Whataburger. The purchase had been made five days ago in Channelview, which was forty minutes away. Kira slipped the receipt into her pocket and then climbed over the console into the back of the van.

Ollie had removed the back-row seating to make room for surveillance equipment, which he kept in a long plastic tub so that it wouldn't attract attention from nosy passersby. Kira scooted over miscellaneous crap: a stack of orange traffic cones, a yellow hard hat, a collapsed tripod. She knelt beside the tub and held the flashlight in her teeth as she opened the lid. On top were several magnetic signs that could be slapped on the side of the van when needed. Underneath an

AT&T sign, Kira found a jumble of photo equipment, including a Polaroid camera, a flash, and several boxes of film.

Beneath the Polaroid was a black nylon camera bag, and Kira's pulse quickened as she lifted it out.

Ollie's Nikon. He loved this camera. It seemed odd that he'd keep it back here, but maybe he'd been using it recently. She unzipped the case and pulled out the camera. Holding her breath, she popped the latch to check for the memory card.

Nothing.

Because that would have been too easy.

Deflated, she zipped the camera back into the bag. The side pocket had a spiral notebook filled with Ollie's messy scrawl. She flipped through a few pages, then checked her watch and glanced at the garage's back windows. She needed to hurry. She tucked the notebook into her pocket, then returned everything to the plastic tub and secured the lid.

The only other place of interest in the van was the tire well. Ollie had replaced the spare tire with a small generator, enabling him to work for hours in the van without running the engine. Kira searched the space but found nothing. She did a cursory search of the rest of the van, checking cushions and seat pockets, but that was it for clues.

Frustrated, she crawled back to the front and switched off the interior light before sliding from the car.

"Find anything?"

She jumped and whirled around.

A giant shadow loomed behind her.

"God!" She aimed her flashlight at Jeremy, and his face looked devilish in the red glow. "What the hell? You scared the shit out of me!"

"What are you doing skulking around here?"

"Nothing."

"Nothing?" He folded his arms over his chest. "I didn't just watch you break into a dead man's car?"

She jerked back. "I didn't *break* anything. And what are *you* doing here? I thought you were off the clock."

"Yeah, well, I'm back on as of midnight. Let's go." He took her arm, pulling her toward the door, and she felt the warmth of his fingers through her long-sleeved shirt.

"What are you doing?" She tripped over a paint can, and he caught her before she did a face-plant.

"Come on."

He opened the door and stepped out ahead of her before towing her with him. His grip was firm as he propelled her down the driveway.

"Would you *wait* a minute?" She tried to shake him off. "I'm not finished here."

"Yes, you are." He stopped and tugged the latex glove off her hand, then stuffed it into his pocket. "Trent picked up on the scanner that there's a possible burglary in progress at this address."

Kira's heart lurched. "Where is he?" She glanced around, but Trent's Explorer was nowhere in sight. She didn't see any patrol cars, either, or hear any sirens, so that was a good sign. Still, her heart was pounding as Jeremy pulled her toward the street.

"Gimme your keys," he ordered.

"Why?"

"I'm driving." He steered her toward her car as the faint wail of a siren sounded in the distance.

"Crap!" she said.

"Come on."

"That sounds far away." She stopped to rummage through her bag. Where were her damn keys? "We've got at least a minute or two—"

"Stop!"

A spotlight blinded her.

Beside her, Jeremy went rigid.

CHAPTER

EIGHT

HANDS UP! Police!"

Kira squinted at the light as she raised her hands in the air.

Jeremy's hands were already up. "Officer, I have—"

"On the ground!" The voice was panicked now. "*Now! Now! Now!*"

Jeremy lowered himself to a knee as the cop rushed forward and shoved him to the pavement. He must have seen the gun.

"I have a concealed-carry permit," Jeremy said. He said something else, too, but Kira didn't catch it because his face was turned away, his cheek flat against the concrete.

"Hands behind your head!" The cop looked at Kira. "You, on the ground!"

Kira's heart sprinted as she lowered herself to the pavement a few feet away. She awkwardly tried to keep her hands above her head as she stretched out on the driveway and rested her cheek on the cool cement.

The cop barked orders at Jeremy as he disarmed him and slapped on a pair of handcuffs.

"Any other weapons?" he asked, patting him down.

"No. I have a concealed-carry permit in my wallet," Jeremy said. "Right behind my driver's license."

Jeremy's voice sounded calm and controlled, which was amazing considering he had a knee in his back and a nervous cop yelling at him.

The officer stood and looked at Kira. "Any weapons?"

"No, sir."

"Don't move."

The cop was short and stocky and had a flat nose. He knelt beside Kira and patted her down, then searched her backpack, keeping his eyes on Jeremy the whole time. Even disarmed and cuffed, Jeremy was obviously the bigger threat.

Kira's chest tightened. The smell of asphalt filled her nostrils as she tried to breathe steadily with her cheek against the ground and her hands on her head. She thought of all the police shootings she'd seen on the news as the wail of sirens grew louder and louder until it was like a bullhorn in her ear.

The cop got to his feet as a car screeched to a halt at the end of the driveway. Two uniformed officers jumped out, weapons drawn, and every muscle in Kira's body tensed. They exchanged words and gestures with the first responder before finally putting away their guns.

Kira looked at Jeremy. His face was still turned away, and his hands were cuffed behind him. His black T-shirt had ridden up, and she could see his lean waist and the empty holster that had once held his gun.

Kira squeezed her eyes shut as her heart jackhammered. He could have been shot. They both could have. They could *still* get shot if some panicky officer pulled up to the scene and misread the situation.

The noise was deafening, vibrating through her body and reverberating off the asphalt. It was unnerving as hell, and she couldn't hear herself think.

All at once, the sirens ceased, and the only sound was the ringing in her ears.

"On your feet."

A hand clamped around her arm and pulled her up. It was the first responder, the stocky one. He spun her toward the headlights of the parked police car.

She looked over her shoulder at Jeremy, still prone on the driveway.

"Officer, if I could explain—"

"You have any drugs on you, ma'am?"

"No, I—"

"This your vehicle?"

"The Toyota. Yes, that's me. Officer, this is my friend's house, and we're just—"

"Any weapons in the car, ma'am?"

"No."

"Step over here."

———

Jeremy sat jammed in the back of the patrol car, his hands trapped behind him, watching the situation unfold as he tried to keep a lid on his temper. Just outside the window, Kira stood talking to a police detective, trying to convince her of something, although Jeremy couldn't make out the words.

The mention of Charlotte Spears had defused a situation that had nearly exploded after the first responder caught sight of Jeremy's SIG. The guy had rookie written all over him, and Jeremy knew all too well that inexperience, nerves, and loaded semiautomatic weapons were a bad mix.

The tall blond detective had arrived looking pissed off, but whatever tale Kira had spun managed to calm her down some. Not enough to free Jeremy from his vomit-scented cage, but at least they weren't being hauled downtown.

Kira wasn't, at least. Jeremy's fate was fuzzier.

The detective stepped over and jerked the door open, letting in a swarm of mosquitoes. Awesome.

"Step out of the vehicle, please."

He squeezed his knees past the seat and swung his legs out. Spears stepped back, and Jeremy levered himself from the car. She motioned for him to turn around, and Jeremy's gaze locked with Kira's as the detective removed his cuffs.

Kira watched him, biting her lip. Jeremy shook out his arms and felt the blood returning to his fingers.

"Mr. Owen, Ms. Vance, you're free to go."

The detective handed over Jeremy's wallet. Even in jeans and worn sneakers, the woman had a professional way about her that suggested she'd been on the job a while.

"My weapon?" Jeremy asked.

She jerked her head at a uniform beside her, and the man pulled Jeremy's gun from the back of his utility belt.

"Good thing your permit's in order," Spears said as the man handed over the pistol. "I would have hated to spend my night hauling you in." She looked at Kira. "No more unauthorized visits. We clear?"

"I told you, I—"

She held a hand up. "Save it. It's past my bedtime."

And with that, she walked off.

Jeremy looked at Kira, conscious of the chilly stares from the remaining cops on the scene. As the officers returned to their cars, Kira took a tentative step forward.

"You okay?"

Jeremy checked his magazine, then tucked his SIG into his holster. "Let's go."

He led her back to her Toyota and slid into the passenger side. He racked the seat back, but it was still a tight fit.

Kira got behind the wheel and looked at him. "Where'd you park?"

"Around the block."

She turned the key, and the engine choked and coughed.

"Don't say it," she said, pulling away from the curb.

Jeremy gritted his teeth.

"I don't need to hear it again."

He looked at her. "You mean hear it about your car? Or the stunt you just pulled?"

"It wasn't a stunt. I was gathering information. It sure as hell wasn't a burglary, because I have a key."

"Bullshit. You lifted the key from his barbecue pit. I saw you do it."

"So what? It's where Ollie keeps his spare, and he told me where it was!"

She got quiet then. Evidently, she hadn't realized that when they said round-the-clock surveillance, they meant round-the-clock surveillance. Whenever she set foot outside her house, they had eyes on her.

"Ollie would be fine with it," she said. "He'd want me to help figure out what happened."

She sounded determined, but Jeremy caught the tremor in her voice. Kira talked a tough game, like she had everything under control, but she was hanging on by a thread. It was only a matter of time before the traumatic events of last night came crashing down on her. He was all too familiar with how PTSD worked.

He glanced at her. Even in the dim light of the dashboard, he could see that her bruise looked worse now than it had this morning. He hated looking at it, and it bothered him that it bothered him.

They reached his pickup, which he'd parked in front of a purple house with a FOR RENT sign in front. Jeremy got out.

Kira waited for him, and he followed her through a string of neighborhoods, avoiding the freeways that might put a strain on her car. When they reached her house, he parked behind her in the driveway and walked her to the back steps without a word.

She unlocked the door. "Would you like to come in?"

"Yes."

Surprise flickered across her face.

"I need to do a once-over."

She ushered him inside and tapped the code into her newly installed keypad.

"Mind if I look around?" he asked.

"Knock yourself out."

"You have any firearms in the house?"

She shuddered. "God, no. I hate guns."

Jeremy did a quick walk-through, examining the sensors and cameras. Trent and Keith did solid work, but it never hurt to double-check things. Years in the Marines had shown him the importance of backing up everything, checking everything twice. *One is none, and two is one,* his CO used to say.

"You have to ignore the mess," Kira said when he returned to the living room. "My laundry's everywhere. It looks like a bomb went off."

"I didn't notice."

Actually, he had. He'd noticed everything—the IKEA furniture, the cheap art on the walls, the smallish closet. The lacy black bra on her bedroom floor had definitely caught his attention.

Her spare bedroom was interesting, too. She had a single bed piled with cables and camera equipment. A door on sawhorses served as her desk. She had no fewer than four computers—a desktop and three notebooks, all top-of-the-line. On the floor beside the desk was a tall stack of case files labeled with block-letter abbreviations. So, yeah, her place was cluttered, but there seemed to be a method to the madness.

"How about a drink?" she asked. "Beer? Bourbon?" She tossed her baseball cap onto the sofa and tugged the elastic thing from her hair, and it fell down her back in a dark wave. "I've got Gatorade, I think." She pulled open her fridge. "And orange juice."

"I'm good."

"Good? You damn near got *shot* tonight. That calls for a stiff drink."

Jeremy had been *damn near* shot dozens of times and actually shot once. Tonight didn't even come close.

"I'm good," he repeated.

"Well, I'm not."

She opened a cabinet above the oven and stood on tiptoes to reach for a bottle of Jim Beam. He could have helped her, but he liked watching her do it.

She turned and caught him staring. "So, what, you don't drink?"

"Not on the job."

She took a glass from another cabinet. "I should have guessed. You guys are professionals." She looked at him. "Why don't you just admit it?"

"Admit what?"

"You're angry."

"I'm not angry."

"Right. You're *not* angry that you spent half an hour handcuffed in a police car."

"Let it go, Kira."

"Why can't you just admit you're pissed off at me?"

"Fine! I'm pissed off!"

He regretted the words instantly and rubbed his hand over his beard.

Kira was smirking now. "See? Was that so hard?"

She poured a generous shot of bourbon, and Jeremy leaned back against the counter and watched her take a sip. He needed to go. There was no legitimate reason for him to be standing in her kitchen, but his feet seemed rooted in place.

"I owe you an apology." She plunked her glass down.

"Apology accepted."

"I can admit when I mess up."

She took another sip, watching him over the rim of her glass.

"I'm upset, but not for the reason you think," he told her.

She looked at him expectantly.

"You need to take us seriously," he said.

"I do."

"You called Trent a beefcake this morning."

Her cheeks colored. "He heard that?"

"We hear everything. We see everything." Jeremy stepped closer, hoping to intimidate her with his height, but she didn't look intimidated at all. "And you need to communicate. Keep us in the loop. This isn't going to work if you don't."

"Is that right?"

"That's right. I know. I've been doing this a while."

She folded her arms. "Okay, so let's play that out. First of all, I didn't know you were on duty tonight. I thought it was Trent—"

"You don't need to worry about who's on duty. We communicate with each other. Telling him is the same as telling me."

"Okay. So say I'd called up Trent and said, 'Hey, I'm going to catch a quick shower and then go sneak into the house of my business associate who was murdered last night.' Trent would have been fine with it?"

"No."

"Right. No. He would have tried to stop me. And this goes to what I said earlier, which is that I have a job to do, and you guys can't get in my way." She rested her hand on her hip and stared up at him.

This was going to be a hell of a case. Jeremy had suspected it the instant he'd seen the client, and it had taken about two minutes alone with her to confirm his suspicions. This woman was headstrong and sneaky as hell.

"Here's the thing, Kira."

She sighed.

"Ultimately, it's up to you. We work for you, not the other way around. So if you want to do something stupid, like go traipsing around a crime scene or go ticking off a bunch of homicide cops, that's your prerogative."

"See, that's exactly my point. What you consider stupid I consider necessary to doing my job. I've got"—she checked her watch—"fifteen hours to develop some real intel on what Ollie was doing right before he died, or Logan's going to fire me. I don't doubt it for a minute."

Jeremy doubted it, but he didn't bother trying to convince her.

"My job matters to me. *This assignment* matters to me, and I intend to deliver."

"Why?"

"*Why?* What kind of question is that? Because I said I'd do this. You probably get a paycheck every two weeks, but I'm paid by the hour. And if I don't do the job the client hired me for, that's it, I'm out. And I have to scrounge around for the next thing to pay my bills."

She looked defensive now. Maybe because moneywise, she wasn't exactly lighting it up.

"Is that the only reason?" he asked.

"What do you mean?"

"You're so dead set on doing this job for Logan, but you almost got killed last night. From where I'm standing, it would make sense for you to sit this one out."

"That's not going to happen." Her eyes turned somber. "Even if Logan hadn't hired me, I'd be doing this anyway. I believe Ollie had just uncovered something important—something that got him killed."

"What?"

"I don't know. But I can't walk away without answering that question. I'm an investigator. That's what I *do*."

But it wasn't just about a professional obligation. This was about Ollie. She didn't have to say it; he could tell just from looking at her. She'd watched the man bleed out in front of her, and Jeremy understood what that did to you. It was the kind of wound that scabbed over but never really healed, and you just had to live with it.

But she'd figure that out for herself.

She glanced down at her nearly empty glass. "It was weird being at Ollie's house," she said quietly. "I still can't believe he's gone. I keep thinking . . ." She trailed off.

"What?"

"Never mind."

Jeremy watched her, wishing she'd keep talking. Which was ironic, because every girlfriend he'd ever had complained that he never wanted to talk. It was the universal feedback that had cut short any long-term relationship he might have had.

"What was he like?" Jeremy asked.

She looked up. "You mean Ollie?"

"Yeah."

She sighed. "God, where to begin? He drank too much." She lifted her glass. "Loved his whiskey, so this is fitting." She tipped her head, mulling his question. "He gambled, too. On the sly. I don't think his family knew about it, but it created some financial strain. What else?" She added another sip of whiskey, and Jeremy started to wish he'd asked for some. "He went through two marriages and a live-in girlfriend that lasted five years. Basically, his personal life was a mess. But he loved his daughter and doted on his grandkids, *and* he was a hell of a PI. Taught me everything I know, including how to be resourceful, how to develop sources, how to be tenacious."

Jeremy made a low noise.

"What?"

He shrugged. "I bet you were tenacious before. It's a trait you either have or you don't."

Her look was suspicious. "Is that a compliment?"

"Yeah."

"Well. Maybe you're right." She took a sip. "Anyway, Ollie didn't give up. He never let go of a lead until he found something. It's one reason I feel so, I don't know, *directionless* right now. What if I'm in over my head?"

The vulnerability in her voice tugged at him. She was grieving. He could see it. And he wanted to say something comforting, but he didn't know what. Jeremy eased closer, and she looked up at him as the moment stretched out.

He cleared his throat. "So did you find whatever you were after tonight?"

And with that, the mood was broken. She turned and set her glass by the sink.

"No. But I found something."

"What?"

"I'm not sure yet," she said. "I still have research to do, which means it's going to be a long night."

It was a pointed comment, like he was keeping her from work, even though she was the one who'd insisted on this discussion.

"Believe it or not, Kira, we're not here to get in your way. We're here to keep you safe. And we'll do it one way or another, but it's a lot easier if you loop us in on what you're doing."

Surprise flickered in her hazel eyes. She gazed up at him, and Jeremy felt a jolt of attraction.

And that was it. Go time.

"You in for the night?" he asked.

"Yes."

"Good." He moved for the door. "I'll be around. Lock up behind me."

CHAPTER

NINE

THE SUSPECT sketch took longer than Kira expected. Two and a half hours, and that didn't include the time she spent talking to Diaz before the artist showed up.

The result was unexpected, too. She stared down at the easel, marveling at the drawing clipped to the board. It looked like a real person. Not only that, but it looked *exactly* like the man Kira had seen—for only an instant—jogging in front of Brock's house. Every detail was there, right down to the cleft in the chin, which Kira had not even realized she'd noticed until the artist coaxed the information from her memory banks.

"I can't believe it," she said. "I thought I didn't really see him."

"People always say that." The artist smiled. Fiona Glass. According to Diaz, she was one of the best in the country. "The mind is a mysterious thing. We absorb so much more than we realize at the time."

Kira studied the picture, done with pastels on pale gray paper. The drawing even showed details about the hooded sweatshirt, including the lime-green drawstrings Kira hadn't recalled until she was in the midst of the interview.

"Now what happens?" Kira looked at the artist. She was dressed in a gauzy peasant shirt and ripped jeans, but her manner was all business.

"Now I spray the fixative." She shook a can of Clairol Maximum Hold hair spray. "And we'll hand this off to the detectives."

"Can you do it without me?" Kira checked her watch. "I'm late for something."

"They'll probably have questions."

She was already reaching for the door. "They know how to reach me."

Kira did her best to escape notice as she hurried for the elevator. She didn't want to get dragged into another interview, so of course, her phone started chiming as she passed the detectives' cubicles. She pulled out her cell, and her heart skittered when she saw the familiar number.

The elevator doors slid open, and Kira jumped inside as she answered the call.

"Hello?"

"Hi, I'm returning a message from Kira Vance?"

"Thanks for getting back to me," Kira said. "I was calling on behalf of Oliver Kovak. I'm his business associate."

"Yeah, Ollie mentioned you. What's up?" The voice sounded curious but tentative. And young, too. Whoever this woman was, she was closer to Kira's age than Ollie's.

"I found your number in Ollie's contacts. May I ask your name?"

"Shelly Chandler."

"And do you work for a law firm?" It was a guess, but Kira went with her gut.

"I'm with Duffy and Hersch. Why? Is this about the package?"

"Package?"

"It should have arrived Tuesday afternoon. Ollie left me a message about it, so I looked up the tracking number, and it's showing it *was* delivered."

"So when you called Ollie yesterday morning, you were returning *his* call?" Kira asked.

"Yes. Why? And what's this about?"

Kira took a deep breath. "Ollie was murdered Tuesday night." Saying the words put a knot in her stomach.

"He—*what?*"

"He was killed. I'm sorry to have to tell you."

The elevator doors opened, and Kira stepped off. She spied Jeremy waiting for her in the lobby instead of Trent, who'd driven her over here. In contrast to yesterday, Jeremy looked showered and rested, and he wore a dark suit.

"Ms. Chandler? You there?"

"I'm here." She sounded even younger now. "I just can't believe it."

Jeremy watched as Kira crossed the lobby. She stopped in front of him, and he looked down at her with concern.

"Listen, I'd like to talk to you," Kira told the woman. "I'm taking over Ollie's cases, and I'm reaching out to everyone he was working with recently."

"But . . . we weren't working together."

"Are you at your office?"

"I'm . . . no." Clearly, she was rattled. "I'm on my way to the post office with a batch of certified mail."

"Downtown post office?" Kira didn't know Duffy & Hersch, but she guessed it was downtown.

"That's right."

"I'll meet you at Café Lu in thirty minutes."

"I really need to get back after—"

"No problem. This won't take long."

Charlotte's crime scene was buzzing with people, but they weren't the ones she'd expected to see here. A pair of workmen with face masks ripped up flooring in the foyer, while another crew was in the courtyard with a table saw, cutting tile for the kitchen.

Diaz walked through the front door, taking off his sunglasses. They'd spent the morning apart and arrived in separate cars.

"You coming from the station?" she asked him.

"Yeah."

"How'd the sketch turn out?"

"Pretty good." He shrugged. "Not that I recognize him or anything. He's not one of our frequent flyers."

"Yeah? And what does the witness think of it?"

"I don't know. She took off before I could ask her about it."

"You're kidding."

"Nope."

"That little sneak."

Diaz glanced around. "He's tearing everything out?"

"It's tough to get blood out of tile grout. Or so I hear." Charlotte sidestepped the workmen and walked into the breakfast room, where someone had cleaned up the mess that had been here on her last visit. Charlotte's favorite CSI stood at the bar setting up a laptop computer.

"What have you got for us, Lacey?"

The blond CSI didn't look up from her work. "Almost ready." She tapped a few keys and pivoted her computer to face Charlotte and

Diaz. "Okay, digital reenactment. I've been working on this since yesterday."

They stepped closer. The screen showed a mannequin-like figure wearing a gray sweatshirt and a ski mask standing in the courtyard in front of Brock Logan's front door. The figure had a black duffel bag on his shoulder, and he held a gun with a suppressor in his right hand. The scene featured details of the courtyard.

"You included the lions. Nice touch," Charlotte said.

"Couldn't resist. You ready? I've got about—"

The deafening buzz of a table saw drowned out whatever she'd been about to say, and Charlotte cringed. When the noise ceased, she looked at Lacey.

"You were saying?"

"It's about four and a half minutes," Lacey said. "Give or take a few seconds. That's about how long I believe the attack lasted."

"And that's based on what?" Diaz asked.

"Witness accounts, the nine-one-one call. It's a pretty solid estimate."

"Okay, let's roll it," Charlotte said, and Lacey tapped a key.

The front door was opened by another mannequin-looking figure. Based on the size and build, this was Oliver Kovak.

"First shot," Lacey narrated as the victim crumpled to the ground. The gunman stepped around him. He immediately pivoted left and ran into the dining room, where he ducked behind the dining table. A female-looking mannequin rushed through the archway leading from the kitchen to the foyer.

"Kira Vance," Diaz said, watching the screen.

"She doesn't see the shooter at first," Lacey said. "That's according to her statement."

Kira dropped to her knees beside the victim.

"Okay, watch." Lacey pointed at the screen. "The shooter waits until Logan enters the foyer, too, and then he rushes through this side door from the dining room into the kitchen. Logan sees him, goes after him."

"Why would he go after a guy with a gun?" Diaz shook his head.

"Maybe he didn't realize he had it," Charlotte said. "Remember, the pistol had a suppressor."

The video continued from the perspective of the shooter as he rushed into the kitchen and turned to confront Logan.

"Okay, two more shots," Lacey said. "Now Logan's down by the cooking island."

The shooter then ran back into the foyer and fired another round.

"That shot was wild," Lacey said. "Ended up embedded in the wall."

"He's in a hurry," Diaz muttered.

The shooter rushed back to the kitchen, dropped his duffel beside the breakfast table, and grabbed items off the table: two cell phones, two laptops. He rummaged through files, snatching up folders and stacks of paper, and shoved everything into the bag.

"According to Logan, he was in the kitchen bleeding and pretending to be dead during this time," Lacey said.

The shooter heaved the duffel onto his shoulder and took a quick look around before running through the back door. Charlotte recognized the patio beside Logan's pool.

"He seems to know his way around," Lacey said, as the animated figure rounded the pool and ran straight for a side yard. He passed some pool equipment and opened the gate, ran through, and then scaled the fence, landing in the neighbor's backyard.

"What's this based on?" Charlotte asked. "It was raining that night, so I heard we had trouble getting footprints. Do we know for a fact he took this route?"

"This is an educated guess," Lacey said, "based on the door where he exited and the witness who saw him on Lark Street."

"The delivery kid," Diaz said.

"Correct. This would be the most likely route between Logan's backyard and the BMW, but we have no witnesses to corroborate it, except for the delivery person who spotted him getting into the vehicle."

Charlotte returned her attention to the screen as the gunman pulled off his ski mask and gloves, stuffed them in his duffel bag, and then emerged from a side yard onto a driveway. He walked briskly down the driveway to the street, where a black BMW was parked.

"What about security cams?" Charlotte looked at Diaz, who'd been responsible for following up with the neighbors.

"Nothing."

The figure reached the getaway car, and the video stopped.

"And that's it," Lacey said.

"Nice work." Charlotte stared at the screen. "If we had more corroboration, we might even be able to show it to a jury at some point."

"Not happening," Diaz said. "We've been by every house twice. Nobody saw him."

"Lacey, thanks for this," Charlotte said.

"Sure thing. Want me to stick around while you do a walk-through?"

"Yes."

Charlotte dug her phone out and pulled up a crime-scene photo that she'd emailed herself to remind her of what the scene had looked like after the murder. She studied the mess in the photo, focusing on the empty spaces at the table where the two laptop computers had been. Charlotte turned to look at the breakfast table, which was empty now and smelled faintly of lemon furniture polish.

"He seems interested in the hardware," Charlotte said. "Almost like the people were secondary."

"Kovak didn't seem secondary. Point-blank range in the chest like that? That's brutal."

"Okay, you're right." Charlotte walked to the back door, studying the lock there. It was a thumb latch, so the shooter wouldn't have had to track down a key to get out, even if the door had been locked. She stepped onto the patio. She remembered the outdoor seating area from the night of the murder. A mop and bucket propped beside the door reinforced her impression that a maid had been here recently, probably yesterday.

Charlotte surveyed the backyard, envisioning the escape route. "What about dogs barking? Gates squeaking? Did anyone at least *hear* anything suspicious?"

"Not until Logan's alarm went off loud enough to wake the dead," Diaz said.

Charlotte walked around the pool, past the wrought-iron patio chair where she'd interviewed Kira Vance. She remembered the shell-shocked look on the woman's face.

She studied the concrete apron, looking for any clues they'd missed around the pool.

"Shame about the rain," Diaz said behind her. "Would have been good to get some footprints, at least."

Charlotte walked through the side yard, where the pool pump hummed softly. The air conditioner was going, too, and she walked past it to the gate. She dug a latex glove from her pocket and tugged it on.

"No prints. We looked," Diaz said. "And no footprints, either."

"I like to double-check things." Charlotte carefully opened the gate, studying the way it glided back without resistance or noise. It should have been locked, but evidently, Logan and his rich neighbors trusted one another too much to bother.

She walked into the neighbor's side yard, where she heard the hum of more pool equipment. She peeked around the corner of some sort of side building, maybe a cabana, and caught a glimpse of a vast blue pool shimmering in the sunlight.

"Must be nice," Diaz said.

"Bet they never swim in it."

No security cameras that Charlotte could see. No vicious guard dog that might have run down their perp for them, saving them a big investigation. She followed the path from the animated video through the side yard to the fence the killer had scaled in the video. The fence was at least seven feet high and looked new.

"Tall fence," she mused.

"So we know he's athletic. Not everyone could get over this thing. Could you?"

"Not with a heavy duffel bag," she said. "And not without falling on my ass."

She scanned the length of fence, making sure there wasn't a gate Lacey had missed seeing.

A scrap of yellow fluttered atop one of the fence boards.

"Well, shit," she muttered, stepping closer.

"What is it?"

"No way."

"What?"

Charlotte's pulse quickened as she pulled out her phone and snapped a picture. And another. And another.

Diaz stepped closer. "What the hell is it?"

"I don't know." But she did know. Or at least, she hoped. She reached up and carefully tugged the scrap of material loose from the fence board.

"Is that latex? Like, from a glove?"

Charlotte held it up, smiling. "Look at that, Diaz. I told you it pays to double-check."

CHAPTER

TEN

THE SIDEWALKS were eerily empty for a clear summer day. When Kira had started working downtown, it was the first thing she'd noticed as she zipped between courthouses and office buildings. Every street was choked with cars, but the sidewalks were nearly deserted, even during lunch hour. It had taken her a full week to figure out where everyone was, and she'd had to get off her bike to do it.

The downtown tunnels were one of the city's best-kept secrets. The subterranean labyrinth included more than six miles of winding passageways connecting Houston's soaring skyscrapers to a climate-controlled underworld of restaurants, shops, and theaters. When the air outside hit triple digits or a crackling thunderstorm rolled in from the Gulf, people took refuge under the city.

Kira and Jeremy reached Brock's building, which had one of the few parking garages connected to the tunnels. "Pull in here," she directed. "Get as close to the elevators as you can. We're running late."

Jeremy found a space and backed in his pickup, setting up a quick departure. "Where are we meeting her?"

"Café Lu. Best Vietnamese coffee in the city."

He lifted an eyebrow at that but didn't comment, and Kira headed straight for the elevator bank. Instead of tapping the call button, she pulled open an unmarked door leading to a long corridor that sloped down. Jeremy walked alongside her without a word.

She glanced at him, still struck by how different he looked from yesterday. His wide shoulders filled out the suit to perfection, and he could have passed for a *GQ* model or a high-priced lawyer. His face was touchably smooth now, but Kira missed the beard. She'd wanted to touch that, too.

He looked at her. "What?"

"You ever been down here?"

"No."

"These tunnels connect everything downtown. Except the courts. That's a separate system."

"How come?"

"I don't know. Maybe security?"

They reached the juncture where the corridor emptied into a spacious lobby with a fountain at its center. People sat along the fountain's concrete edge, munching snacks and scrolling through cell phones as traffic streamed around them. The occasional armed security guard scooted around on a Segway.

Kira led Jeremy through the lobby and into a tunnel. The lunch rush was over, but it was still busy with people running errands or grabbing an afternoon caffeine fix. Kira moved briskly, slicing through crowds, and Jeremy, with his long strides, had no trouble keeping up.

The tunnel branched in two directions. She veered right, then left again when they reached another fork. At every juncture, there were at least a few people standing stock-still, paralyzed with indecision as they tried to get their bearings. The tunnels weren't laid out on a grid, and without street signs and landmarks, it was easy to get lost. Kira took another turn.

"You know your way around," Jeremy said.

"I navigate by food."

"How's that?"

"Restaurant signs. And smells. That empanada place we just passed has amazing chimichurri sauce. And we're coming up on a popular smoothie shop."

Kira veered left at Juices Galore, where the whir of blenders echoed off the narrow walls. The next quarter mile was a straight shot. They passed a shoe-repair place, a drugstore, and multiple clothing shops before reaching a Mexican café, where piped-in mariachi music lured people for an early happy hour.

One last turn, and there it was. Café Lu had small tables out front, and Kira immediately noticed the woman scanning the crowd with a nervous gaze. Shelly Chandler? She had a coffee at her elbow and looked to be waiting for someone. The woman was young and petite, with long chestnut-colored hair and black-rimmed glasses. The glasses looked oddly out of place on her, like one of those eyewear commercials where you can tell all the models have twenty-twenty vision. Kira wondered if she wore the glasses to look older or smarter.

"You want me to hang out or disappear?" Jeremy asked.

Kira glanced at him. "Hang out. I want to get your impressions." She approached the table. "Shelly Chandler?"

The woman nodded.

"I'm Kira Vance." Kira turned to Jeremy, and Shelly's eyes widened when she realized they were together. "This is Jeremy Owen, who works with me." Kira pulled out a chair. "Mind if we . . . ?"

"No, please."

Kira took a seat as Jeremy asked a woman at a nearby table for a chair, snapping her out of her phone trance. She gave him a dazed nod as he commandeered the seat.

"Thanks for meeting with us," Kira told Shelly.

"Sure." She glanced at Jeremy, seeming to accept the coworker explanation, then turned to Kira with a worried look. "What happened to Ollie?"

Kira was prepared for the question, but she still got a knot in her stomach.

"He was working at a client's house Tuesday evening. Brock Logan? I don't know if you know him."

"That was *Brock*? Oh, my God." Shelly covered her mouth.

"You heard about it?"

"I heard some of the partners talking about a murder that happened on Tuesday night. I never imagined it was *Ollie*. I can't believe it. I mean . . . I just talked to him. Was it a robbery?"

"The police are investigating." Kira took out her phone and pulled up her photo of the suspect drawing. "They have a sketch of the man they think did it." She turned the phone to face Shelly. "He look familiar to you at all?"

"No." She shook her head and pressed her hand to her chest. "I just still can't believe someone would do this."

Kira glanced at Jeremy, who was watching her closely, probably wondering what more she planned to reveal.

Not a lot. Kira didn't want to discuss all the details of the case, especially not the detail that she'd been at Brock's house when the shooting happened. This woman already seemed upset.

Kira put her phone away. "Like I said, I'm handling some of Ollie's cases. Part of that is piecing together what he was working on the past few days." She leaned closer. "Could you tell me what you do at Duffy and Hersch? I assume you're an attorney?"

Kira assumed no such thing, but Shelly looked flattered.

"A law student, actually," Shelly said. "This is my second summer clerking for them."

"I see. What can you tell me about the package you sent Ollie on Monday?"

"Not much. I mean, it wasn't from me. Drew called me on Saturday and asked me to send it."

"Drew?"

Her cheeks flushed. "Andrew Spence. One of the junior partners." She cleared her throat. "He called me from the airport on his way to Orlando for vacation. He said he was doing a favor for Ollie, and could I go to the courthouse first thing Monday and request a trial transcript."

"Which courthouse?"

"Sorry. The criminal court. I go by the courts almost every day to file paperwork, so it was really no problem."

Kira itched to pull out her notebook, but she sensed that might make Shelly more nervous than she already was.

"And do you remember the case?"

Shelly shook her head. "Not offhand. I wrote down the number, though. I can text it to you."

"That would be helpful, thanks. So you submitted this request on Monday?"

"Yes. Mr. Spence wanted me to do it in person."

"How come?"

"Sometimes their online orders get backed up, and I think he was in a hurry. He told me to fill out the paper form in person and to go ahead and pay the rush fee."

Kira's heartbeat quickened as she listened.

"And the transcript was ready Tuesday?" Kira asked.

"Monday afternoon, actually. I got a message, and I was over there anyway, so I went by and picked it up. Then I overnighted it to Ollie, like Mr. Spence asked me to."

Kira watched her, desperately wishing she remembered the name of the case. Whatever it was, Ollie had been in a hurry to get his hands on it, which meant it was probably directly related to what he was doing the day of his murder.

"Is it unusual for Drew Spence to call you on a weekend with a request like that?" Kira asked.

Shelly blushed again. Her gaze jumped to Jeremy, then back to Kira. "Not really. He knows I work weekends. And he and Ollie were always doing favors for each other. Why?"

"Just wondering. Where'd you go to overnight the package?"

"Post Place. The one by the noodle shop across from the courthouse?"

"I know it."

"I checked the tracking number, and it was delivered to Ollie's office at four forty-nine the next day."

"But Ollie called you about it? You said he left a message?"

"Yeah, I don't know what that was about. Like I said, I checked the tracking number." Her expression clouded. "Why?"

Kira forced a smile. "Just trying to get a picture."

Shelly looked at Jeremy. "That's all? I can't help wondering if any of this has to do with . . . I don't know, whatever he was working on with Brock Logan."

"I'm not sure," Kira said.

Shelly bit her lip. Then she picked up her phone and checked the time. "I'm late getting back. Was there anything else you needed? You can always call me."

"I will, thanks," Kira said. "And if you think of anything relevant, give me a call. Anytime."

Shelly stood and grabbed her coffee, looking relieved to escape. "Good luck with your work. I'm so sorry about Ollie."

"Thank you."

Kira stayed seated and watched the woman disappear into the river of people. She turned to Jeremy.

"What did you think?" she asked.

"She was nervous. What did you think?"

"I think she's having an affair with Drew Spence, who's probably at Disney World with his wife and kids right now."

"Yeah, I caught that, too," he said.

"And it sounds like Ollie was in a big hurry to get his hands on that trial transcript."

"Any idea what it is?"

"No."

She glanced around the café. "You want to order anything? The line's not bad now."

"I'm fine."

Kira pushed her chair back, and her phone buzzed with a text. She read it as she stood up.

"Wow, she's efficient."

"Who?"

"Shelly sent me that case number. Come on, let's go."

He followed her out, but instead of retracing their steps, Kira led him farther into the warren of tunnels. They passed another shoe-repair place and stopped beside a barbershop with an old-fashioned red, white, and blue barber's pole out front. Kira peered through the glass before opening the door. She caught Jeremy's puzzled look as she went inside.

The shop smelled like shaving cream. New Orleans Saints memorabilia lined the walls. Kira smiled at the tall African American man standing behind one of the occupied swivel chairs.

"Daryl, hi."

He gave her a nod as he skimmed his shears over a customer's neck.

"Mind if I borrow your restroom?" she asked.

Daryl glanced at Jeremy behind her and raised an eyebrow. Then he gave another nod.

"Thanks."

Kira ducked behind the reception desk and grabbed a key that was attached to a clunky wooden fleur-de-lis. Jeremy followed her through the shop, past a series of cramped supply rooms to a heavy gray door.

Daryl knew full well she didn't need to use his restroom. But Ollie was a favorite customer, and Daryl let him and Kira come and go as they pleased in return for the occasional PI favor.

Kira unlocked the door and pushed it open. They were now in a private tunnel beneath a sixty-story office tower, most of which was occupied by an oil and gas company. Kira passed a restroom and a water fountain, then peeked around a corner to check for any security guards. Technically, she needed an ID badge to be down here, and she'd been stopped before.

"Want to tell me where we're going?" Jeremy asked.

"This tunnel links to the criminal courthouse. I need to request that transcript before close of business." She jerked her head. "Come on."

"I thought you said the courts weren't connected."

"I know a back channel."

"Of course you do."

"Hurry." She glanced over her shoulder and caught his look of disapproval. "And try not to be conspicuous."

Charlotte was hiding out in a windowless conference room when Diaz found her.

"What are you doing back here?" he asked, bringing the smoky scent of barbecue into the room with him.

"Close the door, would you?"

He dropped a pair of foil-wrapped bundles on the table and sank into a chair.

"Oscar's truck is out front." He twisted the top off a Dr Pepper. "Two-for-one sandwiches. Want one?"

"No, thanks." She sighed. "I've got a yogurt in the break-room fridge."

He nodded at the binder in front of her. "What's that?"

"The murder book for Ava Quinn. Thought I'd take a look."

He swigged his drink. "McGrath know you're poking around his biggest case?"

"He's not here," she said. "And I'm just perusing."

Cops were extremely territorial, and McGrath was the worst of them all. Even Charlotte *perusing* was enough to get his hackles up.

Charlotte pivoted to the TV screen and aimed the remote control at it. "I've been reviewing the press conference."

"Which one is that?"

"Day after the murder, when Quinn asked for the public's help catching his wife's killer."

She pushed play on the broadcast, and she and Diaz watched as a visibly shaken Gavin Quinn stood in front of the police station with Ava's family, pleading for anyone who had information about the home invasion and murder to contact police. Ava's parents and brother stood beside Gavin, struggling for composure as reporters peppered them with questions. The mom and brother broke down crying, but Gavin held it together.

Charlotte paused the tape, studying the doctor's face for hints of guilt instead of grief.

"Anything interesting in there?" Diaz nodded at the murder book.

"Plenty. For instance"—she leaned back in her chair—"I noticed in both murders, the victims were attacked at home during a robbery. Ava Quinn was confronted by her attacker at her back door, then he bound and gagged her and emptied the safe in the house before shooting her in the back. Logan and his people were also attacked at home around the same time of day."

"Okay, lemme play devil's advocate." Diaz unwrapped a sandwich, and the tangy scent of barbecue made Charlotte's stomach growl. "In *our* case, Oliver Kovak wasn't at home. It was Logan's home, and nothing was stolen except files and electronics." Diaz tossed his tie over his shoulder and picked up his sandwich. "Sounds totally different."

"Not totally. In both cases, someone came in and out of a house in an upper-crust neighborhood without attracting attention."

"Mrs. Quinn's killer didn't attract attention because it was her husband. The crime scene was staged."

"You assume."

Diaz smiled. "No, McGrath does, which is why the doctor was arrested and charged. They got gunshot residue on Quinn's hands, and he had his wife's blood all over him."

"Yeah, I read all that." Charlotte waved him off. "I'll let the lawyers duke it out at trial. My *point* is, in both cases, someone slipped in and out of a fancy neighborhood without attracting notice. And our guy, whoever he is, was driving a BMW."

"You think the crimes are connected?" Diaz asked around a mouthful of food.

"How can they not be? Our perp gunned down Logan *and* his investigator and took off with the files for the Quinn murder case six days before trial."

"So you do think Quinn had something to do with it?" Diaz's brow furrowed. "He's sitting across town under house arrest with a GPS on his ankle. And why would he want to hurt the people trying to get him off?"

"I'm not saying he did," she said. "I'm just thinking about those case files. Why would someone kill for them?"

Diaz wiped sauce off his lip. "Maybe someone didn't like what was in them. Thought Logan was going to expose something damaging in open court."

"Problem is, Logan said he doesn't know what it could be," Charlotte replied.

"And now you're all trusting? Of a *lawyer*?" Diaz smiled. "Just yesterday, you told me half the stuff people tell us is bullshit. For a lawyer, you could probably double it."

She frowned. "You think Logan knows the motive, but he's not telling?"

"Maybe. Defense attorneys hate us, we hate them. It's mutual." He shrugged. "Or maybe he thinks we'd leak the details of his case strategy to the prosecutor. Whose case is it again?"

"John Healy." Charlotte rolled her eyes. "And I wouldn't leak a word to that guy. He's a prick."

"Logan doesn't know that."

"Everyone knows that. At least, every woman does."

"I mean Logan doesn't know *you* think the guy's a prick." He polished off his sandwich with a big bite.

"Still, I don't see Logan holding back if he knows the motive for the murder of his own investigator. Oliver Kovak worked for him for years."

Diaz shook his head. "I don't know, but I'll tell you one thing. I've interviewed Logan three times now, and I get the same impression every time."

"Which is?"

"He says just enough and nothing more. Keeps his cards close."

Charlotte sighed as Diaz unwrapped the second sandwich. "Did you come here just to flaunt your fiendishly high metabolism? Or are you working on something?"

He slid the envelope toward her. "Report came back on the bloody shoeprint from the breakfast room. It's only a partial, so they couldn't determine the size. It's a Nike men's running shoe, and it's their second-most-popular style."

Charlotte grabbed one of the folders in front of her and combed through until she found the eight-by-ten crime-scene photo of the shoeprint on the FedEx envelope.

"In other words," she said, "there were a gazillion sold yesterday."

"Pretty much." Diaz picked up the crime-scene picture and looked at it. "The report says there's some wear on the tread, so *if* we get a suspect and *if* we get a warrant and *if* he happens to have a pair of shoes like this sitting in his closet, we might be able to get a match. Other than that, the shoeprint is a dead end."

"Maybe not." Charlotte took the photo from him and studied it. "I have another idea."

CHAPTER
ELEVEN

WHEN THEY made it to Ollie's office, it was worse than Kira had imagined.

Bookshelves had been toppled, file drawers emptied, pictures pulled off the walls. The mini fridge stood open, the contents pulled out and strewn across the floor. Kira stepped over a sofa cushion that had been gutted with a blade.

"You get clearance from the police to be here?"

She turned to Jeremy. "Spears wants me to make a list of anything missing."

"That's not what I asked."

"Yes, I got clearance."

He really was a Boy Scout about everything.

On the other hand, their last foray into Ollie's world had landed Jeremy in the back of a police car, so she couldn't really blame him for asking.

Kira deposited her messenger bag on a chair. "This place stinks," she muttered.

The office smelled like a combination of mildew and spoiled

shrimp, and Kira held her nose as she stepped around Ollie's big metal desk. All the drawers had been dumped, and the floor was blanketed in papers and office supplies. She crouched beside a pile of pens and legal pads, looking for any sticky notes where Ollie might have jotted his passwords. She didn't find any, and she moved to the credenza, where more drawers had been yanked out. The carpet squished under her feet. She stepped around the toppled file cabinet and found Ollie's forty-gallon fish tank lying on its side. Half a dozen dead goldfish littered the carpet.

"Those bastards." She knelt beside the tank. The filter had formed a dam, blocking several inches of water from escaping, and a tiny orange fish darted about in the pool that remained.

"I thought the police pried their way in," Jeremy said.

Kira stood up and looked at him. He was in the doorway, examining the hinges.

"They told me the landlord met them here with a key," she said.

"No sign of forced entry."

Kira stared at him for a moment before realizing what he was getting at.

"None at all?" She stepped to the door and examined it. No visible damage. The only marks on it were black smudges of fingerprint dust left behind by police.

"Maybe the gunman swiped Ollie's keys from Logan's house when he took the phones and computers," Kira said.

Jeremy grunted a response, still examining the door.

She picked her way across the room, grabbing a bottle of sweet tea that had rolled under a chair. She twisted the top off as she stepped into the cramped bathroom at the back of the office. Ollie had complained that the bathroom had a leaky ceiling and temperamental plumbing, but because it was attached to the office, the landlord charged him the "executive suite" rate.

She glanced around the space now, cringing at the slime along the baseboards and the moldy tile grout. Someone had taken the lid off the toilet and searched the tank.

"Anything missing?" Jeremy asked from the other room.

"Hard to tell. I noticed his CPU's gone, but I don't know what else."

She poured the tea down the sink and then rinsed the bottle.

"What about files?" Jeremy asked. He was standing near an air vent now, examining the metal cover that someone had loosened with a screwdriver. Whoever had searched this place had come prepared.

"I don't know," she said. "Here, help me with this, will you?"

She set the bottle on the desk and then lifted the fish tank. Even almost empty, it was heavy.

Jeremy took the tank from her. "Now I see why it stinks."

"Pour him in here."

Jeremy looked at her. "You're serious."

"Yes."

He tipped the tank, sending pebbles and plastic seaweed sliding as water streamed into the bottle. The fish remained behind, flapping and flailing, and Kira carefully pinched him by the tail and dropped him into the bottle.

Jeremy set the tank down and stepped over to a framed picture that had been pulled off the wall and tossed onto the sofa. It was a copy of the front page of the *Houston Chronicle* the morning after the Astros won the World Series for the first time in franchise history.

A hard lump rose in Kira's throat.

Jeremy picked up the picture. The glass was smashed, and the paper backing had been shredded by someone obviously searching for something.

"He was a 'Stros fan?" Jeremy asked.

"Yeah."

She turned away, settling her attention on the file cabinet. The folders had been pulled out and emptied, and she crouched down to try to make sense of the mess. They weren't case files. Ollie was careful not to keep paper copies of stuff like that. Mostly, it looked like business records—contracts, utility bills, his lease agreement. She combed through the heap, sorting it into stacks, although she wasn't sure what purpose that served at this point. Most of this stuff would probably end up in the trash. Would Ollie's daughter have to comb through it all? Kira could only imagine how painful it would be for her to see her father's office this way.

A commotion sounded in the hall, and Kira whirled around.

"Hey!" a voice yelled.

"What the—" Kira rushed through the door to find Jeremy pushing a man against the wall and pinning his arm behind him. Jeremy yanked a big black pistol from the back of the man's jeans.

"State your name," Jeremy ordered, tucking the gun into his waistband.

"Hey, fuck off. I work here."

"Let him go," Kira said, and the man looked over his shoulder at her.

"You know this guy?" Jeremy asked.

"Emilio Sanchez from next door."

"Jesus, Kira. What the fuck?"

Jeremy let the man go, and he turned around, red-faced. Emilio was short and bulky and had a thick black mustache. Jeremy was a foot taller, but that didn't stop Emilio from glaring up at him.

"What the fuck?" he repeated, looking at Kira.

"We hired security," she said.

"Who did?"

"Logan and Locke. You heard about Ollie?"

"Yeah." Emilio's expression softened. "I heard. Any arrests yet?"

"No. Jeremy, this is Emilio Sanchez, the business owner next door."

"Twenty-four-hour bail bonds." Emilio pulled a business card from his pocket and held it out, all hostility gone. "Hey, can I get my gun back?"

Jeremy darted Kira a look and then returned the weapon. Emilio stuffed it into the back of his pants as he craned his neck to see around Kira into Ollie's office.

"Shit, that's a mess. Did they totally clean him out?"

"I don't know yet."

"The police came by my place yesterday. We didn't hear the break-in, but they wanted a look at our surveillance tapes."

"You turn them over?"

"Sure. Why not? I try to keep things friendly with those guys."

Kira's phone chimed from Ollie's office, and she picked her way through the debris to her bag. She dug the phone out, glanced at the number, and muttered a curse before answering.

"Kira Vance."

"Please hold for Mr. Logan."

It was Bev's voice, and Kira felt a jolt of panic as she checked her watch.

"Hey, Kira, what have you got?"

She took a deep breath. "Some interesting developments."

"Good. We're having a working session at six. I need you there with an update on Ollie."

"I'm working on it. Some things are still unclear at this point, and—"

"Be there at six, or you're off the case." He paused. "That clear enough?"

"Yes."

"Good."

———————

Brock Logan's mansion was no longer a base of operations. While his house was being cleaned up, he'd moved to the Metropolitan Hotel and rented a suite for himself, plus an adjoining one for his security team.

Jeremy stepped into the living room, where luxury furniture had been pushed against a wall to make room for a table covered in computers and surveillance equipment. Erik Morgan stood there now, arms crossed as he monitored footage of the hallway, as well as the meeting taking place in the living room next door. Like Jeremy and Liam, Erik was a former Marine. He had done a stint in the secret service before Liam recruited him to Wolfe Sec.

"How's the principal?" Jeremy asked him, tossing his jacket over a chair. Jeremy hated the suit-and-tie thing, but with corporate clients, it was part of the deal.

"A pain in the ass."

Erik was in charge of Brock Logan's detail, so his assessment wasn't surprising.

"Is he checked out?" Jeremy asked. Some people were so clueless you had to tell them to look both ways before crossing the street.

"Checked in." Erik shook his head. "Wants to micromanage every goddamn thing."

Jeremy loosened his tie as he surveyed the black-and-white footage.

Their team had the hotel's exits on camera as well. The client's bedroom and bathroom had been omitted for the sake of privacy.

Brock Logan's living room was twice as big as this one, and a giant coffee table in the middle was covered in files and legal pads. Kira sat on the arm of a chair, notepad in her lap, as she talked with the man on the sofa beside her.

Jeremy tapped the screen. "This Neil Gautier?"

"That's him. You met him yet?"

"No."

"He's impressive," Erik said. "Junior associate. First in his class at UT Law."

"Age?"

"Thirty-one."

Jeremy watched the scene, and he didn't need audio to know that Kira and Neil were arguing about something.

Brock walked over and offered Kira a short glass of what looked like liquor. She shook her head, and he set it on the table in front of her.

"How's it going with Kira?" Erik asked.

"Fine."

"Yeah? I heard she's a handful."

"She is."

Jeremy watched as she tipped her head back to look at Logan. He towered over her, but she didn't appear intimidated. In fact, she looked annoyed. She'd had that same look last night in her kitchen. That was before the conversation turned personal. Jeremy wasn't sure why he'd asked her about Ollie. It wasn't like him to get personal with a client.

"Who's on her tonight?" Erik asked.

"Trent."

"You good with that?"

Trent was relatively new to the job. He was sharp, though. And he'd already had a wake-up call last night about their protectee.

"He's got it," Jeremy said.

Trent had Kira until six A.M., and Jeremy didn't know why that made him uneasy, but it did.

Kira was unpredictable. And unpredictable was far worse than being clueless or too hands-on.

Brock answered a phone call and left the room. Kira picked up the glass from the coffee table, walked to the minibar, and dumped the drink. She took a water bottle from the fridge and twisted off the top.

Jeremy watched her now that he had the freedom to really *look*. Her body was lithe and compact, and she had feminine curves. Despite her size, she had a take-no-crap attitude that helped her deal with all the men in her orbit, and there were a lot. He wondered whether Brock was sleeping with her. The man was protective and had insisted that she receive the same level of security as all the lawyers on his team, even though she was an outside contractor.

"You worried?"

Jeremy looked at Erik. They'd worked together for years, and his friend picked up on his cues.

It was a loaded question. Clients often hired them based on a hypothetical threat. They'd had concerning phone calls or messages, or an eviscerated pet on the doorstep. Jeremy had seen it all before. The danger was implied, which was still a problem, but not like the problem they were dealing with now.

In this case, Wolfe Sec was a postincident hire. The client had already been the victim of a brazen attack before Wolfe came on board. Kira had narrowly escaped a bullet, which put the threat level much higher than usual. Jeremy didn't like all the unknowns.

He eased closer and watched the monitor. "We still don't know whether she was a true target or a target of opportunity because she happened to be in the wrong place at the wrong time." He shook his head. "And if she wasn't on someone's radar before, she sure as hell is now after taking over Oliver Kovak's work."

Erik turned his attention to the screen. "You want me to trade with Trent tonight? I can pull a double."

Jeremy watched Kira on the monitor. She was in a secure hotel room, surrounded by armed guards, and she had an armed escort home, who would be staked out at her house overnight.

"No, he's got it," Jeremy said.

At least, he hoped so.

———————

Kira glanced at the bedroom and looked at her watch again. She wanted to wrap up this meeting and get out of here. Brock had been on a call for twenty minutes, and Kira's stress level had climbed as she waited for her interrogation. Why couldn't he get off the damn phone? She had way too much to do tonight to be stuck in a hotel suite.

Kira looked at the television, which was tuned to a local news broadcast. The anchorwoman segued into a piece about the upcoming trial of the prominent River Oaks doctor accused of murdering his wife.

As if everyone needed a reminder of why they were here tonight. Kira checked her watch and looked back at the TV. They were playing stock footage of the victim's family standing outside the police station, asking for the public's help in finding Ava's killer. Ava's parents and her brother were weepy and grieving, but Gavin seemed remarkably composed as he addressed reporters. A new clip appeared of Gavin in handcuffs as he was taken into custody, and Neil muttered a curse.

"Great." He tossed his legal pad onto the table. "Just what we need. More tainting the jury pool."

Brock strode into the room and dropped his phone onto a chair. He wore another custom-tailored shirt today and had his sleeves rolled up in a way that made his sling look almost sporty.

"That was Bev at the office. We heard back from Glenda."

"Glenda?" Kira asked.

"The judge's clerk," Neil said.

"The judge has our motions, and we're confirmed for Monday morning."

Neil shook his head. "We're not going to get a continuance."

"I agree, which is why we need to get our shit together." He turned to Kira. "Let's hear what you've got."

She squared her shoulders. Time to wing it.

"Ollie had come into some important information on the day of his death," she said.

"How do you know?" Neil asked.

"He told me."

"He told me, too." Brock sank into the armchair facing her. "Called me on the phone from his car, said he'd explain when he got there." Brock paused, searching Kira's face. "Any idea?"

"I believe he was working on an alternative case theory for the Quinn trial."

Brock leaned back, propping his expensive Italian shoes on the coffee table. "Why do you think that?"

"Because you don't have one. Am I right?"

"Don't need one. Our defendant has an airtight alibi."

Kira watched him. He looked confident, but there was an ever-so-slight defensiveness in his tone that told her she was on the right track here. Ollie had spotted a weakness in Brock's case, and he was trying to fix it.

"This is one of Ollie's things. *Was*." She shook her head. "He was obsessed about finding an alternative case theory, even if the defendant had a strong alibi."

"Why was he so obsessed?" Neil asked. He was relatively new to the firm and had never worked with Ollie on a case before this one.

"In a criminal trial, jurors want someone to pin it on," Kira said. "Especially if it's a murder. Whether they even realize it or not, they feel like it's part of their civic duty to settle the question of whodunit." She looked at Brock, who surely knew this, which was why he was touchy about the case he was planning to present.

"We've got loads of reasonable doubt," Neil said. "We've got an alibi showing Quinn was nowhere near the scene when the murder happened. We've got his cell-phone records. We've got a forensic expert."

"It's not enough," Kira said. "You need to do more than plant seeds of doubt. You need to do more than tell the jury your guy didn't do it. You have to let them know who *did*—or at least suggest it—or you're not likely to get an acquittal."

Brock watched her, his expression guarded.

"This was Ollie's core operating principle, and it didn't change from case to case," Kira said. "I think he was developing an alternative scenario—"

"Meaning an alternative suspect besides Quinn?" Neil asked.

"That's right. I think he found one, and that's what he was working on when he got killed."

"I don't disagree with you," Brock said. "Fact, I suggested the same thing to the detectives who interviewed me. But so far, none of this leads us in a specific direction." He looked at Kira expectantly. "Unless you know something I don't?"

She had *better* know something he didn't was what his tone implied.

"A couple of days before his murder," she said, "Ollie had been in touch with one of his legal contacts to get hold of a trial transcript."

Brock's gaze sharpened. "Who?"

"A lawyer with Duffy and Hersch."

"What trial?"

"Defendant was Andre Markov," Kira said. "It was an aggravated-assault case from two years ago. Ollie wanted the transcript so badly he asked his contact to have a staffer request it in person and put a rush on it."

Brock's and Neil's matching frowns confirmed that this was news to both of them.

"Interesting lead. I'm impressed," Brock said. "Any chance this criminal defendant killed Ollie?"

She shook her head. "I looked up his mug shot. He doesn't resemble the guy I saw at your house at all. He's much too short."

"Why would Ollie go through Duffy and Hersch?" Neil asked. "He could have made the request himself. Or used an admin at Logan and Locke."

"Maybe he didn't want the request tying back to him," Kira said.

"How would it?"

Kira stared at him. Of course, Neil didn't know. He'd essentially been the Heisman Trophy winner of his law-school class, wined and dined and inundated with job offers. He'd clearly never worked as a clerk or a lowly court runner, filling out forms and racing documents around town.

Kira summoned her patience. "When you fill out an in-person request, they ask for a bar number or law firm number," she explained to a man who probably made four times as much as she did. "If Ollie handled it himself, it would trace back to Logan and Locke."

"But what's that case got to do with the Quinn case?" Brock asked.

"I'm not sure, but I've got some ideas," Kira said, stretching the truth like a rubber band. "I've requested the transcript, and I read through a summary of the case online and made a list of names to run down."

"Who was the attorney?" Brock asked.

Kira flipped through her notepad and rattled off the names of the attorneys on both sides.

"You know them?" she asked.

"Not personally." Brock looked at Neil. "You?"

He shook his head. "Who was the judge?"

"Erica Farland."

"She's tough. I've been in her courtroom." Brock shook his head. "Still, none of this rings any bells. What's a two-year-old assault case got to do with Ava Quinn's murder?"

"Whatever this is, Ollie believed it was important. Important enough that it overshadowed everything else we were working on."

Neil looked skeptical. Along with Brock and the rest of the team, he had been working on that "everything else" for months.

"Look, all due respect to Ollie, but this may not even matter," Neil said to Brock. "We've got one of the nation's top gunshot-residue experts ready to testify that the GSR on Quinn's hands was transferred when he tried to render medical aid before the paramedics came. This expert is an amazing witness." He looked at Kira. "She's prepped and ready to go. And besides our forensics people who are going to cast doubt on the physical evidence, we've also got a rock-solid alibi in the form of a respected doctor who was having drinks with Quinn at the time of his wife's murder."

"Yeah, I'm not sure about that," Kira said.

Neil's eyebrows arched. "About what?"

"The respected part."

"What do you mean? The guy's a prominent surgeon and a big philanthropist. The jury's going to love him."

"Don't be so sure," Kira told Neil. "I've been checking him out. He's got issues, including alleged spousal abuse." She turned to Brock. "I told Ollie about it at your house, and normally he'd be freaking out over something like that, but he told me it didn't matter. Whatever he'd discovered trumped the alibi witness being a wife beater."

"Alleged wife beater," Neil said.

Brock leaned forward, resting his uninjured arm on his knee. "You really believe Ollie had discovered a suspect besides Quinn?"

"Yes."

Both men looked skeptical, and Kira felt annoyed.

"Let me ask *you* something," she said to Brock. "Do you really believe Gavin Quinn is innocent? No spin. Do you truly believe that?"

"Yes, I do."

"Why?"

"Lot of reasons," Brock said. "Circumstances, physical evidence, conversations I've had with the guy. Sometimes it comes down to a gut feeling about people, and when he tells me he didn't kill his wife, I believe him." Brock smiled at Neil. "They say an innocent client is as rare as a unicorn. Or maybe a leprechaun, in Quinn's case." His face grew serious as he looked at Kira. "But I'm telling you, the man didn't do it."

Kira studied Brock's eyes. Either he had an excellent poker face, or he really believed what he was saying. Probably both.

"I think it's possible you're right," she said. "And I think Ollie figured out who *did* kill her, and that may have cost him his life."

CHAPTER

TWELVE

JEREMY WAS at Kira's back door at nine A.M. sharp, but she didn't answer. He knocked again and waited. He knew she was awake, because he'd seen her bedroom light go on at 0600, followed by the bathroom light.

Jeremy had watched her house from his truck as the sun came up, and for the first time since he'd started this career, he felt like a stalker.

Kira opened the door with a smile. "Morning."

"You didn't ask who it was."

"Who else would it be? Trent told me you'd be here at nine." She pulled the door back and ushered him inside. "Want coffee? Or a muffin?"

"I'm good."

He stepped into her house and immediately regretted his answer. It smelled like a bakery. Better than a bakery—it smelled like his grandmother's house on Easter morning.

He glanced around, and her kitchen was a wreck. Dishes filled the sink. A carton of eggshells sat on the stovetop. Tupperware bins and plates of banana muffins occupied every inch of counter space.

"Late-night snack attack?" he asked.

"I wish." She poured coffee into a to-go mug. She was dressed nicer than usual today in black jeans and a silky white blouse, and she wore heeled sandals. "These are for Ollie's daughter and her kids."

"Lot of muffins."

"What can I say? People die, we bring food. It's a Southern thing."

"I know."

"Oh, that's right. You're from Florida."

She spooned sugar into her coffee, acting casual, but he could tell she'd mentioned that on purpose. She wanted him to know she'd been checking out his background. It was part of the chess game they had going.

She sipped her coffee. "You mind giving me a ride over?"

"No."

"Or you could follow me, but this might be easier."

"I'll take you," he said, glad not to have to argue about her car.

He surveyed her kitchen again. On the windowsill was a pitcher filled with water, and the goldfish from yesterday was swimming around. Her breakfast table was covered with paperwork and soft-drink cans, and it looked like she'd been up late working. Jeremy's gaze caught on a pair of photographs pinned to the fridge with Snoopy magnets. One was a rosy-cheeked boy in a red wagon—maybe her nephew, he guessed. The other picture showed Kira on a deck with a group of people, half of them guys. He still didn't know whether she had a boyfriend, and he wished he didn't care.

Kira grabbed a file folder from the pile and slid it into her messenger bag.

"Okay, ready." She looked him over. "You really don't want one? I had a failed batch, so I've got lots of extras."

Fuck it, he was hungry. "Sure, thanks."

She plucked a fat golden-brown muffin from a plate and handed it to him, then stacked the Tupperware boxes and balanced her coffee cup on top.

He grabbed the cup off the stack. "Let's go."

Kira engaged her alarm and locked the door as Jeremy scanned the area around her house. He'd parked behind her Toyota in the center of the driveway.

"I understand your neighbor's out of town." He opened the door for her and tried not to stare at her ass as she leaned into the truck and stacked the muffin containers in back.

"She's on vacation with her boyfriend." Kira slid into the passenger seat, and he handed her the coffee. "I filled her in about everything over the phone."

Jeremy went around and hitched himself behind the wheel. "Everything?"

"You know, the new alarm system, the surveillance. I don't want her to get spooked when she comes home and you guys are lurking around here."

"Good call. Where are we going?"

Instead of telling him, she reached over and tapped an address into his navigation system.

"Only twelve minutes away," she informed him. "She lives just across the freeway."

They got moving, and Jeremy glanced at her beside him. Her hair was in loose waves this morning. The bruise on her face had turned greenish-brown, and she'd tried to cover it with makeup.

She glanced at him. "What's wrong?"

"Trent said you were up most of the night."

"How would he know?"

"He had eyes on your house."

She sipped her coffee, then put the cup in the holder. "I was doing research until three."

"On what?"

"The trial Ollie was investigating."

"Find anything?"

"A lot. The defendant has a sheet."

"What's his name?"

"Andre Markov," she said. "And no, he's not the shooter, in case you were wondering. I tracked down his mug shot."

"You're sure?"

"Yes." Her voice was adamant. "His face is all wrong, and he's too small. The man at Brock's house was tall."

"What about connections to Ollie or Brock? Or Gavin Quinn?"

She shook her head. "I couldn't find anything. It was an aggravated-assault case, pretty straightforward. Defendant was accused of pulling a knife during a brawl outside a bar. He was acquitted. I can't figure out what it has to do with anything or why Ollie was so intent on getting the transcript the day he was killed."

"But you haven't actually read the transcript yet, right?"

"Only summaries. I should have an official copy by today."

She sighed, and he could sense her frustration. She seemed tired, too, and he figured it was her third straight night without much sleep.

"How'd you get hold of this guy's rap sheet?" he asked.

"Sources." She gave him a sly look. "I made you a copy, if you're interested."

"I'm interested."

"See, I knew that about you. You guys don't just show up and look scary. You're actually investigating this thing, aren't you?"

"That's correct."

"How come? I mean, I'd expect you to leave it to the police. It's not really part of your job description."

"If it's a threat to my client, it's part of my job description." He glanced at her. "How come *you* don't leave it to the police?"

She looked surprised by the question. "I don't know."

"Yeah, you do."

"I guess . . . because I know how overworked and underfunded they are. And I know they make mistakes."

"Ditto."

"There's also the time factor. The detectives are all over this right now. How could they not be? A murder in the heart of River Oaks is a headline grabber. But give it a few weeks, and some other crime will come along and demand their attention."

She looked out the window, and he wondered if he'd made her uncomfortable talking about threats to her safety. Or maybe it was the prospect of visiting Ollie's family that made her uncomfortable.

He broke off a piece of muffin and popped it into his mouth. Brown sugar melted on his tongue.

"Damn." He glanced at her. "How are these the 'failed' ones?"

"I made the strudel too heavy, and it sank to the bottom."

He shook his head.

"What?"

"You've never lived on MREs for a month. These are awesome."

"It's my grandmother's recipe. Basically the only thing I cook."

They reached the neighborhood, and Jeremy turned onto the

street. Several cars were parked in the driveway and in front of the address.

"I hate wakes and funerals," Kira muttered.

"I thought the funeral was Saturday."

"Yeah, and this is worse. They're going to be looking at photos and picking out Scripture."

Jeremy rolled to a stop at the curb. The expression on Kira's face made him feel a pang of sympathy for her. There were few things he dreaded more than talking to a grieving family. He'd done it way more than he cared to as a Marine, and he'd seen plenty of men shy away from the task or flat-out avoid it.

She rubbed her palms on her jeans.

"You okay?"

She glanced at him. "Yeah."

"We can come back later, if you want."

"No, I need to do this." She looked out the window at the house. "I held her dad's hand right before he died. I need to talk to her."

"I'll walk you to the door. You want me to come in with you or wait outside?"

"Wait outside," she said. "You look like a bodyguard. No offense, but it might be kind of distressing for the family." She reached back and grabbed the muffin boxes. "All right, wish me luck."

A cowbell announced their arrival as Charlotte stepped into the store, followed by Diaz. She took off her sunglasses and read the sign: POST PLACE. FAMILY OWNED FOR MORE THAN A DECADE!

A twentyish kid perched on a stool behind the cash register. He wore a green Post Place golf shirt and had his hair in a bun. He stayed hunched over his phone, oblivious to the cowbell, probably because of his earbuds.

Charlotte waited for him to look up. At last, he did.

"Help you?"

"I hope so." She flashed her police ID, and the kid's eyes widened. "I have a question about a package that was mailed from this location."

He slid off the stool, stuffing his phone into his pocket, and Charlotte got a whiff of cigarettes as he stepped over.

"What package is that?" he asked.

"It was mailed from here Monday. Billed to the account of Duffy and Hersch."

A woman came from the back carrying a stack of brown boxes so tall she could hardly see over them. She set the parcels on the counter and looked Charlotte over, frowning when she noticed her detective shield.

"May I help you?" she asked.

Charlotte once again held up her ID. "We have a question about a package mailed from here." She took out a photocopy of the envelope, which had been strategically cropped to show the return address but not the bloody shoeprint.

"According to the tracking info, this package was picked up at four fifty on Monday and arrived at its destination Tuesday afternoon," Charlotte said. "Were either of you working Monday at that time?"

The woman shot a concerned look at the clerk. "Jason?"

He shook his head. "Yeah, but I don't remember it. We were busy."

The woman's brow furrowed at his answer, and Charlotte studied them side by side. Dark hair, heavyset, underbite. They had a strong resemblance.

"May I get your name?" Charlotte asked with a smile.

"Jean Colton. And this is my son, Jason." She nodded at Charlotte's paper. "May I have a look?"

Charlotte handed over the paper and shifted her focus to the clerk, who was now studiously weighing a padded envelope.

"This is from Duffy and Hersch, the law firm," the woman said. "Have you tried them?"

"We spoke with them earlier," Charlotte said. "The lawyer whose account this was billed to is out of town, so he couldn't have mailed it from here. I'm thinking maybe it's an administrative assistant or someone?"

"It's probably the girl who's always in here." The woman looked at her son. "What's her name? Shari?"

"Shelly." The kid glanced up. "Yeah, it might have been her, now that you mention it. Like I said, we were busy."

"Shelly's one of their summer clerks," the woman said. "She's in here all the time mailing things."

"But you don't recall seeing her on Monday?"

"I wasn't here in the afternoon. Jason, are you sure it was Shelly?"

"Yeah."

"And do you know her last name?" Charlotte asked.

He shook his head without looking up.

Charlotte glanced at Diaz, who was checking out a display of office supplies while listening to every word.

Charlotte thanked them for their time and walked out with another clatter of cowbell. On the sidewalk, she put on her sunglasses.

"That was quick," Diaz said, returning to the Taurus. They traded driving, and today was his turn.

"We're not done yet. Pull around back."

"Why?"

"I want to see something."

Diaz drove around to the back of the strip center, which included a nail salon, a yoga studio, and a liquor store.

"Pull into that loading dock. Just behind the liquor store. See?"

Diaz pulled in and parked beside a dumpster. "Now what?"

"Now we wait."

He cut the engine and looked at her. "The kid was lying. You know that, right?"

"Yep."

"Why didn't you lean on him?"

"I want him alone."

"You're going to wait for him to get off work? That could be hours."

"He smelled like cigarettes, and we just put stress on him. Ten bucks says he'll be out here for a smoke break in less than five minutes."

Diaz eyed the row of back doors. Counting from the end, the mail shop would be the third one down.

"The mom seemed nice enough," Diaz said.

"Yeah, but I don't like ma-and-pop stores, not when they hire their own kids."

"What's wrong with that?"

She dug an emery board from her purse and filed a nail. "It's a bad dynamic. The kids know they won't get fired, so they can be lazy. Or worse, incompetent."

Diaz looked at his watch and sighed.

"What?" Charlotte asked.

"Nothing."

"Not nothing. That was your 'I don't like this plan' sigh."

"Okay, you're right." He tugged at the knot of his tie. "We're on day three of this case, and still no suspects. Why are we wasting our time here? We don't even know what this package has to do with anything, except that our perp happened to step on it at the murder scene. So what?"

"I don't like the timing," Charlotte said.

"What about it?"

"Someone overnighted the victim a package. That implies urgency. And he received that package less than two hours before his murder. That raises a red flag."

"Guy worked for a lawyer. They probably get dozens of packages every week."

"Okay, but whatever was in that package was stolen from the crime scene by the killer."

"Along with laptops, cell phones, and a crapload of other paperwork."

The third door opened, and Jason stepped out. Charlotte put her nail file away. "Ha. There he is."

Diaz looked surprised. "Damn, Chuck."

"That'll be ten bucks."

"I never took the bet." He pushed open his door. "You coming?"

Jason spotted them approaching just as he took a drag. He cast a panicked look at the door but didn't move.

"Hey, Jason. We have a few follow-ups." Charlotte smiled and stopped in front of him.

"I told you everything I know."

"I'm not really getting that impression." She tipped her head to the side. "I think you left a few things out. And I think if I ask to take a look at the surveillance tape from inside your shop, there might be more to the story. What do you think?"

Jason swallowed. He looked at Diaz, and then his gaze flitted to Charlotte. "There was this guy."

She freaking *knew* it. "Who?"

"I don't know, all right? Just some guy who came in after she did."

"After Shelly?" Diaz asked.

"Yeah."

"Did he mail something?" Diaz eased closer, and the kid stepped back.

"No, man. He wasn't a customer. Just some guy who came in and wanted to look at her tracking slip."

"And you showed him?"

"Well . . . yeah."

"Is it your policy to share customers' personal information with people who walk in off the street?" Charlotte asked.

"No."

"How much did he pay you?" Diaz asked.

He cleared his throat. "Fifty bucks."

Charlotte bit back a curse.

"It's not like he wanted her home address." Jason was defensive now. "She was mailing to some business, not like a person or anything."

Diaz made a buzzing noise. "Wrong. That package *did* go to a person. And he's dead now."

Jason's eyes bugged. "What?"

"You heard me."

"But that's got nothing to do with me!"

"That remains to be seen," Charlotte said.

"What did this guy look like?" Diaz demanded.

"I don't know, really. Ow! Fuck!" The cigarette had burned down to his fingers, and Jason flung it away.

"You're going to have to do better than that, Jason."

"I don't know, okay? He had a hat and shades on."

"Indoors?" Diaz sounded skeptical.

"Yeah, okay? I barely saw him. He came in right after Shelly and asked to see the tracking slip, and he paid me a fifty and then he left. That's it."

"Do you have the fifty?" Charlotte asked, even though fingerprinting money was about as useful as lifting DNA off a gas-station urinal.

Jason shook his head. "I spent it."

Of course he did.

Charlotte gave him a cool stare, then looked at Diaz. She could read her partner's mind. This was a good lead, but they were in for a long day. They were going to have to bring this guy in for a formal interview and also get access to the surveillance footage from inside the mail shop, which could require a warrant.

"Is that all?" Jason asked. "I have to get back to work now."

Diaz laughed. "No, Jason, that's not all. Not by a long shot."

Kira worked off some of her tension at her gym while Trent waited in the lobby, attracting stares from every woman in the place and a few men. Jeremy's promise of his team keeping a low profile was not panning out, but it was only the gym, so Kira let it go. For now, at least. She wasn't footing the bill for her security, and their transportation was reliable, so that was a perk.

Kira gathered her gym bag off the floor of Trent's SUV as he pulled into her driveway. Gina's car was back in its customary spot, and Trent parked behind it.

"Thanks for the ride," Kira said.

"No problem. Are you in for the night?"

"Think so." Not exactly a yes. "I've got a lot of work to do."

His gaze narrowed with suspicion as she grabbed her water bottle and jumped out. He walked her to her back step, scanning the surrounding area as she unlocked the door and tapped in her alarm code.

"Well, good night," she said as she noticed Gina's blinds shifting.

"Call if you need anything," Trent told her.

"I will."

After he left, Kira stood by the door and listened to him back out of the driveway.

By anyone's standards, Trent was extremely good-looking. He was tall and muscular and had an adorable dimple that showed when he laughed. He was friendly and easygoing, too, so of course, Kira wasn't attracted to him at all.

She dropped her bag on the sofa and cursed her stupid taste in men. She was drawn to the strong, silent types. The cool and unreadable ones who almost never let their guard down. She had a history with such men, and it wasn't pretty. The relationships—if you could even call them that—started with a bang and soon flamed out, and she was left wondering why she kept on torturing herself.

Gina said her problem stemmed from a taciturn father who withheld approval. Kira thought it was much simpler. Men who didn't talk had less chance of pissing her off before she decided to sleep with them, hence, she did. It wasn't until later that she realized they were either (a) assholes, or (b) emotionally closed off and she was wasting her time.

A knock sounded at the back door, and Kira wasn't surprised to find Gina there.

"How was Padre Island?" Kira asked.

"Hot." Gina stepped inside, smelling like coconut oil. With her windblown brown hair and sunburned cheeks, she looked like she'd just come off the beach.

"How are *you*?" Gina asked, giving her a hug. "I'm so sorry about your friend."

"Thank you." Kira's stomach knotted at the words. She thought of Ollie's daughter this morning with her puffy pink eyes and the shoe-box of photos in her lap.

"It must have been awful," Gina said with a look of concern.

"It was." Kira stepped into the kitchen. "Would you like a muffin? I just made some."

"No, thanks. And you're changing the subject."

"I know." Kira leaned back against the counter. There was no dodging Gina's worried look as she pulled out a breakfast chair and sat down. They'd been friends since the day Kira moved in and Gina showed up at her door with a bottle of wine, which they'd shared while they unpacked Kira's kitchen. Gina was like the sister Kira had never had. They swapped clothes and work troubles and dating nightmares. But this new nightmare was all too real, and Kira wasn't ready to talk about it.

"So was *that* your bodyguard I just saw?" Gina asked, kindly shifting to a lighter topic.

"One of them."

"Wow."

"They stay out of sight, mostly."

Gina smiled. "That's too bad."

"I meant to tell you," Kira said, "the security company offered to install an alarm system on your side of the duplex, if you're interested. You wouldn't have to pay for it."

"Don't tell me Bruce is paying. I asked him about an alarm system before I moved in here, and he wouldn't even consider it," Gina said.

"My client is paying."

"Wow. What did Bruce say?"

"I haven't mentioned it yet."

Gina lifted an eyebrow.

"He'll either bitch about me 'damaging' the place and threaten to keep my security deposit, or he'll say it's an improvement and try to raise the rent."

Gina rolled her eyes. "He's such a weasel. And sure, I'd love to get something if someone else is picking up the tab. I just ran over a damn nail and had to get a tire replaced. I swear, I don't know what I'd do if my boyfriend wasn't a mechanic."

"That reminds me, you think Mike would mind if I asked him to look at my car? It's making that noise again."

"Sure, no problem. Just swing by the shop. I'll tell him you're coming."

"Thanks."

"Hey, you want to come out with us tonight?" Gina asked. "We're meeting Rowan and Luke over at the Tap House."

"I have to work tonight."

"You sure? It might do you good to get out."

"Next time, maybe. I really have to get some stuff done," Kira said. "And honestly, I'm not up for a crowded bar tonight anyway."

Gina stood and gave her a sympathetic look. "Well, text me if you change your mind."

"I will."

Gina hugged her and left, and Kira locked the door behind her but didn't set the alarm. With a sigh, she surveyed her house. Her kitchen was still a mess, and her dishes hadn't managed to wash themselves while she'd been gone. She stepped over to the breakfast table, where she'd spread out her paperwork. She'd spent hours last night combing through Ollie's notebook and searching for leads.

Ollie's cryptic scrawl stared up at her. She'd managed to decipher some of it. He'd gone out on a series of surveillance jobs and taken notes each time. Kira had flagged a few items that caught her attention. He'd written "L.H." and "to L.H." several times, and there had been three mentions of "XS co." Was L.H. a person? A place? Was there a company called XS? Or was he running surveillance on an extra-small company? Between Ollie's odd shorthand and his terrible handwriting, Kira had come up with more questions than answers.

She picked up the fast-food receipt she'd found in his van. The time stamp said he'd been at Whataburger in Channelview at 10:18 last Friday, exactly a week ago. She tried to recall that night. She'd wanted to go jogging after work, but it was raining, so she'd gone to the gym instead. She remembered talking to Ollie on the phone, and he'd vaguely said he was "working" but didn't mention any details.

Kira checked her watch. It was nine fifteen. She felt a flutter of nerves as she walked into the guest room. The twin bed was piled with surveillance equipment. She unpacked her Canon camera and checked the memory card. Then she went to the window and peered out at the vacant house down the street.

Trent's black SUV wasn't in its spot anymore. Instead, it was Jeremy's gunmetal-gray pickup truck.

Kira took a deep breath. She knew what she needed to do tonight. She'd known since yesterday. The question was, how to do it?

Ultimately, it's up to you. We work for you, not the other way around.

Had Jeremy meant that, or was that a tactic meant to placate her?

She pulled out her phone and called him.

"Hey, it's me."

"I know." His low, masculine voice put a tingle inside her. She loved the way he sounded.

"I need to ask a favor."

Silence.

"Jeremy?"

"Where are we going?"

CHAPTER

THIRTEEN

JEREMY DROVE, and Kira navigated. Aside from giving him directions, she didn't talk. Her focus was on a spiral notebook in her lap, and she kept flipping through the pages and shaking her head.

"I never should have turned in that damn phone." She huffed out a breath and shoved the notebook into the cupholder. "It was the best lead I had, and now all I've got is a pile of chicken scratch."

He glanced at her in the seat beside him. She was dressed like a cat burglar again and had her hair pulled back in a ponytail.

"What good would Ollie's phone do you? You didn't know the code," he said.

"At least I'd have his incoming calls, and I could run the numbers. Now I've got zip." She glared at him, as if he were the reason she'd turned the phone over to the police and not her conscience.

"Not zip."

"Almost zip."

"You've got Shelly Chandler, who pointed you to a court case," he said. "And you've got the location of his last stakeout."

She darted a glance at him.

"What's that mean?"

She looked out the window.

"Kira?"

"*Probable* location." She wouldn't make eye contact. "I have reason to believe he was running surveillance in Channelview, but I'm not a hundred percent."

Of course, she was mentioning this now, after he'd already driven half an hour across town to help her run down a lead.

"What's this based on?" he asked.

"A fast-food receipt."

"That's it?"

"That's solid. It lines up with Ollie's MO. Whenever he went on a stakeout, he would load up on fast food, usually from Whataburger, and then go set up someplace."

"So you don't know exactly where we're going?"

"I've got an idea."

Jeremy shook his head.

"He made notes about a company called Ballard Shipping, which just happens to be less than three miles from the Whataburger in Channelview. That's a solid lead."

Jeremy didn't argue with her. Not because he agreed but because he didn't want to get her all worked up. He liked it too much when she got that way, and he was determined to stay focused on the job tonight.

Kira was getting to him. He wasn't sure if it was her looks or her words or her step-off attitude that directly contradicted the flirty glances she gave him when she wanted something. Probably, it was all of it, and the fact that he couldn't pin her down was messing with his head. She wasn't like any client he'd had before, and he was beginning to wish he'd been assigned to one of the lawyers.

Jeremy looked at her beside him. Her hair was still damp from her shower, and he could smell her shampoo.

He'd never been so distracted on a job before. It was probably a combination of jet lag and the op that had gone sideways, but whatever it was, he needed to get over it and focus on the task at hand.

He trained his gaze on the road.

"I have to tell you, I'm surprised you agreed to this," she said.

"To what?"

"Coming out here with me."

With her. Like she'd be out here alone in her piece-of-shit car if he hadn't agreed.

"You have a job to do. I get that," he said. "Would I like it better if you holed yourself up in a sixty-story office building and did it from there? Yes, I would."

"That's not how investigations go."

"I know."

He was resigned to it. Which didn't mean he had to like it, and didn't mean he had to let her do whatever the hell she wanted. They were going to check out this lead, and then he'd get her home so she could spend the rest of the night tucked safely into bed.

"Okay, heads up. This is our exit," she said.

He coasted off the freeway and spotted the orange-and-white striped roof of the burger place.

"Turn right at this light." She consulted her phone, then looked around. "Okay, get in the turn lane and hook a left at the next street. It's right up here. Slow down."

Jeremy followed instructions. Her bossy voice turned him on, which was the dead-last thing he ever planned to tell her, but it was true.

"Cross the tracks, and then take a right on Waterfront Road. See it?"

He glanced at her. "We're headed for the ship channel."

"I know."

They bumped over the railroad tracks and picked up a two-lane highway paralleling the shore. The ship channel connected the Gulf of Mexico to the Port of Houston, and traffic up and down it was one of the primary drivers of the city's economy.

The neighborhood quickly became industrial. Warehouses. Concrete lots filled with heavy equipment. More lots filled with endless rows of shipping containers. All the properties were surrounded by high security fences, some topped with razor wire.

Jeremy glanced to his left, where a wall of trees blocked the view of the businesses located directly on the waterfront. A white glow above the tree line indicated that several of the places were up and running, even this late at night.

"One more mile," she said.

Through a gap in the trees, he caught a glimpse of the ship channel. Not the water itself but the towering steel cranes that lined the shore.

"Okay, see the sign up here?"

They neared a sign for Ballard Shipping. A chain-link fence surrounded a big lot, five acres at least. But the lot was empty. Not a light anywhere, and stalks of weeds sprouted through cracks in the concrete.

Kira sighed. "Shit."

Jeremy drove past the lot without stopping.

"We should pull over and look around," she said.

"Not yet."

A high pair of headlights moved toward them on the narrow high-

way, and Jeremy could tell from the silhouette that the vehicle was law enforcement.

Kira seemed to notice them, too. She watched as they passed the SUV that had a fence buster on the grate and a light bar mounted on top.

"ICE," Jeremy said.

"How can you tell?"

"The crest on the door."

Jeremy watched in the rearview mirror. When the taillights faded to nothing, he found a side road and turned onto it.

Kira was tapping away at her phone. "I looked up the company. They're in business still, so they must have moved locations."

"What kind of business?"

"Industrial shipping."

"That's every place out here."

"No kidding."

Jeremy turned around and headed back for the empty lot.

"What a waste," she said. "Why did Ollie write this name down if there's nothing here? And what are all these notes about? He had to have been staked out here for hours. He must have—wait! Stop!" She smacked the dashboard. "Stop, stop, stop!"

Jeremy halted and backed up, stopping before he reached the gate so they wouldn't attract attention.

"Xavier Shipping Company." She whirled to face him. "This is it!"

"What is?"

"Something called 'XS co.' from Ollie's notes. This has to be it."

Jeremy shifted gears and resumed a normal speed.

"We need to stop and look around," she told him.

"We need to not draw attention."

He surveyed the area for a better vantage point. About half a mile ahead, he spotted a long berm that likely served as a dam for storm surges.

At the next juncture, he made a turn. About fifty yards later, he found a gravel road that ran atop the berm. On the downside, it wasn't a well-traveled road, which meant they might attract suspicion. On the upside, it was an elevated vantage point.

Jeremy turned onto the road. Superior vantage point won every time.

"Where are we going?" Kira asked.

"Getting a better view of the property. I assume you brought binoculars? Or a zoom lens?"

"Both," Kira said, dragging her bulky duffel into her lap.

The berm traversed an empty field. Beyond it was a stand of trees. Jeremy eased onto the shoulder, then pulled a three-point turn and positioned the truck near a dense thicket. Someone would have to drive right up on them to see them here. The location had flaws, but it was better than being right on top of the surveillance target.

Kira handed him the binoculars case. Then she attached a big lens to her camera and peered through it.

She checked her watch. "It's ten twenty, which is when Ollie was in Channelview exactly a week ago."

Her voice was tinged with excitement, and Jeremy watched as she adjusted the lens.

"This is perfect." *Click. Click. Click.* "I can see the gate from here."

Jeremy unsnapped the case and pulled out the binoculars. Leupold BX-4 HDs. He looked at Kira, amazed.

"You bought these?"

"Yeah."

He examined the high-def lenses, and his respect for her took another leap. "These are military-grade."

"Yep." She lowered her camera. "Ollie recommended them. I blew my whole second paycheck on those things. First one went to this." She lifted her camera and snapped another photo.

"You've got some serious cash invested in your equipment."

She shrugged. "Tools of the trade."

Jeremy peered through the binos, and the world became a tunnel. He moved the diopter adjustment dial, and everything came into focus, sharp as a blade. The scene had a hyperreal look to it, from the textured shingles on the gatehouse to the glint of razor wire on top of the security fence.

Jeremy whistled. "Nice."

"I know." Kira lowered her camera. "Now comes the fun part."

He looked at her.

"Waiting."

Jeremy peered through the binoculars again, zeroing in on the guard inside the gatehouse. The man had a shaved head and a thick neck. The interior of the building was dim, but his face was lit blue from a screen. He was probably watching a game or looking at porn, oblivious to his surroundings. He picked up a fast-food cup and sipped from a straw.

Night watchmen never ceased to disappoint. Working after hours, they seemed to assume they could sit around and jerk off, when the late shift was a peak time for criminal activity.

"How'd you get into this, anyway?"

He looked at Kira.

"Working for Liam Wolfe," she added.

"He recruited me."

Kira dug a shiny red apple from her bag and offered it to him. "Want one?"

"No."

She took a bite, and Jeremy tried not to think about her mouth as she chewed.

"I'd take some water, though, if you have some."

"Nope. Rule number one for female PIs: water on a stakeout is a bad idea." She chomped the apple again. "What made you want to join Liam? It's a pretty big leap from being a Marine, right?"

"True."

He lifted the binos again, scanning the fence around the property. No security cams visible, but that didn't mean they weren't there. Judging by sheer size, Xavier Shipping seemed to be a small-scale operation compared to some of the others on the waterfront.

"That's all?"

He looked at her. "What do you mean?"

"I'm curious how you got into this."

She'd been doing her homework. Or else hitting up Trent for info. Jeremy had told her almost nothing about himself, not even his military background—although it didn't take much to figure that out.

She shook her head and looked away. "Like pulling teeth."

"What is?"

"Getting you to talk about yourself. You have an entire *file* on me, and I know almost nothing about you, except what's readily available online."

He frowned. "Which is what?"

"Past addresses, criminal history, marriages, bankruptcies. Oh, and the occasional mention in *Stars and Stripes*."

"I've never been arrested or married or filed for bankruptcy."

"I know." She smiled. "But this conversation makes you uncomfortable, doesn't it? I mean, it's kind of weird realizing someone you just met knows a bunch of personal stuff about you." She nibbled her apple, watching him.

Jeremy lifted the binoculars. She was making a point.

And he didn't blame her, really. A lot of clients weren't thrilled about the scrutiny that occurred when they hired a top-notch firm like Wolfe Sec. They weren't rent-a-cops, not like the guys who worked graveyard shifts at some of these shipping terminals. Most of those guys were hired because some insurance company required it, and although they carried sidearms, their training was a joke.

Kira tucked the apple into the cupholder and picked up her camera again. "You still haven't answered my question. How'd you get into protection work?"

So much for stonewalling.

He looked at her. "You really want to hear this?"

"Yes."

"I was in an elite MARSOC unit in Afghanistan. That's special operations. Liam was there, too, and we provided security to VIPs visiting the area. Military brass, visiting politicians, people like that."

"Sounds exciting."

"Not usually. They showed up for photo ops, and we made sure they didn't get blown up or picked off by a sniper."

"Whoa. I can't even imagine living in a war zone like that. What was it like?"

He thought for a beat. "Dusty."

She just looked at him.

"Dust was everywhere. In your eyes, in your socks, in your weapon. I got to where I could've cleaned my gun in my sleep."

He remembered the colors, too. A million shades of brown. Coming home after his first tour, the world had seemed like a Disney cartoon. He'd gotten a headache just looking at it.

"What was the work like?"

Jeremy turned to look at her. Interest flashed in her eyes, and she sounded genuinely curious, not like she was making small talk. He felt compelled to be honest with her.

"Sometimes it was hell."

Her brow furrowed.

"Other times . . . it was a lot like this."

"This?"

"Yeah, a lot of waiting. Sitting around watching a place and waiting for shit to go down. Then, in the blink of an eye, everything could go sideways."

Sometimes he still dreamed he was back there in a firefight, with mortars shrieking overhead. Even more unnerving were the roadside IEDs. Even when you were vigilant and knew what to look for, sometimes it all came down to shitty luck.

"I can't imagine being in a place with bullets flying around," she said.

"You get used to it. You'd be surprised." He gazed through the windshield, surveying the area, as he thought back to all those long, dusty days. He looked at Kira, and something about her openness made him want to keep talking.

"When you're over there, it's different. You're not afraid of death so much as failing. Not being there when your brothers need you." He shook his head. "It's hard to explain, but it's like a family. Tighter than a family."

"Do you have any real brothers?"

"Two," he said. "But I'm closer to the guys I served with, when it comes down to it. Something about being over there together. Everyone depends on each other for everything. I miss that sometimes."

He looked at her, and she was watching him closely. "So why'd you leave?" she asked.

She didn't say "quit," and he felt strangely grateful.

"Things were winding down. And there was an incident. Liam took a bullet." Jeremy didn't mention that the bullet was nearly fatal or that he personally took out the man who fired it. "Liam decided he wanted to get out and get something else going, and he asked me to be part of it."

Kira's gaze narrowed, as if she knew he was omitting a lot. But he didn't want to get into it now. Maybe someday. Or maybe not.

He lifted the binoculars. "Heads up. We've got action."

CHAPTER

FOURTEEN

KIRA ZOOMED in on the car. It was a blue Mini Cooper, tinted windows, and she couldn't see how many people were inside.

The car veered around a row of oil drums and pulled to a stop beside a double-wide trailer that looked to be some sort of operations center.

She shifted her focus to the other side of the lot.

The gatehouse was empty.

"Hey, the guard's gone," she said.

"He opened the gate three minutes ago and left his post," Jeremy reported.

"How did I miss that?"

"You were talking instead of looking."

She ignored the jab. "Think his being gone was intentional?"

"Oh, yeah."

"Damn it. I should have snapped a picture of him." She lowered her camera and scanned the broader area. No more cars on the road. So was the driver of the Mini meeting someone? Picking someone up?

"Here, let me see those," she said.

Jeremy handed over the binoculars.

She sighed. "I didn't get a good angle on the license plate. Did you?"

"No."

She lowered the binoculars and spotted another vehicle speeding down the road. It was a pickup truck, and its lights went off as it neared the gate.

Kira's nerves fluttered as the truck turned into Xavier Shipping, where the gate was still open.

"This feels sketchy," she said.

"Yep."

The truck veered around the same line of oil drums and parked alongside the Mini. No one got out, and again, Kira didn't have a good angle on the license plate.

"I want those tags."

Jeremy looked at her.

"They could be important," she added.

"Why?"

"A clandestine meeting exactly one week after Ollie was here running surveillance right before his murder? This has to be related."

"You're assuming a lot. This may not be a 'clandestine' anything. You don't know for sure that Ollie was ever here. And this may not be a regular meeting."

"What if it is? Look at them." She nodded toward the property. "The guard disappears. Two cars show up. They're sitting there waiting for someone. I need to know who they are and what they're doing there."

Jeremy rubbed his chin as he stared out the window. The beard was gone, but he had some major five o'clock shadow going tonight, and she was *not* going to think about how good he looked. She loved his sharp cheekbones and the intense expression in his eyes when he was on a job. There was nothing sexier to her than a man on a mission.

His overprotectiveness was starting to get under her skin, though. He'd trained in an elite military unit, and she didn't have a shred of doubt that if it weren't for her, he would be halfway across that field by now, stealthily approaching the action, so he could figure out what was going down.

"We need intel," she said. "Let's get closer and take a look at those tags."

Even in the dimness, she could see his jaw tighten.

"Jeremy, come on. Otherwise, what are we here for? We're wasting our time."

He looked at her, and she saw the conflict in his eyes. She considered batting her lashes and flirting, but she had a feeling he wouldn't go for that.

"You want to leave me here and you can go?" she asked.

"No."

She'd known he wouldn't agree to that. She simply looked at him and waited.

"We'll get closer," he said finally. "But we do this *my* way. Understood?"

"Roger that."

"Don't be glib."

"I'm not." She looped the camera strap over her head. "I'll follow your lead."

He waited another moment, maybe second-guessing his decision. Then he reached up and switched off the interior light before quietly opening the door of the truck. Kira followed suit. She walked around the front of the pickup and waited for instructions.

The August air was thick and humid, and the low hum of cicadas surrounded them.

"We'll hug the trees to the west," he said.

"Sounds good." She had no idea which direction was west.

"Stay low, and don't create a silhouette. Don't talk. And keep close to me. Got it?"

"Yes."

He set off into the knee-high grass and aimed for the nearest clump of trees. Kira followed, staying as close as she could without bumping into him. Cool water seeped into her sneakers, and it soon became clear that this "field" was more of a marsh. The air smelled faintly of fish and rot, and she hoped they weren't traversing a septic field.

Jeremy moved briskly, staying low and close to the trees. He reached back and caught her arm as the ground sank abruptly and she nearly tripped. She eased closer and focused on keeping her footing while he navigated the way. Her ankles were underwater now, and bog seemed to suck at her feet. Her socks squished with every step, but Jeremy's footsteps were silent, and she made a note to ask him how the hell he did that.

It was dark with only a half-moon to guide them, which should have been a good thing, but she was feeling a little freaked out as they moved deeper and deeper into the marsh. There had to be snakes in here. Moccasins or maybe copperheads. Stifling a shudder, she tried not to picture them slithering up her jeans.

Jeremy reached back, catching her again as she stumbled into him. Somehow he was able to predict her movements without watching her.

She tucked her fingers into the waist of his jeans. His body felt warm against her knuckles, and he either didn't notice or didn't want to acknowledge her hand there.

Glancing around, she saw that they'd almost reached the other side of the field, which meant the highway was just ahead. The ground became firmer. Jeremy moved closer to the trees as the grade increased.

He suddenly reached back and clamped her wrist, pulling her down.

A pair of headlights appeared in the distance. Kira crouched low beside him as the vehicle drew closer. It was a sleek silver gas rig. The truck roared past, sending dust swirling. Kira blinked and turned away, trying not to cough.

Jeremy leaned close, and she felt the heat of his body. "We'll cross the highway. There's a clump of bushes east of the guardhouse. We should be able to see the cars from there."

She nodded.

"On my count." He craned his neck, looking for traffic. "Three . . . two . . ." He clasped her hand in his, and they darted across the street. When their feet touched grass again, he went straight for the trees and ducked behind them.

Kira immediately saw the advantage of this location. In addition to the mesquite bushes, the guardhouse provided a nice dark shadow for them to hide in, with an unobstructed view of the two cars parked beside the trailer.

Both cars were still waiting, engines running, and she heard a *thump* of bass coming from the stereo inside the pickup.

"Get your shots quick," Jeremy ordered.

She was already zooming in and adjusting the focus. *Click. Click.* She cringed at the noise, which may as well have been cymbals clanging. But she was being paranoid. No way someone could hear a camera shutter from inside a vehicle probably fifty yards away. She took several more shots, just in case something turned out blurry.

Jeremy touched her arm. *Time to go*, his look said, and she nodded.

Suddenly, the trailer door opened, and a tall man stood in the rectangle of light. He trekked down the steps and went for the pickup. Without a word to the driver, he heaved a long black duffel bag into the truck bed.

Click.

Kira waited until he turned and tried to catch his face. *Click. Click.*

He walked to the Mini and passed something through the driver's-side window, then turned and trekked back up the stairs and into the trailer.

Both sets of taillights glowed red. The pickup backed out first, cutting in front of the Mini as it veered around the oil drums. Kira's nerves skittered. She crouched low as headlights swept over the bushes between their hiding spot and the fence. The truck zoomed through the gate and barely slowed as it skidded onto the highway. The Mini followed but turned in the opposite direction and sped away.

Kira crouched there, heart thudding. Jeremy peeled her fingers from his arm, and she realized she'd had it in a death grip.

He gave her a nod, then signaled with his fingers this time. *Three . . . two . . .* He took her hand, and they dashed across the road. They ran back to the cover of the trees, and this time, she welcomed the cool water in her sneakers, because it meant they'd almost made it. She tucked her fingers into his jeans again.

Jeremy jerked her down beside him and pressed her head against the grass.

"What—"

"Shh."

Kira waited, her knees sinking into the cold mud.

The light shifted, and she turned her head slightly. Jeremy crouched low, shoulders hunched forward as he looked and listened intently.

Light skimmed over the tops of the reeds, and Jeremy pressed her head down. She was on her hands and knees now, mud oozing between her fingers as she ducked as low as she could without putting her face in the muck.

Had someone seen them? Did they have a flashlight trained on them? A spotlight?

Seconds ticked by. Jeremy was as still as a stone, a big warm rock beside her, and his hand on the back of her head kept her from looking around. She tried not to move a muscle or even blink, but her heart felt like it would pound right out of her chest.

A minute ticked by. Two. Three. Kira's mouth felt dry.

Finally, his hand disappeared, and she turned her head to look at him. His eyes were dark and serious.

He pointed toward the trees and nodded. She nodded back. He eased close, and she felt his hot breath on her ear.

"Stay low."

She nodded again, and he took her arm, helping her off her knees. He laced her hand through his and moved toward the trees, ducking as low as his tall frame would allow. She didn't dare look around. She focused on the pockets of his jeans and on trying to keep her footing as he towed her behind him. The marsh gave way to firm ground, and they had to be nearing the truck.

Pop!

Jeremy yanked her to the ground and shoved her head down. His body pressed against her back, compressing the air from her lungs.

Panic surged through her, and she bucked against the weight. Someone was shooting. *Shooting.* It was happening all over again, and she wanted to sprint for the trees—not wait here until she was riddled with bullets. She tried to wiggle free, but Jeremy was heavy. Immovable.

Don't panic. Don't panic. Don't panic.

She squeezed her eyes shut.

Stay still. Stay still. Stay still.

She could hear the words, but he wasn't moving or making a sound, so maybe it was all in her head. Opening her eyes, she saw his big forearm beside her hand. The muscles were taut, and she realized he was holding himself up, supporting his weight to keep from crushing her completely, but she could still feel the pressure against her hips and the solid heat of his chest against her shoulder blades.

Her lungs felt tight. She was going to suffocate here in this stinky swamp. Or else someone was going to hunt them down right here and spray them with bullets. Panic zinged through her as she pictured it. Her fight-or-flight instinct kicked in, and her brain was screaming *Go!* as loud as it could. She pushed against Jeremy, but his body didn't budge except for the curl of his big fingers on the back of her head.

"Shhhh . . ."

The word was a low whisper in her ear, barely a word at all. More like a warm breath.

Kira closed her eyes, fighting the tears. She didn't want to die tonight. Not here in this vile swamp.

Jeremy's body was warm, and she tried to focus on that instead of the icy fear pulsing through her veins. He could get them out of this.

He was armed and trained and loaded with quiet confidence. She just needed to trust him.

Suddenly, the weight shifted and disappeared. She turned her head to see Jeremy crouched low beside her. She searched his face and then noticed the black gun gripped in his hand. She didn't remember him pulling it out.

With his free hand, he helped her up and nodded toward the trees, and this time, she hunched so low she was practically duckwalking as she hurried for cover. She didn't look back, didn't even dare look over her shoulder, for fear of seeing some man standing on the road and pointing a gun at her.

Jeremy's grip was firm as he dragged her alongside him, and she realized he'd positioned her closest to the trees, putting his body between hers and any bullets.

Kira's shoes squished despite her efforts to keep quiet, but finally, they reached the far edge of the field. Jeremy pulled her behind a mesquite tree and stopped, standing upright. He released her hand and dug his keys from his pocket, and only then did she realize they were standing right beside the gravel road. She glanced behind him, and there was his truck, a dark shadow within a shadow. He steered her toward it, still surrounding her with his bulk as he guided her to the passenger door and opened it.

The light didn't come on, and she felt a rush of relief that he'd thought of that detail ahead of time. She scrambled into the cab, and he pressed her head against the console and motioned for her to keep it there. Then he closed her door with a quiet *snick*.

Kira closed her eyes, waiting and listening with dread for any more gunshots.

It had been a gunshot. Distant, maybe, but it *had* been a gunshot.

Otherwise, why would he have yanked her to the ground like that? She unlooped the camera from her neck and stowed it on the floor.

Jeremy slid behind the wheel and stayed low in his seat as he shoved the key into the ignition and started up the truck.

"Don't move," he ordered.

He swerved onto the road and punched the gas, leaving behind a spray of gravel. Still no lights, and her heart skittered as she pictured them careening into a ditch.

Then they *did* careen into a ditch, and her head smacked against the dashboard.

"Sorry."

"What—"

"Shortcut."

They bumped and bounced over the uneven terrain, and she gripped the door for support. Another burst of speed, another bounce. The truck caught air, and they came down with a jaw-rattling *thunk*, and suddenly, they were speeding over smooth pavement. He switched on the headlights, and the dashboard lit up green.

He looked at her. "You can sit up now."

She didn't move.

"It's okay."

Slowly, she lifted her head and looked over the dash. They were on a paved road. Two lanes. No lights anywhere except the tunnel created by their headlights.

She glanced over her shoulder, and the lights of the dock were nothing more than a distant glow above the tree line. She couldn't even see the towering cranes.

Jeremy trained his gaze on the road ahead.

He didn't speak. Didn't explain. Kira still felt the heady buzz of adrenaline, and he just stared straight ahead as if nothing had just happened.

He checked the rearview mirror. Suddenly, he hit the brakes and swung onto a dirt road. He skidded to a halt and thrust the truck into park.

He reached across the console and clutched the side of her face. "You okay?"

She nodded.

"You sure?" His blue eyes bored into her, and she felt the intensity coming off him, right through his fingertips.

"Who was that?" she croaked.

"I don't know."

"That was a gunshot, right?"

He nodded, and she studied his face. She'd thought he was fine, but she saw now that he wasn't fine at all. Even in the dimness, she could see the taut muscles of his neck, the hard set of his mouth, the beads of sweat glistening at his temples.

His fingers in her hair tightened. "I shouldn't have let you come here."

"You didn't *let* me anything. I—"

He cut her off with a kiss.

CHAPTER

FIFTEEN

KIRA FROZE. Then he burrowed his fingers into her hair, and she moved into him.

Jeremy was kissing her. *Kissing her.* And it was loaded with all that pent-up intensity she'd felt from the moment she met him. She slid her hands up around his neck and pulled herself closer.

He tasted so, so good, and she couldn't get enough as he angled her head and delved into her mouth. She ran her fingertips over that stubble that she'd been dying to touch for days and pressed her body against him, as close as she could get with the damn console between them. Her heart lurched as he grabbed her hips and dragged her over it and into his lap. His erection was like a steel rod, and she squirmed against him.

He tipped his head back. "Kira—"

"Shut up."

She pulled him closer, and she was surrounded by the solid heat of his body. He was so good, everything about him, from his sharp taste to his strong arms. His skin felt hot, and she ran her fingertips down his sweat-dampened neck, as he kissed her with a fierceness she never would have expected.

Except that she had. She'd *known*. From that first morning, that simmering look in his eyes had warned her about what was buried under all that cool self-control. His palm slid over her T-shirt and closed over her breast, and she arched against him. She wanted both his hands on her. She wanted to straddle his lap and pull her shirt off and feel his mouth on her, too, but all she had right now was the teasing brush of his thumb through the fabric.

A loud hum made her jerk away. She looked up at him, panting. The raw lust in his eyes sent a surge of heat through her.

The noise again.

She spotted her glowing phone beside her mud-smeared camera on the floor of the truck. Recognizing the number on the screen, she scrambled off his lap and grabbed it.

"This is Kira."

Silence.

"Hello? Shelly?"

"Kira, hi."

She fell back against the seat and tugged her shirt down. Her skin tingled. She glanced at Jeremy as he ran his hand through his hair and gave her a look she couldn't read.

"I hope it's not too late," Shelly said. "You said anytime, so . . ."

"It's fine." Kira checked the clock and went on alert. "What's wrong, Shelly?"

"I just . . . maybe I'm being paranoid, but I thought I saw something. Twice, actually."

Kira shook her head, trying to shake off the daze. In the background of the call, she heard music. Was Shelly calling from a bar? A restaurant?

"*What* did you see twice?" Kira asked her.

"I'm not sure. Not really. But you know that picture you showed me?"

Her blood ran cold. "The police sketch?"

"I thought I saw him at a stoplight downtown. In the car behind me? But then I thought it was nothing, because I made a turn, but the car didn't turn, and I figured I was just imagining it. Then I thought I saw him *again*."

"Where?"

Jeremy put the truck in gear and pulled back onto the highway.

"You know Mulligan's?" Shelly asked.

"The sports bar."

"I was there with some friends, and I could have sworn I saw him at the bar as I was leaving."

"Where are you now?" Glancing at Jeremy, Kira motioned for him to go faster. "Shelly?"

"I'm on my way home."

"Where do you live?"

"Avalon Lofts on Kirby Drive."

"Lock your door, all right? Did anyone follow you?"

"No. I looked. In fact, I drove past the police station on my way, thinking I might pull in, but . . . he wasn't back there. No one was. No one was following me, and I felt dumb. Honestly, I'm not even sure it was him. It just looked like it *might* be him, and I thought I should tell someone."

"I'm going to text you a number for the lead detective on the case, and I want you to call her, okay? Tell her I gave you her number, and then tell her what you just told me."

Silence.

"Shelly?"

"Isn't that a little much? I'm not even sure it's the guy from the sketch. And it's after eleven."

"Don't worry about that. Contact this detective. And also, keep your phone on you and call nine-one-one if you see anything suspicious."

No response.

"Shelly?"

"Okay."

"I'm serious. Anything at all."

"I got it."

———————

Shelly dropped the phone into her lap and replayed Kira's words in her head.

I want you to call her.

Right. Like she was going to call up some homicide detective this time of night and tell her . . . what? That somewhere between her second and third raspberry mojito, she'd slipped off to the bathroom to check her phone, and she'd *maybe* seen a guy who *might* have looked like the guy in that police sketch?

Shelly was half-drunk, and even she knew how stupid that sounded.

She shouldn't have come out tonight. Especially not with her law-school friends. They were wrapped up in their perfect little overachieving lives and didn't understand what she was going through.

I want you to call her.

Shelly pulled up to a stoplight and checked her mirrors. No odd looks from other drivers. No creepy cars following her. She hadn't been lying about the police-station thing. She really *had* driven by there a minute ago and even made a loop around it, but she'd seen no one suspicious, and no one was following her.

Someone honked behind her. The light was green. She was distracted tonight. What the hell had possessed her to order that third mojito?

Ren's been wanting to go.

Ren. Her real name was Renee. And every time Drew used her nickname, Shelly felt a sharp pang in her chest.

Shelly coasted through traffic lights, green, green, green, trying not to obsess. For days, all she'd been able to think about was Drew with his wife and his kids, walking through the Magic Kingdom. She pictured them watching fireworks together and eating ice-cream cones and riding Space Mountain.

Well, maybe not Mia. She was only three, definitely not big enough for a roller coaster. But Drew was a doting father. He'd probably take her on Mr. Toad's Wild Ride instead, and Shelly pictured Mia's blond curls flying as she shrieked with glee. Or maybe not. Would she even know what Mr. Toad's Wild Ride was? Had Renee read her children *The Wind in the Willows*? Probably so. Renee was a good mother, of course, and she had good, beautiful kids who would someday become good, beautiful adults.

Although Shelly had had a good mother, too, one who read stories and took her to church, and look how Shelly had turned out. She was a bitch. A home-wrecker.

She was the kind of woman she'd never imagined in a million years she'd be, the kind who met someone else's husband in expensive hotel rooms and did things to him that his wife didn't do anymore, things that made his eyes glaze over as he groaned her name.

The phone in her lap dinged, making her jump. She checked the screen and saw a text from Kira Vance with the detective's phone number. Charlotte Spears. She bit her lip and once again wished she'd never gone to that damn bar tonight. But she'd wanted a distraction.

I want you to call her.

There had been an urgency in Kira's voice. An intensity. Much like the look in her eyes when they'd met at the coffee shop. And the other detective with her? Whoa. He took intensity to a whole new level.

"Screw it."

Shelly tapped the phone number as she neared her apartment. Her nerves danced as she tried to work out what to say. *Hello, detective, you don't know me, but I've got a hot tip for you . . .*

She turned into the driveway of her building and rolled to a stop at the gate. As it slid open, she checked her mirrors again and thought about the man in the bar. He'd been attractive. Much more attractive than that suspect sketch. They didn't even really look alike, come to think of it.

But . . . there had been that glance. He'd caught her eye on her way to the bathroom, and he'd looked at her a second too long. Only a second, but it had been enough to turn Shelly's skin cold. Enough to make her call Kira Vance on her way home.

A woman's voice sounded in her ear, low and throaty, like Kathleen Turner. *You have reached the voice mail . . .*

Shelly hung up, relieved. She'd call Detective Spears in the morning. Or maybe she'd wake up and realize the whole thing was stupid, and she wouldn't call anyone.

Shelly pulled into a parking space and checked her surroundings. The building formed a U shape, with narrow balconies looking out over a pool. She saw lights in several units and the flicker of a few televisions, but the parking lot wasn't full. Many of her neighbors were probably still out for the evening. Shelly dropped her keys into her purse, then grabbed her tube of pepper spray. It was sticky and covered with lint, and she peeled a gum wrapper off it before clutching it in her hand and getting out of her car.

The air smelled of chlorine and grass clippings. Shelly strode across the lot, gripping her key card in one hand and her pepper spray in the other, and the heels of her sandals clacked against the concrete. She glanced around, checking the sidewalks and the shadows between cars. She passed through a hedge to the landscaped courtyard, where a glowing blue pool was surrounded by a wrought-iron fence. The pool was empty now, except for a pink foam noodle drifting listlessly in the corner.

Shelly scanned the hedges, trying to calm her nerves. She shouldn't have called Kira. The PI had gotten her all worked up, and now she wouldn't be able to sleep tonight. Maybe she'd have one last drink just to smooth her nerves and block out the images of Drew and his family on their perfect vacation.

She reached the door and swiped the key card over the panel. The light blinked green, and she felt a surge of relief. Home sweet home.

"Michelle."

She whirled around, and her heart jumped.

Charlotte needed to get home.

She'd been running nonstop for eighteen hours, and now she wanted to eat, shower, and crash. She hadn't had a midnight callout in weeks, and she was overdue for being pulled out of bed and losing half a night's sleep.

She exited the police-station parking lot, but instead of turning

right toward the freeway, she hung a left toward Allen Parkway, making her way to Avalon Lofts for what would be the second time today.
She and Diaz had stopped by earlier after convincing the Duffy &
Hersch receptionist to give them Michelle Chandler's address. They
had wanted to interview the woman, but she hadn't been home, and
they figured she was probably out for the evening, kicking off her
weekend, which was where she and Diaz would be tonight if either of
them had a life outside of work.

Charlotte's phone buzzed, and she tapped the button to put it on
speaker.

"I thought you went home," she said.

"I'm on my way." Diaz's voice surrounded her in stereo. "You listening to the scanner?"

Charlotte tensed. "No."

"Unresponsive female at Avalon Lofts."

"You're kidding."

"No. I'm on my way over there now, ETA ten minutes."

"I'll meet you."

Charlotte floored the gas, wishing she were in a police unit instead
of her personal vehicle. Pushing her Mustang to its limit, she swerved
around traffic and sped through three consecutive yellow lights before
reaching the apartment complex. Nearing the gate, she spied a pair of
patrol units in the lot, red and blue strobes spinning. An ambulance
was there, too, but the lights were off.

"Shit." She pounded her fist on the steering wheel.

The gate to the complex stood open, and a uniformed officer
manned a barricade between the parking lot and the building's courtyard. It was a large complex. Hundreds of units. An unresponsive fe-

male could mean anything. Maybe some woman had choked on a chicken bone or had a few too many beers by the pool.

But Charlotte's gut told her otherwise.

The uniform by the barricade was tall and had a buzz cut. Charlotte didn't recognize him. She parked her car and approached the man, flashing her ID.

"What do you have?" she asked.

He nodded toward the building, where several officers stood under a covered patio area with a barbecue pit.

"Caucasian female, twenty to thirty, gunshot wound," he reported. "Neighbor found her on the sidewalk and called nine-one-one."

"She's—"

"Dead."

Charlotte took a deep breath. "Any ID?"

"Not yet. Scene's taped off, but the ME isn't here yet, so no one's touching anything."

She glanced at the parking lot behind her. A white Honda Accord was parked in a nearby row, and Charlotte read the plate. It was the car she and Diaz had been looking for earlier when they'd stopped by. Charlotte dug a glove from her pocket and pulled it on as she walked over to check the car out. Doors locked. Clean interior. She touched the hood. Still warm.

"*Damn* it."

The uniform watched her curiously as she strode past him and followed the courtyard path to the pair of officers. One she recognized. The other looked barely out of braces.

"Gonzales." She nodded. "Catch me up."

"Call came in about eleven thirty-two. GSW, close range." Gonzales gestured toward the building, and Charlotte looked over. Beyond the yellow tape, she saw a low hedge and a woman's feet peeking out. White sandals. Red toenail polish.

"Anyone report a gunshot?" she asked.

"To my knowledge, no."

The knot in Charlotte's stomach tightened.

"Detective Spears?"

She turned around as Buzz Cut walked over.

"There's a woman here who wants to talk to you," he said.

"Where?" *God, please don't let it be her mom or sister.*

"Over there." He nodded at the barricade. "Kira somebody? She said she knows you."

CHAPTER

SIXTEEN

S HE LOOKS bad," Diaz said in a low voice.

Charlotte followed his gaze to the patrol car, where Kira Vance stood with her arms crossed, staring at her feet, while her security guy scanned the scene with an eagle eye.

Former military, Charlotte would bet on it. She'd meant to run his background, but she'd gotten sidetracked with about ten other aspects of this crazy investigation.

"Think we should take her in?" Diaz asked.

"Let's keep it informal. We'll probably get more out of her."

Kira and her bodyguard had been here for a while now, waiting outside the gate. An officer had already interviewed Kira and relayed the basics, but Charlotte had some follow-up questions. As she walked over, Jeremy Owen's gaze homed in on her.

"Ms. Vance?"

Kira looked up. Her face was pale, and she had the same blank expression Charlotte remembered from Brock Logan's patio. Once again, they were standing a stone's throw away from a bloody crime scene where someone had been shot at close range.

"Get you some water?" Charlotte asked.

"No."

"I have a few follow-up questions about your interactions with the victim."

"Okay." Kira shuddered and wrapped her arms tighter around herself. She wore an oversize flannel shirt that swallowed her, but she still seemed cold. The knees of her jeans were damp, and her shoes were muddy.

"What about her?" Kira asked.

"How exactly did you find her? At this address?"

"She told me where she lived over the phone."

"This was when she called you from her car?"

"That's right." Kira cast a wary look at the crime scene, where the ME's people were still huddled around the body.

Charlotte dug out her notepad and flipped it open. According to Kira's initial statement, the victim had done some work for Oliver Kovak shortly before his death, so Kira had interviewed her to learn more about it.

"How did *you* find her?"

Charlotte glanced up. "Me?"

"I noticed you were already here when we arrived," Kira said, "but another detective's in charge of the crime scene."

Sharp girl. And maybe she wasn't as out of it as she looked.

"We'd been trying to reach her for an interview," Charlotte said.

"Why?"

"We believe she's connected to the Kovak case."

Another glance at the crime scene. "Do you think—" She halted and looked down, like she might get sick. Her face turned a sickly shade of green.

Jeremy eased closer and touched her elbow. "Kira?"

She shook him off and looked at Charlotte. "Do you think I might have led him to her? Whoever killed her?"

Charlotte considered how much to reveal. She sensed she might get more from this witness if she shared some information.

"That's unlikely."

Kira's brows arched.

"We have reason to believe that on Monday afternoon, someone followed her to a mail store, where she sent a package to Oliver Kovak."

"Post Place, by the courthouse."

Charlotte frowned. "How'd you know that?"

"She told me."

Charlotte studied the PI. Clearly, she knew a hell of a lot more about this case than she'd volunteered in her multiple interviews. She was withholding info, and it needed to stop.

"We believe the person followed Michelle Chandler and learned where the package was going," Charlotte stated, "and then killed Oliver Kovak shortly after he received it."

Kira stared at her.

"Does that fit with what you have?" Charlotte asked.

A slight nod.

"So what was it?" Charlotte asked Kira. "The package she sent to Kovak? We recovered the envelope at Logan's but nothing inside."

"I don't know," she obviously lied.

Charlotte stared at her, and it was a battle of wills. Why was this woman so guarded? Was she protecting someone, or was she simply being difficult? Kira Vance had turned up at two murder scenes in less than a week, and Charlotte wanted answers.

"Detective?"

She turned around to see Diaz walking over, notepad in hand. He looked from Kira to Charlotte and seemed to know he'd interrupted something important.

"The ME's people are wrapping up," he said.

In other words, she'd better catch them now if she wanted their input without having to wait for official reports.

"Be right there." She turned back to Kira. "Before you leave, Detective Diaz needs to get an official statement."

She gave a brisk nod. "Fine."

Charlotte stepped closer and lowered her voice. "I suggest you share whatever it is you have, Ms. Vance. Keeping investigators in the dark is never a good idea. And it won't work anyway. We always find out."

"I know." Her gaze was steady. "I'm an investigator, too."

Kira rode in Jeremy's truck, head pressed against the window, eyes closed, wishing the vibrations would lull her to sleep. They didn't, but she didn't mind pretending so she wouldn't have to talk.

Jeremy smoothly navigated the streets to Kira's neighborhood, and she pictured a map in her mind's eye. She tried to visualize every turn and stoplight before it happened. Anything to occupy her thoughts and keep her from puking right here in Jeremy's truck.

Her stomach roiled, and she squeezed her eyes tighter.

Do not throw up.

His truck was nice and tidy, and she could tell he took pride in keeping it that way, even though there was muck on the floor mats now from their trek through the marsh. Jeremy had lent her a flannel shirt, but Kira's skin was still cold and clammy under her damp clothes, and the sensation wasn't helping the nausea.

She kept picturing Shelly. One minute she'd been on the phone, and the next she was dead. Kira had caught a glimpse of her pale foot at the crime scene, and the realization had smacked her: Shelly was *gone*. Just like that. Just like Ollie. One second she'd been talking to Kira, and then she was dead.

Acid swirled in her stomach, and Kira clenched her teeth, trying not to think about it.

Another turn, right this time. Damn it, she'd lost track. But then Jeremy slowed and made a smooth turn into a driveway, and Kira opened her eyes to see the yellow light of her carport. It was empty. Gina wasn't home, and Kira's car was in the shop now.

Jeremy put the truck in park, and Kira reached for her door.

"Wait."

She sighed as he got out and went around, but she was too tired to protest as he opened her door and accompanied her to the back step.

"I need to do a walk-through," he said as she dug out her key.

"Sure."

When they were inside, she tapped in the alarm code and kicked off her shoes, then peeled off her wet socks and dropped them on the floor. She went straight to the bedroom, where she stripped off her damp clothes and got a dry shirt out of a drawer. It was a faded gray Astros jersey, and the softness against her skin brought tears to her eyes.

She was losing it. That was the only explanation for why a ratty old sleep shirt could make her want to cry.

She heard Jeremy in the guest room fiddling with the window lock as she returned to the kitchen. Ollie's fish was in a pitcher on the windowsill. She gave him a pinch of food and watched him dart around.

Kira felt more than heard Jeremy walk up behind her. He had a knack for stealth.

"Everything okay?" she asked, turning around.

"All good."

"I'll wash your shirt and get it back to you."

He didn't respond, just gazed down at her. She couldn't read his expression. The kitchen was dark except for the light under the microwave, and she remembered the look on his face after he'd kissed her in his truck.

Kira's stomach fluttered. She didn't trust it, so she stepped to the sink and washed her hands.

"Sorry about earlier." His voice was gruff.

"It was just a kiss." She turned around. "Forget it."

"I meant the op. Taking you down there." He rubbed the back of his neck. "I should have scoped it out first."

"I wouldn't call it an 'op,' really." She felt annoyed now for no apparent reason. "Skulking around taking pictures? I do that all the time."

So he *wasn't* sorry about the kiss? Or he just wasn't saying he was sorry? Her brain was too tired to analyze it.

She rubbed her forehead. "Why were they shooting at us?"

"Not they," Jeremy said. "One guy with a pop gun, and he was well out of range."

"A pop gun?"

"A twenty-two pistol."

"You can tell that just from one sound?"

"I've spent a lot of years around a lot of weapons." He paused, watching her. "Corporate security is a mixed bag. You get what you pay for. Some outfits are trained and disciplined. Some are just yahoos with guns. Some will take potshots at anything that moves, whether it's an armadillo or a trespasser."

"You think that was a potshot?"

"A warning shot. He was trying to scare us off."

Jeremy sounded so sure. Not worried at all. Meanwhile, just thinking about it had Kira's heart racing. She'd been on countless stakeouts—some boring, some not—and typically she relished a little excitement. But never had she been shot at during one.

Jeremy stepped closer, staring down at her in the dimness. He was a strong, solid presence. Her eyes dropped to the mean-looking gun in his holster, and she had no doubt he was well trained. She thought of how easily he'd put himself between her and a bullet. Why? Because he was a professional.

She looked up and tried to read his thoughts. Could he read hers? She wanted to pull him into her bedroom. She wanted to peel off his shirt and run her hands over his skin, and she wanted him to replace the disturbing images in her head with something better.

"Erik's on his way over," he said.

Erik.

"You've met him, correct?"

"Briefly, yesterday." She stepped back. "But why? I thought you were on tonight."

"I have to take care of something."

Lights swept across the window, and Jeremy stepped over to look through the blinds. Kira watched him numbly. What the hell did he have to take care of at this time of night, after everything that had happened?

He reached for the door. "Get some sleep, Kira."

Yeah, right. No problem. She'd sleep like a baby, just like the past three nights. The mere thought of the restless hours ahead of her made her eyes sting.

"Okay?"

She nodded. "Sure, okay."

———————

Jeremy left her standing there, still shocked and shaky and looking like she was going to puke. He didn't want to leave. The desire to stay with her clawed at him, which was exactly why he needed to hightail it out of there.

Erik's truck was parked on the street. He lowered his window as Jeremy approached.

"Thanks for this."

Erik nodded. "How is she?"

"Rattled."

"You think it's connected?"

"Yes." Jeremy glanced back at Kira's house, then looked at Erik. His hair was mussed, and Jeremy knew he'd dragged him out of bed to come here, but it didn't matter, because Jeremy would have done the same for him.

"GSW, point-blank range," Jeremy said. "No one heard a gunshot, so they're thinking he used a suppressor."

"Shit."

"Exactly. Cop said she had an unused tube of pepper spray in her hand, so sounds like an ambush. And the victim was working on something with Kovak right before his death, so that's not good, either."

"Liam wants to double up agents until the police know more," Erik said.

"I won't argue with that."

"Where you going now?"

"Recon."

"The ship channel?"

Jeremy nodded. He'd given Erik a brief update over the phone. "Should have done it earlier," he added. Before letting Kira anywhere near the place.

What the fuck had he been thinking? Jeremy glanced at her house again, where the kitchen light was on now. He hoped she'd go to bed, but more likely she'd be up all night working, because she was too wired to sleep. Jeremy knew the feeling well.

Erik was watching him closely. Too closely. If Jeremy wasn't careful, he was going to figure out that this client was getting to him.

Jeremy pulled out his keys. "You got this?"

Erik nodded. "Watch your step, man."

"I will."

CHAPTER

SEVENTEEN

I T WAS a triple-digit day, with a neon-blue sky and wispy white clouds that gave no relief from the sun. Charlotte put on her Ray-Bans as she crossed the church parking lot. Heat shimmered up from the blacktop, and she didn't envy Diaz in his dark suit. She slid behind the wheel of their car and got the AC going.

"Private burial, correct?" Diaz asked, tossing his jacket into the back seat as he got in.

"It's tomorrow. And yes, it's private."

"Thank God."

Charlotte watched the doors of the church as the last of the mourners emerged. Kira Vance stepped onto the sidewalk, accompanied by Brock Logan and several other attorneys. Two of their bodyguards trailed behind them, dressed in suits and trying—unsuccessfully—to blend into the crowd.

Brock had chosen a seat beside Kira at the service, and Charlotte had watched them in the pew together, hoping to get a read on their relationship. Despite Kira's evasiveness, Charlotte was starting to trust her. Brock was another story. Maybe it was simply her bias against lawyers, but she still didn't feel like he was being straight with her about a number of key issues.

"What did you think?" Charlotte asked as she skimmed the faces. She'd gotten to where she could read people in a heartbeat. Body language was everything, which was why she came to these things.

"Big turnout," Diaz said. "He seemed to have a lot of friends and contacts for a one-man shop."

"People say he was a nice guy. Even his two ex-wives came, which tells you something." She glanced at Diaz. "Anyone strike you as off?"

"No."

"What about the bail bondsman? Sanchez?"

"He seemed okay. Why?"

She shrugged. "He seemed a little slimy to me."

"I didn't notice. And hasn't he been cooperative? He gave us those surveillance tapes from his office."

"Yeah, and there was nothing useful on them."

"Still, we haven't had any pushback from him."

Charlotte sighed. She scanned the crowd one last time before backing out of the space. She hated to admit it, but the funeral had been a bust in terms of leads.

"What's the word on that vehicle list?" Diaz asked.

"Still working it. I've got Phan giving me some help." At her request, Phan had culled through a list of black BMWs registered locally, checking for owners who had a criminal record. "He's turned up a few leads, but so far nothing that really pops. What about the tape from Avalon Lofts?"

"I'm supposed to hear back from the building's security company." He pulled out his phone and checked. "Looks like I missed a call. Hang on."

Diaz listened to the message as Charlotte edged her way through the crowded parking lot. A white Subaru cut her off, and she muttered a curse.

"Don't do it," Diaz said.

"What?"

"You can't use your horn at a funeral."

"What, is that written somewhere?"

He shook his head. "You're going to give yourself an ulcer. Okay, I've got a message from the security firm. Guy says he emailed me the files I wanted, including the two-hour window leading up to the crime."

Charlotte inched her way into the line of cars. "Maybe we'll get lucky and someone scouted the scene ahead of time in a black BMW."

"That's not the kind of luck we're having lately."

"You're right." She glanced at him. "We need to interview Kira Vance again. I say we bring her in. Or better yet, show up at her house uninvited."

"Why?"

"She talked to *both* victims minutes before they were murdered. Doesn't that seem weird to you?"

"Yeah, but you just want to show up and hope she'll talk to us?"

"Why not?"

"Might piss her off."

"Exactly. She needs a push."

Charlotte's phone vibrated with a text. She grabbed it from the cupholder and checked the number. "Hey, get this. It's her."

"Who?"

"Kira." Charlotte skimmed the text. "She wants to meet at her office in one hour. It's over on McKinney Street."

"What's she want to meet about?"

"The case, I guess. I told you from the get-go she was holding out on us."

Diaz combed his hand through his hair and smoothed his tie.

"You look fine."

He ignored her and checked his watch. "Let's stop first. I could use some lunch."

"You just had a breakfast taco."

"So?"

"Okay, but make it quick. This girl's been dodging questions for days, and now she wants to talk. I want to catch her before she changes her mind."

Kira was relieved to be out of that church. Since the very first hymn, she'd had a knot in her chest. She didn't know whether it was the sight of Ollie's casket—the simple pine box his daughter had said he wanted—or the droning minister or the cloying scent of lilies. Whatever it was, Kira spent the entire service battling a tight, suffocating feeling, like someone was squeezing her heart in a fist, and it wasn't until she got out of there and stood in the sweltering parking lot that she could breathe again.

"Feel better now?"

She glanced at Jeremy beside her. He'd noticed her acting strangely and steered her to a drinking fountain as soon as the service let out.

"Fine."

Being in his truck felt better. Now that she wasn't near funeral flowers or Brock's cologne, she could take a normal breath. Jeremy's truck had a simple, earthy smell—probably because of all the mud and grass they'd tracked in last night. Or maybe it was the work boots he kept stashed in the back seat. Whatever it was, she liked it, just as she liked his steady presence beside her. Trent was steady, too, but it wasn't the same.

She slid another glance at Jeremy. What was it about him? What was it about his long, silent looks that made her feel better? There was something in his eyes when he looked at her, a flicker of something that maybe only *she* saw. It had been there last night in his truck and again when they'd stood together in her dim kitchen. That look of his put a tingle inside her and made her feel warm all over.

Or maybe she was coming down with a damn fever. Just what she needed this week.

Jeremy looked at her again. "You sure you want to talk to the police right now?"

"I'd rather talk to them on my terms than go back to the station."

Kira pulled her purse into her lap. She didn't normally carry one, but her messenger bag didn't fit with her black linen dress and heels. She found a compact and checked her face. People had been staring at her, and now she saw why. Her bruise was in its final stages of healing and was a hideous shade of green, and her attempts at makeup didn't really conceal it. Kira dabbed on some powder, then gave up and dropped her purse to the floor.

Jeremy turned onto McKinney. He knew exactly where she worked without having to be told. Evidently, he'd committed her file to memory.

"Park right in front," she instructed. "The meters are free on weekends."

Jeremy pulled up to the building. It was a three-story walk-up on the far edge of downtown. The neighborhood was in transition, and she figured she had about six months left until she'd have to look for something cheaper.

She started to open her door, but Jeremy shot her a look.

Wait.

He didn't have to say it anymore, and she sat patiently as he came around to her side. She stepped onto the sidewalk, wobbly in her heels, and he caught her arm, sending a jolt of heat through her.

"Thanks," she said without eye contact.

She wouldn't think about that kiss. Or those arms. Or the possessive way he'd slid his hand over her breast. Flashes of memory had slipped through during the funeral, and she hadn't been able to block them. Jeremy had been stationed by the door at the back of the church, and she could practically feel his gaze on her throughout the service.

She took her key card from her purse and swiped it through the card reader. The door clicked open, and she stepped inside.

"I'm on two," she said, leading him across a small foyer and up a narrow flight of stairs. At the top was another locked door, this one with the WorkWell logo etched across frosted glass.

"It's a communal office." She glanced over her shoulder and caught him looking at her ass. "You ever seen one?"

"No."

She unlocked the door and stepped into the common area, where tall windows facing the street let in a flood of light. It was a large, open space surrounded by small private offices. Clusters of tables—not cubicles—occupied the center to "foster dialogue," according to the WorkWell brochure. Beanbags filled the room's corners. At the far end of the space, three young men in jeans and T-shirts were crowded around a computer screen. One glanced up and did a double-take.

"Hey, Kira."

"Hey."

All of them were staring at her now, probably because they'd never seen her in a dress before. Or maybe it was Jeremy who had their attention. With his dark suit and holster, he looked like a secret service agent.

Kira glanced back at him. "I need coffee. You?"

"I'm good."

She led him into the break room, passing the purple hammock dangling from the ceiling. He lifted an eyebrow at it but didn't comment. She fired up the Keurig and started a cup of Donut Shop Blend, then took a water from the fridge and handed it to him. He liked to stay hydrated, she'd noticed.

Jeremy twisted off the top, watching her as he took a long pull.

Kira tried not to shift under his gaze as the coffee maker hissed and gurgled. She poured sugar into her coffee and led him to her office.

"Well, this is it," she said, unlocking the door. "It's small, but it's plenty of room for me."

She flipped the light on and was dismayed to see the mess she'd left when she last visited. Her desk was covered with files and soda cans. A pile of mail occupied her chair as a reminder to catch up on her bills. After her wire transfer from Logan, she'd managed to pay her rent, but she was still late on everything else.

Jeremy stepped in behind her. The room seemed to shrink with him in it, and she once again marveled at his size. He eased around her without a word and peered through the vertical blinds. Kira had a view of the street—something she'd been proud of when she first signed the lease here. In retrospect, she should have saved the fifty bucks a month and gone with an alley view.

He looked at her. "Why do you keep an office here?"

His tone wasn't judgmental but curious. She found a free space on her desk and set her coffee down.

"Security reasons."

His brow furrowed.

"I needed a business address different from my home. Early on, I was doing a lot of cheating spouses, and I didn't want people finding me. This gives me a PO box and a secure server for sensitive files. Plus a conference room for clients who don't want to meet in public." She shrugged. "The security thing doesn't come up that much now that I'm working mostly for lawyers and insurance companies. But I'm used to it."

Cheers erupted in the common room, probably over some videogame milestone.

"And the other tenants?" He nodded toward the door.

"Two of those guys are app designers, and the other's some kind of consultant, I think. I don't actually know what everyone here does, and I kind of like it that way. We stay out of each other's way."

Jeremy watched her silently. It felt strange to see him in her tight little office. It seemed intimate somehow, as though she were letting him into another room of her life. The more time they spent together, the more she let her guard down. And she had to remind herself that to him, this was an assignment. Regardless of what had happened in his truck last night, he was getting paid to be with her, and this was his job.

Sun streamed through the blinds, catching the dust motes between them, and Kira held his gaze, wishing she could read his thoughts. Something flickered in his eyes, and her pulse sped up. Was he thinking about last night? She'd been drawn to him all day, and she wanted to kiss him again, right here in her messy office. She wanted to tug his tie loose and unbutton that starched shirt.

He turned to the window. "They just pulled up."

Of course. Perfect timing.

"I'll be right back," she said. "We'll meet in the conference room."

Kira went down to open the door for Spears and Diaz. The detectives still wore their funeral attire, and Diaz carried a to-go cup from Dairy Queen.

"Glad you could make it," Kira said as they followed her up the stairs.

"No problem at all," Diaz replied.

Kira didn't know whether Spears shared his view that it was no problem to come here. She probably would have preferred to talk at the police station, which was exactly why Kira wanted them here.

Kira led them into the conference room, and Spears stopped short as she caught sight of the beanbag corner.

"Interesting work space." Spears glanced around the conference room, where giant whiteboards covered three of the four walls. She took a leather swivel chair at the head of the table as Kira ducked into her office to grab her coffee and the notebook from her purse.

Jeremy claimed a chair beside Kira, and she was glad he'd opted to sit in. She wanted his take on the investigation.

"Anything new since last night?" Kira asked Spears.

"We're working on it." She looked from Kira to Jeremy. "I need to ask if either of you has seen a black BMW around recently."

"No," Kira said.

"What about in Brock Logan's neighborhood on the night of the murder?"

"I don't remember one. Why?"

"A witness spotted someone in a gray hoodie getting into a black BMW a few minutes after the shooting."

"Where?" Jeremy asked.

"It was parked on Lark Street, right behind Logan's house."

"So you have another witness?" Kira leaned closer. "Did they give a description?"

"Not much of one. He saw this person from behind, and he mainly noticed the car."

"I haven't seen a black BMW around." She thought of her last conversation with Shelly and wished she'd asked about the car Shelly had noticed at the stoplight. "But why hasn't that detail been released? And what about the suspect sketch?"

Spears darted a look at Diaz, and Kira sensed she'd hit on a sensitive topic.

"The department wants to hold off releasing the sketch," she said.

"How come?"

"With the hood and the sunglasses, it's pretty . . . inconclusive, I think is the term they used."

"It's so generic, they're worried we'll be flooded with tips," Diaz added. "Which means we'd have to devote a lot of time and resources to running them down, when we could be following up on concrete leads."

"Until we have something more specific, they want to use the sketch internally," Spears said.

Kira glanced at Jeremy, who was watching her closely, probably wondering why she'd called this meeting. Kira flipped open her notebook and unclipped a business card. On the back, she'd written two license-plate numbers and vehicle descriptions. She slid the card across the table to Spears.

"What's this?"

"Two tags." She'd been up late running them through a database she had access to as a licensed PI. "One comes back to a shell company called FC Incorporated. The other is an individual, Andre Markov. I believe Ollie was watching him in the days before his murder."

"Watching him?" Spears asked.

"Doing a background search, probably some surveillance." Kira glanced at Diaz. "I don't think Markov is the gunman. I looked up the guy's mug shot. He doesn't look like the man I saw, and his height is wrong."

Diaz's eyebrows arched. "So he has an arrest record?"

"Yes. But, like I said, he wasn't the guy at Brock's house. And I have reason to believe he was in Channelview when Shelly Chandler was killed last night."

"Why do you think that?" Diaz asked.

"Because his car was there. That's where I got these tags."

Spears watched her for a moment, then picked up the business card and studied the info Kira had written down. "So you don't think Markov is a suspect—"

"I didn't say that. I don't think he's the *shooter*," Kira said. "I do think he's involved somehow. I thought you could do some background, see what comes up."

Spears looked from Kira to Jeremy. "Both of you do background checks, too, if I'm not mistaken."

"True," Kira said. "But you have more tools than I do. You can dig deeper."

"Does this Markov have anything to do with the package that Shelly Chandler mailed to Ollie Kovak right before his death?" she asked.

Kira nodded.

Diaz crossed his arms. "We'd like you to tell us about that."

"Sorry." Kira smiled thinly. "I would, but that's confidential."

"In other words, it has to do with a legal case you're working on," Spears said. "The Quinn case, I assume?"

"That's right. My work product is privileged."

Spears muttered something about lawyers.

"We'll check out Markov," Diaz said. "But any idea *why* Kovak would have eyes on this guy?"

"Ollie was working exclusively on the Quinn case," Kira said, "so I believe it's linked to that. Before his death, Ollie was trying to identify Ava Quinn's real killer."

Spears looked annoyed. "Her *real* one? As opposed to the made-up one we arrested?"

"Our investigators say her husband did it," Diaz said.

"I'm aware," Kira replied. "And I know a defense attorney who plans to show a jury otherwise."

Spears tapped the business card on the table. "Thanks for the vehicle tags. We'll check these out."

She looked at her partner, and they stood to leave. Kira and Jeremy stood, too.

"Let me know what you find out," Kira said, although she doubted they would. Kira was holding back info, so why shouldn't they? Given that she was working for Gavin Quinn's defense team, her cooperation could only go so far. Still, Kira wanted to help them as much as she could.

"We'll be in touch." Spears looked at Jeremy. "In the meantime, watch your back." She nodded at Kira. "Hers, too."

CHAPTER

EIGHTEEN

THE BULL pen was nearly empty when Charlotte returned from a grueling three hours at the ME's office.

Big surprise. Not many of her coworkers chose to spend a summer weekend holed up in the office. Even Diaz, who was almost as dogged as she was, had knocked off for the day, citing "plans," which could mean anything from drinks with his cop buddies to a hot date.

Charlotte had no such diversions in her future—just a long night ahead of her trying to forget the grisly images of a twenty-eight-year-old law student on an autopsy table.

Charlotte dropped her keys onto her desk and sank into her chair with a sigh. Shelly Chandler's death had been up close and personal. Very up close, according to the pathologist. It looked like she'd been approached from behind and turned around to find herself face-to-face with her killer, right there at her own back door. Her last moment must have been terrifying, and Charlotte got angry just thinking about it.

Yet no one—not one of the apartment residents police had interviewed—reported hearing a gunshot, leading investigators to believe the assailant had used a suppressor.

Just like in the Oliver Kovak case.

"You're here."

She turned to see Lacey coming from the elevators.

"I am, unfortunately. Working on the Kovak case. Why are *you* here?"

The CSI looked like she'd just come off a baseball field. She wore a dusty blue uniform and a ball cap, and the tops of her cheeks were pink.

"Got called in for that house fire in Meyerland. Three fatalities."

Charlotte cringed. "I heard. Kids?"

"Yeah, and I'm hearing rumors it was arson."

"Damn. That's awful."

Lacey dropped a file onto her desk. The folder had a white envelope paper-clipped to the top. "That's from Grant."

Charlotte brightened. "Already?" Their fingerprint examiner was notoriously backlogged, and she hadn't expected to hear from him today.

"He asked me to hand-deliver it. Said you've left him about a hundred messages?"

"I may have left a few."

"The envelope's from me," Lacey said. "I put the crime-scene video on a flash drive for you. I tweaked the mockup to show where he tears his glove climbing over the fence."

Lacey was always thorough, which was why Charlotte liked working with her.

"Thanks."

"Sure." She sighed. "I'm off to analyze carpet samples for accelerants."

"Good luck."

Lacey walked away, and Charlotte cleared the clutter off her desk and opened the file from Grant. He'd put a beautiful eight-by-ten glossy of the fingerprint on top.

Damn, she loved that man. Too bad he was married.

Grant was a legend in cop circles for his ability to get a print off anything. Fabric. Leather. Human skin. She'd once seen him develop a thumbprint off an electrical cord that had been used to strangle a thirty-year-old mother while her children slept in the next room. The print was only a partial, but it had generated a hit in the system and led police straight to the killer's door.

Charlotte studied the photograph. The print was bright yellow against a purple backdrop, suggesting he'd developed it using fluorescent powder and then photographed it with an alternative light source to create maximum contrast. Even from such a small scrap of latex, he'd been able to get an amazing level of detail. It probably helped that people left better prints when they were nervous and sweating, and people fleeing murder scenes tended to be both.

Charlotte slid the photograph aside and skimmed the report.

No match with the FBI database, which contained fingerprints from more than seventy million subjects in the criminal master file. Also, no DNA hits.

Grant had scrawled a handwritten note beneath the typed report. He drew a zero with a line through it and added, "Still trying a few more things. More TK. —G."

Charlotte chewed her lip. Grant could get creative. And clearly, her case had his attention, which was good.

What *wasn't* good was that anyone with a record like Andre Markov's would have his prints in the system, and possibly his DNA, unless the sample hadn't been entered yet due to bureaucratic logjams—which were known to happen.

At any rate, the prints would be there, so whoever had murdered Ollie, it wasn't Andre Markov.

Kira had essentially told her that already, but Charlotte needed to check. And she had. Markov's physical description didn't line up with the eyewitnesses, who had seen an approximately six-foot-tall man at Brock Logan's residence and fleeing the scene. According to Markov's booking photo, he was five-three.

So even if Kira was right and Ollie *had* been tailing Markov right before his death, and even if Ollie *had* been trying to pin Ava Quinn's murder on the guy—which might give Markov motive to want to kill him—Markov hadn't been the hooded gunman who'd fled the River Oaks murder scene.

Charlotte recalled Kira's face as she'd handed over this lead. She recalled the imploring look in her eyes and how convinced she'd been that Markov was somehow involved. Charlotte had a hunch she was right. Kira had sharp instincts, and she would have made a good cop if she hadn't decided to work in the private sector.

The elevators dinged, and Charlotte glanced up as two detectives walked into the bull pen. Goldstein and McGrath, sarcastically known as the Twins because of their completely different builds. Goldstein was short and chubby, while McGrath was a beanpole.

Goldstein ducked into the break room, and McGrath went to his cube. Charlotte got up and strolled over.

"Hey, Rick."

He looked her up and down, lingering on the silky gray blouse she'd worn for the funeral.

"How's the Kovak thing coming?" he asked, pushing his chair back to stretch out his long legs. He wore jeans and a navy HPD T-shirt today.

"Working on it now. I wanted to ask you about something." She propped her hip on the corner of his desk. "When you were working the Ava Quinn homicide, you ever come across the name Andre Markov?"

He frowned. "No, why?"

"Name came up in the Kovak case."

"What's that got to do with me?"

She crossed her arms, annoyed by his defensiveness. "Well, let's see. Kovak was working for Brock Logan at the time he was killed. And Brock Logan goes to trial Monday representing Gavin Quinn." She watched him and waited for a reaction. Every cop in the department knew the details, and Oliver Kovak's murder had been splashed all over the news for days.

"We ran a tight case."

"No one says you didn't."

"Yeah?" His brow furrowed. "Then how come you've been nosing through my murder book."

"*Your* book?"

"Don't give me that shit, Spears. I know what you've been doing."

She tipped her head to the side. "What, you mean investigating?"

"Let me tell you something. Ava Quinn was dumping her husband. She'd just met with one of the best divorce lawyers in town and withdrawn twenty-five grand from her account for a cash retainer. We got the bank records to prove it."

This was news to Charlotte, but she tried not to look surprised.

"The woman was getting a divorce." He pointed a finger at her. "Her husband offed her, and we proved it six ways to Sunday, and I don't need you and Diaz going around stirring up shit."

Charlotte rolled her eyes. "No one's stirring up anything."

"Then keep your nose out of my case."

She got up and walked away, ticked off. She should have come at him a different way. Or asked his partner.

He stalked into the break room, no doubt to go bitch about her to Goldstein.

Charlotte stood at her desk, gazing down at the photo of the big yellow print. She traced her fingertip over the loops and whorls.

Keep your nose out of my case.

If he'd wanted her to butt out, he'd picked exactly the wrong tactic.

Brock's office was a ghost town on Saturdays, and Kira and Jeremy zipped straight up to the thirty-seventh floor.

The reception area was dark, and Sydney's desk was cleared of everything except a black phone and a thick pink message pad.

Kira followed the low sound of voices to the back, where she found Brock and Neil in a glass conference room. Both had changed from their funeral clothes into jeans and button-down shirts.

"Hey." Brock sat forward as Kira stepped into the room. "Any word from HPD?"

Brock had hit her up at the church—in the pew, no less—for details about Shelly's murder, but Kira had little to share.

"Nothing they're telling me." She set her bag on the table and watched as Jeremy ducked into the conference room across the hall. Erik and Liam were seated at a table, deep in conversation. Kira turned her attention to the paperwork spread out in front of Brock. "How's it going here?"

Neil shot him a look.

"What?" Kira pulled up a chair.

"We've decided to switch gears," Brock said.

"Gears?"

"The trial strategy," he elaborated. "Instead of focusing on the alibi—which is mortally wounded since you dug up the restraining order against Peck—"

"The prosecutor may not know about it," Kira said.

"He knows." Brock shook his head. "Or we have to assume he knows. He's not an idiot. So we're making adjustments. We're shining the spotlight away from Quinn and onto the real killer."

Kira arched her brows, waiting. Brock and Neil just looked at her.

"And that would be . . . ?"

"Whoever murdered Ollie," Neil said. "And now Shelly Chandler. The theory is, they uncovered his identity—either wittingly or unwittingly—and he killed them on the eve of trial to prevent exposure."

Irritation welled in Kira's chest. The way Neil was talking, it sounded like a movie trailer.

"That's a *theory*," she said.

Neil nodded. "A well-supported theory."

She looked at Brock. "You're not really going to put this in front of a jury, are you?"

"Why not?" He leaned back in his chair. "It's an excellent piece of detective work, and we plan to use it."

Kira felt flattered. But they had a long way to go before her theory was ready for the courtroom.

"Where's the proof?" she asked. "And how are you making a connection between Ava Quinn's murder and Ollie's and Shelly's?"

"The connection is Markov," Brock said. "You said so yourself."

"I believe he's connected, yes, but I don't think he killed Ollie or Shelly. I've seen Markov's mug shot, and he looks nothing like the person I saw jogging in front of your house that night. Not to mention that his car was in Channelview when Shelly was killed."

"So if Markov isn't the killer, who is?" Neil asked.

"I don't know."

"We need to figure out what Ollie's death has to do with Markov," Brock said.

Kira sighed and closed her eyes. She rubbed her forehead. Four days of too much stress and too little sleep was starting to catch up with her. She rested her arms on the table and looked at Brock.

"I believe Markov is a trip wire," she said.

Brock's gaze narrowed. "How do you mean?"

"Look at the timeline. Ollie was running surveillance at a dock in Channelview the Friday before his murder. I think he spotted Markov's car and took down the license plate, exactly like I did last night. I think he ran Markov's name and hit on his arrest record, like I did. I think he then called his lawyer buddy Drew Spence—on a Saturday, mind you—and asked him to get him Markov's trial transcript ASAP. Ollie was in a hurry, and he didn't want his fingerprints on the request."

Brock watched her, and she couldn't tell whether he was buying any of this. "Walk me through it."

"Okay, so last Saturday, Drew is getting on a plane to Florida for vacation," she said. "So he hands off Ollie's request to his clerk, who goes to the courthouse and fills out a request."

"The trip wire," Brock said. "Maybe some guy at the courthouse had a flag on the record?"

"Who?" Neil asked.

"I don't know." Kira shrugged. "But everyone's got a 'guy at the courthouse.' Someone who does favors, tips you off to gossip, flags interesting filings that come through."

Neil looked intrigued. "Who's yours?"

She snorted. "I'm not telling. I don't even know who Ollie's guy was, but there was definitely someone."

"Get back to your story," Brock said.

"So when Shelly gets the trial transcript, she overnights it to Ollie's office. He gets the package, then arrives at your house excited about this hot new lead he's found."

"He told me he had something big," Brock said.

"He told me that, too." Kira's stomach clenched as she thought back on the conversation. She could still see the sparkle in Ollie's eyes. "Minutes later, someone shows up and kills him. And a few days later, that same someone kills Shelly."

Had the murderer been following Shelly when she went to meet Kira at the coffee shop? Kira didn't know. The thought filled her with guilt. She liked to think that she or Jeremy would have spotted a tail, but she didn't know for certain and probably never would.

If only Shelly had never been involved. If only Ollie hadn't called Drew and he hadn't passed the favor off to his clerk. If only, if only, if only . . .

"So Markov's case is the trip wire," Brock stated.

Kira nodded. "That's my theory."

"Why, though?" He picked up a thick file and dropped it onto the table. "I read the whole damn transcript, and I'm not seeing it. How is a two-year-old aggravated assault outside a bar connected to the murder of Ava Quinn?"

"I don't know, but I know that it is."

"But Ava and Gavin aren't mentioned." Brock turned to Neil. "Did you come up with anything?"

He shook his head. "Whole thing seems off."

"I thought that, too," Kira said. "I mean, why's an aggravated assault going to trial in the first place? That's the sort of thing that normally gets pleaded down, right? But the aggravated assault is the original charge."

"You're saying he should have copped a plea," Brock said. "I thought that, too."

"The prosecutor was playing hardball," Neil said. "Maybe he was using the threat of a trial to pressure Markov to flip on someone else, a bigger fish. What are Markov's connections?"

"We need to find out," Brock said. "But whoever they are, it doesn't sound like he cooperated. He rolled the dice and went to trial and ended up getting acquitted."

"So Markov took a risk," Kira said. "What does that tell us?"

Neil shrugged. "Could be he thought he'd get a friendly jury. Or he had the judge in his pocket. Though I'm not sure that's a can of worms we want to open."

Brock closed his eyes and tipped his head back. "I hate this case. I really hate it."

Kira did, too.

"Okay, so assume Markov somehow got a lock on an acquittal," Brock said. "We still don't know what the trial has to do with Ava Quinn. How does any of this give Ollie a suspect to pin Ava's murder on?"

"What about the obvious?" Kira asked. "Maybe Markov killed her."

"I thought of that." Brock's voice was edged with frustration. "But where's the evidence? And *why* was Ollie so excited to get his hands on this transcript? It doesn't spell out Markov's connection to my case, and yet Ollie was acting like it was a gold-plated Get Out of Jail Free card for Gavin Quinn. Why?"

"I don't know," Kira said. "But I plan to find out."

Jeremy stuck his head into the room. "Kira. We need a word."

"What is it?"

"Logistics."

She looked at Brock, and the expression on his face put her on her guard. "What's wrong now?"

"Another change of plan." Brock nodded at Jeremy. "Go ahead and fill her in."

Irritated, Kira followed Jeremy across the hall into the conference room where Liam and Erik were waiting. She took a chair at the end of the table, suddenly self-conscious about all the testosterone in her midst.

"What's up?" she asked.

"New plan," Jeremy stated.

"We're increasing the number of agents staffed to you and your colleagues," Liam said.

Colleagues. Like she had a law degree and a fat salary to go with it. She almost laughed, but the serious look on Liam's face stopped her.

"What else?" she asked.

"We're recommending that we consolidate operations at the Metropolitan Hotel," he said. "That makes it easier for us to conduct round-the-clock surveillance and also facilitates communication between agents."

"So . . . you're saying you want us to work there?"

"Live there," Liam said. "For at least the time being."

Kira barked out a laugh. "Are you kidding? I couldn't afford to buy an omelet at that place, much less *live* there."

"The law firm is covering expenses."

She glanced through the glass into the opposite conference room. Brock stood at the whiteboard now, debating something with Neil as he sketched out a timeline.

She looked at Liam. "How long are we talking about?"

"Until we get a handle on this threat or until police make an arrest."

"Or both," Erik added.

"But that could take weeks."

"We know," Jeremy said.

Kira stared at him. He looked so serious, with his sleeves rolled up and his arms folded across his chest, and she caught a glimmer of the expression he'd had on his face last night, when he'd been standing in her kitchen.

"Of course, it's up to you," Liam said. "We can't *make* any one of you do anything."

Jeremy shot a glance at him. "We can recommend." He gave Kira a steely look. "And this is our recommended course of action, based on what we know about the current threat level."

Threat level. It sounded unreal. She wasn't a political figure or some celebrity. And yet they wanted her to move into what amounted to a luxury fortress and have round-the-clock protection. If it was hard to do her job now, she could only imagine what it was going to be like going forward.

She looked directly at Liam. "You're the security experts, so I'll defer to you."

Liam nodded. "Good." He pushed back his chair.

"On one condition."

All three men looked at her.

"I have a job to do. Now more than ever. And I can't be a hostage in some hotel room, so don't try to get in my way when I tell you I need to leave."

Liam's gaze flicked to Jeremy. "Sounds reasonable. Jeremy?"

Based on his look, Jeremy didn't think it was reasonable at all. Kira waited, and finally he gave a slight nod. "Fine. Agreed."

CHAPTER

NINETEEN

GAVIN QUINN'S house wasn't what Charlotte had envisioned. She'd expected a mansion like Brock Logan's, an imposing monument to the ego of the city's top heart surgeon. But the doctor's home was low and understated, hidden from view behind a tall hedge in an expensive neighborhood.

Charlotte passed through the gate and parked her unmarked unit between a pair of black Range Rovers with tinted windows, probably belonging to Quinn's security crew. Beside the Range Rovers was a silver Escalade. Was this more security, or did the doctor have a visitor?

A black fence with horizontal slats faced the driveway. The gate stood ajar, and Charlotte walked into a stony courtyard with a modern sculpture that looked like a rusted Easter egg. She approached a pair of tall black doors and was searching for the bell when one of the doors swung open.

"Well, hello." She fixed a smile on her face. "Nice to see you again, counselor."

"Likewise."

Brock ushered her into the house. The foyer was dim and empty.

It looked out on yet another courtyard with another rusty egg in the center.

She turned to face the lawyer. Unlike Charlotte, he'd had a chance to change since the funeral. He now wore jeans and a tailored shirt that fit nicely over his muscular shoulders, and he looked so athletic she almost didn't notice his black sling.

"How's the arm?" she asked for lack of something better to say.

"Fine." He smirked. "I take it you're surprised to see me here?"

"Not really."

He walked down a hallway, and she followed him. She'd guessed Brock would be Gavin Quinn's first call as soon as he hung up the phone with her.

The house was dim throughout, the only light coming from narrow niches where spotlights shone down on more arty sculptures on pedestals. All the surfaces in the house were stone, glass, and metal, and the rugs and fabrics covered a range of gray. The look was sophisticated yet muted, and she figured either Quinn had hired an expensive decorator or his late wife had a flair for design.

Brock led her down a glass corridor past a wall of trees. Charlotte halted.

"Wow." She looked out at the view. An evening shower had soaked everything, and a vibrant green lawn covered a sloping hill. "Is this all his?"

Brock nodded. "He's got two acres. It's a pie-shaped lot. Doesn't look like much from the street."

Quinn's flat-roofed home was like a tree house, she saw now, with expansive views overlooking the bayou.

"Nice, isn't it?"

She sniffed. "Beats the hell out of the Harris County Jail."

Charlotte didn't bother to hide her annoyance with the way the system worked for people like Quinn. The judge had ordered Quinn to surrender his passport and granted a one-million-dollar bail. Most accused murderers couldn't afford anything close to that amount and ended up awaiting their trials as guests of the county, three hots and a cot, and your chance of an assault-free stay was low if you had the wrong tattoos or none at all. Meanwhile, rich guys like Quinn got to await trial at home.

Brock led her through yet another glass corridor, nodding at an armed security guard as he stepped into a living room. The guard was bald and bulky, with hands like baseball mitts. Charlotte couldn't imagine him handling the Glock on his hip.

She looked at Brock. "Is he with your outfit? Wolfe Security?"

"No, Gavin's got his own guys. He's had them for months. Been getting death threats since the arraignment."

This was news to Charlotte, but she didn't react.

"Wait here," Brock told her, then disappeared down another hallway, leaving her alone with the guard.

Charlotte stepped closer to the window and tried to admire the view. But she couldn't. You could not give her two acres backing up to Buffalo Bayou. What looked like a harmless creek had become a surging torrent when Hurricane Harvey stalled over the city and dumped trillions of gallons of rain. Charlotte had joined the cadre of emergency workers who'd boated and waded through chest-deep water to pull stranded residents from houses. She remembered the slime. The stench. The fear in people's eyes as they abandoned their homes, clutching their kids and their pets, leaving all their earthly possessions behind. Charlotte had gone home each night filthy, exhausted, and deeply grateful for her no-frills second-floor apartment in the Heights.

"Detective Spears."

She turned around.

Gavin Quinn entered the room, followed by his attorney, and Charlotte was struck by the sight of them together. Brock Logan was tall and strong and virile. Even with the sling, he was a picture of health.

Gavin Quinn was . . . not. The doctor had pasty skin, slumped shoulders, and a listless look on his face. His gray eyes were bloodshot and watery, and the bluish circles under them made Charlotte think of a NyQuil commercial. The man's rust-red hair had gray streaks, and he'd grown a beard since that press conference he'd given in front of the police station. The detectives had nicknamed him "the Leprechaun" when they were working his case, and she could see where they'd gotten that. But he didn't look very sprightly now, much less lucky.

"Have a seat." Quinn gestured at the general area of a seating arrangement and sank into a chair. He wore loafers without socks, and his ankle bracelet was clunky and black against his pale skin.

Charlotte perched on the end of the L-shaped sectional. Brock sat in an armchair across from her and reached up to switch on a standing lamp.

Quinn winced at the light. "What can I do for you, Detective?"

The man sounded tired. The kind of tired that wouldn't be cured with sleep.

"Thanks for making time to meet with me." She darted a look at Brock and took out the file she'd tucked into her purse.

"Well, not like I've got much else to do. What's this about, anyway?"

Charlotte pulled out a copy of the suspect sketch. Brock raised an eyebrow when he saw it.

She passed Quinn the picture. "I wanted to see if this man looks familiar to you."

The doctor fished a pair of reading glasses from his pocket and nestled them on his face. Now he looked even older than his forty-three years and more doctorly.

"No." He looked at her over the tops of the lenses. "Why? Who is this? This is a police sketch, so this person obviously committed a crime."

"This is a suspect seen around your lawyer's house the night he and his investigator were shot," she said.

Quinn turned to Brock. "This man killed Oliver Kovak?"

He nodded.

"Is this sketch from you?"

"No," Brock said. "I never saw his face, remember? He was wearing a ski mask."

"You're sure he's not familiar to you?" Charlotte asked, pulling Quinn's attention back to the sketch. "Really look."

Quinn looked. He stroked his beard, and she noticed his fingernails were bitten to the quick.

He took off the glasses. "I don't know him." He handed her the picture and leaned back in the chair.

She tucked the folder back into her purse. "Dr. Quinn, did your wife owe anyone money that you're aware of?"

"No."

"What about you?"

"No." A heavy sigh. "We went through all this back when it happened. We owe money on the house and the cars. That's it. I paid off my med-school loans five years ago."

"What about anyone who owed *her* money? Or you?"

"No, okay? We didn't loan money to people. Even people who hit us up all the time, like her deadbeat brother. We had a thing about it, especially family. 'Just say no' was our motto."

"Why'd you have a thing about it?" Charlotte swept her gaze over the room. "Seems like you and your wife had money to spare."

"Yeah, well, you'd be surprised. I had the med-school loans. And then all the insurance I'm required to carry. *Was* required to. Before my practice went to shit." He shot a look at Brock. "And now there's my security, my legal fees. This thing's eating me alive." He rubbed his hand over his face.

"I can imagine."

"No. You really can't."

She took out her notebook. "Doctor, does the name FC Incorporated mean anything to you?"

"No."

"Are you sure?"

"Yes."

She watched his eyes closely. "What about Markov? You know anyone by that name?"

"Mark Hoff?"

"Markov. A last name."

"No." His brow furrowed. "What's the first name?"

"Andre Markov."

"Never heard of him." He looked at Brock. "Why?"

"We're looking into possibilities," Charlotte said vaguely. "Do you remember your wife ever mentioning anyone by that name?"

Quinn's face clouded at the mention of his dead wife. His jaw twitched. "No."

"You're sure?"

"Yes."

"Maybe you could take a look in her address book, if she kept one. Just to be sure."

He nodded. "I will. Now, you want to explain what this guy Markov has to do with Ava?"

"I'm not sure. Maybe nothing."

Quinn leaned forward on his elbows, and his eyes looked intent. Feverish. "Did he do it? Is that what you're saying?"

"I'm not saying anything, Dr. Quinn. I'm merely asking questions."

He shot a look at his lawyer.

"We'd like to understand what this is about," Brock said reasonably. "Can you elaborate?"

Charlotte studied Brock's eyes. She got the impression this wasn't the first time he'd heard the name Andre Markov, and she figured he knew more about what Kira Vance was up to than she did, which pissed her off because it was her damn case.

Brock's client, however, seemed surprised by the name. He was still watching Charlotte, on high alert, his cheeks flushed pink now.

"Who is he?" Quinn persisted.

"I don't know."

"Was he having an affair with her? Is that what this is?" His face crumpled, and he rubbed his hand over his eyes.

"His name came up in connection with a case. That's all. Are you sure you don't know him?"

A slight head shake. He rubbed his eyes with the back of his hand. "No."

The man looked haggard, well beyond caring whether a stranger saw him cry. Or maybe the tears were generated for her benefit. She'd certainly seen all the tricks.

Charlotte checked her watch. "I appreciate your time tonight."

His face fell. "That's it?"

"That's all for now. I'll call you if any more questions come up." She stood, and the men stood, too. She turned to Brock. "Thank you for coming."

"Of course."

She picked up her purse and looked at the doctor. "You mind if I use your bathroom before I leave?"

"Sure. Down the hall on the left."

Charlotte felt their eyes on her as she walked away. She entered another windowed corridor with a view of the treetops. Dusk was coming early because of the rain, and the house was utterly gloomy without any lights to speak of. She passed several doors and found a small powder room.

Charlotte turned on the faucet and then took out her notepad and jotted some notes. She liked to get things down while they were fresh in her mind. Then she flushed the toilet and stepped out.

The corridor was quiet and empty. She peered to her left but didn't see anyone lurking about. She crept to a doorway and peeked inside. It was a small guest bedroom, from the looks of it. The queen-size bed was rumpled, and throw pillows littered the floor. Charlotte noted a highball glass on the nightstand beside a TV remote and a stack of books. Beside the stack was a framed photograph of a dark-haired woman.

Ava Quinn.

Another glance down the hallway, and Charlotte crept to the end. Peering through the doorway, she found a spacious master suite. The giant bed in the center was piled with pillows, and a huge stone fireplace occupied the wall opposite a large window overlooking the treetops.

She studied the bed again with its perfectly arranged pillows. Plush gray carpet covered the floor, and she noted the vacuum lines.

Ava Quinn had been murdered right in this room. She'd been bound and shot between the shoulder blades while she lay prone on the floor. The carpet had obviously been replaced since then, and Charlotte wondered if the room had been slept in. Probably not.

"I didn't kill her."

She turned around, cursing herself. Gavin Quinn stood behind her, silent as a mouse.

"It happened in here?" she asked. No point in pretending she wasn't snooping.

"By the closet." He nodded at the door beside the fireplace. "That's where the safe is."

Charlotte didn't comment. She knew the details already, right down to every hair and fiber recovered, from reading through the murder book.

Quinn watched her intently. He had a fire in his eyes now. He'd had it since she mentioned the name Markov.

"Well." She smiled slightly. "I'll get out of your way."

He stepped aside to let her pass him. She backtracked to the living room as Brock stepped in from the hallway, looking suspicious. "Everything okay back here?"

"Fine."

Brock led her to the front door and opened it, and Charlotte stepped into the muggy August air. Clouds gathered overhead. They were in for more rain.

She looked at Brock. "Thanks for meeting."

"No problem." He gave her a thin smile. "And next time you want to talk to my client, call me first."

CHAPTER

TWENTY

A FEELING OF dread nagged at Jeremy as he stepped into Kira's hotel room. It had been hard enough being around her at her house, but it was going to be even harder now, cooped up in a two-room hotel suite with a bed just footsteps away.

Trent was perched on the sofa arm, flipping through TV channels. He'd been responsible for getting Kira and her stuff moved to her new luxury accommodations. The agents were still staying at their original motel ten minutes away.

"How'd it go?" Jeremy asked.

Trent shook his head. "She had a shit-ton of luggage, but fine other than that."

Jeremy crossed the suite to the bedroom. Standing in the doorway, he surveyed the two queen beds with pristine white linens. A pair of large black suitcases lay on the bed closest to the window. Shopping bags lined the wall, and another black suitcase was parked beside the dresser. Looking at all of it, someone might think Kira was a clothes freak, but Jeremy had seen her tiny closet.

Kira was out on the balcony with her back to the door, talking on the phone and gesturing as she gave someone an earful. Brock Logan, maybe? Jeremy hoped so.

Again, he surveyed the clutter. On the dresser were several Tupperware containers of muffins, along with the glass pitcher he recognized from Kira's kitchen. She'd even brought her damn goldfish.

"I wouldn't have pegged her for a techie."

He glanced at Trent. "What's that?"

"Kira. You wouldn't believe all the stuff she brought with her. Check out her camera equipment." Trent indicated a small dining table, where Kira had her Canon camera and two telephoto lenses spread out. "And look at this." Trent walked past him into the bedroom. "She was sorting through it all earlier." Trent flipped open the unzipped top of one of the suitcases. It was chock-full of surveillance equipment. Trent picked up something shaped like a satellite dish.

"I don't even know what half this shit *is*."

"That's a parabolic collector dish," Jeremy said.

Trent's eyebrows arched.

"Picks up conversations from about a hundred yards away. Put it back."

He dropped it into the suitcase and closed the lid. Jeremy glanced at the balcony, where Kira still had her back to them.

"She's a trip." Trent folded his arms. "So what's the schedule? Are you on or off?"

"On until midnight. Then it's you and Keith from twelve to seven."

"Works for me." Trent checked his watch. "If you're good now, I was thinking I'd get some food. With the schedule shuffling, I missed dinner."

"Go."

He left, and Jeremy watched the door close behind him, feeling a twinge of regret over giving him the night shift. But this was for the better. Really. The dead-last place Jeremy needed to be tonight was in a hotel with Kira, even if he was a room away or stationed outside the door.

The slider opened, and she stepped in from the balcony. She wore black yoga pants and a loose white T-shirt, and her hair was twisted up in a knot.

"Where'd you disappear to?" she asked.

"Had something to take care of."

She walked to the minibar and took a bottle of water from the fridge. " 'Something to take care of.' Like last night?"

He'd known she'd bring it up. "That was recon."

"You went back to Channelview, didn't you? I freaking knew it." She plunked the water onto the desk. "I should have come with you."

No, she shouldn't have.

"What did you find?" She folded her arms. "And don't even *think* about leaving anything out. Or making stuff up. I can spot a lie a mile away."

Jeremy hadn't planned to lie. But he also hadn't planned to tell her everything he'd seen.

A sharp rap on the door had her turning around. She grabbed her messenger bag off the sofa and pulled out some money.

"Wait." He caught her arm and walked around her to check the peephole. "Did you order a pizza?" He looked at her over his shoulder.

"Yes."

He held out his hand for the bills. She rolled her eyes and passed him the money. "Give him a good tip."

"It's a she."

The woman had a long blond ponytail and a butterfly tattoo in the middle of her neck. Jeremy accepted the warm box that smelled like pepperoni and handed her the money as she eyed Kira's expensive camera equipment.

"Keep the change," he said, and closed the door.

Kira was busy moving chairs around and tossing decorative pillows to the floor. Jeremy set the box on the coffee table as she dropped onto a pillow.

"Sit," she ordered.

Yes, ma'am.

She opened the box, and Jeremy's stomach growled. He sat on the edge of the sofa, putting some space between them.

"So this recon was so urgent you had to go right back out in the middle of the night?" she asked.

He watched her, and he didn't want to tell her that was only part of the reason he'd left. The other part was that he didn't trust himself in her house alone with her. Not after that kiss.

Jeremy was known for his self-discipline, but he didn't want to test it. He wasn't sure what had possessed him back at the ship channel, only that yanking her to the ground after the gunshot and then hustling her to safety had kicked off a reaction inside him. He'd pulled over to make sure she was okay, but then he'd made the mistake of touching her, and that was it. Game over. Next thing he knew, he was dragging her into his lap, shocking the hell out of both of them.

He should have known better. He *did* know better. And he had to rein this in. If they slept together, he'd have to resign from her detail, and he couldn't do that. He wouldn't. He'd been committed before, but Shelly Chandler's murder had ramped up the stakes.

"Hello? Earth to Jeremy?"

She was still waiting for an answer.

"It was important," he said. "I couldn't wait till morning."

She lifted an eyebrow. "Well, I want to hear what you found." She picked up a slice of pizza, snipping the ropy cheese with her fingers, then handed it to him. "Don't edit anything out."

"I went back to Xavier Shipping."

"I figured. Careful, that's hot." She picked up a slice for herself and folded it like a taco. "You park in the same spot?"

"No." He chomped into the pizza, burning the roof of his mouth.

"What'd you see?"

"Couple interesting things."

She got up and walked to the minibar, where she grabbed another water bottle. She handed it to him and sank onto the pillow again, folding her legs.

"Such as?"

"The cars were gone," he said. "Only one I spotted was the night watchman. I got his tag, if you're interested."

"I'm interested."

Jeremy was, too. The guy's convenient disappearance last night right before the two vehicles pulled up told him the man was involved in the operation, whatever it was.

Kira sipped her water, watching him and waiting for more.

"I found some evidence of trafficking in and out of the location," he said.

She didn't look surprised. "You mean like drugs or people?" She licked sauce off her finger.

"Maybe both. Definitely people, but I'm guessing some contraband, too, based on the handoff we saw."

"You mean the duffel bag."

"Yeah."

"Why do you say 'definitely people'? What are your tip-offs?"

"ICE, for one," he said. "They were patrolling that area for a reason."

"Maybe just as a deterrent."

He shook his head. "Remember the ten-foot security fence? I found a hole in it on the east side, closest to the highway. It was cut out with wire cutters, and it was big enough for a man to squeeze through. Also found a faint path through the grass from the hole in the fence to a clump of trees."

"Yeah, but . . . the ship channel?" She looked skeptical. "Seems like a tough entry point."

He shrugged. "It's an entry point. You have to assume people are coming through. Stowaways on the tankers. Maybe some of the boat workers themselves. People get picked up at the docks, then hit the city and disappear."

She sighed. "Damn it."

"Yeah."

He studied her face, fairly sure she was thinking the same thing he'd been when he first saw that handoff. The target Ollie had been surveilling last week—presumably Andre Markov—was involved in something big. And he was likely just the tip of the iceberg.

Kira took another sip of water. "The question is, who's Markov working for? His age and his rap sheet don't line up with him being in charge."

"I agree."

"Maybe Brock will find something," she said.

"More likely, Spears and Diaz will."

"Don't underestimate Brock Logan. He's very resourceful." She glanced at the TV, where a muted news anchor was giving the top-of-the-hour headlines. It was after eleven, and Jeremy needed to go.

"So." She took a deep breath. "That brings us to Shelly Chandler."

"What about her?"

"I believe the same person who killed Ollie also murdered Shelly Chandler. So do the police. They think it's all connected. But you and I both know Ollie was focused on Markov, and it was Markov's car we saw at the ship channel last night at the same time someone followed Shelly home from a bar. So Markov probably didn't kill her. And anyway, the man I saw at Brock's house looks nothing like Markov's mug shot, which means someone else is the triggerman."

"Sounds logical."

"And that means we're talking about multiple people, and they've got multiple targets. So far, Ollie, Brock, and Shelly, all of whom—"

"Don't forget *you*."

"And myself, yes. All of us are working on—or *were* working on—the Gavin Quinn case, which goes to trial in less than two days. Seems obvious someone wants to derail that trial, and they're willing to kill to do it."

Jeremy just looked at her. She sounded so calm and matter-of-fact about it, but underneath that, he knew she was deeply unsettled.

Just the other night, she'd seen her friend gunned down. This morning, she'd been to the funeral, but she hadn't shed a tear, although she'd come out looking white as a sheet. From what he could see, she was processing everything the way he did, putting her emotions on lockdown.

Kira leaned back against the sofa. "So what are we dealing with? In your expert opinion?"

"Expert?"

"Wolfe Sec is a world-renowned firm. You deal with people targeted by crazies and assassins all the time. What do you think this is about? *Who* is doing this?"

He finished off his pizza crust, stalling for time. Then he dusted his hands on his jeans.

"I'm not sure what you're looking for, but Liam would be the one to tell you about motive. His brother's a criminal profiler and weighs in on some of our cases."

"Seriously? I didn't know that."

"He used to work for the FBI."

"Interesting," she said. "But what about you?"

"What about me?"

She rolled her eyes. "What do *you* think? You've dealt with all sorts of threats. How does this rank? How worried should I be?"

Jeremy studied her face, trying not to stare at the damn cut on her cheek. But the cut said it all, really. She'd caught a piece of shrapnel in her *face*. How worried should she be? Very.

Jeremy had been asked that question before. Sometimes the clients wanted reassurance or soothing words. Sometimes they were in denial that the threat against them was real.

Kira wasn't in denial, and she didn't want reassurance or platitudes. She was a realist, and what she wanted was information. But could she handle it, or would it freak her out?

She watched him, waiting for his answer.

He cleared his throat. "There are several kinds of threats we see a lot of. On American soil, most attacks are carried out at close range and with a handgun."

"What's close range?"

"Less than twenty-five yards."

She nodded.

"Then there are long-range attacks. That's with a rifle, sometimes hundreds of yards away. Shooters like that tend to be ideological killers."

She frowned. "Give me an example."

"The abortion doctor who was murdered last fall. Guy shot him with a Remington seven hundred at two hundred yards."

"Was he a sharpshooter?"

"No, but he had military training. Guys like that—ideological killers—they get in, do the job, get out. They have a plan of escape and no desire to get caught."

"Who *would*?"

"You'd be surprised. Some of these up-close shooters—people like John Hinckley, who shot Ronald Reagan—that's exactly what they want, especially if their target is a celebrity. The second they pull the trigger, they go from a life of obscurity to instant fame. They may not even care who the target is, as long as it's someone famous enough to get them in the news. Or maybe the target is interchangeable. In those cases, personal security is everything."

"How come?" She looked skeptical. He could tell from the worry line between her brow.

"An attacker like that takes one look at us and sees a hard target. It's going to be a lot tougher for him to get what he's after, which is attention. So he switches targets. The identity of the target may not even matter."

"How does it *not matter*?" she asked. "If someone is willing to risk their life and their freedom, I'd think the target would mean everything."

"Maybe it's symbolic." Jeremy leaned forward, resting his arms on his knees. "The job I just finished? That's exactly what it was. Our guy was an American business mogul. Didn't matter his name or what his company did—just that he was a rich American traveling in their backyard. That's why he was targeted by Islamic extremists, and they should never have gotten near him, but we screwed up."

"What happened?"

Kira looked riveted. And he hadn't meant to tell her this shit, but now it was too late to go back.

He looked her in the eye. "There were six of them, divided into three vehicles. They surrounded his car and ran it off the road, hoping to either kidnap him or murder him on the spot. They hosed Roland's car down with bullets. Missed him but managed to kill a kid who was standing on the sidewalk next to his mom. She was hit, too."

"Oh, my God."

"Course, that didn't make the headlines. Even though a six-year-old died, it was barely mentioned."

"Where were you?" Kira asked.

"Car behind, passenger side. It was a two-vehicle convoy."

The whole thing had lasted less than a minute, but at the time, it had felt like slow motion. The seconds dragged out as Jeremy saw everything unfolding, right there in front of him, and all he could do was jump from the vehicle and try to put a stop to it, but he was two seconds too late.

"It never should have happened." He shook his head. "This group should have gotten one look at our client's security and picked another target."

"Why didn't they?"

Jeremy gritted his teeth. "Social media. They had a critical advantage. Leo Roland's PR flack posted his day's events online, and they were waiting for us when we pulled up. That's why we prefer unpredictability. Unscheduled arrivals, unscheduled departures. Don't tell people exactly what you're doing and when, because it gives them an edge."

"Sounds to me like the PR flack was the one who screwed up, not you," she said.

"Same result. And it's part of our job to control the information that goes out, or at least be aware of it. We could have had agents on the rooftops when our guy arrived, but we thought his schedule was private, so we didn't take that step, and a child got caught in the cross-fire of something that never should have happened."

"I'm so sorry."

Jeremy could still hear that mother wailing as she bent over her son. He wished he could erase the sound. Erase the whole day.

"I went to see her in the hospital. The kid's mother." He shook his head. "She was catatonic. Her sister and the rest of her kids were with her, but she couldn't even talk."

Kira just watched him, her eyes somber.

"Leo Roland's been racked with guilt over it. He's going to take care of them financially, but nothing he can do will bring that boy back. And all because some gutless fanatic wanted to grab a headline and post a video."

"God. Did they?"

"Yeah, it's out there." He raked a hand through his hair. How had they gotten on this topic? She'd been asking about her case, not the job he'd just come from. He shouldn't be dumping this on anyone, least of all someone he was protecting.

But he was. Something about Kira made him want to tell her things straight.

"But back to your question." He leveled a look at her. "What kind of threat is this? How worried should you be?"

Her eyes turned wary, and it looked like she was bracing herself.

"In my opinion, both shootings were professional jobs."

She watched him steadily.

"By professional, I mean that the gunman was hired, not that he's very good at it. He's an average shot if you look at the ballistics."

She smiled nervously. "Great. So I shouldn't be worried?"

"No. You should. The problem is he's brazen. He walked right into that house and fired rounds at three people, then calmly filled a duffel bag and left. He may be a crappy shot, but he has nerves of steel, and that's concerning."

"*Concerning*. Yeah."

"Also, he knows how to blend in. The clothes, the car, the confidence. All of it tells me he's comfortable in his targets' environment, and when you combine that with the BMW? That tells me he has money, or at least he's around it."

"Someone rich is paying him."

Jeremy nodded. "And when you combine *that* with this new evidence that Andre Markov is involved in some kind of shady business down on the ship channel . . ." He trailed off, and she waited for him to finish. "It's looking more and more like a crime syndicate."

She shuddered.

"I'm not trying to scare you, but—"

"Sure you are. If I'm scared, I'm less likely to push back when you guys tell me what to do. You want me scared. You want all of us scared." She stood abruptly.

"Hey."

"No, I get it. I'd do the same thing if I were you. Tell the client she's on a hit list, that some *crime syndicate* is after her, ensure full cooperation."

He stared up at her. She looked pissed now. And rattled, too. And okay, *yes*, that had been part of his objective from the start of this conversation.

She carried the pizza box to the minibar and tossed it onto the counter.

"Sorry." She rubbed her forehead. "I know I started this."

"It's okay."

"No, I'm being a bitch, it's just . . ."

Jeremy stood and walked over. It was dim beside the window with the drapes closed, but he could still see the strain on her face.

"It's been a long day, with the funeral and the detectives, and everything last night . . ." She trailed off again and looked away.

And she hadn't been sleeping. He could tell just by looking at her that she was on edge and had been for days. He knew how to relax her and get her mind off everything, but he was *not* going to go there, and he needed to get the fuck out of her hotel room. Where was Trent?

He checked his watch. "Listen, Kira—"

"Do me a favor, will you?" She stepped closer, and her eyes looked different now. Heated, but in a way they hadn't been a second ago. And he got the sense she knew exactly what he'd been thinking about.

She eased closer, close enough for him to smell her hair again, that subtle floral scent he noticed every time he was around her.

"Will you?"

He cleared his throat. "What is it?"

"Stay."

CHAPTER

TWENTY-ONE

I WANT TO keep talking. We don't have to talk about the job or anything, just . . ." She looked around. "Let's have a drink."

He gazed down at her, and she could see some sort of battle going
on in his head. He wanted to stay. She could tell. She sensed he wanted
to do a lot of things, but he was determined to hold back.

She tipped her head to the side. "Please?"

The muscle in his jaw twitched, and she knew she had him.

"One drink," he said.

She opened the minibar and crouched to examine the contents.
She spied the bottle of Jameson and felt a pang in her chest. Ollie had
given her a bottle for Christmas last year, and it was collecting dust in
the back of her cupboard. It seemed like fate that the same brand was
here in her minibar tonight.

Without looking at Jeremy, she flipped over the pair of glasses on a
silver tray and poured them each a shot. She handed him a glass and
took a deep breath.

"To Ollie." She wanted to say more, but there was suddenly a rock in her throat. She clinked her glass with Jeremy's and took a swig.

Jeremy watched her as he took a sip. She turned and pushed aside the curtain to open the slider and step outside. The suite's balcony overlooked a swimming pool. Rain pitter-pattered on the water, dimpling the surface.

The lights went off, and Kira turned around.

"You don't want a silhouette," Jeremy said as he stepped out.

It took her a moment to get it. "Oh. You mean in case—"

"Yeah."

She stifled a shudder, even though it was eighty-five degrees out. She couldn't imagine thinking about assassins all the time.

Kira knew she was more aware than the average person, given what she did for a living. It was second nature to her to watch her mirrors and check her reflection in windows to make sure she didn't have a tail. But all that was different. She wasn't used to being a target.

"We've got a man in the courtyard." Jeremy nodded toward the pool four stories below, and Kira noticed the uniformed guard stationed beside a lamppost. She'd noticed him earlier when she'd been out here on the phone.

"I thought he was with the hotel?"

"He's ours. Uniform is just for show. And we've got another agent on patrol of the perimeter."

"Sounds like you thought of everything."

He didn't comment.

Kira leaned back against the wall, watching the rain as the whiskey began to warm her. Jeremy propped his shoulder against the wall and looked at her. He hadn't brought his glass out, she noticed. That had been for show, too. He wasn't actually going to be her drinking buddy tonight. He was holding back, keeping his distance, and she knew it was because of what happened before.

Kira took another sip and looked out over the pool. The scent of chlorine wafted up, and she remembered the same scent at Brock's the other night.

"You all right?"

She looked at him, and his face was shadowed, but she could still see the outline. He had strong cheekbones and a chiseled jaw. And then there were those beautiful blue eyes that she couldn't really see right now. But she knew from the furrow in his brow that he was worried about her.

"I'm fine." She sighed. "Just thinking about the day." She shook her head. "I hated seeing Ollie's family hurting. He was nuts over those grandkids. They're really going to miss him."

She was really going to miss him. She already did.

"You know, Ollie was my one real friend in the business. All my contacts at the courthouse—they're passing acquaintances. Ollie was different. He took an interest in me from day one and set me on a career path. He was my mentor every step of the way. Even when he was driving me crazy, I learned from him."

She took another sip, and the whiskey slid down her throat, smooth as velvet.

"Liam's like that for me."

"Yeah?"

He nodded. "We don't always agree, but I always respect his judgment. He's a good man."

"I respected Ollie, too." She hadn't realized how much until now. "Even when he used me, I didn't mind."

"How do you mean?"

She looked at Jeremy in the darkness, suddenly tuned in to his wide shoulders and big arms. He was in one of those black T-shirts again, and she wanted to slip her hands under the sleeves and feel the warmth of his skin.

"Ollie liked me to go out and interview witnesses, develop sources," she said. "He liked me to play the petite woman card. You know, dupe people into thinking I was harmless, and they could let their guard down. It usually worked, too. I'd interview witnesses for our case—or the prosecution's case. I'd figure out who was credible and who was stretching the truth or outright making stuff up. I can always spot the fakers. Ollie called me a human polygraph." She smiled at the memory. "He'd been pressing me about pursuing that career-wise."

"Pursuing it how?"

"Jury consulting," she said. "I've had a chance to sit in on quite a few trials as part of the defense team. I watch the voir dire. You know, jury selection? People answer questions, and I observe their body language while the lawyers are talking and giving details about the case. Some people try to lie their way onto a jury because they've got an ax to grind. Or maybe they think they're going to write a screenplay, or maybe they're just plain bored. Whatever it is, if they're misrepresenting themselves, we need to know about it, so I would watch and pass my opinion along to Ollie, who would pass it along to the lead attorney."

"You like the work?"

"Absolutely. It's challenging. And the money potential is a lot better than what I'm doing now, so . . . I guess I have Ollie to thank for yet another aspect of my career."

Kira sighed. She felt a little dizzy now that the whiskey was kicking in. She looked out at the rain on the pool, and her eyes burned.

She wasn't going to cry.

Four full days, and she hadn't lost control. And she sure as hell wasn't going to start right now, in front of Jeremy.

He touched her shoulder, and her heart lurched.

"I'm sorry."

"For what?" She wanted him to keep his hand on her shoulder, but he tucked it into his pocket as if he regretted touching her.

"For what you're going through right now."

"I'm fine. It's his family I'm worried about."

Kira looked at him in the darkness, and she couldn't read his expression. But she sensed his mood. Tense restraint. If she let herself cry, she had a feeling he'd wrap his arms around her. And she felt a deep-down ache, hoping he'd do just that. How nice would it be to rest her head on his chest and just feel safe for a moment and let everything fall away?

Kira held his gaze. Maybe she should just get it out there. It wasn't like her to hide from things. Maybe she should just say it. *You've probably figured this out already, but I'm dying to touch you, and the way you're keeping your distance is making me crazy. How about if you get me another bodyguard, so you can stop being so uptight and we can see where this goes?*

Yeah, right. He'd never agree to that. Even more intense than the attraction flaring between them was his dedication to his work. He took it *very* seriously, and whatever fling they might have together—and she had no doubt that to him, it would be a fling and nothing more—would never be worth letting down Liam or his teammates by removing himself from an assignment and leaving them in the lurch. Kira didn't know Jeremy that well, but she knew loyalty was a big thing for him.

Thunder rumbled, and Kira glanced up. As the rain fell harder, she knew it was going to be another restless night. She'd had this hang-up since Hurricane Harvey. Unceasing rain put her on edge.

Jeremy stepped away, once again putting distance between them. He leaned against the rail and looked out.

"I need to tell you about Monday," she said, mustering her business voice to cover her disappointment.

"What about it?"

"Brock wants me to sit in. He wants my input on the jury pool."

Jeremy didn't respond, but she could see his shoulders stiffen. His brow furrowed, too, and he seemed to be thinking of the logistics.

"When did he tell you this?" Jeremy asked.

"Tonight. Right before we got off the phone earlier. It's a good opportunity for me. I've never done any jury consulting for him before, so I'd like to do it if we can make it work. But I realize it's not ideal. Everyone knows when the trial is starting. It's been in the news for months, so showing up at the courthouse—"

"Not exactly a low profile."

She nodded.

He blew out a sigh. "We'll make it work."

"Really?"

"You have a job to do. I get it. I'll talk to Liam, and we'll figure out the logistics. We'll be there anyway for Brock."

"Thank you." She folded her arms, a bit chilled now, and she wasn't sure why.

Maybe because now it was official. She was going to venture out in public over the next few days, and she was trusting Jeremy and his team to keep her out of the way of any bullets. But she refused to stay holed up in a hotel suite. She felt suffocated, and she'd only been here a few hours.

He stepped closer. "What's wrong?"

"Nothing, I just . . ."

"What?"

"It's just that I hate this. I keep thinking about Ollie. And about Shelly clutching her damn pepper spray. And I feel like a sitting duck."

"You're not."

"It's all just so callous and calculated. I feel like . . . prey."

"Don't think that way." His voice had an edge now. "You are not prey. He is. If he gets near any of you, he's going down."

His voice was cold. Resolute. She stared up at him in the dimness, wanting to believe him. She wanted to trust him, but she wasn't used to trusting other people to handle her problems for her.

"I mean it, Kira."

The light went on, and both of them turned. Trent was back. He set a to-go cup on the dining table and shot a curious look out at the balcony.

"I need to go."

She looked at Jeremy.

"You're in good hands with Trent."

"Thanks," she said, not sure what to make of that statement. Or of the sharp disappointment she felt now that he had to leave for the night. Did Jeremy feel it, too? Was he even tempted? He gazed down at her, but his blue eyes gave nothing away.

"Come on."

He slid open the door and ushered her inside.

Charlotte stared at her screen, and her attention started to drift. She needed to go home. Seriously. She'd been on since this morning, and it was a Saturday, one she should have had off. Plus, it had been five days since her last callout, which meant it was only a matter of time until another case fell into her lap.

But she still hadn't solved this one.

It was a puzzle. She'd been manipulating the pieces for days now, and all she'd come up with was something vaguely resembling an edge. The picture in the middle was still a mystery.

"What's your story?" she muttered under her breath. She leaned closer to the screen, trying to memorize every detail of Andre Markov's face. She studied his eyes, his mouth, the jagged scar through his eyebrow that was probably from a knife fight. She studied the tattoo on his neck—a faded skull with some sort of cryptic writing beneath it that she couldn't read. She flipped to his rap sheet and read about his past.

"Tell me you've been home tonight."

She glanced up to see Diaz walking across the bull pen. He wore a navy Astros jersey and his favorite baseball cap.

"Not yet," she said.

"Damn, don't you ever take a day off?"

"I just had seven, as a matter of fact." She swiveled in her chair to face him and nodded at the ball in his hand. "You catch a pop-up?"

He grinned. "Yep." He dropped into a chair nearby and tossed the ball up, then caught it one-handed.

"I heard we won."

"Seven-zip," he said. "Want to come to Milo's and grab a drink? I hear some of the guys are still over there, even though the game wrapped up."

"I should skip it." She glanced at her computer.

"So what gives? You've been here all weekend."

"Kovak and Chandler."

"Shelly Chandler isn't ours."

"She should be. We know they're connected."

He spun the baseball in his hand. "What's new?"

"I'm stuck on Andre Markov. What's his connection to all this? Oliver Kovak was surveilling him the week before he died, and the paperwork he received that day had Markov's name all over it. It has to be related."

"Gavin Quinn have any ideas?"

"No." She folded her arms over her chest. The blouse she'd worn to the funeral that morning was beyond wilted, and she really needed to get home. "And his lawyer didn't appreciate my asking."

"How surprising. Bet McGrath didn't appreciate it, either."

"I didn't ask him."

Diaz winced. "Remind me not to be here when he gets wind of it."

"He won't."

"What about records on the victim's phone? Anything come back yet?"

"I checked this morning. It'll be Monday at the earliest."

Diaz pulled forward and picked up the spiral notepad on her desk. If any other detective had done that, she would have had to stab his hand with a pen. But she and Diaz had no secrets.

He knew, for example, that she'd spent her week's vacation here at

home instead of cruising the Caribbean, as she'd been planning for months. He also knew that she'd found out her boyfriend was cheating on her three weeks before the trip, which, unfortunately, was too late for a refund.

Charlotte had definitely wanted a refund. Not just for the cost of the cruise but for the ten months of her life she'd spent with the guy.

Diaz knew both of these embarrassing details about Charlotte's life, but he kept his mouth shut, because that was the kind of partner he was, and she thanked her lucky stars every day that she hadn't been paired with McGrath or Goldstein.

"Who's Craig Collins?" Diaz looked up.

"Gavin Quinn's deadbeat brother-in-law."

"What about him?"

She shrugged. "It came up in conversation. Thought I'd check it out."

"He have a sheet?"

"Couple of DUIs. In fact, one of them is for the evening of his sister's murder, so he has an alibi, too."

Diaz arched his eyebrows. "Convenient."

"Forget it. I looked into it already."

"So you're back to Markov."

"That's right." She rubbed her eyes. "I feel like I'm chasing my tail here."

"Go home. Get some rest." Diaz stood and tossed the ball into the air, turning and catching it behind his back this time. "With our luck, we'll get smacked with another case soon, and you'll be wishing you'd taken the sleep when you could get it."

"I know, I know."

"I'm out," Diaz said. "Sure you don't want to join us at Milo's?"

"I'm sure."

"Catch you tomorrow." He waved over his shoulder.

Sighing, Charlotte closed out of the screen she was in and shut down her computer. Diaz was right. She needed to get some rest and come at this fresh in the morning.

Her phone buzzed on her desk, and she checked the number.

Damn it.

"Spears."

"Is Diaz with you?" her captain asked. "He's not answering his damn phone."

"What's wrong?" she asked, already grabbing her notebook, knowing her work on the Kovak investigation was about to get derailed by a new case.

"We've got a gunshot wound at Ben Taub Hospital. You guys are up."

CHAPTER

TWENTY-TWO

JEREMY CROSSED the wooden deck and held the door open for Kira. The scent of grilling burgers wafted out as they stepped into the restaurant. He'd never been here before, but it was fairly crowded on a Sunday evening, so he took that as a good sign.

"Man, I love this place." Kira inhaled a deep breath and closed her eyes. "Best onion rings in town." She turned to look at him, and again he was struck by her pretty hazel eyes. She'd skipped makeup today, and Jeremy liked her natural look. Her hair was down, and all afternoon he'd watched her twisting it absently as she sat in her hotel suite working on her laptop.

Kira approached the register and glanced at him over her shoulder. "You trust me?"

"How do you mean?"

"It's a simple question: Do you trust me?" When he didn't respond, she smiled slyly. "Well, too bad. You're going to have to." She turned to the woman behind the counter. "Two Burger Daddies all the way, two chocolate shakes with extra whip, and an order of rings." She pulled her wallet from her bag. "Oh, and two waters."

She glanced at him. "Don't look at me like that. I worked out this morning."

Jeremy was aware that she'd worked out, just as he was aware of practically everything she'd done over the past twenty-four hours. Trent had told him, for example, that Kira had had trouble sleeping last night and spent much of it on the sofa watching TV.

Kira insisted on paying and then took a plastic number and led Jeremy to a circular booth. He waited for her to scoot in before sliding in beside her and glancing at the door.

"What time is this guy meeting us?" Jeremy asked.

"Seven fifteen."

He checked his watch. "It's seven twenty."

"He'll be here."

Jeremy scanned the restaurant, cataloging the exits and checking out patrons, while Kira scrolled through her phone.

"He's on his way," she said. "I just got a text."

He looked at her beside him. Today she wore a snug black T-shirt and cutoff shorts, and her bare legs were proving to be a major distraction.

"Tell me about this guy again," Jeremy said.

"Emilio Sanchez. You threw him against a wall the other day."

"I didn't throw him against a wall."

"You absolutely did." She sipped her water. "He hears things about people. And he has a steel-trap memory. I think maybe he can help me. Here he is now." She shot Jeremy a look. "Try to be civil this time."

Sanchez spotted Kira, and his look turned wary as he walked over. He nodded at Jeremy. "Hey, chief."

Jeremy nodded back, and Sanchez turned to Kira. "You eat yet?"

"Just ordered."

"I can't stay long." He glanced at his watch. "I've got to go meet a client." He scooted into the booth on Kira's side. "I checked out that guy for you. Andre Markov."

"You come up with anything?"

"You could say that. I put Guillermo on it."

Kira leaned closer. "What did he find?"

"This guy Markov, he's unlucky. That's the word."

"Unlucky how?" Kira asked.

"Horses, sports. Freaking dog racing. He likes to bet, and he doesn't usually win."

Kira glanced at Jeremy. "Okay, so . . . you think maybe he owed people money?"

"Not so much. He's got his old man's money to back him up. Anatoly Markov." Sanchez leaned back in the booth. "Now, *that* guy you want to watch out for."

"Why?"

He shook his head. "Serbian-born businessman. Been over here almost thirty years. Started out small-time, and now he's got some big business on the ship channel."

"Xavier Shipping. He imports oil-drilling equipment," Kira said. "I read up on it."

"Yeah, I hear that's a front for some other imports, you know what I'm saying? Other thing you probably didn't read about is Markov's business practices." Sanchez glanced at Jeremy. "You do not want to cross this guy."

"Markov Senior," Kira clarified.

"Anatoly, yeah. Word is he's connected, he's violent, and he holds a grudge. If you work for Anatoly and you fuck up, you're liable to take a ride on a barge and never come back."

Kira shuddered beside him. "He have an arrest record?" she asked.

"Yeah, but it's old. He's been keeping his nose clean. Or maybe he's paying people off."

A teenage waiter appeared with a tray full of food. He unloaded red plastic baskets heaped with burgers and onion rings, then put two tall milkshakes and two waters in front of them.

"Anything else?"

Kira smiled. "We're good, thanks."

When the kid walked away, Sanchez checked his watch. "I gotta go." He slid to the edge of the booth.

"Thanks for this." Kira put her hand over his. "I really appreciate it."

"*De nada.*"

Kira pulled her hand away, and Sanchez nodded at Jeremy. "Later, chief."

"Later."

When he was gone, Jeremy looked at Kira.

"You were right." She took a deep breath. "A crime syndicate, like you predicted. We guessed Markov was shady, and now we have confirmation. What I still don't know is *why* was Ollie obsessed with young Markov's court case on the day he died? I feel like that's key to everything, and when I know that, I'll know why all this is happening."

Jeremy watched her, trying to get a read. He sensed that this info from Sanchez bothered her more than she was letting on.

She plucked the toothpick from the top of her burger and picked it up with both hands.

"Who's Guillermo?" Jeremy asked.

"Emilio's skip tracer. He's good."

She chomped into her burger and closed her eyes as a look of bliss came over her face. Jeremy ignored the powerful shot of lust.

He needed to get a handle on this thing with her. Kira was his client. Full stop. She needed him for protection, and he couldn't get distracted by her legs or her mouth. Or by watching her eat dinner, for Christ's sake. He scanned the crowded restaurant and tried to rein in his thoughts.

Kira was right about the food. Everything was good and greasy, and for a while they didn't talk. Jeremy enjoyed the quiet almost as much as he enjoyed watching her take down a half-pound hamburger, no problem, along with most of the onion rings. Midway through, she paused to scroll through her email and tap out a message to someone on her team.

Jeremy admired her commitment. She worked days and nights, weekdays and weekends. Since the moment he'd met her, she'd been running full speed. She was driven, and he didn't know if it was because this case was personal or if she tackled every case this way.

She glanced up at him and dabbed her mouth with a napkin. "What is it?"

He ate an onion ring. "Do you trust that guy?"

"Who? Sanchez?"

"Yeah."

"Absolutely."

No hesitation. She was certain, and she was a good judge of people, supposedly. A human lie detector. And evidently, Logan thought she was good enough to be his jury consultant.

Jeremy wasn't sure why that irked him, but it did. Actually, he did know why. He didn't like the guy around Kira. The man was rich and successful and manipulative, and Jeremy had clients like that all the time. He hoped Kira was smart enough not to fall for his bullshit.

She picked up her shake. "Why do you ask?"

"There's something off about him."

She rolled her eyes. "You're being paranoid."

Jeremy shook his head. He couldn't put his finger on it, but that didn't matter. When it came to people, he'd learned to trust his instincts.

Kira seemed to read his mind, because she started shaking her head.

"You're wrong," she said. "Sanchez is solid. I mean, yeah, he comes off kind of sleazy, but that's because of the business he's in. He's a stand-up guy. Has five kids and another one on the way."

"You ever checked him out?"

"Yes, as a matter of fact. He's clean, okay?"

Jeremy nodded. "Glad to hear it."

She picked up the last onion ring. "Mind?"

"No."

He pushed his basket away, and Kira checked her watch. "Ready?" she asked, sliding out of the booth.

They returned to his truck in silence, and he scanned the shadows in the parking lot as he opened the door for her. Dusk was coming early again tonight after an evening drizzle, and the air felt steamy. Jeremy cataloged the various vehicles in the parking lot, taking note of a black Jeep like one he'd noticed yesterday.

He hitched himself behind the wheel and drove past the Jeep as they exited the parking lot.

"What is it?" Kira asked.

"Nothing."

"It's the Jeep Wrangler, isn't it? I noticed it yesterday."

He glanced at her and lifted an eyebrow. She was more observant than he gave her credit for, and she was already tapping the tag number into her phone.

"I'll look it up," she said.

Jeremy planned to do the same.

"So where to?" he asked. "The hotel?"

"I need to swing by Ollie's first."

He pulled up to a stoplight and looked at her. "Home or work?"

"Work."

"Not happening."'

"What do you mean, not happening? I need to check something."

"What?"

"None of your beeswax."

He looked at her.

"I need his Rolodex," she said. "I'm trying to run down that name from his surveillance notes. Someone called 'LH'? This person's all over his notes, and I want to find out who it is."

"He really uses a Rolodex?" Jeremy hung a right on the street leading back to the hotel, and she glared at him.

"Um, hello? You agreed *not* to infringe on my work. Remember that? We need to stop by Ollie's office."

"I'll go by there."

"What about me? We're together. If you go, I go."

"I'll drop you at the hotel first."

"*Why?*"

Jeremy took out his phone and sent a quick text to Erik. He glanced at Kira, whose eyes flashed with temper as she waited for an answer.

"The first time we went by Ollie's office, it was under surveillance by an unknown person," he said. "The second time we went there, it had just been ransacked. Ollie's office is not a safe location for you to be snooping around, and I'm not taking you over there."

She muttered something and looked away.

"What's that?"

"You're being paranoid. And anyway, *you* are my security detail right now. I should go where you go."

"I'll drop you off with Erik at the hotel."

She huffed out a breath and looked away.

Jeremy let her fume and didn't say anything as he pulled into the Metropolitan Hotel's long, tree-lined driveway. They reached the grand entrance, where several uniformed valets were parking luxury cars. Jeremy pulled over behind a white Mercedes.

Kira dug into her bag. Without comment, she handed over a key.

"I'm looking for an actual Rolodex?" he asked. "Not something digital?"

"Yes." She still sounded annoyed. "Ollie was totally old school. He kept his contacts on paper."

"Okay, I'll bring it back."

Right on cue, Erik appeared beside the truck. Kira pushed open her door before he could open it for her and slid out without saying goodbye. Erik ducked his head in to look at Jeremy.

"Everything all right?"

"Keep an eye on her," Jeremy told him.

Erik nodded. "Roger that."

Ollie's office looked as bad as the last time Jeremy had seen it and smelled worse. Even before the spilled fish tank, the place had been a dump, and Jeremy wasn't surprised the landlord hadn't been in here yet with a cleaning crew. The stench was strong enough to overpower the smell of grilling meat from the Korean restaurant below.

Jeremy swept his flashlight around the room, illuminating trash and paperwork and tufts of sofa stuffing. He kept the lights off so as not to attract attention from the street as he picked his way through the debris to the overturned drawers around Ollie's desk. No Rolodex in sight. Jeremy poked through a heap of office supplies. He found a stack of business cards bound with a rubber band and also a pair of keys attached to a pocketknife keychain. The smaller key looked like a safe-deposit key or possibly a PO box. Maybe Ollie's daughter would know, and Kira could ask. Jeremy tucked the keychain and the stack of business cards into his pocket and stood up to look around.

On the credenza, he spotted it: an old-fashioned Rolodex, just as Kira described. It was fatter than he'd expected. Ollie had a lot of contacts, evidently. Jeremy flipped through the "H" section but didn't see anything with a first initial *L*. Still, he grabbed the Rolodex and dropped it into the plastic trash bag he'd brought from his truck. Glancing around, he tried to imagine what else Kira might want if she were here.

The smell got worse as Jeremy picked his way across the room, and he tried to ignore it. The only thing that had made the place bearable last time was Kira, and he missed having her alongside him with her running commentary. But bringing her would have been an unnecessary risk, and he wasn't sorry he'd dropped her off.

Jeremy beamed his flashlight over the mess, cursing himself. He'd developed a thing for a woman who rode a bike to work. And hated guns. And rescued fish.

She was totally not his type, except for the attitude. *That* he loved. Kira had guts. She wasn't afraid to go toe to toe with a veteran trial attorney. Or argue with a homicide detective. Or talk to a grieving family. Plus, she was observant—which was something they had in common.

And besides that, she was incredibly sexy. Ever since Friday night in his truck, Jeremy had been thinking about that kiss. He'd been thinking about her plump mouth and her tight breasts. He'd been picturing that long dark hair fanned across his pillow. He'd been thinking about all that and more, and he needed to stop.

His flashlight beam landed on a white envelope tucked beneath an accordion file. Jeremy moved the file with his foot and picked up the envelope, squinting at the scrawl. "Lorraine." Inside was a pair of tickets to an upcoming baseball game, Astros versus Red Sox.

Thunk.

Jeremy switched off his flashlight. The noise came from outside on the stairwell. Jeremy eased closer to the window and looked out. He could only see the base of the stairwell, but it was empty.

Jeremy surveyed the half dozen vehicles that had been parked along the block when he pulled up. He'd taken an empty metered space in front of a dry cleaner two buildings down.

A dark green pickup eased down the street. The taillights glowed red as the truck slowed for a stoplight. Jeremy waited a full, silent minute before grabbing his trash bag and creeping to the door. He exited the office and silently locked up and tucked the key into his pocket. For a moment, he listened. Nothing suspicious. Scanning the area around the building, he walked down the outdoor staircase, taking care to keep his boots quiet on the metal stairs. When he reached the bottom, a blur of movement caught his eye.

A dark figure sprinted down the alley. Jeremy dropped the trash bag and took off after him. The man darted around the corner of the dry cleaner.

Jeremy's boots smacked against the pavement as he raced down the alley, which smelled of garbage and cooking oil. The man glanced over his shoulder, then tripped and fell, catching himself against a dumpster before grabbing a wooden pallet and heaving it into the path behind him. Then he darted around the corner.

Adrenaline fired through Jeremy's veins. He hurdled the pallet and ran around the corner. The man was three buildings away now, sprinting along a narrow sidewalk behind the buildings, passing the occasional parked car, and Jeremy took in details about the subject: tall, medium-build, fast. He wore a baseball cap, so Jeremy couldn't see his hair.

Another glance over his shoulder, and then the man darted sideways and slid over the hood of a low-slung convertible before racing across the street. Jeremy kept after him. The man was in the open now, running down a narrow strip of grass between the street and a chain-link fence. On the other side was a wide easement and a set of railroad tracks.

Jeremy turned on the speed, pumping his arms and legs hard as he closed in. He gripped his SIG, ready to take a shot if needed, but the subject was empty-handed.

A faint rumble in the distance caught Jeremy's attention. He ran faster as a pinprick of light grew steadily bigger. The noise increased until it was a thunderous roar, and the man he was chasing was a long silhouette against the blazing white. He kept glancing to the side, and Jeremy knew what he was thinking. Suddenly, the man turned and leaped onto the chain-link fence, clawing his way up, pausing at the top to yank his shirt free.

Jeremy darted right, grabbing the fence with both hands and scaling it in two moves. Up ahead, the guy leaped down from the fence and scrambled to his feet. Jeremy jumped and rolled, then sprang to his feet and took off again.

Jeremy was gaining, shrinking the distance. The train sped closer and closer, so loud Jeremy felt the ground vibrating through the soles of his boots. He pounded after his target, heart hammering as he steadily closed the gap. The man was trapped. He'd locked himself in between a fence and a freight train. Jeremy estimated four seconds until he was close enough to tackle him.

Up ahead, Jeremy spied a tall streetlight at the top of the rise. Bells clanged as a pair of arms swung down, blocking nonexistent traffic from crossing the tracks.

The subject looked back, and Jeremy caught a glimpse of his face. Only a glimpse, but he could read the panic. The man turned again, and Jeremy spotted the gun in his hand.

Pop!

Jeremy hit the ground with a flash of pain, then lifted his SIG and returned fire. The figure lurched sideways, and Jeremy cursed his crappy shot as the man sprang back up and kept running. The guy darted a look at the train tracks, and Jeremy understood the move the instant before it happened.

The man lunged right, scrambling up the rise and over the tracks, a small black blur before the blinding white light. Jeremy started after him but halted as the man vanished from view and a wall of shrieking metal rushed by him.

Jeremy stood there, chest heaving. He tipped his head back, then leaned forward, planting his palms on his knees as he gulped down oxygen. The deafening noise reverberated through his body as the seconds and minutes ticked by. His arm burned. His body ached. Finally, he stood and watched with fury as the final cars rushed by.

When the train was gone, he stared across the tracks at an empty field between himself and some abandoned warehouses. His ears rang, and the vibrations seemed to linger in his chest. Gradually, the noise faded until there was only the distant clang of bells again as the arms lifted at the railroad crossing.

Cursing, Jeremy tucked his pistol away. Frustration burned in his gut as he started walking back.

CHAPTER

TWENTY-THREE

CHARLOTTE SPOTTED the patrol car parked along the lonely strip of road paralleling the train tracks. She pulled in behind it and dropped her phone into the pocket of her blazer before getting out.

Jeremy Owen leaned against the back of a pickup truck, arms crossed, talking to an officer who looked up from his clipboard as Charlotte approached. She vaguely recognized the officer, but he seemed to know her.

"Detective Spears." He gave a crisp nod. "We're about wrapped up here. Mind if I make a few calls?"

"Not at all." He returned to his patrol unit and opened the door, and Charlotte turned her attention to Jeremy. "You keep showing up at crime scenes."

He didn't comment. This man didn't talk much, she'd noticed, but he seemed wise beyond his thirty-three years. Combat would do that to you. Charlotte worked with enough veterans to know.

She nodded at his elbow, which was wrapped in a T-shirt. "What happened to your arm?"

"He nicked me."

"He *nicked* you? Why didn't you mention that over the phone?"

"Didn't seem relevant."

Charlotte stared at him.

Over the past two days, she'd had a chance to research Jeremy Owen, and what she'd learned impressed her. The former Marine had a Purple Heart and a Bronze Star, not to mention a five-year tenure with one of the top private security firms in the country. So maybe she shouldn't be surprised that when he'd called her to report scaring off a potential burglar at Oliver Kovak's office, he'd neglected to mention being *shot* by the guy.

"Run me through what happened," she told him.

"Like I said over the phone, I arrived here at approximately eight fifty to pick up some items from Kovak's office."

"What items?"

"An address book. Kira needs it for work."

Charlotte crossed her arms. "Okay, then what?"

"As I was leaving, I heard a noise on the outside stairwell. When I went to look, the guy took off down the street at a dead run, which made me think he'd been planning to break in."

"Makes me think that, too. Then what happened?"

"I went after him. He jumped that chain-link fence there. I followed. He turned and took a shot at me with a black pistol."

"Suppressor?"

"No. Then he darted across the tracks there right before the train came, and I lost him."

"He ran in front of a train," Charlotte stated.

"That's correct."

She closed her eyes. "Jesus." She shuddered to think how close she'd come to having another gruesome crime scene on her hands this weekend.

When she looked at Jeremy again, he was checking his makeshift bandage where the blood had seeped through.

"You need to get that looked at."

He gave a noncommittal nod.

"You stated over the phone you think it's our suspect," she said. "Why do you think that?"

"The face, the build."

"You got a look at him?"

"Yes."

She glanced around the area, but it was dark and desolate. Oliver Kovak's office was on the periphery of downtown—not exactly a happening neighborhood at this hour on a Sunday night.

She looked at Jeremy. "How sure are you about this ID?"

"Very. He closely resembled the suspect sketch."

"But it was dark, and you were running. How can you be sure?"

He just lifted his eyebrows.

Charlotte looked out over the train tracks to the row of warehouses beyond. The suspect could be anywhere by now.

"It's unclear how he got here," Jeremy added. "Before the officer showed, I did a few laps around the block, looking for a black BMW."

"And?"

"Didn't see one. There was a dark green pickup in the vicinity that I noticed from the window of the office, but I don't know if it's related."

She sighed. "Would have been good to have a vehicle."

"Yep."

"Maybe we'll get lucky and a surveillance cam picked him up. What do you think he wanted at Kovak's office?"

"No idea. Documents? Photos? Maybe something he was looking for at Logan's house but didn't find on the night of the murder."

She looked at the bodyguard, who stood there stoically talking to her, as though he hadn't been shot at an hour ago. He was calm and composed, offering detailed observations. Yet another person who would have made a good cop if he hadn't been lured away by the private sector.

"So no license plate," she said. "Guess that would be too lucky, huh?"

"We've got a print, though."

"A print?"

"A palm print." He glanced across the street and nodded. "When I was chasing him, he planted his hand on the hood of that black Mustang and slid over it."

"What Mustang?" She turned and looked across the street, spotting a black Mustang parked along the curb. It was a GT, same as hers, only about ten years older.

Charlotte's pulse picked up. "He touched the hood of that car? You're sure?"

"I saw him do it."

"Show me."

Kira sat on the floor of her hotel suite, her laptop in front of her on the coffee table, alongside the box of leftover pizza from last night. She nibbled on a slice as she scoured the Web for anything linking Andre Markov to Gavin Quinn or his murdered wife.

There had to be something. Ollie was a good PI. The best in town. He'd been sure he was onto something big on the day of his death. But again, what was the link between a two-year-old assault outside a bar and the murder of a prominent doctor's wife?

Kira went back to her copy of Markov's trial transcript. As she finished off her pizza slice, she thumbed through the thick sheaf of papers. Then she slid it aside and took out the backup materials. Once again, she scanned the witness list from Markov's defense team. This time, she got hung up on a name: Craig Collins. He was subpoenaed to testify, but it looked like he never actually got called to the stand, which happened sometimes.

Collins. Collins. She'd seen that name somewhere earlier today.

She reached for her accordion file on the Ava Quinn murder, which she'd been building ever since Brock had hired her. She flipped through the original police report, the autopsy report, several news clippings from the *Houston Chronicle*. She came upon the obituary.

Ava Collins Quinn, beloved wife, daughter, and sister, died on Thursday evening . . .

Kira's breath caught. Could that be it? She skimmed to the bottom of the obit. *She is survived by her parents, Michael and Margaret Collins of Houston; her brother, Craig Collins . . .*

Craig Collins. She'd seen him on the news with Ava's parents and Gavin. Kira scrambled to her feet. She snatched her key card off the counter, then rushed out of the room, startling the guard stationed in the hallway between her suite and Brock's.

"Is he in there?" she asked Joel, striding down the hallway.

"Who, Mr. Logan?"

Not waiting for an answer, she rapped on the door.

Brock answered the door. He wore jeans and an untucked white shirt with the sleeves rolled up.

"Hey. What's up?"

"I found it." She brushed past him into his suite. It was a mess, with legal pads and files blanketing the coffee table. A room-service cart loaded with the remnants of a steak dinner sat beside the desk.

"Found what?" Brock asked. With his uninjured arm, he reached for the TV remote and muted the baseball game.

"The link between Markov and Ava Quinn." She waved the obituary. "It's right here in the obit. Ava *Collins* Quinn, survived by her parents and her brother, *Craig Collins*."

Brock's brows arched. "So?"

"So it's in the trial materials. Craig Collins is on the witness list for Markov's trial! He was supposed to testify for the defense, but he never got called to the stand. But his name on the wit list means he was probably at that bar that night when Markov assaulted the guy with the beer bottle, which means he and Craig are *friends*, which means—"

"Whoa, whoa, whoa." Brock held up his hand. "Slow down. You're saying Ava Quinn's brother knows Markov?"

"Yes." Kira's heart was thrumming now. She had that adrenaline rush that always accompanied a break in a case. It was the same adrenaline rush that had put a spark in Ollie's eyes on the night of his murder.

"With all his sketchy business dealings, the last thing Andre Markov wants is investigators linking him to a murder suspect. Or looking at *him* as a murder suspect."

Brock rubbed his jaw. "You're saying Markov was worried that the Quinn trial might put heat on him?"

"Yes. I mean, imagine it. If Gavin's defense team casts suspicion on Ava's brother, and Ava's brother is a known associate of a character like Markov, police might suddenly take a long, hard look at the Markov family business."

Brock took the obituary from her and frowned as he read it. "You know, I met Craig before at Gavin's house one time."

"You did?"

"He looks just like his sister." He handed back the obituary and sauntered to the minibar. "Want a drink?"

"I'm good. Listen, are you understanding how big this is?"

Brock opened an ice bucket and dropped some cubes into a glass he already had going. He poured bourbon over the ice. "No, I get it."

Didn't sound like he did. Kira crossed her arms.

"The age would work, in terms of them being friends," he said, "but we don't have proof this is the same Craig Collins on Markov's witness list. Collins isn't exactly an unusual name."

"We'll get proof."

Brock lifted an eyebrow skeptically.

"I'll get it."

He sank into an armchair. His sipped his drink and looked up at her. "Ollie told me you were like this."

"Like what?"

The corner of his mouth ticked up. "A pit bull when you got hold of something."

Ollie had called her a pit bull to Brock? Her heart swelled.

"Sit down. You look tense."

"I'm fine." She glanced at her watch, wondering what was taking Jeremy so long. She'd expected him back an hour ago.

"Seems like you could use a drink," Brock said. "Why don't you join me? We should relax before tomorrow." He smiled slightly. "Juries don't like uptight lawyers. Makes them think we've got something to hide."

"Hmm."

"You don't agree?"

"I don't know. I'm not a lawyer."

"Yes, but you're on the team." He held up his glass. "Sure I can't talk you into a drink?"

"Really, I'm fine."

Truthfully, Kira would have loved a drink, but something about Brock's demeanor tonight put her off. He looked like he'd already had a few. He had a certain gleam in his eye, and she was suddenly self-conscious about her cutoff shorts and bare feet. He was attracted to her—she'd figured that out already. But he was her employer, and the last thing she needed to be doing was hanging out in his hotel room, tossing back bourbon. If he wanted to get toasted on the eve of a big trial, that was his business, but she wasn't going there.

He was still watching her. She glanced at the door.

"I need to research this some more, so . . ."

"Let me know what you find," he said.

She walked to the door.

"Oh, and Kira? We've got some pretrial motions in the morning, so jury selection won't start until after lunch. I won't need you till then."

"Got it."

Kira walked out and nodded at Joel in the hallway.

"Hey," she said.

"Hi."

She opened the door to her suite and stopped short. Spread out on the coffee table was a black trash bag. Sitting on it was the fat Rolodex she remembered from Ollie's desk.

Kira walked over and examined it. She ran her finger over the alphabetical cards, as Ollie must have done a thousand times. Beside the Rolodex was a red pocketknife keychain and an envelope with "Lorraine" scrawled across it in Ollie's handwriting.

The balcony door slid open, and Erik stepped into the room, followed by Jeremy.

"You found it," she said.

Jeremy nodded. "Yeah."

She looked from Jeremy to Erik, then back to Jeremy again. "What's wrong?"

"Someone showed up while I was there," Jeremy said. "I think he planned to break in."

"Again?"

"Yeah. He looked like your guy from the suspect sketch."

"Wait, you saw him?" Her stomach lurched. She noticed the white bandage above his elbow. "What happened to your arm?"

"I chased after him, and he grazed me."

She looked from the bandage to Jeremy's eyes. All the air left her lungs as she realized what he meant.

"You . . . chased after him, and he *shot* you?"

"He shot *at* me. He missed."

Kira stared at him. Her chest tightened. She opened her mouth to say something but clamped it shut again and turned around. She strode into the bedroom and shut the door behind her.

Someone had *shot* him. The man who'd killed Ollie and probably Shelly, too, had *shot* him.

Kira felt sick and dizzy, both at once. Her heart was racing. Her skin tingled. She looked around, panicked, as tears burned her eyes. She pictured Ollie on the floor in Brock's house, and she felt something cracking and breaking inside her.

She couldn't think about it. But she couldn't *stop* thinking about it, and she'd been trying for days.

She stepped into the spacious bathroom and closed the door. She turned the shower on as high as it would go, then she stripped off her clothes and stepped under the spray. Hot water sluiced over her as the floodgates opened and tears streamed down her cheeks.

Why was all this happening? What had Ollie ever done to deserve this? Or Shelly? And now they were gone. *Dead.* Gunned down by some soulless person who'd taken aim at their lives and squeezed a trigger and blown everything apart.

Kira tipped her head back and let the water thrum against her chest. She tried to breathe and calm herself. But her heart wouldn't stop racing, and the tears kept coming. She grabbed the bar of soap off the shelf and lathered up fiercely, rubbing the mint-and-rosemary-scented foam over her body. Then she washed her hair and stared down at the shower floor as the sudsy water swirled down the drain.

She pictured Ollie's shocked face again, and she closed her eyes, wishing she could block out the image, block out everything that had happened for the last six days.

A tapping noise made her turn around. She shut off the water.

Someone was knocking on the door. Probably Jeremy.

"Kira?"

"Go away."

She squeezed the ends of her hair and stepped out of the shower. She didn't want to talk to him or anyone else right now. She just wanted to go to bed.

Where she would toss and turn all night and spend hours staring up at the ceiling, trying to get those horrible images out of her mind.

Tap tap tap.

"Kira?"

She grabbed the fluffy white robe off the hook. She shrugged into it and wrapped the belt around her waist, cinching it tight. Then she yanked open the door.

"What?"

Jeremy stood there, a worried look on his face. "Why are you crying?"

Why? She wanted to slap him. Instead, she stalked past him and snatched her brush off the dresser. She dragged it through her hair, catching a glimpse of herself in the mirror. Her eyes were pink and puffy, and a fresh wave of tears welled up, these from frustration. She hated crying, and she hated Jeremy seeing her like this.

He stepped over, and she met his gaze in the mirror as she ran the brush through her hair.

"I'm upset, okay? First Ollie. Then Shelly. Now you. You go off to do me a favor and end up *shot*, and this whole thing is out of control! I don't see why the police haven't arrested anyone. It's been six days!"

He took her arm and turned her to face him. "I'm not shot. It's nothing."

She tried to pull away, but he wouldn't let her go.

"Look at me."

"No."

He tipped her chin up.

Kira stared up into those potent blue eyes. Her stomach seemed to drop, and she got that panicky feeling again. But it was a different kind of panic, because he was standing so close and she could feel the heat of his fingers through the terry-cloth sleeve of her robe. Her heart thrummed inside her chest as she watched the conflict in his eyes.

He bent his head down and kissed her, and the panic gave way to excitement as he tilted her head back. His kiss was deep and hungry, and she stood on tiptoes and slid her fingers around his neck. His body felt warm and solid, and he tasted good again, so good she couldn't seem to get enough, even when he cupped his hand over her butt and pulled her tight against him.

This was what she wanted. What she needed—Jeremy's tongue in her mouth, and his solid body, and his hand tugging at the belt of her robe. She eased back so he could get it loose, and then the fabric parted, and his warm palms slid over her bare hips, pulling her closer. She felt a rush of nerves and kissed him harder, and he made a low groan. God, she wanted this. Him. Now. She wanted his mouth and his hands and his hard, powerful body. Desire rushed through her, making her pulse pound, pushing away all the ugly thoughts and replacing them with need. His hand slid to the small of her back, and she felt the steely ridge of him through his jeans. She reached for his belt.

His hand closed around her wrist. "Kira."

She fumbled with the buckle, and his grip tightened.

"What?" She pulled back and looked up at him, breathing hard. His gaze dropped to her open robe, then snapped back up.

"I can't." The pleading look in his eyes was like a kick in the gut.

She eased away. "But—"

"I'm sorry."

He released her hand and pulled the sides of her robe together. She watched with disbelief as he retied the belt he'd just undone. She looked up at him and saw that he was serious, and all that hot desire turned to ice in her veins.

"Sorry," he said again.

He turned and walked out—just like that—leaving her hot and confused and even more shaken than she'd been before.

CHAPTER

TWENTY-FOUR

KIRA SIPPED her coffee, careful not to scald her tongue, as the office buildings of downtown whisked by. She'd gone with plain drip this morning instead of the mocha Frappuccino she would have liked, because the coffee place was packed, and the drive-through line had curved around the building.

She glanced at Jeremy beside her, silent as he navigated rush-hour traffic. The *swish-swish* of wiper blades on the windshield was the only sound. He hadn't said a word about last night. He acted as though everything were normal, as though he hadn't seen her naked and had his hands all over her.

Kira eyed his fingers on the steering wheel and felt a rush of embarrassment. She gazed out the window again. To distract herself, she nibbled on a store-bought banana muffin that wasn't nearly as good as her grandmother's.

"Want some?" she asked.

"No."

He didn't even look at her. He was in bodyguard mode. Eyes forward. Muscles tense. Attitude heavy on the grim, especially when they stopped at traffic lights. It was as though he thought a crew of assassins might pop up out of nowhere and ambush them. He hadn't even wanted to stop for coffee, but Kira had insisted, and he'd finally agreed to take her to a Starbucks drive-through.

Sipping her drink, she glanced at his hands again and remembered his warm palms gliding over her hips and pulling her close. Then she remembered those same hands retying the belt of her robe, and she felt another flood of embarrassment—and irritation, too. She was mad at herself more than at him.

The irony was thick here. Last night she'd rejected Brock and then promptly thrown herself at a man who *didn't* want her. Brock was smart. Successful. Interested. So naturally, she wasn't attracted to him at all.

It was a curse, she decided. The Curse of the Strong Silent Type. The only men who turned her on were uncommunicative or emotionally unavailable or both. Jeremy was a particularly vexing example because she *knew* he was attracted to her, and yet he seemed burdened by this misplaced sense of duty to keep her at arm's length.

The muffin tasted like sawdust, and Kira dropped the remainder into the bag and stashed it on the floor. She looked out the window through the rain-slicked glass. It was for the better, really. Jeremy didn't even live here, and she had no business getting hung up on him, which was exactly what would have happened if they'd slept together.

It may have happened already. In fact—if she was being honest with herself—she knew it had. She *liked* Jeremy, even though he was guarded and taciturn and infuriatingly tight-lipped about his feelings. She liked him anyway, whether he'd rejected her or not, and it was going to suck when this whole crisis was over and he had to leave.

Well, not completely. Some aspects of this crisis being over would be good. Such as having her freedom back and being able to go about her life without the constant threat of violence lurking around every corner.

"That's the parking garage right there," she said as they neared the building beside the courthouse.

Without a word, Jeremy buzzed his window down and pulled into the garage. He tapped the button for a ticket, waited for the arm to go up, and rolled through.

"You can pull into one of those spaces there," Kira directed. "This shouldn't take long."

"Those are reserved."

"So?"

"So they belong to someone."

She felt a flash of annoyance. "It's not like this is a hospital! Don't be such a Boy Scout."

He lifted an eyebrow at that and pulled into a space.

Kira shoved her door open before he could get out and come around. She was in a bitchy mood, but she couldn't help it. She'd been up all night, tossing and turning, too fired up to sleep, and not just because Jeremy had rejected her. The constant thrum of rain outside the window had grated on her nerves throughout the night.

She grabbed her bag off the floor, and Jeremy closed the door. Because of their prime parking space, they were on level one, and she walked briskly toward the doors leading to the courthouse, her heels clacking against the pavement. Today she wore her typical courtroom attire of black slacks and a white silk blouse with a pearl-gray tank underneath. It was more conservative than her normal fashion tastes, but she was mindful of making a good impression on people in legal circles. She never knew where her next client might come from.

"You still haven't told me what we're doing here," Jeremy said as he pulled open the heavy glass door.

"The envelope you found at Ollie's office."

"The one addressed to Lorraine?"

"I've got a hunch about it," Kira said. "I think she's the 'LH' I've been looking for."

Kira skirted around a huddle of lawyers and made her way to a stairwell.

"Lorraine works in the basement." Kira's words echoed off the cinder-block walls as they descended the stairs. "She's a clerk here."

"This is a federal court building," Jeremy said behind her. "What's that got to do with your murder case?"

"I don't know yet, but I plan to find out."

At the bottom, Jeremy reached around her to open the door and insisted on stepping through first. Despite her foul mood, he was vigilant as ever, and she felt guilty for being such a grouch earlier.

The basement offices were already buzzing with people. Clerks and interns and paralegals streamed through the corridor, each on a mission to track down some obscure document for some VIP who probably worked in one of the city's soaring skyscrapers. With the exception of the occasional tattoo-covered messenger in spandex, most people down here adhered to a business dress code.

She passed a plexiglass window and stopped at a door marked EMPLOYEES ONLY. She glanced over her shoulder.

"Try to look like you belong," she told Jeremy.

That wouldn't work, but she hoped to find Lorraine before anyone questioned their presence here. She passed through half a dozen cubicles and reached a small office. The placard beside the door said LORRAINE HARTMAN, PUBLIC RECORDS.

Lorraine was at her desk, facing her computer. She wore a cheerful yellow blouse and fake pearls, and as she glanced up, her face brightened.

"Kira, hi. How are you?" Her brow furrowed, and she pressed her hand against her chest. "I heard about Ollie. My *stars*, hon. That's just awful."

"It is."

"I wanted to get to the funeral, but I was sitting my grandkids Saturday. Did you go?"

"I did. It was really nice," Kira said, then realized that sounded awkward. "Well attended," she added.

Kira stepped into the little office and hoped Jeremy would linger outside, but the look on Lorraine's face told Kira she'd noticed him.

"This is my friend Jeremy. He's working with me today."

They traded nods, and Lorraine gave Kira a puzzled smile.

"Sorry to just drop by, but I have something for you." Kira reached into her messenger bag and pulled out the envelope. "Ollie wanted you to have these." She handed Lorraine the envelope and watched the anguished look on her face as she read her name in Ollie's distinctive scrawl. She opened the envelope and pulled out the baseball tickets.

"Oh, Lord." She shook her head. "I can't believe he did that." A tear slid down her cheek. She swiveled in her chair and reached for the tissue box behind her. "He didn't need to do that." She dabbed her eyes. "He was always such a sweetie."

"He was."

She looked from Kira to Jeremy. "Sorry. I still can't believe he's gone."

Kira gave her a sympathetic smile. "Neither can I."

"He asked me for a favor last week. Some paperwork he wanted. I

told him I didn't mind getting it for him, and he sure didn't need to get me Astros tickets."

It was Ollie's way. *You gotta scratch backs to get shit done in this business.*

"The paperwork he requested, did he ever pick it up?" Kira asked.

Lorraine dabbed her nose with the tissue. "No. Why, do you want it?"

"I do, actually. I've taken over some of his cases."

Lorraine glanced at Jeremy and looked self-conscious about her tears. "Sorry." She swiveled in her chair again. "Where did I put it? I swear, this place is such a clutter. Oh—here." She dug a blue folder out from beneath a tall stack of files. She opened the folder, then closed it. "This is it," she said, handing it over.

Kira tucked it into her bag. "Thank you. It's a big help."

"Not at all. Sorry I'm a mess."

"I understand. We can catch up later. I'd love to take you to lunch soon," Kira said, wanting to ramp up her networking effort.

Lorraine smiled through her tears. "I'd like that."

Burning with curiosity, Kira led Jeremy back through the cubicles and left the office. When she was back in the crowded corridor, she ducked into an alcove beside a water fountain and opened the file. Her heart lurched when she spotted the name Craig Collins at the top of the page.

Jeremy's shadow fell over her, dimming her light as he shielded her from people.

"What is it?" he asked.

"I'm not sure yet." She skimmed the top page. As she flipped through the papers, her pulse picked up until she could hardly breathe.

"Holy hell," she murmured.

"What, Kira?"

"Two years ago, Ava Quinn's brother filed for bankruptcy."

His eyebrows went up.

"He had creditors, too," she said. "Some of them are listed here. I wonder if he had any *unlisted* ones."

"You're thinking of Andre Markov."

"Right." She looked up. "I mean, Markov's dirty. Not the kind of guy you want listed in your court documents, especially if what you owe him for is something illegal, such as drugs or whatever. But Craig Collins might have owed him money."

"You're saying Craig killed his own sister and cleaned out her safe?"

"Craig had an alibi. He got a DUI on the night of the murder." She shook her head. "But maybe he hired it out. Or *maybe* Markov did it, and it was some kind of trade."

"A trade like . . . 'I'll help you murder my sister and steal her cash, and then we're square'?"

"Exactly." Kira's heart pounded as all the pieces fell into place. "It makes sense, right? Her brother probably knew she was having marital problems. She might have mentioned she was hiring a fancy divorce lawyer, and he spotted an opportunity to intercept that big fat retainer."

"It was cash?"

"Her attorney handles divorces, so money can be tricky. He only takes cash and wire transfers, and she probably wanted to hide the transaction from her husband. So say Craig pumped her for information about it, so he knew when the money would be in her safe, and he picked the timing for the murder."

"And then he got himself arrested for a DUI, giving himself an alibi," Jeremy said. "Damn, that's cold."

"Yes." She checked her watch. "I need to call Brock. I think I just found the alternative suspect Ollie was looking at."

"Two suspects," Jeremy said.

"Right. And I think we have their motive right here."

Charlotte bumped into Diaz as she was leaving the police station. The fast-food cup in his hand told her he'd already had lunch.

"Hey, check this out." He handed her a stapled stack of papers.

"What is this?"

"Just got this from my FBI contact. I asked him about Andre Markov."

Charlotte stepped out of the traffic flow beside the door as she skimmed the top page.

"This is an arrest record for Anatoly Markov."

"Andre's father," Diaz said.

"He was busted for drugs. And . . . check fraud. But this is old. The most recent arrest was twenty years ago."

"Yeah, *but* I hear the feds have him on their radar. Him and his businesses. They're looking at RICO charges, and my friend told me he's rumored to be behind an unsolved murder in Channelview."

That got her attention. "Tell me more."

"One of Anatoly's dock workers got popped on drug charges—intent to distribute. He managed to get his throat slit two weeks before trial."

"Interesting."

"Yup. Like I said, the feds don't have it all nailed down, but they're looking at this guy hard, and he's Andre Markov's father."

Charlotte skimmed the papers again. "Mind if I keep this?"

"It's yours. Where you headed?" he asked, holding the door open for her.

"I got a message from Kira," Charlotte said. "She wants to meet, and she says it's important. You want to come?"

"Sure." He fell into step beside her on the sidewalk.

"She's at Logan's law office. Their team is on a lunch break. I'm going to meet her there before I head over to the courthouse. The Quinn trial is starting, and I want to sit in."

"Why?"

"You know. Get a read on the players. Watch Logan. Get a feel for his case."

Diaz smiled.

"What?"

"Nothing," he replied.

"That was definitely a look," she said as they crossed the parking lot. "What is it?"

"You and Logan."

"*Me* and Logan?"

"Yeah, I noticed you're interested in him."

"I am *not* interested in him. I hate lawyers."

Diaz shook his head.

"*What?*"

"Nothing."

They reached the car, and Charlotte slid behind the wheel. She grabbed the accordion file from the passenger seat to make room for Diaz. As he got into the car, she slid the new paperwork into the file and pulled out a forensics report.

"Read that," she said, handing it to him. "It's from Grant."

Diaz skimmed the paper as she backed out of the parking space.

"This is from the car hood last night?" he asked.

"Yes."

"Says the prints aren't in AFIS."

"That's right."

"But he got a full handprint?"

"That's right."

Charlotte exited the parking lot. She glanced at Diaz, and he was frowning at the page. "I don't get it. Sounds like a dead end."

"Keep reading."

She changed lanes so she could pick up Smith Street, which would take her straight to Logan's building.

"One of the prints matches the glove from Brock Logan's back fence."

Charlotte smiled. "Bingo."

"So whoever it was at Kovak's office last night is our shooter."

"Yep. *And* Grant's still working. He said he had another lead on the print, but he had to confirm something first."

"That's vague."

"Yes, but given Grant's track record, that's good, right? He turns over every stone."

Charlotte fought her way through the lunchtime traffic. The streets were still wet from the drizzle earlier, which made people forget how to drive. Diaz didn't talk, and she took advantage of the quiet to sort through her thoughts about the case.

The shooter was after something. As in *some thing*, a physical object. Otherwise, why grab up all the electronics from Logan's house? And ransack Ollie's office looking for something? And then *return* to that office as if whatever it was still needed to be found?

But Charlotte couldn't figure it out.

So much paperwork was digital now. Why would the killer want a physical copy of something? It had to be something unique. And uniquely incriminating. Such as a piece of biological evidence, maybe. Or a murder weapon. Or a stash of money. Some *thing* with value in and of itself. But that theory didn't tie in with the theory she'd come up with originally, that the shooter had shown up at Logan's home and gunned down Gavin Quinn's defense team and stolen their computers and files in order to throw a wrench into their court case.

Who the hell was this guy, and what was he after? And why was he so certain that whatever it was, Oliver Kovak was in possession of it at the time of his death?

Kira knew much more than she was saying. If she wasn't careful, her secrets were going to get her killed.

"You're quiet over there."

Charlotte looked at her partner. "Just thinking. Mind?" She picked up his drink from the cupholder.

"Finish it. I've had enough caffeine."

She took a slurp. It was real Coke, cold and sugary, and she wished she'd had time to grab a bite of lunch. She wasn't looking forward to sitting in court on an empty stomach.

Charlotte pulled into the parking garage beside Brock Logan's office and took a ticket from the dispenser. There was a row of spaces marked reserved, and she pulled into one, adjusting the police hangtag on her rearview mirror, which she hoped would keep her from getting ticketed.

They crossed the garage to the door, where they were met by a wall of frosty air. An all-glass tunnel led to the main lobby of Logan's building. It was a three-story atrium with a huge black sculpture in the center. The sculpture was an oblong-shaped glob on two spindly legs, and Charlotte thought it looked like a charred flamingo.

She scanned the lobby for any sign of Kira.

"There she is," Diaz said, and Charlotte followed his gaze to a group of people walking from the elevator banks. Charlotte spotted the PI. She was dressed like a lawyer today in slacks and high heels, and she had her hair pulled up in a ponytail. Evidently, she planned to be in the courtroom this afternoon, too.

At her side was Jeremy, who was half a head taller than everyone else in the lobby and looked intimidating in his dark suit. He'd skipped the tie today, but he appeared every bit as grim as he had at Ollie's funeral Saturday.

Spotting Charlotte and Diaz, Kira crossed the lobby and stopped in front of them.

"Thanks for meeting me," she said to Charlotte.

"Sure. What's up?"

"A lot." She pulled a blue folder from her bag. "Take a look at this."

Kira watched as the detective skimmed the paperwork and knew the exact moment her gaze landed on the name Craig Collins. She glanced up.

"Where did you get this?" Spears asked.

"The courthouse this morning."

She looked at her partner. "This is the deadbeat brother-in-law Quinn mentioned."

"What about him?" Diaz asked, peering at the folder.

"It's a bankruptcy filing. Ava Quinn's brother has money problems."

Watching Spears flip through the pages, Kira felt a swell of relief. Clearly, she understood the implications in terms of a new suspect in Ava Quinn's murder case.

Brock emerged from the crowd near the elevator bank. He was flanked by two bodyguards, Erik and Trent, and the three of them made an imposing trio in their black suits. Brock noticed Kira and walked over. The entire legal team had spent the lunch break in the conference room, strategizing about how to incorporate Kira's latest bombshell into their client's defense.

Gavin, meanwhile, had stood beside a window, silently gazing out over the downtown skyline. The man had looked shell-shocked. And he probably was. Kira couldn't even imagine the betrayal he must be feeling right now.

Brock's entourage stopped beside Kira.

"You show her?" he asked.

"Yeah."

A shrill scream pierced the air.

Kira whirled around, searching for the source as the screams continued.

Hands clamped around both her arms.

"What—"

"*Go!*" Jeremy commanded as he and Trent propelled her across the lobby. They were on either side of her, and her feet barely touched the ground.

"*Move, move, move!*" Jeremy said, slicing through people as they hustled her to a corridor. They rushed down the hallway and stopped at a solid gray door marked EMPLOYEES ONLY. Jeremy opened it, and she noticed the pistol in his hand as he pulled her inside.

"What—"

"Get down," he ordered, cutting her off again.

She dropped into a crouch beside the wall, and Brock joined her.

"What happened?" she asked Brock.

"I heard someone say something about a gunman."

"Where? I didn't hear anything."

"Don't move," Erik ordered. "I'll be right outside."

Kira's chest clenched as the door whisked shut, leaving them alone in the dingy room. It was a staff break room, from the looks of it, with a table and chairs in the middle and a coffeepot on the counter.

"Where's Gavin?" Kira asked.

Brock was already on his phone. "Fuck," he muttered. "He's not answering."

Kira's chest tightened again. She tucked her forehead against her knees and tried to breathe.

The door burst open, making her jump, but she saw that it was Jeremy.

"Quinn's been shot."

She jumped to her feet. "Where is he? Where's the gunman?"

"He fled the building."

"He?"

"They think it's a he."

"Who's 'they'?" Brock demanded.

"Quinn's bodyguards," Jeremy said. "Come on."

Taking Kira by the elbow, Jeremy guided her to a door she hadn't noticed before. He opened it and stepped into an adjacent room that was bigger and brighter and crowded with people. A long counter on the far wall was filled with video monitors.

Erik leaned over one of the screens, pointing at something and talking to two uniformed security guards.

Brock turned to Jeremy. "What happened?"

"Quinn was stepping out of the elevator when someone shot him," Jeremy said. "He went down right there, and the woman beside him started screaming."

Brock cursed. "Is he—"

"Paramedics just showed up. We don't know."

Jeremy turned to Kira and rested his hand on her shoulder. "You all right?"

"Yes—I didn't hear gunshots. I didn't hear anything, except for the screams."

Jeremy stared down at her, his gaze intense. And then she understood.

The hallmark of this shooter was that he used a silencer. He'd probably scoped out the lobby and waited in the crowd by the elevator until Gavin stepped off.

Kira closed her eyes. Jeremy's hand tightened on her shoulder.

"You okay?" he asked.

"Yeah. I . . . I can't believe this is happening again."

"Kira."

She turned to look at Erik.

"Come take a look at the monitors. We're searching for a tall male wearing a black baseball hat, according to an eyewitness."

She crossed the room to the row of screens and studied the footage. She recognized the concrete pocket park in front of the office building. People milled around and sat on benches, seemingly oblivious to what had just happened.

"Anyone look familiar?" Erik asked. "You and Jeremy might be able to ID him."

Kira studied the figures. The camera was placed at a second-story vantage point. She searched for someone running or jogging or even walking briskly away from the scene. She moved to the next monitor, which showed a view of the attached parking garage. The next monitor showed footage of the sidewalk on the building's north side as a police car raced up to the curb and stopped.

Diaz stepped over. "See anything?"

"Not yet," Jeremy said.

Kira turned to Erik. "Are we sure he fled through a street-level exit? What about the tunnels?"

"A witness said he went out the front door, walking quickly."

"Walking?" she asked.

"Yeah."

"There." Jeremy leaned forward and tapped on the monitor. "That's him."

"Is that Rusk Street?" Diaz leaned closer. "Okay, we've got an update," he said into his phone. "He's moving east on Rusk. I repeat, east on Rusk."

"Who's he talking to?" Kira asked Erik.

"Detective Spears. She went after him."

Kira eased closer to Jeremy, peering around him to look at the monitor. She immediately saw what had his attention: a tall man walking quickly down the sidewalk. He wore a baseball cap and had both his hands stuffed into the pockets of a heavy jacket that didn't fit the ninety-degree weather.

"That's him." Jeremy pulled Kira closer. "Take a look."

She studied the man's gait, his build. "Yeah, I think that's him," she said.

As he neared an intersection, the man pulled off his jacket and wadded it into a ball. He walked past a trash can and stuffed it inside.

"He's at Rusk and Travis, and he just ditched something. Maybe the weapon," Diaz said. "You see him? Looks like he's headed into the Southwest Bank Tower, west entrance. You copy?"

Kira's heart pounded as she watched the man enter the building. "That bank lobby has direct access to the tunnels." She looked at Diaz. "You guys are about to lose him."

CHAPTER
TWENTY-FIVE

WEST ENTRANCE?" Charlotte demanded, pressing her phone to her ear as she ran as fast as she could.

"Affirmative."

She raced for the revolving glass door, where people streamed in and out. She still hadn't spotted the man in the black ball cap, so she was blindly following Diaz's directions over the phone.

"We have units en route," Diaz said. "Should be there in . . . one to two minutes."

Faint sirens sounded in the distance as Charlotte reached the door. "Tell them to hurry." She entered the lobby, where she was hit by a cold blast of air-conditioning. She skimmed her gaze over all the people, searching for a black ball cap, or even someone tall moving suspiciously quickly. Baseball caps were easy to ditch, and she couldn't get hung up on that detail.

"I'm told there's an escalator there," Diaz said.

"I see it. *Shit*." She was already rushing toward it. "He might be going for the tunnels."

"You have visual ID?"

"No." Charlotte hopped onto the escalator. All the way at the bottom was a man in a black ball cap. "Wait, *yes*. I see him!"

She elbowed past people, rushing down the steps and trying not to trip. Her Glock was gripped in her hand, but no one seemed to notice as she squeezed past them. She reached the bottom and found herself in a long, narrow hallway filled with throngs of businesspeople moving to and from lunch spots.

"You have him?" Diaz asked.

"Not anymore," she said as she jogged down the corridor, dodging huddles of people who'd stopped to talk or read their phones. "I need backup here ASAP."

"It's coming."

"I'm hanging up now so I can run."

She stuffed the phone into her pocket and increased her speed, moving as fast as she could through the congested corridor. She'd lost sight of the ball cap and didn't even see anyone tall ahead of her anymore.

"Shit," she muttered, cutting through the crowds.

The corridor emptied into a huge atrium with a food court centered around a giant water fountain. People sat on the wall of the fountain, eating lunch and looking at their phones. Others lined up at restaurants and food kiosks.

Charlotte scanned the crowd, desperately looking for the baseball cap. She spotted it, and her heart lurched.

She took off across the atrium, straining to keep the baseball cap in her sights as she jogged through the crowds.

She caught a blur of movement to her left just as something hit her like a Mack truck. She went down hard, catching herself with her elbow as she struggled to keep hold of her gun.

"Sorry!"

The Mack truck turned out to be a teenage kid on Rollerblades. Charlotte scrambled to her feet, cursing as pain lanced up her arm. She looked around frantically. Where was her guy? She'd lost sight of the ball cap.

"Are you okay?" the kid asked.

"Fine. Go."

His eyes widened as he noticed the gun in her hand.

"HPD," she said, moving her jacket to show her badge.

She jogged to the fountain and found a gap between people. Jumping onto the wall for a better vantage point, she scanned the atrium. No ball cap. No tall guy running away.

Her phone vibrated in her pocket. She pulled it out as a Segway zoomed over, piloted by a portly security guard.

"I lost him," she told Diaz.

"Ma'am. You need to get down from there." The ruddy-faced Segway cop glared up at her. "Ma'am?"

Again, she moved her jacket to show her badge. "I'm in pursuit of a suspect. Tall, jeans, black baseball cap?"

He shook his head.

Charlotte hopped down from the fountain, and pain lanced through her shoulder as her feet hit the floor. She'd wrenched something in her fall, but she couldn't worry about that now as she scanned the crowd. There had to be hundreds of people in this atrium and hundreds more in the many corridors that radiated out from it like spokes. Frustration churned inside her.

"You there?" Diaz asked.

"I'm here."

"Your backup should be there now."

"It's too late, Diaz. He's long gone."

———————————

Kira was tired and hungry when she stepped off the elevator into the lobby of the police station. She caught sight of the big, broad-shouldered bodyguard standing beside the door with his back to her. He wore a black leather jacket, and she noticed the bulge of a weapon at his hip.

He turned around, and she realized it was Liam, not Jeremy.

Liam Wolfe, of Wolfe Security, was here to pick her up.

Kira crossed the lobby and stopped in front of him. "Wow. VIP treatment."

"Are you finished here?" he asked.

"I hope so."

He nodded and led her to the door, which he pushed open as he smoothly cut ahead of her. These guys had the ladies-last thing down pat.

A shiny black Escalade was parked right at the curb—miraculously, without a parking ticket on the windshield. Liam reached for the passenger door and helped her inside. As she clicked her seat belt, he walked around the front, his gaze scanning the area.

The inside of the Escalade smelled of new leather. The dashboard was sleek and high-tech, with a navigation system that looked like it belonged in the cockpit of a fighter plane.

She glanced in back to see four empty bucket seats and windows tinted so dark she could hardly see through them.

Liam got behind the wheel and quickly pulled away from the curb.

"So," she said, searching for small talk. "You guys are really pulling out the big guns, huh?"

He shot her a look.

"Is it my imagination, or is this glass extra thick?"

"It's bulletproof," he said.

Her nerves did a little dance. "And the doors?"

"Armored."

"Damn. I feel really important."

He exited the police-station parking lot. "Why do you say that?"

"Because this is like a presidential motorcade."

He glanced at her, and she was struck once again by his intense look.

Of course, all the Wolfe guys were intense, including Jeremy. It had to be a prerequisite for getting hired.

"We don't operate that way," Liam told her.

"What way?"

"VIP treatment. Each client's protection plan is determined by the threat assessment, not some organizational pecking order. Or who is footing the bill."

"Good to know," she said. "Any updates on Gavin Quinn?"

"He's at Methodist Hospital, still in ICU."

Kira's chest tightened as she thought of him. From the security headquarters of the office building, she'd watched on the monitors as paramedics loaded Quinn onto a gurney and whisked him away. Detective Diaz had told her he'd been shot in the abdomen.

"I can get you an update when we reach the hotel," Liam said. "We've got an agent at the hospital."

"I thought he wasn't your client?'"

"He isn't. But we're coordinating with his people now, along with local authorities." He glanced at her. "Information sharing is a win-win in situations like this."

Situations like this.

Situations like . . . murder. Attempted murder. Ever since she'd sat on Brock's patio talking to those detectives, Kira had felt like she was living in an alternate universe.

She cleared her throat. "I'd like to thank you. And your agents."

He gave her a questioning look.

"For reacting so quickly," she explained. "It was instantaneous. One second we were standing around the lobby talking, and the next second we were in some windowless room. How'd they even know to take us there?"

"We scouted the location ahead of time."

"Seriously?"

"We scout all the locations."

"That's very thorough."

He smiled slightly. "Standard procedure."

"And your agents are very professional. You must have a tough recruiting process."

He nodded.

"I'm guessing it's extremely competitive?"

He nodded again.

Kira knew this already from her research, but she was trolling for details. Wolfe Security was guarded about its inner workings, and the firm's website gave out scant information. But there had been a handful of articles written over the years, mostly by reporters covering celebrities, and Kira had gleaned a few interesting details.

"Is it true all you guys have military backgrounds?" she asked.

"Not all but most. And it's not all guys, by the way." He looked at her. "We've got quite a few women in our ranks."

"Interesting. And you, Erik, and Jeremy, you were all Marines?"

"That's correct."

"And you served together?"

"Yes."

Another interesting tidbit. She wished she knew more about Jeremy's background, but he'd been so stingy with information. From her digging, she'd learned he was from Jacksonville, Florida, and had gone to college on an ROTC scholarship. Clearly, his military service was a major part of his life, but the only time he'd spoken about it was that night at the ship channel.

She thought of the way he'd opened up to her, if only for a few minutes. He'd talked about death and fear and brotherhood.

And she thought of the way he'd dragged her into his lap and kissed her. He was a man of few words, which made his actions all the more thrilling.

"Jeremy saved my life once."

She looked at Liam, afraid that if she said anything, he would stop.

"We were in Afghanistan. Suicide attack. Jeremy was on overwatch."

"You mean, like . . ."

"He was on a rooftop. Took out the threat. Saved twelve people that day, including eight Marines."

"Wow."

"I take it he didn't mention it. He doesn't talk about himself much."

"Yeah, I noticed."

He looked at her. "He's very good at his job, though."

"I noticed that, too."

"He excels at reacting. There's no hesitation—he's pure focus. That's how he's wired."

Kira looked at him, wondering why he was telling her all this.

"You should know you're in good hands," he said.

She glanced away, not sure what to say to that. She didn't want to be in anyone's hands. She didn't want to be part of *any* of the things that were happening, but here she was anyway, caught in the middle of it.

If only she'd pieced the clues together sooner, none of this would have happened. Why hadn't she put together the puzzle when Ollie did? If she had, he might be alive today, along with Shelly Chandler. And Gavin Quinn—who was looking more and more like an innocent man, falsely accused—might not be stuck in the ICU fighting for his life.

He's pure focus.

Something about those words snagged Kira's attention. Maybe Liam was on to her. Was that the underlying message, in addition to *you're in good hands*?

Jeremy was one of Liam's top agents, and she was messing with his focus. Did he somehow know that she had feelings for Jeremy? But how could he know that?

Well, the man made a living by being observant. Maybe he'd figured it out.

They reached the hotel's tree-lined driveway. Liam pulled under the porte cochere, where wealthy hotel guests were sliding out of Benzes and Bentleys.

Valets and bellmen jumped to attention, taking their cars and their luggage off their hands, so they were free to check into their luxury rooms or hit the spa or maybe get a drink in the Metropolitan's swanky bar. Kira had been here two nights, and she felt disconnected from all of it. Despite the sumptuous linens and pillows, she'd barely managed a few hours of sleep.

Liam parked the Escalade and turned to face her. Something in his eyes told her she could trust him.

"How long does it take to get past it?" she asked him.

"Get past . . . ?"

"Nearly getting shot and killed." She looked out the window. "I've hardly slept in a week."

"Insomnia is associated with PTSD. You should talk to someone professional."

"Did you?" She looked at him. "Talk to someone professional?"

He hesitated, and she thought he was going to duck the question.

"No," he said. "I usually talk to my wife. She's in law enforcement, so she knows what it's like."

Kira was surprised by his candor. And she felt a pang of envy. It must be nice to have a relationship like that, one where you could help each other through problems. All her adult life, Kira had been on her own. For years, she'd been trying to prove her independence to her parents and her brother and herself. Now she wondered what it would be like to have someone to share things with.

She wanted to talk to Jeremy. She thought of how he'd reacted last night after her shower meltdown. He'd been comforting and kind and hadn't given her a lot of platitudes. Mostly, he'd distracted her by kissing her until she was so turned on she couldn't think of anything else. That was one kind of therapy.

Trent stepped out of the hotel and strode straight up to the Escalade. Evidently, she was being handed off to yet another agent who wasn't Jeremy. Trent opened the door, and Liam held up his hand.

"Give us a sec."

Trent closed the door.

"You should really talk to someone," Liam repeated.

"I'll check into it," she said.

But by the look in his eyes, he knew that was a lie.

Charlotte sat at the bar at Bud's BBQ two blocks from the police station, watching ESPN as she waited for her to-go order. She picked up her drink and sipped through the slender red straw. In the mirror behind the bar, she watched as the door opened, and Diaz stepped into the restaurant. It took him about two seconds to spot her, and he walked over.

"Where'd you go?" he asked, sliding onto a stool. "I thought you were coming back after dinner."

"Got sidetracked," she said. "Ended up spending two hours in the emergency department at Methodist Hospital."

"What'd they say about your shoulder?"

"Nothing broken." She moved it slightly and winced as pain zinged through the joint. "They gave me a fancy ice pack and sent me home, so I stopped to pick up some dinner. How'd you find me?"

"Spotted your car."

Charlotte looked Diaz over. Her partner appeared bone-tired, and his hair was doing that spiky thing it did when he ran his hand through it too many times.

"How'd it go with the tapes?" she asked.

"Still nothing."

The pretty young bartender walked over with a smile for Diaz, which seemed to perk him up somewhat.

"What can I get you?" she asked.

He nodded at Charlotte's drink. "What is that, rum and Coke?"

"Straight Diet Coke."

He frowned. "You working after this?"

"Maybe."

"I'll have a Coke," he told the bartender. Then he looked at Charlotte. "If you're thinking about going back in, I wouldn't bother. The tapes are a bust."

After Gavin Quinn's assailant vanished into the tunnel system, detectives had spent all afternoon combing through security footage from Brock Logan's office and surrounding areas. By evening, they'd found nothing, such as a suspicious vehicle or possible accomplice, that might give them a clue to the shooter's current whereabouts. Much like the River Oaks murder, the perpetrator had waltzed right up to his target, shot him, and calmly left the scene.

Charlotte had been a cop for twelve years, and she found the attacks particularly disturbing. Not that the perp was a great shot—if you included Shelly Chandler, he was two for five in terms of lethality—but he was brazen.

"I gotta say, the guy's got balls," Diaz said, reading her mind, as usual.

"I know."

"I mean, an office building in broad daylight? With a bodyguard right there? It's almost like he's daring us to catch him."

"Or he doesn't think we can."

"I've been nosing around about Anatoly Markov," Diaz said.

"Word is, people who work for him are accident-prone. One of his dock workers got hit by a truck last year. Another fell off a crane."

"No kidding?"

"Yeah. I talked to a detective in Channelview. They investigated foul play but could never prove it. Evidently, Markov's son Andre is involved in the business, but he's not really suited for it."

"Why not?"

"I hear he's a hothead. When he's not busy wrecking cars and getting into fights, he puts a lot of money up his nose."

Charlotte shook her head. "What'd I tell you about family businesses? What do you want to bet we find out this whole mess comes down to Anatoly trying to protect his kid from his own stupidity?"

The bartender delivered Diaz's drink with a smile. He sipped it glumly, and Charlotte knew he'd much rather be drinking a beer.

"So what's left tonight?" he asked. "And do you need a wingman?"

"Nah, I got it. I just have to stop by the Metropolitan Hotel and interview those Wolfe agents. They're observant. Maybe they can tell us something useful."

"I'd say they're a hell of a lot better than Quinn's people. His guy didn't even pull his weapon before his client was on the ground. You believe that?"

"You get what you pay for," she said. "Wolfe Sec is the best of the best, but they're expensive, and Quinn's buried in legal bills in addition to everything else."

"Why don't you let me do the interviews?" He nodded at her shoulder. "You go home and ice that injury."

"I can handle it."

"I know you can handle it. I'm offering to do it for you."

She eyed him suspiciously. "Why?"

"Because. I know you've had a shit day, and I know you hate hospitals. You wouldn't have gone in unless you were in serious pain. You should put some ice on it and call it a night."

She watched him, trying to think of something to say that didn't sound sappy.

"I don't deserve you, Diaz."

"Yeah, tell me something I don't know." He took a big sip of his drink and plunked it onto the bar. "Such as . . . what did you do to piss off McGrath?"

Charlotte didn't know, but she smiled at the thought. "He's pissed off?"

"He showed up in the bull pen an hour ago, flinging files and cursing your name. What'd you do?"

"Maybe he's mad about his murder case not being wrapped up with a nice red bow, like he thought it was."

"You think they collared the wrong guy?" Diaz asked.

"Don't you?"

"Maybe."

"How else would you explain the attempted assassination of Quinn's entire legal team and the theft of their work product just before trial?" Charlotte asked. "And what about the murder of Shelly Chandler, who was doing errands for the defense? Seems pretty obvious someone is hiding something. And that person is hell-bent on keeping Quinn's trial from happening."

"You're saying they're afraid of exposure?"

"Exactly."

"But if this was all about Gavin Quinn, why not take him out a long time ago? Why wait for his trial to start?"

"Man's been under house arrest. He's had security. His trip down-town today was the first time he's been in public in months, and it was a scheduled appearance. It would have been easy for someone to tail him from the courthouse to his lawyer's office for lunch, then set up an ambush there in the lobby."

Diaz combed his hand through his hair. He looked almost as whipped as she was. But at least he wasn't going home with a black-and-blue shoulder. She'd crashed hard today, harder than she'd realized when she'd been hot on the heels of her suspect. She'd thought she might have fractured something, but an X-ray had ruled out broken bones, so it was only a nasty bruise.

Diaz had guessed right that she'd had a shit day. What she needed now was a big dinner, a hot bubble bath, and a solid night's sleep with no interruptions. But given her luck lately, she'd probably get a callout the minute her head hit the pillow.

The bartender was back with a brown paper bag.

"Bud's Rib Combo, double coleslaw?" she asked.

"That's me." Charlotte handed her a credit card as Diaz took out his phone.

"Crap," he muttered.

"What?"

"The sergeant wants us back. You got this, too."

"Does he say what it's about?" Charlotte pulled out her phone to read the message.

"No, but he's also got McGrath on here, so I bet it's about the Quinn case. I hope he didn't croak in the hospital."

Charlotte skimmed the message, and her pulse picked up as she read the list of names. "Grant's on here, too."

"Grant, the CSI guy?"

"Yep." She slid off her bar stool. "I think I know what this is about."

"What? And why are you smiling?"

"I think we may have finally caught a break."

———————

Jeremy answered his phone as he crossed the hotel lobby.

"Where are you?" Erik asked.

"Just starting my shift. Why?"

"You're at the hotel?"

"Yeah."

"Meet me by the bar. I just did a walk-through with the security chief."

Jeremy checked his watch, annoyed. He didn't want to talk to Erik right now. He wanted to talk to Kira. He hadn't seen her since they'd parted ways at the police station, and she'd been looking pretty shaky.

Erik stood beside the hotel bar, scrolling through messages on his phone.

"How'd it go at the station?" he asked Jeremy.

"Fine. No new leads from the security tapes."

"I heard. Listen, we talked to the hotel manager. They've approved two extra cameras for both the main driveway and the employee entrance to the property. Keith just got started installing them."

"I thought he was with Kira?"

"Trent's with her. There they are now."

Jeremy turned to see Kira crossing the lobby with Trent at her side. She caught Jeremy's eye and changed directions. She wore workout gear and had a white towel around her neck, as though she'd just jumped off a treadmill.

"Hey, you're back," she said.

"I thought you were upstairs."

"I was getting antsy, so I decided to work out."

Jeremy shot Trent a look.

"We were in the spin room," Kira said. "It was empty. We had the place to ourselves."

Jeremy gazed down at her, swallowing all the words he wanted to say. Her cheeks were flushed from exertion, and her hair was damp.

"Are you on tonight?" she asked.

"Yeah."

"You want to come up with us?"

"I'll be up in a minute."

Her brow furrowed. "What's wrong?"

"Nothing."

"Okay, whatever."

She rolled her eyes and walked off with Trent, and Jeremy stared after them.

"He scoped it out beforehand."

Jeremy looked at Erik. "What's that?"

"The fitness room."

Jeremy looked at his friend and realized his frustration must be written all over his face. So what if Trent had scoped it out ahead of time? Taking her down there at all was an unnecessary risk, and he never should have done it. Knowing Kira, she'd been determined to get her way and probably poured on the charm until he agreed.

"You okay?" Erik asked.

"No." Jeremy blew out a sigh. "I heard they're thinking of pulling us off," he said, referring to Logan & Locke.

"I heard that, too."

"That's a bad plan."

"Yeah, well, the trial's been postponed indefinitely. The defendant's in the hospital."

"It's not just about the trial," Jeremy said. "That law clerk was killed because of something she saw or knew. She wasn't involved in the trial, except tangentially. The same thing could happen to Kira."

Erik nodded. "You should take it up with Liam."

"I will."

"But the law firm's paying the bills. Not much you can do if they've pulled the plug."

Jeremy's gut clenched at the thought. Even if the trial never happened, he couldn't shake the feeling that Kira might be in more danger than ever.

He glanced at Erik, who was watching him with a wary look in his eyes. He knew where Jeremy's head was. And Jeremy didn't care. He didn't care about much of anything right now except seeing this thing through.

Which meant that—job or no job—he wasn't going anywhere until the threat they were dealing with had been eliminated.

"I'm going up," Jeremy said.

"Let me know how it goes with Liam. And let me know if I can help."

"I will."

Jeremy made his way to the elevator but then decided to take the stairs, hoping to work off some of his frustration on the four flights up. He didn't like that Trent had taken Kira to the fitness center. He didn't like that she'd acted so blasé about it. And he didn't like that he'd had this clench in his gut ever since those screams rang out in the lobby, and he'd realized they had an active shooter situation, and Kira was *right in the fucking middle of it.*

Jeremy didn't get emotional about work. At least, he never had before. He had nerves of steel and laser-sharp focus, and both of those traits had served him well throughout his career.

So what was happening now? And why did he feel so ticked off all the time? Jeremy had known from the beginning that he wasn't in shape for this job. He didn't have his head on straight, and it was affecting his concentration.

The irony wasn't lost on him. He hadn't wanted this assignment in the first place. He'd flat-out rejected it, then relented and signed on, purely out of a sense of duty. But now the thought of walking away from this job made him livid with anger. He wouldn't do it. He refused. One way or another, he planned to see this thing through. The threat to Kira was still out there, and until it was gone, Jeremy wasn't leaving.

He reached the fourth floor and exited the stairwell. He shed his suit jacket as he walked down the corridor, then turned the corner to the hallway where Logan & Locke had booked every single suite. Joel sat in a chair in the hallway, stationed between Brock's suite and Neil's.

"Where's Brock?" Jeremy asked him.

"He and some of the lawyers are working."

"Is Kira in there?"

"She was." Joel nodded toward her door. "She went back to her room. Think she's in the shower. Trent's in the control room. Said he's almost done for the night." Joel checked his watch. "You on now?"

"I am."

Jeremy took out his key card and let himself into Kira's suite. She wasn't in the living room, and her bedroom door stood ajar.

He walked over and tapped on the door with his knuckles. No answer. He leaned his head into the room, which was warm and steamy, as though she'd just stepped out of the shower. One of the beds still had a big black suitcase on it, and Kira's clothes were strewn everywhere, but she wasn't there.

The curtain shifted, and she stepped in from the balcony. She wore the same white robe as last night, and Jeremy's heart gave a kick. Her long hair was wet and freshly combed.

"That was Brock," she said, putting her phone on the dresser. "He just got word from the hospital. Gavin's still in ICU."

"I know."

She turned to face him and crossed her arms. "So what's with the attitude?"

Jeremy stepped closer, looking her over. Her cheeks were pink, either from her workout or her shower or both.

"What attitude?"

"You're being an ass."

"*I* am?"

"You're mad that Trent took me to the fitness center. It was *my* idea, not his, so get off his case about it."

He stared down at her. Temper flashed in her eyes, and Jeremy's pulse picked up. His gaze dropped to the belt of her robe.

"Oh, no you don't." She stepped back.

"Don't what?"

"Don't even think about pulling that crap again."

He stepped closer.

"I mean it. You lay a hand on me, and that's it. No takebacks."

He gazed down at her. She meant it. He could see it in her eyes—her frustration, her anger, her wounded pride over last night. It was all right there, on full display.

"I mean it, Jeremy."

"I know."

———

Kira watched as he turned and walked to the door, and the pain was sharp. It was like he'd landed an arrow smack in the center of her chest, and fury filled her all over again. Not fury at him but at herself, because she'd misread him *again* and somehow gotten her hopes up.

He reached for the door. She heard a soft *click*, and he turned around.

He held her gaze as he crossed the room again. He dropped his suit jacket onto the chair, and Kira's heart lurched as she read the look in his eyes.

"Jeremy . . ."

He stepped closer, and whatever she'd planned to say evaporated. His gaze was hot. Intense. And either she was really, really misreading him, or he wasn't going anywhere.

He reached for the tie of her robe and gave a hard tug. She held his gaze even as she felt a draft against her bare skin.

He leaned his head down and kissed her, sliding his hands around her waist and pulling her up on tiptoes. She slipped her hands around his neck, lacing her fingers together in case he tried to pull away. But he didn't. His mouth was eager and determined. And the next thing she knew, he was moving her backward, steering her toward the bed until the backs of her legs hit the mattress. She slid her hands down his shirtfront, feeling the hard contours of his chest underneath. She rested her palm against his heart, and she could feel it thudding through the fabric, and as she looked into his eyes, she knew this was happening. Now. *Finally.* After two false starts and countless fantasies. His gaze was resolute, and his warm hands slid over her butt, pulling her against him.

She went up on tiptoes and kissed him again, letting her fingers glide down his sides, and her hand came to rest on his holster. She pulled back and trailed her finger over the grip of his gun, and just the hard feel of it made a shiver go through her.

"Take this off." She looked up at him. She wanted him to be there as himself, not as her bodyguard.

He didn't move. And she realized she'd given him another out, another chance to stop and think and come up with some logical reason why this was a bad idea.

His hands went to his belt, and he smoothly unbuckled it. With efficient movements, he removed his holster and stepped over to the nightstand, where he set everything beside the alarm clock. Next came his wallet and keys, and then he turned to face her.

The light from the bathroom made the shadows on his face sharp. She walked over and reached up to trail her finger over his jaw. She liked his cheekbones and his chin and the layer of stubble. It reminded her of the long, stressful day that had happened since the last time they'd been alone in this room together.

He pulled her against him and kissed her, hard, in a way that told her he was done waiting and making excuses. His hands moved over her shoulders, and she heard a soft *whoosh* as her robe hit the floor. Kira's nerves fluttered. And then his hands were on her again, stroking over her bare skin. She ran her fingers down his shirt, unbuttoning the buttons, one by one, as his hands rested on her hips. He didn't help her at all, and she glanced up to see him looking down at her intently.

"What?" She tugged his shirt from his pants and undid the button.

"I like watching you do that."

She smiled up at him as she lowered the zipper. He shrugged out of his shirt and tossed it on the nearby chair, and then he was standing before her, half naked, and her stomach clenched as she saw the bandage around his arm.

She touched it lightly, cringing at the thought of how close the bandage was to his vital organs.

"Jeremy—"

He tipped her back onto the bed and stretched out over her, caging her in with his arms. Then he kissed her, once again cutting off conversation. He settled his weight between her legs, and the hard ridge of his erection made her forget everything except him and all the pent-up desire she'd been feeling since the moment she first met him. She hooked her leg around his and kissed him, arching against him.

He kissed his way down her body, pausing to look at her as he reached her breast, and she ran her fingers into his hair. Then his mouth was on her nipple, hot and teasing, and she tipped her head back and moaned. She'd been thinking about this, and now it was happening, finally, and the need deep inside her started to build.

The bed creaked as he pulled away and stood up. She sat up on her elbows, watching impatiently as he kicked off his shoes and got rid of the rest of his clothes, and then he stretched out over her again.

"Whoa." She rested her hand against his chest. "Time out."

"What?"

She stroked her hand down. "I want to look at you."

He kissed her, clearly attempting to distract her from that plan, and she pushed against his shoulder.

"I mean it. Roll over."

He stared at her.

"Roll over. *Now*."

He eased onto his back and watched warily as she got to her knees.

Kira had imagined his body, but her imagination hadn't even come close. His shoulders were wide and muscular, and his torso was perfectly sculpted. He looked even bigger without his clothes on, and she thought about her size compared to his.

He propped himself up on his elbows, and his muscles rippled.

"Come here." He reached for her, but she scooted back on the bed.

"No."

"Please?"

The word sent a warm shiver through her, and she scooted closer, smiling down at him as his gaze heated. She straddled his hips and leaned forward to kiss him. He settled her on his lap, gripping her hips as her tongue tangled with his. She moved against him, loving the hard feel of his erection as his grip on her tightened. He was so intent. So focused. And the prospect of having his undivided attention on her body made her flush with excitement. Then his hands were on her breasts, and he teased her nipples with his thumbs, and she felt that delicious yearning deep in her core.

She eased back and looked around the room. Her cosmetics case was all the way in the bathroom, so she reached for his wallet on the nightstand.

"Any chance you have a condom in here?"

He took it from her and dug one from the inner pocket. It looked shiny and new, and she wondered if he'd put it in there for her.

"Yes."

She looked at him. "Yes, what?"

"I know what you're thinking." He tossed his wallet back on the nightstand and rolled over her, pinning her against the bed with his hips. He kissed her deeply, and she wrapped her legs around him, pulling him as close as she could. She wanted him inside her. She wanted them joined together, but he seemed determined to make her wait. He eased down her body, and she felt a rush of heat as his mouth closed over her nipple.

She combed her fingers into his hair, squirming against him as the need built and built. He moved to her other breast, and she felt the hot pull of his mouth just as his hand slid between her legs. She arched against him, gasping, as his fingers slid inside her.

Kira moved against him, loving the way he touched her, loving the way he set her on fire with his mouth and his hands, the whole time watching her responses. He seemed to read her, because he knew just how to touch her, just how to take her right to the edge but never quite over. She closed her eyes and gave in to him, and the pleasure went on and on and on, until she started to feel dizzy.

"Jeremy." She opened her eyes and looked up at him, and the raw attraction in his eyes made her giddy. "Now."

He gazed down at her for a moment, and she pulled him closer with her leg. She reached for the condom and handed it to him, and he knelt between her legs and put it on.

"Careful," she whispered.

"I know." He watched her expression as he shifted her legs and pushed into her. She closed her eyes and tipped her head back, and it was painful and exhilarating, both at once.

"Kira?"

"Yes. More."

He drove into her, and she pulled him close, as close as she could, as he started moving against her. He felt good, and she stroked her hands up his back and clutched him as close as she could as the need inside her burned brighter and brighter. She loved the heat of him and the slick, hot power of his body as he thrust into her again and again, driving right up to the edge, until she thought she'd lose her mind. She dug her nails into his back and tightened her legs around him.

"*Jeremy.*"

Everything got hotter, faster, and she moved with him, desperately trying to keep up with his pace. She wanted to wait for him, but then she couldn't hold on anymore, and the climax flashed through her, bright and blinding, and she gave him everything she had. Her body shuddered, and she held on, clutching him tight until he gave a final powerful surge and came, too.

Kira held on to him, not opening her eyes, because she wanted to let the moment stretch out.

She didn't want to talk. Or move. She just wanted to absorb the solid feel of him, completely inert on top of her, except for his hammering heart. Never in her life had she felt anything so physical. She stroked her fingers into his hair, and it was damp from sweat, and she smiled because she'd made that happen.

He pushed up on his elbows and stared down at her, searching her eyes.

"You all right?"

She nodded.

He rolled away and sat up, and her heart squeezed as she noticed his bandaged arm again. He stood up, and she watched him walk into the bathroom.

Kira stared up at the ceiling. On the other side of the wall, she heard the faint sound of a TV. Through the sliding glass door, she heard rain drumming against the balcony. While she'd been having mind-blowing sex, it had started pouring outside, and she hadn't even noticed.

Kira looked around at the room. Her robe was on the floor beside Jeremy's pants. His shirt was draped over the chair where he'd tossed it. His holster was on the nightstand beside his wallet.

What now? Was he going to suit back up and return to work? It was his shift, after all, which meant he might spend the night watching TV in her living room. Or stationed in the hall in that damn chair.

Jeremy switched off the bathroom light, and the room went black. The mattress creaked as he stretched out beside her. He didn't peel the comforter back, but he slid his arm under her shoulders and pulled her against him. He kissed the top of her head, and Kira's heart squeezed because it was such a sweet thing to do and not what she'd expected.

What *had* she expected?

She had no idea. She hadn't planned this. Not really. Not beyond satisfying the relentless yearning she'd felt since the day they met.

She hadn't thought about keeping her emotions out of it and how knotted up she'd feel if this turned into anything more than a one-night thing.

She didn't want him to leave.

Not just leave town—she didn't even want him to leave her room. She wanted him to spend the night with her. She wanted to wake up with him in the morning and have breakfast together and see where things stood.

Which was crazy.

He stroked his hand over her arm. Softly up and softly down, without saying a word.

She didn't want to talk about it. And neither did he. That she knew for a fact—and for once, she didn't mind his silence.

She rolled toward him, nestling her head against his chest, and the gentle stroking on her arm made her feel sleepy, dreamy, more relaxed than she'd felt in ages. Kira sighed deeply. She absorbed his warmth and his silence and let her mind drift.

CHAPTER

TWENTY-SIX

KIRA AWOKE in a dark room. Her eyes felt gritty, her limbs heavy. She shifted beneath the cool comforter and noticed the band of light peeking between the drapes. She looked for the clock.

It was 8:04.

Kira bolted upright and realized she was naked. She didn't remember falling asleep. She didn't remember getting under the covers. And she definitely didn't remember Jeremy leaving.

The bathroom light was off, and the only light came from the bright stripe of sunshine streaming through the window. Her bedroom door was closed, and on the other side she heard voices.

She strained to identify the speakers.

Trent. She couldn't make out the words, but he was talking to someone.

Jeremy.

Nerves fluttered in her stomach. Kira glanced at the nightstand. All his things were gone. The suit jacket he'd tossed onto the chair last night was gone, too, and now her robe was draped neatly over the arm.

He must have put it there, because she distinctly remembered it whooshing to the floor.

Kira got up and wrapped herself in the plush terry cloth. She tied the belt and glanced at the door as she made her way to the bathroom. A few moments later, she took a deep breath to brace herself and opened the door to the living room.

"Morning," she chirped.

Jeremy and Trent turned around. Both wore suits and ties and appeared freshly shaven.

"Morning." Jeremy looked her up and down.

"Brock wants you to call him," Trent informed her. "He left for the courthouse already."

"Oh?" She looked at Jeremy, noting his pale blue dress shirt. Yesterday's had been white.

He seemed to notice her staring at him, and she glanced away. Her gaze landed on the espresso machine on the minibar. She stepped over to it and opened the fancy wooden box that held the supply of shiny coffee pods that was replenished daily.

"Any word from the hospital?" she asked, dropping a pod into the machine.

"Gavin stabilized," Jeremy said. "They moved him from ICU into a private room."

"That's great news. When?"

"Sometime overnight."

"We also got a call from Detective Spears," Trent said. "They have some big new developments in the case."

The coffee maker whirred, and he waited for it to finish.

"They were able to match a fingerprint from Oliver Kovak's murder scene to a suspect," Trent continued. "The person is a known associate of the Markov family."

"Who?" Kira asked.

"Name is Bruno Duric. He's Serbian," Jeremy said.

"And turns out, he has a partner," Trent added. "His wife."

"His *wife*?" Kira looked at Jeremy.

"This tip came from Interpol," Jeremy said.

"Yeah, apparently, these two do wet work for the Markov family on two continents," Trent said.

Kira stared at him.

"That's, you know, murders for hire," Trent told her. "Fixing problems, cleaning up loose ends."

She looked at Jeremy, who was watching closely, gauging her response to this news. Kira turned away. She tore open a sugar packet and dumped it into her coffee, and she could feel them waiting for her reaction.

"What time did Brock leave?" she asked.

"Ten minutes ago," Trent said. "He has a hearing at nine."

She took her coffee to the sliding glass door and stepped out onto the balcony. The air felt warm and humid, but the sky was a dazzling blue, suggesting the rain had probably cleared for at least a day. Kira squeezed past the wrought-iron table and chairs and sat down on a chaise at the far end of the balcony.

Wet work. A Serbian team. A husband and wife, no less. Kira cringed just thinking of it.

Had she been there, too, on the night of Ollie's murder? Kira tried to recall a woman in the neighborhood. But she only remembered the plodding jogger in the gray hoodie and the sprinting valet attendant.

Kira sipped her coffee and gazed through the glass wall at the sparkly blue pool down below. The lounge chairs around it were arranged in perfect rows, and each had a rolled white towel at the end. The water shimmered invitingly, but no one was in it, and the only sound came from the gurgle of the tiered fountain at the end of the patio.

The sliding door opened, and Jeremy stepped out. He squeezed past the chairs and gazed down at her for a moment before lowering himself onto the end of her chaise.

She smiled tentatively. "Hi."

"Hi."

He rested his hand on her knee, and her heart melted a little. He glanced up, and his eyes looked bluer than ever because of that shirt.

"You crashed last night," he said.

"I guess so." She set her cup on the table. "When did you change?"

"When Trent came on at six, I went by my motel." He nodded at the door. "I spent the night on your sofa watching TV, by the way."

"How come?"

"There's a security camera in your living room. I didn't want people speculating."

She shrugged. "I don't care."

He picked up her robe tie and rubbed the end between his fingers, and she thought about his hands on her body last night.

"Word is, Logan and Locke is pulling us off the job."

She watched him, waiting for more.

"They don't want to continue paying to protect an entire legal team for a client who's no longer headed to trial. Sounds like police have reopened Ava Quinn's murder case in light of new evidence pointing to her brother." He searched her face. "You don't look surprised."

"I'm not." She sighed. "When is this happening?"

"Today. We have a wrap meeting at ten."

"What's that?"

"To tie up logistics." He paused. "I'd like to stay."

"Where?"

"Here in town. With you."

Hope bloomed inside her chest.

"Until an arrest is made, I don't feel good about leaving," he added.

Kira looked away to cover her disappointment. She didn't know why his words stung.

Or maybe she did. Maybe she'd thought that he wanted to stay here for her, that he wanted to turn their one-night fling into something more.

She looked at him. "You don't need to do that."

"I want to."

"If your team's been pulled off—"

"This would be personal," he said. "I've accrued plenty of vacation time. I don't mind using it."

"That isn't necessary. I'm not your responsibility."

"I didn't say you were."

She felt a surge of annoyance—with herself. *One* night with him, and she'd allowed herself to get attached. She'd allowed herself to hope that their relationship might be going somewhere. Which was foolish. She liked him, yes. She could admit that. But he lived a hundred miles away, and he wasn't even there most of the time. He worked crazy hours at a crazy job that had him traveling forty weeks a year.

He was watching her with those serious blue eyes, and Kira's chest tightened. Maybe she should just summon her courage and tell him how she felt.

The door opened again, and Trent poked his head out. "Erik called to say he'll meet you in the lobby."

"Thanks."

The door slid shut. Jeremy stood, and Kira tried to keep her face neutral.

"We can talk about this later," he said. "I'll be back after my meeting at the law firm."

"You don't need to stay with me."

"I want to."

"Jeremy—"

"Kira, I want to." He bent over and dropped a kiss on her head. Then he walked back into the suite.

Kira stared down at the pool, trying to sort through her feelings. She was all over the place today. She tipped her head back against the chair and closed her eyes. She felt rested—finally—and more energized than she had in a long time. But she still had that gnawing sense of anxiety.

Wet work. She shuddered. And she knew Jeremy was right to still be concerned. Even if Gavin Quinn's trial was off, and even though the prospect of Ava Quinn's real killer being exposed in open court was no longer a threat, Kira still didn't feel safe. And she wouldn't feel safe until whoever was responsible for murdering Ollie and Shelly was in custody.

She heard the faint *thud* of the door closing inside, meaning Jeremy had left. She got up and returned to the living room, where she found Trent seated at the dining table with his laptop in front of him.

He nodded at the TV. "Mind if I have the news on?"

"Not at all."

Kira glanced at the coffee table, where her own laptop sat beside the flattened black trash bag. Ollie's Rolodex was still there, as well as a stack of business cards and the red keychain Jeremy had retrieved from Ollie's office. Kira set her coffee cup on the table and perched on the edge of the sofa. She picked up the keychain and examined the two bronze keys. One was the same size and shape as her key to Ollie's office, and she suspected it was a duplicate. The other key was smaller, maybe to a post office box? Or a safe-deposit box? Ollie's daughter might know. Kira turned the keychain over in her hand. The pocket-knife had two small blades and a tiny button that activated a mini flashlight. On the other end was a small notch. She pressed the notch with her thumb, and a USB drive popped out.

Kira stared at it. Heart thudding, she pulled her computer over and turned it on. As the system booted up, she gazed down at the USB drive. Then she popped it into the port and waited.

After what seemed like an eternity, the password screen appeared, and she entered her code. She opened the drive and found only one file, labeled with a six-digit number that looked oddly familiar. It was a date. The same date she'd seen on that fast-food receipt she'd discovered in Ollie's van.

She opened the file.

A dim image filled the screen. The video had been taken at night, and the scene included a wire fence and a gatehouse. Kira's heart skittered as she recognized the location.

Xavier Shipping.

The guardhouse was empty. The camera panned left and zoomed in on a familiar double-wide trailer with a floodlight above the door. The cars parked in front were different this time. Instead of a Mini Cooper and a pickup truck, it was a black Mercedes sedan and a light-colored Honda.

"Day two of my investigation into Craig Collins," Ollie said quietly.

A chill snaked down Kira's spine. She'd never expected to hear his voice again.

"I'm here at Xavier Shipping," he narrated, zooming in on the Honda's plates. "I tailed Collins to this location, and it looks like he's meeting someone." He panned the camera again, this time focusing on the Mercedes.

"Aaaand . . . looks like we got action."

He zoomed out, and Kira watched as the Honda door opened. A thin dark-haired man got out. This would be Craig Collins. Then the door to the building opened, and a man stepped outside. He went down the steps and moved into the glare of the floodlight, and Kira caught a glimpse of his face.

She hit pause. Andre Markov.

"Son of a bitch," she murmured.

Her pulse picked up as she hit play again. Markov handed Ava Quinn's brother a black duffel bag. Craig handed over something small—maybe an envelope?—and they exchanged words.

The camera jerked left as the trailer door stood open again, and a tall figure emerged. Icy fear gripped her as he stepped into the light.

It was him. Ollie's killer.

Kira studied his face, his build. This would be Bruno Duric. The man spoke to Markov. Then he turned to go back into the building and stopped, his attention fixed on something across the highway.

The camera jerked down. Ollie cursed, and the screen went black.

Kira stared at the computer, her heart pounding against her ribs. She was sweating now.

He'd been made. Ollie had tailed Craig Collins to the ship channel and been made. He knew he'd screwed up, too, but he didn't realize the gravity of it. He didn't know that the man who'd caught him spying would somehow uncover his identity, figure out what he was doing there, and then track him down and kill him.

How had Bruno done it? Possibly from Ollie's vehicle or some security footage somewhere. Or maybe he'd done something as simple as follow him home when he left the area. Or maybe Bruno had *sent* someone to follow him. Someone who probably looked harmless and wouldn't arouse suspicion. Someone such as his wife.

They do wet work . . .

Kira's stomach roiled, and she leaned forward.

She forced herself to watch the video again, looking for any figures in the background or details she'd missed.

"You okay?"

Kira glanced up to see Trent giving her a worried look.

"Yeah, I just—yeah." She cleared her throat. "I'm fine."

She copied the file to her computer and then ejected the flash drive. She still didn't know where the original memory card for Ollie's camera was, but Ollie had probably hidden it somewhere. He'd understood the value of this evidence enough to copy it to a USB drive and stash it in his office.

Kira had to get this video to the police. It provided a conclusive link between Craig Collins and Andre Markov—who had likely murdered Craig's sister—and Bruno Duric. *This* was the mystery evidence tying all three men together. It was the thing Bruno had been looking for at Brock Logan's house and later at Ollie's office. Bruno was searching for this video footage, as well as anyone who knew about it, and he was willing to kill for it.

Andre's reckless move to get mixed up in a murder scheme was sure to draw attention to his father, especially after Ollie uncovered a concrete link between Andre and Craig Collins. So Anatoly sent someone to fix the problem, making sure Gavin's case never went to trial and an alternative murder suspect was never exposed.

Kira's heart thudded as all the pieces clicked into place. She ducked into her bedroom and closed the door. She tossed the USB drive onto the bed and grabbed her phone off the dresser.

"Spears," the detective answered.

"It's Kira Vance."

"I know."

"I have something."

"Something . . . ?"

"It's important evidence that you need to see."

"I'm putting you on speaker, okay? I'm in the car with Detective Diaz." Background noise came through the phone. "Okay, tell me about this evidence."

Kira took a deep breath. "I found a USB drive that belonged to Ollie, and it has a video clip dated a few days before his murder. Craig Collins is on it, along with Bruno Duric and Andre Markov. There's some kind of transaction going down, maybe a drug deal."

Silence.

"Detective?"

"Yeah, I'm here. Where are you?"

"I'm at the hotel. I can bring this to the police station." She glanced down at her robe and looked around. Half her clothes were strewn across the room. She grabbed a pair of yoga pants off a chair.

"Don't go anywhere," Spears said. "We're not far from your hotel. We can swing by there."

"You sure?"

"Yes. Just sit tight. We'll be there in ten minutes."

"Okay, I'll meet you in the lobby."

Kira threw on a T-shirt and yoga pants and slipped her feet into sandals. Then she hurried into the bathroom and spent a few quick minutes washing her face and putting her hair in a ponytail. She grabbed the USB drive and walked into the living room.

"I need to run down to the lobby."

Trent frowned. "Why?"

"I'm meeting Detective Spears. I have to hand over some evidence." She held up the flash drive.

Trent stood up. "I'll go." He grabbed his suit jacket off the back of the chair.

"She's expecting me."

"I'll handle it."

"But—"

"I'm under strict orders not to let you out of this room."

Kira's mouth fell open.

"Sorry. Let me rephrase." He cleared his throat. "I've been instructed not to take you anywhere without authorization. That includes the fitness center, the restaurant, and anywhere else."

"Jeremy can't just—"

"This is from Liam."

Kira closed her eyes and gritted her teeth. She hated having her movements dictated. But these guys were security experts, supposedly. And so far, they had an excellent track record of keeping her alive.

"Fine." She handed Trent the flash drive. "But do *not* lose that. It's important."

———

Jeremy checked his watch again and glanced impatiently across the lobby at the gift shop. Finally, Erik made it to the front of the line and paid for his breakfast. After getting his change from the cashier, he collected his purchases and walked over.

"Hungry?" he asked, offering Jeremy one of his two protein bars.

"No, thanks. I'm parked out front." Jeremy nodded toward the driveway, where he'd left the Escalade parked, much to the displeasure of the valet attendant.

As he and Erik reached the door, Detective Diaz walked through it. He wore a dark suit, no tie, and had a big manila envelope in his hand.

"Hey." He looked from Erik to Jeremy. "Is Kira with you?"

"She's upstairs. Why?"

"I've got copies of those mugs for you guys. Bruno and Sasha Duric."

Diaz handed over the envelope, which wasn't sealed. Jeremy pulled out several pages, each showing eight-by-ten photographs of Anatoly Markov's hired gun. The top two pictures were candids, evidently taken when Bruno was under surveillance.

"You recognize him?" Jeremy handed the photos to Erik, who studied them and shook his head.

The next photo was Bruno's mug shot. Based on the words at the bottom, he was in the custody of Italian authorities when the photo was taken. The last page was Sasha Duric's mug shot, also apparently taken by Italian authorities.

Jeremy stared down at the picture. His pulse quickened. "I've seen her," he said.

"Who? The wife?" Erik edged closer.

"Yeah, Sasha Duric."

Jeremy stared at the woman. She had long dark hair in the picture, and her eyes looked familiar. And the tattoo on her neck—a butterfly.

"The delivery." He handed the picture to Erik. "She delivered a pizza here two nights ago."

"Wait," Diaz said. "Sasha Duric was *here?*"

"Hey, what's up?"

Jeremy turned to see Trent standing there. Jeremy glanced over the man's shoulder. "Where's Kira?" he demanded.

"Up in the suite."

"You left her alone?"

"I'm bringing her evidence down for the detectives." Trent frowned. "Why? What's the problem?"

Jeremy rushed for the elevator. He jabbed the button, then looked up to see that both elevators were on the tenth floor. Cursing, he ran for the stairs.

CHAPTER
TWENTY-SEVEN

KIRA STOOD beside the bed that she and Jeremy had shared last night. She heaved her suitcase onto it and unzipped the top. Inside was her surveillance equipment. She scooted her camera over and stuffed a pile of dirty clothes in beside it. She needed to do laundry, and unlike Brock, she hadn't availed herself of the hotel's same-day service, which charged twelve dollars a shirt. She moved her tripod over, stuffed another pile of clothes in, and then went into the bathroom to pack her cosmetics bag.

Kira's phone chimed just as someone rapped on the door to the living room. She glanced at the phone on the dresser and let the call go to voice mail as she crossed the suite.

"Yes?" she asked, looking through the peephole.

"Room service."

"I didn't order anything."

"Champagne breakfast, compliments of Logan and Locke."

They'd sent her champagne?

Kira opened the door, and a uniformed server pushed the cart inside. On it was a silver dome and a goblet of orange juice covered in cellophane.

"Are you sure this isn't for next door?" Kira asked the woman as she wheeled the cart into the center of the room.

She said something, but her back was turned, and Kira didn't hear it. The server removed the dome from the plate, and the scent of scrambled eggs wafted over.

Kira watched the server with interest. She was tall and slender and had a long blond ponytail. Her uniform was much too small, and Kira could see two inches of skin between her black sneakers and the cuffs of her pants. Kira noticed the bulge beneath her jacket.

The back of Kira's neck prickled.

The woman whirled around and pointed a gun at Kira's face.

"Where's the camera?" she asked.

Kira stepped back, bumping into the couch. The gun had a silencer affixed to the end.

"Where is it?" She aimed at Kira's chest. "The memory card for Oliver Kovak's camera. Where?"

Kira's throat went dry. Her mouth wouldn't work. Her phone started chiming again from the bedroom.

"*Where?* You have three seconds!"

"I—It's . . . in my suitcase."

She grabbed Kira's arm and shoved her toward the bedroom. "Get it."

Kira stumbled into the bedroom. She darted a glance at the door to the hall, but it was too far away, and even if she made a dash for it, the security latch was still engaged.

"I want the camera *and* the memory card." The woman shoved her from behind. "And you're going to show me what's on it, so I know it's real."

Kira approached the bed with the suitcase on it. "It's still in the camera." She glanced over her shoulder and came face-to-face with the gun. Her stomach knotted as she turned and opened the suitcase. "It's right here." She reached for the camera but grabbed the tripod instead. Ducking and spinning, she swung the tripod like a bat, hitting the woman's arm. She yelped with surprise.

Kira bolted into the living room. A hand clamped around her arm, and Kira whirled back, smashing the tripod down on the woman's hand.

She shrieked in pain, and the gun cartwheeled across the carpet.

Kira lunged for it.

Pain zinged up her arm as the woman jerked her back, yanking her off balance. Kira caught herself on a table as the woman scrambled for the pistol. Kira jabbed an elbow into her ribs, then kicked the gun, sending it sailing underneath the sofa.

The woman shouted something in a foreign language. Pain blazed across Kira's face as she landed a blow. Kira staggered back, dazed, then rushed forward, shoving the woman aside as she made a dash for the door, but the woman caught her arm and threw her against the wall as she managed to flip the security latch.

She whirled to face Kira, and her expression was feral. Kira glanced at the door behind her, frantic for an escape. The only other way out was the bedroom, but she had to reach the door with enough time to flip the latch and get out. Which meant she had to disable someone who outweighed her by probably thirty pounds.

Kira ducked her head and plowed into her, sending her reeling backward against the food cart, and everything crashed to the floor.

———————

Gripping his pistol, Jeremy took the last flight of stairs three at a time and reached the top. Kira's voice emanated from the phone in his left hand. *I'm sorry I missed your call* . . .

Cursing, Jeremy plowed through the door into the hallway and sprinted down the corridor. Turning the corner, he stuffed the phone into his pocket and pulled out the key card to Kira's room.

———————

Kira raced for the bedroom. Her attacker hauled herself to her feet by the food cart and chased after her, grabbing Kira by the ponytail. Fire blazed up her scalp as the woman dragged her backward by her hair.

She slammed Kira to the floor and flipped her onto her back, then landed on Kira's chest with her knees, knocking the wind out of her. The woman's face was flushed and furious as her big hands closed around Kira's throat. Panicked, Kira bucked and twisted, but the woman didn't budge. Kira gripped the woman's wrists, but they wouldn't move. Kira's throat burned. The edges of her vision started to blur.

"Kira!"

Jeremy.

The door opened but caught on the security latch.

"Police! Open this door!"

———————

Jeremy peered through the gap.

"Who's in there?" Diaz asked behind him.

"Call backup!"

Jeremy raced down the hall and found a glass cabinet containing an ax and a fire extinguisher. He broke the glass and grabbed the ax, then sprinted back to the room, where Diaz was taking aim at the security latch with his Glock.

"Move! And cover me!" Jeremy raced up to the door and swung the ax. The latch burst apart, and Jeremy kicked open the door and reached for his pistol.

A toppled food cart was on its side, plates and glasses spilled everywhere. Where the hell were they? Diaz darted into the bedroom.

A wheezing noise came from behind the armchair. Jeremy rushed over to find Kira on the floor, coughing and sputtering.

He dropped to his knees as she rolled onto her side, struggling to catch her breath.

"Where are they?" he asked.

Kira looked up at him, her eyes red and watery. "She's . . . balcony," she croaked.

Jeremy whirled around. The balcony door was closed. He yanked it open and readied his pistol.

Glass shattered on the neighboring balcony as Jeremy stepped outside. He leaned over to look, just in time to see a blur of movement. A metal chair sat inside the hotel room on a pile of glass.

Jeremy raced back inside.

"The bedroom and bathroom are clear," Diaz said.

"She's next door."

Kira was on the sofa now, bending over and catching her breath. She looked at Jeremy and seemed to read his conflict.

"I'm fine. Go."

"Take my SIG."

"No."

"Take it, Kira." He put it into her hand and folded her fingers around the grip.

Grabbing the ax from the floor, he raced into the hallway after Diaz. The detective stood before the neighboring door, aiming his gun at the open door.

"Police! On the ground!"

Sasha Duric looked unarmed. The woman was flushed and panting, and the sleeve of her black jacket was torn at the shoulder. She started to rush back into the room, but Jeremy lunged forward and grabbed her.

"On the ground!" Diaz commanded.

She shot a furious look at Jeremy. Then she dropped to her knees. Diaz took out his handcuffs as Jeremy gripped her arm.

"On your stomach, hands behind you," Diaz ordered.

Jeremy stepped back as Diaz slapped the cuffs on. He patted her down, but she didn't have a weapon. At least, not anymore.

"You got this?" Jeremy asked him.

"Yeah."

Jeremy rushed back into the suite. His heart lurched when he saw that it was empty. Then he heard water running in the bathroom.

Kira stood at the sink, his SIG on the counter beside her. She tipped her head and examined a ring of red welts around her neck.

Jeremy's chest clenched. She'd needed him, and he wasn't there. It was his worst combat nightmare come true. He stared at the marks on her neck, and the floor seemed to sink under his feet.

She met his eyes in the mirror. "Did you—"

"Diaz has her." He closed the door behind him and locked it, then turned Kira to face him. She'd almost died. Thirty more seconds, and he could have lost her forever.

Kira glanced down at the ax in his hand, and he let it drop.

"Come here." He pulled her into his arms and held on tight.

Charlotte checked the clock on her phone. Where the hell was Diaz? She glanced at the hotel entrance, but didn't see her partner, only the stocky valet attendant who'd been glaring at her since she pulled in.

He walked over, and Charlotte reluctantly lowered the window.

"I'm sorry, ma'am, but I'm going to have to ask you to—"

"HPD." Charlotte held up her ID. "I'm waiting for someone."

The man stared at her a moment. He started to say something but then seemed to think better of it and walked away.

Charlotte looked through the windshield and sighed. Up ahead—also illegally parked—was a dark green pickup truck. There was a black Escalade sitting out here, too, and Charlotte could see why the valet guy had his shorts in a twist. Deciding to do her good deed for the day, she put her Taurus in gear and pulled in behind the pickup, freeing up space in the driveway.

Charlotte gazed at the pickup with its dented bumper. A man sat behind the wheel, probably waiting for someone like she was.

Jeremy Owen's words from the other night niggled at her. *There was a dark green pickup in the vicinity . . .*

Charlotte studied the truck, the driver. Her heart rate quickened. She pushed open her door and slid from the car. Resting her hand on her service weapon, she slowly approached the vehicle.

Suddenly, the engine roared, and the truck surged forward.

"Damn it!" Charlotte rushed back and jumped behind the wheel as the truck took off down the divided driveway. Charlotte thrust the car into drive as she reached for the radio and called for backup.

The truck was halfway to the main gate, and Charlotte punched the gas. She swerved, bouncing over the curb as she careened over the grassy median, then bouncing again as she hit the street.

A horn blared, and she swerved, narrowly missing an oncoming car. She set her gaze on the gate up ahead and stomped the gas, and her trusty V6 responded with a throaty growl. She was almost there, almost there, almost . . .

Charlotte reached the end of the median and jerked the wheel right, then hit the brakes. Tires shrieked, and she braced for impact.

He hit her like a torpedo, and the car spun out. Charlotte shoved it into park and blinked down at the steering wheel, dazed, for maybe a second. Then she drew her pistol and jumped out.

Bruno Duric was fighting the airbag and struggling to get his door open, but it was smashed to hell. He scrambled over the seat as Charlotte rushed to the other side.

"Don't move!" She pointed her gun at his chest. "Hands up!"

She saw the fury in his eyes. Not just that he was caught but that he was caught by a woman with a badge.

"Hands up, asshole! Now!"

Slowly, his hands went up, and Charlotte stepped closer, amazed that he looked exactly like the suspect sketch, right down to the dimple on his chin. But the look in his eyes now was pure hate.

CHAPTER

TWENTY-EIGHT

KIRA STEPPED into her house and disabled the burglar alarm as Jeremy brought her luggage inside.

"Where do you want these?" he asked.

"Um . . . that's mostly equipment, so it goes in the office."

He walked past her, carrying her two giant suitcases like they were lunch boxes.

What a long, strange day. Her suite at the Metropolitan had become a crime scene, so Kira had decided to check out. She would have left soon anyway, now that Logan & Locke had discontinued her security arrangement and was no longer footing the bill. And she was eager to get home.

After Diaz and Spears arrested the Durics, a horde of law-enforcement officials had descended on the Metropolitan—police detectives, FBI agents, even a few ICE guys. It turned out that Anatoly Markov's business was already under investigation by the feds. It sounded like the shipping company was a front for a drug- and people-smuggling operation, and Craig Collins may have been involved as a low-level employee who got in over his head and owed Andre Markov money.

Kira and Jeremy had spent several hours talking to investigators at the scene before going to the police station for additional interviews that had dragged on and on. When that was finished, Jeremy had taken her to check out of the hotel and offered her a ride home. They'd even stopped by the store to buy a few groceries—which felt totally bizarre, as though they were some normal couple picking up dinner for a quiet night in together.

Kira set a bag of groceries on the counter now and returned Ollie's goldfish to the kitchen windowsill. Then she grabbed her roll-on bag and wheeled it down the hallway.

Jeremy stepped from the office. "Want everything else back here, too?"

"It can wait by the door," Kira said. "I have to sort through some of it and put stuff in the laundry."

He flipped the light switch on the wall and looked down at her, his brow furrowed with worry. He reached up and lightly traced his finger over the bruise on her neck from where Sasha Duric had tried to strangle her. Jeremy had been looking at her neck all afternoon, his eyes tormented.

"I'm fine," she insisted. "But I'd like to jump in the shower before dinner. You mind?"

"Take your time. I'll get the grill going."

"It hasn't been used in a while, so I'm sure it's really dirty."

He kissed the top of her head. "I'll handle it."

He walked away, leaving her staring after him and wondering what the hell she was doing.

She hadn't formally invited him home with her, it had just been understood that that was what was happening as they left the hotel. She was glad he'd come. Relieved. And not just because of how rattled she felt after being attacked. She didn't want to be alone tonight, but she also didn't want to deal with saying goodbye to him yet. Her emotions felt raw right now, too close to the surface, and she worried about what she might say if she got into a serious discussion with him.

Kira went into her bathroom and stripped off her clothes. She stood under the hot shower spray, letting it steam up the room as all the events of the day swirled through her mind. Despite the two arrests, they were still waiting for news from Charlotte Spears. Police had attempted to pick up Andre Markov for questioning, but he seemed to have disappeared, which catapulted him to the top of the FBI's Most Wanted list.

What had started as a straightforward PI job had spun out of control, and Kira felt as though her life had been hit by a tornado. It had ripped through everything with dizzying ferocity, and she didn't know how to get her equilibrium back, or if she ever would.

She stepped out of the shower and toweled off, feeling ridiculously grateful to be back in her own house, in her own shower, with towels that smelled like her laundry detergent. She would sleep in her own bed tonight—with Jeremy—and just the thought of it put a warm tingle inside her.

She dressed in cutoff shorts and her softest sweatshirt and was combing her hair when someone knocked on the back door.

After checking the window, Kira opened the door for Gina.

"Oh, my God, *wow*." Grinning, Gina stepped inside and gave Kira a hug.

"What?"

"Your smoking-hot bodyguard."

"That's Jeremy," Kira said. "And he's no longer my bodyguard."

Gina smelled like perfume, and she was dressed to go out in a sexy black top. She craned her neck to see out the kitchen window. "What's he doing back there?"

"Getting the grill going." Kira sat on the sofa arm. "We're making hamburgers tonight."

"Seriously?"

"Yep."

Gina smiled. "Well, isn't *that* romantic?"

"It's just burgers. You can join us if you want."

"Thanks, but I wouldn't want to crash your *date*." She stepped closer, and her smile vanished. "Hey, what happened to your neck there?"

"Long story."

"Holy *shit*, don't tell me he—"

"Jeremy had nothing to do with it. He helped apprehend the person who did, so—"

"What on earth happened?"

Kira cast a glance through the kitchen window, and she could see Jeremy scrubbing down her grill with a metal brush he'd found somewhere. Her heart fluttered at the sight of him on her patio. He wore jeans and an untucked flannel shirt that made him look like a lumberjack. The weather was too hot for a long-sleeved shirt, but he wore it to conceal his gun.

She turned to Gina, whose brow was furrowed with worry. Kira gave her the nutshell version, and Gina's jaw dropped when she got to the attack in the hotel room. So she downplayed everything and emphasized the two arrests, making it sound like the case was all wrapped up.

"Oh, my *God*, Kira. Are you really all right?"

She glanced out the window again. "Jeremy's here, so . . . yeah." She forced a smile. "How are *you*?"

"Great, compared to you. I'm headed out with Mike, but I wanted to let you know your car's ready at the shop. You can pick it up tomorrow."

Guilt needled Kira, because she'd completely forgotten about it.

"Thank you. And tell Mike how much I appreciate it. I'll get Jeremy to take me over there."

Gina eyed her warily, and a smile spread over her face. "You really like him, don't you?"

Kira shrugged, but she didn't deny it. "He has to leave soon, though."

"Why?"

"He lives up in Cypress Springs."

Gina tipped her head to the side. "That's not that far."

"And he travels a lot."

"Yeah, so what? When was the last time you fell hard for a guy?"

Kira stared at her. She couldn't answer because she didn't remember. It had been years since she'd felt anything remotely like this. Maybe she never had.

The door opened, and Jeremy stepped inside. Sweat beaded at his temples, and in his hand was a filthy metal brush.

Kira cleared her throat. "Jeremy, this is Gina."

He nodded at her. "Nice to meet you."

"Likewise." Gina smiled and looked at Kira. "Well, I'd better run. You guys have a nice dinner."

"You and Mike don't want to join us?"

"We've got plans, but thanks. Bye, Jeremy."

She slipped out, and Kira watched her leave, sure she was going to hear all about Jeremy's hotness later. She glanced at him, and he looked tense suddenly.

"What's wrong?" she asked.

"Charlotte Spears just called me."

Her stomach knotted. "What now?"

He walked into the kitchen and dropped the metal brush into the sink. Kira's heart started to pound as he turned around.

"They located Andre Markov."

"Oh, thank God." She breathed a sigh of relief. "I thought you were going to tell me something bad."

Jeremy just looked at her, and she walked over to him.

"What is it?" she asked.

"The feds apprehended him at the airport in Dallas. He was about to board a flight to Amsterdam. He's in custody now and being charged with capital murder in the death of Ava Quinn." He paused and watched her. "Craig Collins is being charged, too, because it looks like he arranged the hit on his sister to square up a debt."

Kira just stared at him. She'd known about this. She'd helped come up with this theory and uncovered evidence to support it. But theorizing about it was different from knowing that people had actually been arrested and charged with such a twisted scheme. She couldn't imagine what Ava's parents must be feeling right now. Not to mention Gavin, whose whole life had been destroyed.

"So . . . that's four arrests in one day," she said. "Everything's happening fast."

He nodded. "That's the best news we could have had. Everything Andre Markov's been trying to hide—the video evidence, his connection to Craig, his role in Ava's murder—it's all been exposed. Investigators have proof now, and he's no longer a threat to you or anyone else involved in Gavin's trial. The feds are closing in on his father, too."

"No, I get it. It's all good." She stepped around him to unpack the groceries.

"Hey."

She turned around. "We should eat. I'm hungry."

He smiled and took her arm, gently tugging her toward him. "You know, for someone who's a human lie detector, you're pretty bad at it."

"Okay, fine. It's *not* all good. But I don't want to dwell on this. I want to put it behind me."

"I understand."

She gazed up at him. Then she hitched herself onto the counter, so she'd be closer to his eye level. "So . . . I'm wondering what comes next for you."

His eyes turned serious. He nodded, as though he'd expected the question. "My next assignment starts Friday."

Disappointment needled her, but she tried to keep her expression blank.

"We're headed to Bangkok with a client," he said.

"Another business mogul?"

"No. This time, we're going to an island off the southern coast. A magazine is shooting a swimsuit issue, and their cover model's been getting death threats. Once the shoot wraps up, we go with her to a film festival in Hong Kong, so it's about three weeks, door-to-door."

"You don't sound excited."

"I'm not."

She laughed. "Are you kidding? A tropical photo shoot with a bunch of supermodels?"

"It's going to be a pain in the ass. It's some remote island, with bad cell reception and no AC."

She snorted. "I thought you were a big, tough Marine."

"I am."

He leaned in and kissed her. She draped her arms over his shoulders and gave in to it, even though she knew she was just sliding further and further down a slippery slope. He tasted so good, and it was the first time she'd kissed him this way since last night.

He pulled back and rested his forehead against hers. "I travel a lot."

She sighed.

"Is that a deal breaker for you?"

She eased back. "I didn't know we were making a deal."

He looked down at her, his blue eyes serious. "I like you, Kira. I like spending time with you." He paused. "I'd like to see if we can make this work."

She kissed him again, because she didn't know what to say. Her heart was pounding, and she didn't have the words for how she felt. She only knew that she liked him, too—a *lot*—and the thought of him surrounded by swimsuit models and movie stars for the next three weeks put a painful knot in her chest.

But for right now, she had him. She wrapped her legs around him and pulled him closer, and his hand slid under her sweatshirt, and he gave a low groan as he discovered she wasn't wearing a bra. She combed her fingers into his hair, kissing him until she couldn't breathe, and finally she came up for air.

His gaze was heated. But she could tell he was still waiting for a response to what he'd said.

He kissed her forehead. "I don't want to pressure you."

"You're not."

"I know you're dealing with a lot right now."

She ran her fingers through his hair. "I want to see where this goes, too."

He looked at her, and she summoned her courage.

"I wish you didn't have to leave."

"It's not that long. I'll come see you as soon as I'm done."

Kira wanted to believe him. But he was making promises he might not want to keep, and this was why she hadn't wanted to have this conversation today. She felt too emotional.

She cleared her throat and looked out the window at the grill. "Looks like your fire's ready."

"You're changing the subject."

"I know."

He slid his arms around her. "Let's eat later."

She smiled. "You sure?"

"Yes." He picked her up, and she clamped her legs around his waist as he carried her to the bedroom.

CHAPTER

TWENTY-NINE

KIRA HUNG the picture on the hook and stepped back to check it. It was crooked, and she reached over to nudge up the corner. Tears welled in her eyes, and she blinked them back. Ollie had loved this newspaper clipping, and his daughter had offered it to Kira when she went over to the office to help sort through the mess. Kira had replaced the broken glass and reframed the clip, grateful to have a reminder of Ollie in her new space.

"You're an Astros fan?"

She glanced over her shoulder to see Brock standing in the doorway.

"It was Ollie's."

"Nice." He stepped into the room filled with half-unpacked boxes. "You're making progress," he said, glancing around.

"Yep."

"Sorry you don't have a window."

"I don't mind."

Kira couldn't care less about a window. She could hardly believe she had an actual office, with four walls, at Logan & Locke.

Brock had offered to bring her in-house for a hefty salary, and she'd jumped at the chance. At least for a while. She'd see how things went, and she could always go it alone if it didn't work out. The new arrangement meant giving up her space at WorkWell and her other clients, but she didn't mind. For the first time in her life, she didn't have to wonder where the next gig was coming from.

Brock reached over a cardboard box and handed her a stack of papers.

"What's this?" she asked.

"Some background on my case for next week. I'd like your help with voir dire."

She felt a flutter of excitement. More jury consulting. "Sounds good."

"We start at eight thirty Monday. Bev will get you the details, but I wanted you to have something to read over the weekend."

"Got it."

She put the papers on her desk and looked at Brock. He had started to say something else when her desk phone rang, and Kira reached for it, glad for the distraction. The last time Brock had stopped by her office at five o'clock, he'd asked her out for a drink, and she'd politely declined. She needed to establish boundaries with him if she wanted this new job to work.

The call was from Sydney at the reception desk.

"Yes?" Kira said.

"You've got a delivery here."

Brock gave her a nod and stepped out.

"I'm heading out for the day, so I'll leave it on my desk," Sydney added.

"Thanks. See you on Monday."

Kira hung up and looked around her office. *Her* office. It was small and crowded and, yes, windowless. But it was hers, and she felt a swell of pride every time she stepped into it. She had several more boxes to unpack and organize, and she still had to set up her computer, but she could do all that later. She'd made enough headway for one day.

Kira slid Brock's papers into her messenger bag, excited by the prospect of more jury consulting work, as well as the chance to prove herself to Brock and his partners. And she was glad to have something to do this weekend that would take her mind off Jeremy, who had barely talked to her in three days. Their last phone call had been rushed and distracted, and he'd caught her at four in the morning because of the time difference.

He'd said he missed her. But as soon as they hung up, Kira was flooded with doubts. She hated phone calls. She wanted to see his body language. She wanted to read his eyes and know what he really felt when he said the words.

Lately, she'd found herself doing silly, pointless things. Like checking the weather in Thailand. And sleeping in the flannel shirt she'd borrowed. And stopping in the middle of her workday to wonder whether he missed her even a fraction as much as she missed him. She yearned for him so much it was a physical ache in her chest—one that subsided when she was busy but never truly went away.

Kira grabbed her bike helmet and clipped it to her messenger bag. She cast a last look at Ollie's news clipping on the wall before switching off the light and heading out. She wended her way through the labyrinth of cubicles and saw that some of the lawyers were still around, but most of the support staff had left for the day.

Kira stepped into the reception room, where Sydney was clearing off her desk and gathering up her purse.

"Special delivery," Sydney said with a grin. She nodded at the window.

Jeremy stood there, watching her.

Kira's heart skittered.

"You're back," she said, crossing the room.

He slid his arm around her waist and kissed her forehead.

"I thought you got in Monday?"

"I grabbed an early flight." He smiled down at her, and she felt a flood of nerves.

"Good night, you guys."

"Night." Jeremy nodded at Sydney, then looked at Kira.

She gazed up at him, speechless. He wore jeans and his scarred leather jacket, and he was tall and solid and wonderful. His face was tan, and she thought of all the hours he'd spent on a beach surrounded by gorgeous women while she'd been missing him like crazy.

"You're leaving?" he asked.

"Yeah."

He took her hand, and they walked toward the elevators.

"This way," she said, tugging him to the service elevator, where they'd have a better chance of being alone.

Sure enough, the car arrived empty. They stepped onto it, and Jeremy must have read her thoughts, because he pressed the button and kissed her as the doors closed. He tasted so good, and he kissed her with the same pent-up desire she'd been feeling for weeks.

Finally, he pulled away, and the heated look in his eyes made her nerves flutter.

He tapped the lobby button, and the car whisked down.

"I take it your car's in the shop?" He nodded at her helmet.

"Actually, it's gone." She sighed. "Finally gave up the ghost last week. I'm headed to CarMax this weekend."

The doors dinged open, and they stepped out. The ground level was bustling with people heading home for the night, and Kira couldn't believe that less than a month ago, Gavin Quinn had been shot and nearly killed in this same lobby.

"Where to?" Jeremy asked.

"I'm right out front."

He put his hand on the small of her back, and Kira felt another flurry of nerves as they walked to the doors and stepped outside. The summer heat had finally broken, and a gentle September breeze wafted over them.

She glanced up at him as they walked toward the bike rack.

"When did you arrive?"

"This afternoon," he said. "Hong Kong to LAX to Houston."

"I can't believe you're here." She shook her head as they stopped beside the row of bikes.

"I said I'd come."

"I know."

He was a man of few words. But the words he said he meant. She looked up at him, and his blue eyes were filled with such sincerity it made her heart hurt. And she knew that she loved him. There wasn't a doubt in her mind. She wanted to tell him, but she decided to save it for a time when they weren't surrounded by people and noise and car exhaust.

He bent his head down and kissed her again, and it was even hotter than before in the elevator. She slid her hands around his neck and pressed her body against his, loving the solid feel of him. She'd missed him desperately, and she hadn't even realized how much until this moment.

He eased back, looking as dazed as she felt.

"Will you stay the weekend?"

He sighed. "I was hoping you'd ask that."

Her heart squeezed, and she knelt to unlock her bike. She remembered the moment she'd met him, right here on this sidewalk. She'd had no idea that her life was about to change forever.

She unlocked the chain, and he picked up the bike.

"Can I give you a ride?" he asked.

She smiled up at him. This time, she didn't argue.

ACKNOWLEDGMENTS

S O MANY people helped make this book possible. Thank you to my talented editor, Lauren McKenna. I am grateful to the amazing team at Simon & Schuster, including Abby Zidle, Jean Anne Rose, Hannah Payne, Maggie Loughran, and Matthew Monahan, as well as Paul O'Halloran and the foreign rights group. A very special thank-you to Jen Long, Jen Bergstrom, and Carolyn Reidy. As always, I owe a huge thanks to my longtime agent and friend, Kevan Lyon.

I'm incredibly grateful to my readers, who make writing the best job in the world, as well as the many book bloggers out there who spread their love of reading. And finally, a heartfelt thanks to my family for always believing in me. I love you guys!